Marie-Claude
Roussel

ROMÉO ET JULIETTE

SHAKESPEARE

Roméo et Juliette

NOUVELLE TRADUCTION DE FRANÇOIS LAROQUE
ET JEAN-PIERRE VILLQUIN

Préface et notes de François Laroque

LE LIVRE DE POCHE

Cet ouvrage a été réalisé sous la direction de Michel Jarrety.

Ancien élève de l'École normale supérieure, François Laroque est professeur de littérature anglaise à l'Université Paris III-Sorbonne Nouvelle. Il a publié *Shakespeare et la fête* (PUF, 1988), *Shakespeare comme il vous plaira* (Gallimard, coll. « Découvertes », 1991), et traduit en collaboration avec Jean-Pierre Villquin *La Tragique Histoire du docteur Faust*, de Marlowe (Garnier-Flammarion, 1997).

Jean-Pierre Villquin, professeur agrégé et maître de conférences honoraire, a enseigné à l'Université de Nantes. Il a traduit plusieurs pièces élisabéthaines et jacobéennes et a publié de nombreux articles sur le théâtre de la Renaissance anglaise.

© Librairie Générale Française, 2005.

ISBN : 2-253-08210-4 - 1ère publication - LGF
ISBN : 978-2-253-08210-1 - 1ère publication - LGF

PRÉFACE

Après *Titus Andronicus* (1592-1593), *Roméo et Juliette* (1595-1596) est la deuxième tragédie de Shakespeare. Avant cela, il avait principalement écrit des drames historiques, notamment la première tétralogie (qui comprend les trois parties d'*Henri VI* et *Richard III*) et le début de la seconde avec *Richard II* (1595), ainsi que des comédies (*La Comédie des erreurs*, *La Mégère apprivoisée*, *Les Deux Gentilshommes de Vérone*, *Peines d'amour perdues*). Avec cette première tragédie amoureuse, Shakespeare porte à la scène le mythe de l'amour qui avait été répandu en Occident par le roman médiéval de *Tristan et Iseult* et que l'on trouve dans des sources multiples. Il espère pouvoir ainsi toucher un large public, comme cela avait déjà été le cas avec la fresque sanglante de l'histoire nationale ou les horreurs de la vengeance sénéquéenne. Et, en décidant de faire de l'amour non plus la matière de la seule comédie mais le thème central d'un nouveau type de tragédie qu'il reprendra à deux reprises avec *Othello* (1603) et *Antoine et Cléopâtre* (1607), Shakespeare montre qu'il n'hésite pas à prendre des risques pour innover.

Roméo et Juliette est en effet une tragédie hybride qui commence comme une joyeuse comédie avant de virer au noir à la scène 1 de l'acte III, après la mort de Mercutio, l'ami de Roméo, et le duel à mort entre Tybalt et Roméo. Ce basculement d'un extrême à l'autre est résumé par le père de Juliette, lorsqu'il est confronté au macabre spectacle de sa fille morte le matin de ses noces[1]. L'influence de la comédie est également perceptible dans les nombreux jeux de mots de la pièce et dans les dialogues où l'esprit fuse et pétille (I. 1, v. 1-26, II. 3, v. 36-100, III. 1, v. 46-50), ainsi que dans le recours à la rhétorique et aux effets de style les plus artificiels. Stanley Wells parle justement ici « d'intellectualisme et de jeu littéraire aussi conscient qu'ostentatoire[2] ».

Roméo et Juliette porte également l'empreinte des sonnets que Shakespeare commence à écrire à cette époque. Les prologues de l'acte I et II sont des sonnets et c'est encore un sonnet que se partagent les deux amoureux lors de leur rencontre au bal des Capulet (I. 5, v. 91-104). Le dramaturge n'hésite pas à combiner formalisme littéraire et lyrisme amoureux. Cependant, l'évolution de Roméo, lorsqu'il oublie Rosaline, dont il se disait pourtant éperdument amoureux, pour s'adonner corps et âme à sa passion pour Juliette, montre toute la distance qui sépare ces deux modes stylistiques. Il y a d'un côté ce qui, chez le jeune Montaigu, obéit à la mode, à l'air du temps et à la posture (la mélancolie amoureuse qui sert d'aiguillon poétique aux pétrarquistes) et, de l'autre, ce qui relève de la fulgurance et de l'illumination. Les figures de l'oxymore, qui associent les contraires et qui sont utilisées à la fois par Roméo (I. 1, v. 172-177) et par Juliette (III. 2, v. 73-85), renvoient aux clichés de l'amour véhiculés par les disciples anglais de l'amoureux de Laure, Sir Thomas Wyatt et le comte de Surrey, Sir Philip Sidney ou Edmund Spenser. Les exclamations creuses, les lamentations, l'indignation, qui se rattachent au mode emphatique et déclamatoire, sont clairement dénoncées à la

---

1. Voir ci-dessous p. 155, vers 84-90.   2. Wells, Stanley, éd., *Romeo and Juliet and its Afterlife*, *Shakespeare Survey* 49, Cambridge, Cambridge University Press, 1996, p. 6.

scène 5 de l'acte IV après la découverte de la fausse mort
de Juliette pendant la nuit. Jamais le décalage entre action
et discours n'a été aussi grand. Ainsi, on y entend la mère
de Juliette, pourtant plus que froide dans ses rapports
avec sa fille, s'exclamer que cette dernière était « toute [s]a
joie et tout [s]on réconfort » (IV. 5, v. 47). Visiblement,
le monde des adultes n'a que peu de chose à voir avec la
sincérité brûlante et l'exigence d'absolu de la jeunesse.

Par contre, les images qui véhiculent l'éclat lumineux
de l'amour et transmettent la violence de sa déflagration
sont comme un coup porté en plein cœur. Il est en effet
question de l'incandescence des torches au milieu de la
nuit (I. 5, v. 42-43) ou encore des « violents plaisirs [qui]/
… comme le feu et la poudre/… explosent en s'embrassant » (II. 5, v. 9-11). Les feux du désir, l'été à Vérone,
sont aussi explosifs que la poudre et font de la passion un
poison dangereux. Aimer c'est jouer avec le feu. Les
torches qui flambent tout autour de Juliette et la miné-
ralisent pour en faire un joyau merveilleux, dont l'éclat
est encore rehaussé par la joue de la nuit, produisent
un décrochement du réel, où George Steiner voit un
exemple de ce qu'il appelle la « dictée surnaturelle[1] »,
c'est-à-dire une forme de révélation mystérieuse. L'amoureux réussit en effet à lire indirectement ici le nom de
celle qu'il ne connaît pas encore dans une forme de rébus
érotique (en anglais, le mot *jewel* renvoie en effet à « Jule »,
le surnom que la Nourrice a donné à Juliette). Juliette
aura beau ensuite relativiser l'importance du nom (« Qu'y
a-t-il dans un nom ? », II. 1, v. 86), cette kabbale mystique
unira les amoureux jusqu'au bout comme un lien
magique autant que fatidique. Nous sommes ici en pré-
sence d'une forme de transcendance de la vision poétique
qui se trouve en accord avec les pulsations de l'émotion et

---

1. *Grammaires de la création*, Paris, Gallimard, 2001, p. 114.

du désir et dont la force se situe aux antipodes de la mécanique pétrarquiste comme des injonctions patriarcales. L'amour romantique s'oppose aussi à la grivoiserie, voire à l'obscénité, de la Nourrice et de Mercutio, qui présentent tous deux l'amour comme une série de gestes ou de figures simples (tomber en arrière, se dresser, pénétrer un cercle et retomber), toutes liées à ce que Mikhaïl Bakhtine appelle le « bas matériel[1] ». Ce langage rabelaisien et coloré, qui donne lieu à des répliques souvent un peu crues, sert de contrepoids aux envolées lyriques des amoureux. Mais on peut aussi voir dans les joutes oratoires, où les jeunes gens font assaut d'ingéniosité et multiplient les allusions salaces, un équivalent des duels et des rixes, où les provocations verbales ne sont pas moins importantes que les coups de lames. La proximité phonétique des mots « Jule », « jewel » ou « duel » en anglais montre à quel point l'amour est proche de la haine (lors du bal des Capulet, Roméo suscite la haine de Tybalt juste avant son coup de foudre pour Juliette). L'entrecroisement des mots et des épées apparaît donc bien comme le négatif des embrassements amoureux, le combat de rues comme l'antithèse et l'antichambre de l'érotisme. *Roméo et Juliette* est une pièce paradoxale où la haine et l'affection se tournent le dos tout en se donnant la main.

Outre ces paradoxes, dont Shakespeare joue avec virtuosité, les jeux de lettres (en particulier sur le « O » et le « R ») sont modulés sur les blasons du corps comme autant de signes tirés de quelque alphabet érotique, mais ce sont aussi des jeux de l'être. Afin de faciliter les

---

1. *L'Œuvre de François Rabelais et la culture populaire au Moyen Âge et sous la Renaissance*, traduit du russe par Andrée Robel, Paris, Gallimard, 1970, p. 30 et *sq.* Voir aussi Ronald Knowles, « Carnival and Death in *Romeo and Juliet* : a Bakhtinian reading », Romeo and Juliet *and its Afterlife*, *Shakespeare Survey*, p. 69-85.

correspondances et les résonances internes, le dramaturge recourt à des effets de parallélisme et à des contrepoints au sein d'une architecture d'ensemble à la fois solide et subtile. Le prologue donne les grandes lignes de l'action dans des anticipations que les prémonitions des deux rôles-titres soulignent et reprennent en sourdine, tandis que les récits comme ceux de Benvolio ou de Frère Laurent rappellent sur un mode narratif ce que le spectateur a déjà vu. Là où certains ont vu une maladresse de construction, s'élabore en réalité tout un jeu délibéré de préfigurations et de retours en arrière dont la principale raison d'être est d'intensifier le moment présent. L'espace-temps de la pièce est en effet très particulier dans la mesure où, du fait d'une funeste conjonction astrale, tout est déjà consommé dès le début[1]. En montrant que la mort est déjà présente à l'origine même de la vie, Shakespeare emprunte ses images à l'érotisme macabre des gravures et des tableaux de la Renaissance des pays du Nord[2]. Dans le monologue de Juliette à la scène 3 de l'acte IV ou de Roméo à la scène 3 de l'acte V, il anticipe sur le futur genre « gothique » qui fera la fortune du roman anglais de la fin du XVIIIe siècle. Dans la mesure où le baiser des amoureux au bal préfigure le baiser de mort final, on voit bien que les dés sont pipés au départ et que seules l'intensité, l'énergie et les fulgurances de la verve poétique pourront réussir à créer l'illusion de la vie et de l'action.

De même, la forme brève du sonnet, utilisée à plusieurs reprises dans la pièce, offre un contraste saisissant avec les longs monologues : soliloques de la Nourrice (I. 3) et de

---

1. Voir sur ce point l'image des *star-crossed lovers*, c'est-à-dire des amoureux nés sous une étoile contraire, dans le premier prologue, vers 6.   2. Notamment dans les gravures de Peter Flötner et des frères Beham ainsi que dans les toiles de Hans Baldung Grien. Voir à ce sujet la monographie de Jean Wirth, *La Jeune Fille et la Mort. Recherche sur les thèmes macabres dans l'art germanique de la Renaissance*, Genève, Droz, 1979.

Mercutio (I. 4), monologues de Frère Laurent (II. 2), de Juliette (III. 2 et IV. 3) et de Roméo (V. 3). L'autre système d'opposition binaire divise le temps en deux avec, d'un côté, le régime essentiellement nocturne de l'amour (Roméo et Juliette se rencontrent le soir, échangent leurs serments au cours de la nuit et se quittent à l'aube après une brève nuit de noces) et, de l'autre, le monde du soleil et de la chaleur du jour qui correspond au temps du duel et de la rixe. L'amour s'oppose à la rage caniculaire des « dog days », censés sévir de la mi-juillet à la mi-août et ainsi nommés parce que cette période se situait sous l'enseigne et l'emprise de la constellation du Chien, comme la nuit s'oppose à la clarté diurne.[1]

La structuration quasi symphonique de l'œuvre permet d'effectuer des rappels d'un passage de la pièce à l'autre. Ainsi la scène du bal préfigure en filigrane la scène de la descente au tombeau des Capulet : dans un cas comme dans l'autre, Juliette est décrite comme une intense source de lumière, tandis que le baiser de mort rappelle en écho le premier baiser d'amour. C'est là que Roméo va être « blessé » par celle qu'il a blessée en retour alors qu'il n'était venu là que pour apercevoir la cruelle Rosaline. La première scène de l'acte III fait du duel entre Mercutio et Tybalt une sorte de valse ponctuée par les piques et les bons mots, notamment les calembours en série sur les termes musicaux de *consort* et de *minstrels* et sur les archets qui servent à désigner les épées (*fiddle-sticks*). Lors du duel, Tybalt « assaisonne » Mercutio, lui portant un coup mortel destiné à Roméo, qu'il était venu défier. Ce dernier va donc en découdre avec celui qu'il aurait voulu aimer. Roméo, au

---

1. Voir l'article de Philippa Berry, « Between idolatry and astrology : modes of temporal repetition in *Romeo and Juliet* », *in* Richard Dutton, Alison Findlay and Richard Wilson, éd., *Region, Religion and Patronage. Lancastrian Shakespeare*, Manchester, Manchester University Press, 2003, p. 68-83.

bal, s'était involontairement substitué à Pâris et Juliette
à Rosaline. Lors du duel, Mercutio relève le gant pour
Roméo et trouve la mort au moment où ce dernier
essayait de séparer les deux adversaires dans un geste
qui se voulait pacificateur. La fête comme le duel ne
sont donc que l'autre face d'une longue danse macabre
où se trame le sinistre jeu de dupes imaginé par le
destin. À Vérone, c'est la mort qui mène le bal, de
sorte que Roméo peut s'écrier à juste titre «Oh! Je suis
le jouet de la Fortune» (III. 1, v. 140).

D'un autre côté, on ne joue pas impunément avec la
mort. Frère Laurent l'apprendra à ses dépens en acceptant
de donner à Juliette un puissant somnifère qui simulera la
mort. Tentant de mettre un terme à l'enchaînement fatidique des événements, il joue les apprentis sorciers. Face
à la ronde infernale de la malchance, les jeunes gens, au
nom de la foi et de la merveille qu'est leur amour,
adoptent une fidélité à toute épreuve, alors que le monde
de la comédie, qui fait de l'amour et du sexe une loterie,
s'accommode plus aisément des contrariétés comme de
l'adversité. Avec son gros bon sens populaire et son réa-
lisme à courte vue, la Nourrice a vite fait d'indisposer
Juliette qui se sent trahie et la traite alors de «vieille
sorcière».

Car les jeunes gens qui s'aiment hors la loi sont de
simples fétus de paille face à des querelles familiales qui
les dépassent et les débordent. Ils ne maîtrisent rien. La
vendetta à laquelle se livrent les deux grandes familles de
Vérone paraît aussi âpre et inéluctable que les ravages de
la guerre des Deux-Roses décrite dans les trois parties
d'*Henri VI* et qui fait presque pâle figure par rapport
aux horreurs de *Titus Andronicus*. L'idée brillante du
dramaturge aura été de mettre ici la vengeance en
arrière-plan pour braquer le projecteur sur une jeune
passion que l'on voit naître sur fond de haine ancestrale,
montrant ainsi les affres autant que la beauté d'un

amour impossible contrarié tour à tour par les étoiles et la lutte des clans. Car ce n'est qu'au nom d'un idéal aussi puissant que l'aspiration au bonheur que Shakespeare pouvait réussir à légitimer l'idée de la désobéissance à la loi.

De fait, les scènes d'amour de la pièce sont l'occasion d'arias et de duos sublimes, où le dramaturge donne libre cours à toutes les expressions de son art. Mais ce nouveau culte de l'amour, qui trouve des expressions inédites dans le déploiement et l'orchestration des sonorités, des rythmes et des images, prend aussi l'allure d'une religion hérétique qui s'oppose aux lois de la cité comme aux règles non écrites de l'honneur et de la *gens*. La force virtuellement pacificatrice de l'amour (II. 2, v. 91-92) n'est ainsi comprise ou même admise par personne ou presque. Le secret et la clandestinité font que les attitudes des amoureux prennent le contre-pied des projets des parents, provoquant en retour un redoublement de la rage ambiante. Avec son cortège d'associations panthéistes ou païennes, l'idolâtrie amoureuse s'oppose alors aussi bien à l'iconoclasme érotique d'un Mercutio, qui ne cesse de déboulonner les statues de leur piédestal mythologique ou poétique, qu'aux règles patriarcales qui régissent l'ordre familial et politique à Vérone. Le sacrifice d'une jeunesse fauchée dans la fleur de l'âge évoque les martyrs – le mot est utilisé par Capulet à propos de la mort de sa fille (IV. 5, v. 59) – et la persécution religieuse à l'encontre des Jésuites et des prêtres catholiques. C'est ainsi qu'Edmund Campion et que le poète Robert Southwell allaient être atrocement torturés puis exécutés à Tyburn en 1581 et en 1595[1].

---

1. Voir sur ce point l'analyse de Richard Wilson, *Secret Shakespeare. Studies in theatre, religion and resistance*, Manchester, Manchester University Press, 2004, p. 139-141.

Avec l'image de l'histoire écrite en lettres d'or,
la *golden story* dont parle Lady Capulet (I. 3, v. 92), on
pense en effet à *La Légende dorée*, le célèbre recueil de
Jacques de Voragine qui raconte la vie des saints et des
martyrs chrétiens, à la fois l'un des premiers manuscrits
imprimés à Londres par Caxton (1483) et l'un des
ouvrages les plus lus en Angleterre jusqu'à la Réforme.
On trouve dans la pièce quelques allusions indirectes à
ce livre qui servent à décrire aussi bien la beauté phy-
sique que la douceur du baiser (I. 5, v. 105-108).
Conformément à l'étymologie de son nom[1], Roméo se
présente comme un pèlerin, tandis que Juliette est assi-
milée à une sainte dont il vient adorer le sanctuaire.
L'imagerie catholique se trouve ainsi utilisée pour faire
passer un message d'amour et de beauté esthétique.
D'un autre côté, les amoureux sont aussi ceux dont la
main a « signé le livre de l'amère infortune » (V. 3,
v. 82), eux dont le destin tragique était déjà écrit
d'avance, en quelque sorte.

Le paradoxe tragique naît donc de leur écartèlement
entre la situation réelle qui est la leur, puisqu'ils sont
l'un et l'autre pris dans les mâchoires de la mort, et
leur furieux désir de vivre qui se double d'une tentative
désespérée de prolonger l'instant. Car, à chaque fois
qu'ils se quittent, aucun d'eux ne sait s'il reverra l'autre
un jour. Ils ont tous deux la mort aux trousses, et leur
frénésie amoureuse est telle qu'ils ne cessent, au moins
en images, de s'abîmer dans la « petite mort ». Juliette,
plus encore que Roméo, traduit son désir par ces
images d'étranglement et de fusion cosmique[2], tandis

---

1. Romeo, ou *romitaggio*, désignait en effet un pèlerin se rendant à Rome.
En anglais, le mot *roamer* signifie errant. Voir John Florio, *A Worlde of Wordes*
(1598). La définition est citée par Philippa Berry *in* « Between idolatry and
astrology », *op. cit.*, p. 73.   2. Dans *Histoires d'amour*, Paris, Denoël, 1983,
rééd. Gallimard, « Folio Essais », 1988, Julia Kristeva insiste sur le fait que, selon
elle, « le désir féminin [...] est davantage ombiliqué à la mort », p. 271.

que son suicide à la fin prend l'allure d'une pénétration phallique :

> O happy dagger
> This is thy sheath. There rust, and let me die
> (V. 3, v. 168-169)[1]

Par effet d'hypallage, le *happy dagger*, « l'heureux poignard », devient l'instrument de la jouissance quand il est planté dans le cœur-fourreau, le mot *sheath* traduisant littéralement le latin *vagina*. En anglais, la première partie du deuxième vers semble quasiment imprononçable, ce qui montre que la jouissance, comme le moment de la mort, est effectivement de l'ordre de l'indicible.

Comme pour les martyrs, l'extase n'est atteinte que dans la souffrance et dans la mort, et ce déplacement d'Éros en direction de Thanatos paraît d'autant plus cruel que les amoureux débordent de vie et d'énergie. C'est dans cette vacance, au sein de ce manque, que se joue la tragédie du désir, où le plein est constamment figuré par le vide, par la lettre « O » qui, pour Shakespeare, signifie à la fois le chiffre zéro et le sexe féminin[2].

Grâce à sa virtuosité prosodique et rythmique, la pièce réussit à porter à l'incandescence toute la gamme de l'émotion et du désir, faisant ainsi de la poésie dramatique un puissant vecteur d'une passion amoureuse tour à tour présentée comme pathétique ou merveilleuse.

François LAROQUE.

---

1. Voir la traduction ci-dessous, p. 174.   2. Voir à ce sujet mon article, « *Antoine et Cléopâtre* ou l'esthétique du vide », *Études anglaises* n°4 (octobre-décembre 2000), Paris, Didier Érudition, p. 404-407.

Note sur la traduction

Cette nouvelle traduction de *Roméo et Juliette* est le fruit d'un travail à quatre mains où les deux collaborateurs se sont efforcés de se tenir à égale distance du littéralisme et d'une adaptation trop libre qui ne respecterait pas les inflexions et les images du texte d'origine. Quant aux rimes, auxquelles Shakespeare recourt parfois, ils les ont maintenues quand c'était possible. La cadence générale du texte correspond à celle de l'alexandrin, plus naturel que le décasyllabe en français, sans que cela ait été fait de manière systématique par crainte d'une certaine monotonie. Sans ignorer l'importance des détails, des jeux de mots, de la richesse et de la complexité de certains réseaux d'images qu'ils ont essayé de rendre aussi fidèlement que possible, les traducteurs ont eu à cœur de rechercher à tout instant un principe d'équilibre entre la forme et le sens.

F. L.

La très excellente et très pitoyable
tragédie de Roméo
et Juliette.

[William Shakespeare]

*Nouvellement corrigée, augmentée
et améliorée :*

telle qu'elle a souvent été jouée en public par
les serviteurs du très honorable Lord Chambellan.

Londres

Imprimée par Thomas Creede, pour Cuthbert Burby,
vendue en sa boutique près de la Bourse.

1599

Personnages

LE PRINCE de Vérone, Escalus.

PÂRIS, jeune noble, parent du Prince.

CAPULET, ennemi de Montaigu, père de Juliette.

MONTAIGU, ennemi de Capulet, père de Roméo.

ROMÉO, fils de Montaigu.

MERCUTIO, jeune noble, parent du Prince et ami de Roméo.

BENVOLIO, neveu de Montaigu et ami de Roméo.

TYBALT, neveu de Lady Capulet.

FRÈRE LAURENT, moine franciscain.

FRÈRE JEAN, moine franciscain.

BALTHAZAR, valet de Roméo.

SAMSON, valet des Capulet.

GRÉGOIRE, valet des Capulet.

ABRAHAM, valet des Montaigu.

PIERRE, valet de la nourrice de Juliette.

APOTHICAIRE.

UN COUSIN de Capulet.

LE PAGE de Pâris.

LADY MONTAIGU, épouse de Montaigu, mère de Roméo.

LADY CAPULET, épouse de Capulet, mère de Juliette.

JULIETTE, fille de Capulet.

LA NOURRICE de Juliette.

UN OFFICIER, hommes du guet, serviteurs, le chœur, musiciens, citoyens et bourgeois de Vérone.

La scène est à Vérone et à Mantoue.

La très excellente et très pitoyable tragédie de Roméo et Juliette

Prologue

[*Entre le Chœur.*]

LE CHŒUR

Deux maisons l'une et l'autre égales en dignité,
Dans la belle Vérone où se tient notre scène,
Se déchirent à nouveau pour d'anciennes querelles,
Souillant leurs mains du sang qu'elles font couler.
5 Des fatales entrailles de ces races rivales
Sont nés deux amants sous une mauvaise étoile ;
Leur chute infortunée autant que pitoyable
Enterre avec leur mort les haines ancestrales.
Le cours d'un amour destiné à la mort,
10 La haine héréditaire que se vouent leurs parents,
Éreinte seulement par la mort des enfants,
Vont deux heures durant occuper notre scène.
Et si vous nous prêtez une oreille attentive,
Notre zèle essaiera d'en effacer les fautes[1].

[*Il sort.*]

---

1. Le prologue a la forme d'un sonnet (quatorze vers composés de deux quatrains et deux tercets). Lors de leur rencontre au bal des Capulet, le premier dialogue entre les deux jeunes gens épousera également ce mode poétique, alors très présent à l'esprit de l'auteur.

ACTE I

Scène 1

Entrent Samson et Grégoire de la maison des Capulet,
armés d'épées et de boucliers.

SAMSON

Grégoire, ma parole, on ne va pas se laisser marcher sur les pieds.

GRÉGOIRE

Sûr, autrement on pourrait nous traiter de pieds-plats.

SAMSON

Je veux dire que si on nous échauffe le sang, on va tirer l'épée.

GRÉGOIRE

5 C'est vrai, dans la vie, il faut toujours essayer de s'en tirer.

SAMSON

J'ai le bras leste quand on m'énerve un peu.

GRÉGOIRE

Oui, mais avant de te battre, tu es plutôt lent à t'émouvoir.

SAMSON

Un chien de la maison des Montaigu peut m'émouvoir.

GRÉGOIRE

S'émouvoir, c'est s'mouvoir. Être brave, c'est faire front, donc,
10   si t'es ému, tu décampes.

SAMSON

Un chien des Montaigu m'émeut assez pour que je fasse front.
Je ne céderai le haut du pavé à personne, homme ou femme,
qui appartient à cette maison.

GRÉGOIRE

Ce qui prouve que tu n'es qu'un faible esclave, car c'est le plus
15   faible qui se bat le dos au mur.

SAMSON

Vrai, c'est pourquoi les femmes, étant du sexe faible, se font
toujours presser contre le mur ; en conséquence de quoi, je
chasserai du mur les valets des Montaigu et j'y presserai leurs
servantes.

GRÉGOIRE

20   La querelle est entre nos maîtres et entre nous, leurs valets.

SAMSON

C'est le même combat. Je vais jouer au tyran, une fois les
hommes vaincus, pas de quartier pour les pucelles, quel que
soit leur âge.

GRÉGOIRE

L'âge des pucelles ?

SAMSON

25   Oui, l'âge des pucelles ou leur pucelage, prends ça dans le sens
que tu veux[1].

---

1. Une sorte de pétrarquisme généralisé semble régner à Vérone, où les
serviteurs font les premiers assaut de jeux d'esprit. Ici, deux mots indépendants
(« âge » et « pucelle ») se trouvent reliés pour obtenir un sous-entendu grivois.
Pour un effet du même style, voir le monologue de la Nourrice en I. 3, v. 13-15.

GRÉGOIRE

Celles qui le sentiront devront bien y trouver un sens.

SAMSON

C'est moi qu'elles sentiront, tant que je pourrai tenir le coup, et
on sait que je possède un joli bout de chair!

GRÉGOIRE

30 Heureusement que tu es plus chair que poisson, sinon tu ne
serais qu'un minable maquereau. Tire ton engin, en voici venir
deux de la maison des Montaigu.

Entrent deux serviteurs [Abraham et Balthazar].

SAMSON

Mon arme est dégainée. Toi, tu cherches querelle, moi, je reste
derrière, afin de te couvrir.

GRÉGOIRE

35 Quoi! derrière moi pour mieux filer?

SAMSON

Ne crains rien.

GRÉGOIRE

Ce n'est sûrement pas toi que je crains.

SAMSON

Mettons la loi de notre côté, laissons-les commencer.

GRÉGOIRE

Je vais les regarder de travers en passant près d'eux, et qu'ils le
40 prennent comme ils veulent.

SAMSON

Non, comme ils peuvent, s'ils osent. Je vais leur faire la nique,
c'est une injure s'ils n'y répondent pas.

ABRAHAM

C'est à nous que vous faites la nique, monsieur ?

SAMSON

Je fais la nique, monsieur, c'est vrai.

ABRAHAM

45 C'est bien à nous que vous faites la nique, monsieur ?

SAMSON [*bas à Grégoire*]

A-t-on la loi pour nous si je réponds oui ?

GRÉGOIRE [*bas à Samson*]

Non.

SAMSON

Non, ce n'est pas à vous que je fais la nique, je fais la nique,
voilà tout, monsieur.

GRÉGOIRE

50 Vous cherchez querelle, monsieur ?

ABRAHAM

Querelle, monsieur ? Non, monsieur.

SAMSON

Mais si c'est le cas, monsieur, je suis votre homme, le maître
que je sers vaut bien le vôtre.

ABRAHAM

Mais pas davantage ?

SAMSON

55 À votre gré, monsieur.

Entre Benvolio.

GRÉGOIRE [*apercevant Tybalt, bas à Samson*]
Dis qu'il est meilleur, car voici venir un des parents de mon
maître.

SAMSON
Si, monsieur, il est meilleur.

ABRAHAM
Vous mentez.

SAMSON
60 En garde, si vous êtes des hommes! Grégoire, n'oublie pas ta
botte fatale.

Ils se battent.

BENVOLIO
Séparez-vous, imbéciles que vous êtes, rengainez, vous ne savez
pas ce que vous faites.

Entre Tybalt.

TYBALT
Quoi, tu croises le fer avec ces vauriens sans courage?
65 Retourne-toi, Benvolio, regarde la mort en face.

BENVOLIO
Je ne fais que maintenir la paix. Rengaine ton épée,
Ou sers-t'en pour m'aider à séparer ces hommes.

TYBALT
Quoi, l'épée à la main, et tu parles de paix? Je déteste ce mot
Tout autant que l'enfer, les Montaigu et ta personne.
70 En garde, lâche!

[Ils] se battent.

*Entrent trois ou quatre bourgeois armés de gourdins
et de pertuisanes.*

BOURGEOIS

Porteurs de massues, de piques et de pertuisanes, frappez, ter-
rassez-les ! À bas les Capulet ! À bas les Montaigu !

*Entre le vieux Capulet, en robe de chambre,
accompagné de sa femme.*

CAPULET

Quel est ce bruit ? Holà ! qu'on me donne ma grande épée.

LADY CAPULET

Une béquille, une béquille ! pourquoi demander une épée ?

CAPULET

75 Mon épée, mon épée, vous dis-je. Le vieux Montaigu est ici,
Et me nargue de ses moulinets.

Entrent le vieux Montaigu et Lady Montaigu.

MONTAIGU

Infâme Capulet ! Ne me retenez pas, laissez-moi faire.

LADY MONTAIGU

Non. Pas un pas de plus pour aller affronter un ennemi.

Entre le Prince Escalus accompagné de sa suite.

LE PRINCE

Sujets rebelles, ennemis de la paix,
80 Vous qui souillez vos armes du sang de vos voisins,
Allez-vous m'écouter ? Êtes-vous des hommes ou des bêtes
                                                      [sauvages,
Vous qui noyez le feu de votre rage pernicieuse
Dans les flots pourpres qui jaillissent de vos veines ?
Sous peine de torture, que vos sanglantes mains

85 Déposent à mes pieds ces armes de haine
    Et écoutez la sentence d'un prince courroucé.
    Trois rixes civiles sont nées de vos paroles,
    À cause de toi, vieux Capulet, et de toi, Montaigu,
    Troublant à trois reprises le calme de nos rues,
90 Poussant les vénérables citoyens de Vérone,
    À faire fi de leur rang et de leur dignité,
    À saisir dans leurs mains ridées de vieilles pertuisanes
    Que la paix a rouillées pour trancher la haine qui vous ronge.
    Si jamais vous troublez à nouveau la cité,
95 Votre vie répondra de la paix de nos rues.
    Aussi, pour cette fois, que chacun se disperse :
    Vous, Capulet, vous m'accompagnerez.
    Quant à vous, Montaigu, venez l'après-midi
    À notre vieux palais de Villefranche, notre cour de justice.
100 Encore une fois, sous peine de mort, que chacun se retire.

Tous sortent, à l'exception de Montaigu,
de Lady Montaigu et de Benvolio.

MONTAIGU

Qui a rallumé cette ancienne querelle ?
Dites-moi, mon neveu, étiez-vous là quand elle a commencé ?

BENVOLIO

Les serviteurs de votre ennemi et les vôtres
S'affrontaient corps à corps, bien avant que j'arrive.
105 Je dégaine pour les séparer, quand survient
Tybalt fulminant, l'épée tirée au clair.
Et, tout en me crachant des insultes au visage,
Il fait des moulinets, veut pourfendre les airs
Qui, sans en souffrir, lui sifflent leur mépris aux oreilles.
    Comme nous étions là à échanger des coups,
Chaque camp grossissant de nouveaux partisans,
Le Prince arrive alors pour séparer les camps.

LADY MONTAIGU

Où donc est Roméo ? L'as-tu vu aujourd'hui ?
Je suis très heureuse qu'il soit resté à l'écart !

BENVOLIO

115 Madame, une heure avant que le soleil glorieux
Ait dardé ses regards vers la fenêtre dorée de l'Orient,
Le trouble de mon âme m'incita à sortir,
Et là, sous le bosquet de sycomores
Qui se dressent à l'ouest, aux abords de la ville,
120 À cette heure matinale, j'aperçus votre fils.
J'allai à sa rencontre mais, se méfiant de moi,
Il disparut alors sous le couvert du bois.
Moi, mesurant sa peine à l'aune de la mienne,
Moi qui cherchais un lieu que rien ne pût troubler,
125 Étant déjà de trop, près du triste moi-même,
Je suivis mon humeur sans poursuivre la sienne,
Heureux de fuir un homme si heureux de me fuir.

MONTAIGU

Bien des fois, le matin, on l'a vu par là-bas,
Ajoutant ses larmes à la fraîche rosée,
130 Et gonflant les nuées de ses profonds soupirs.
Mais, dès que le soleil qui réjouit l'univers
Au plus loin de l'Orient commence à écarter
Les rideaux sombres du lit de l'Aurore,
Mon fils, accablé de soucis, fuit le jour qui se lève,
135 Il rentre à la maison, se cloître dans sa chambre,
Ferme ses volets, chasse la lumière du jour
Et se crée une nuit tout artificielle.
Cette humeur noire ne peut qu'être funeste
À moins qu'un bon conseil n'en dissipe la cause[1].

---

1. L'amoureux était couramment assimilé au type humoral du mélancolique qui associait la nuit, les larmes et la bile noire. Voir à ce sujet l'ouvrage de Timothy Bright, *Traité de la mélancolie* (1586), éd. et trad. Éliane Cuvelier, Grenoble, J. Millon, 1996.

BENVOLIO

140 Mon oncle, connaissez-vous la cause de tout cela ?

MONTAIGU

Non et lui ne veut rien m'en dire.

BENVOLIO

Est-ce que vous l'avez véritablement cuisiné ?

MONTAIGU

J'ai essayé, moi comme beaucoup d'amis.
Mais lui, seul confident de sa propre passion,
145 Reste (qui sait s'il est sincère ?) aussi insondable,
Aussi impénétrable et tout aussi fermé
Que le bouton de fleur que ronge un ver jaloux
Avant qu'il puisse ouvrir ses pétales fragiles,
Et offrir sa beauté au soleil.
150 Si nous pouvions savoir la source de ses maux,
Nous voudrions les guérir autant que les connaître.

Entre Roméo.

BENVOLIO

Tenez, le voici qui arrive. De grâce, tenez-vous à l'écart.
Je saurai la raison de sa peine ou j'essuierai son refus.

MONTAIGU

Puisses-tu en restant avoir la chance
155 D'apprendre la vérité. Venez, madame, retirons-nous.

Sortent Montaigu et Lady Montaigu.

BENVOLIO

Bonjour, cousin.

ROMÉO

Le jour est-il si jeune ?

BENVOLIO
                    Neuf heures viennent de sonner.

ROMÉO
Dieu, que les heures tristes semblent longues !
Est-ce mon père qui s'en allait si vite ?

BENVOLIO
Oui. Quelle est cette peine qui allonge les heures de Roméo ?

ROMÉO
160   Le fait de ne pas avoir ce qui les rendrait brèves.

BENVOLIO
L'amour ?

ROMÉO
L'excès.

BENVOLIO
D'amour ?

ROMÉO
L'excès de froideur de celle pour qui je brûle.

BENVOLIO
165   Hélas ! pourquoi l'amour, si doux en apparence,
Est-il si tyrannique et si dur à l'épreuve ?

ROMÉO
Hélas ! pourquoi l'amour dont les yeux sont bandés,
Peut-il, aveugle, si bien voir les chemins du désir ?
Où dînons-nous ? Mon Dieu ! Quel était ce tapage ?
170   Non, ne me le dis pas, car j'ai tout entendu.
Il y a beaucoup de haine mais encore plus d'amour.
Quoi ! Ô amour querelleur, ô amoureuse haine !
Ô je ne sais quoi par le rien engendré,
Ô pesante légèreté, sérieuse vanité,

175 Informe chaos fait d'harmonieuses formes !
Plumes de plomb, fumée lumineuse, feu glacé, santé malade,
Sommeil éveillé qui n'est pas ce qu'il est ![1]
Cet amour que je sens ne m'inspire pas d'amour.
Mais toi, tu ne ris pas ?

BENVOLIO
Non, cousin, je préfère pleurer.

ROMÉO
180 De quoi, noble cœur ?

BENVOLIO
Pleurer du chagrin de ton noble cœur.

ROMÉO
Voilà donc bien comment l'amour passe les bornes.
Mes propres peines pèsent sur un cœur déjà lourd,
Et tu les multiplies en le chargeant des tiennes.
L'amour que tu m'as témoigné ajoute
185 Un nouveau poids à l'excès de mes peines.
L'amour, c'est la fumée qu'exhalent les soupirs,
Attisé, c'est le feu dans les yeux des amants,
Contrarié, c'est la mer que viennent grossir leurs larmes.
Qu'est-il encore ? Une folie des plus sages,
190 Le fiel qui étouffe et le miel qui nous sauve.
Adieu, mon cousin.

BENVOLIO
Doucement, je te suis.
Tu me portes grand tort, si tu me laisses ainsi.

---

1. Cette succession d'oxymores (figure de rhétorique qui associe les contraires) fait de l'amour un art autant qu'un artifice, de sorte que l'amoureux de l'invisible Rosaline fait de sa prétendue passion une pose. Roméo apparaît ici comme un apprenti-poète disciple de Pétrarque.

ROMÉO

Va, je me suis perdu, je ne suis pas ici.
Ce n'est pas Roméo, il est allé ailleurs.

BENVOLIO

195 Dis-moi sérieusement qui tu aimes.

ROMÉO

Tu veux donc que je gémisse et te le dise ?

BENVOLIO

Non, ne gémis pas mais dis-moi sérieusement qui tu aimes.

ROMÉO

Demande à un malade de faire sérieusement son testament,
Mot bien mal venu pour qui se sent déjà mal.
200 Sérieusement, cousin, j'aime une femme.

BENVOLIO

J'ai visé assez près, devinant ta passion.

ROMÉO

Tu as visé fort juste, et celle que j'aime est belle.

BENVOLIO

Et plus la cible est belle, beau cousin, mieux on peut la toucher.

ROMÉO

Là, tu manques ta cible, car elle ne se laissera pas toucher
205 Par la flèche de Cupidon. Sage comme Diane
Sous l'armure d'une imprenable chasteté,
Elle vit à l'abri de l'arc enfantin de l'Amour.
Elle refuse qu'on l'assiège avec des mots d'amour.
Elle se détourne des œillades meurtrières,
210 Elle ferme son giron à l'or qui séduirait une sainte,
Oh! elle est riche en beauté et elle ne sera pauvre

Que le jour où la mort emportera sa beauté.[1]

BENVOLIO

Elle a donc juré de vivre toujours chaste ?

ROMÉO

Oui. C'est ainsi qu'épargnant sa vertu, elle gaspille ses biens.
215 Car la beauté affamée par une telle abstinence
Retire à la beauté toute postérité.
Elle est trop belle, trop sage, trop sagement belle,
Pour jouir du bonheur de me désespérer.
Elle a juré de ne jamais aimer, serment
220 Que je ne te rapporte que comme un mort vivant.

BENVOLIO

Suis mon conseil, abstiens-toi de penser à elle.

ROMÉO

Alors, apprends-moi comment m'abstenir de penser.

BENVOLIO

Rends à tes yeux toute leur liberté,
Qu'ils puissent examiner d'autres beautés.

ROMÉO

                                        C'est le moyen
225 De rappeler encore plus la sienne, si exquise.
Les jolis masques sont un baiser au front des belles,
Eux dont la noirceur fait croire qu'ils cachent la beauté.
Frappé de cécité, l'homme ne peut oublier
Le trésor précieux des yeux qu'il a perdus.
230 Si tu me montres une femme incomparable,

---

1. Roméo joue ici sur les clichés mythologiques de la chasteté qui
font de Rosaline une nouvelle Diane et une anti-Danaé (nymphe séduite
par Jupiter transformé en pluie d'or). Voir Ovide, *Métamorphoses*, VI, 113.
Ce thème se retrouve dans les *Sonnets* de Shakespeare (le sonnet 4, par
exemple).

Que sera sa beauté sinon un mémento
Où je lirai le nom d'une beauté plus grande[1] ?
Adieu, tu ne peux pas m'apprendre à oublier.

BENVOLIO

Quitte à mourir endetté, je veux bien payer cette leçon.

Scène 2

Entrent Capulet, Pâris et un serviteur.

CAPULET

Mais Montaigu est comme moi condamné
À une même peine. Il n'est pas difficile, je pense,
Pour des gens de notre âge de maintenir la paix.

PÂRIS

Vous êtes l'un et l'autre honorés, estimés,
5 Et il est dommage d'être si longtemps brouillés.
Mais au fait, monseigneur, quelle suite à ma requête ?

CAPULET

Je te répète ce que j'ai déjà répondu.
Mon enfant est encore étrangère à ce monde,
Elle n'a pas encore atteint ses quatorze ans.
10 Laissons donc deux étés se flétrir en leur éclat

---

1. Cette image qui associe le livre et la beauté (on pense aux enluminures médiévales, mais aussi aux nombreux beaux livres illustrés parus à la Renaissance) se retrouve dans l'éloge que Lady Capulet fait de Pâris (I. 3, v. 82).

Avant qu'elle soit mûre pour une bague au doigt.

PÂRIS

De plus jeunes qu'elle ont fait d'heureuses mères.

CAPULET

Mais elles se fanent trop vite, ces mères trop précoces.
La terre a englouti tous mes espoirs sauf elle,
15 Elle est mon héritière sur cette terre.
Mais courtisez-la, Pâris, gagnez son cœur.
Ce que je veux n'est qu'une part de son consentement.
Et si elle dit oui, sachez que son libre choix
Aura aussi mon accord et mon consentement.
20 Selon la tradition, j'offre ce soir une fête
À laquelle j'ai convié de très nombreux amis
Qui me sont chers. Vous en faites partie
Et serez bienvenu pour en grossir le nombre.
Dans mon humble maison, attendez-vous à voir
25 Des étoiles terrestres qui vont illuminer le soir.
La joie qu'éprouvent les fringants jeunes gens
Quand avril bigarré marche sur les talons
De l'hiver boitillant, vous la ressentirez ce soir
Chez moi devant toutes ces filles en fleur.
30 Écoutez et regardez-les toutes, puis aimez
Celle qui le mérite le plus. Après avoir
Bien regardé, ma fille sera peut-être l'une d'elles
Même si en soi le chiffre un ne fait pas nombre !
Venez donc avec moi. [*Au serviteur.*] Va, bon à rien, arpente
35 Notre belle Vérone et trouve les personnes
Dont le nom figure sur cette feuille. Dis-leur
Que, s'ils le veulent, ils seront bienvenus chez moi.

Sortent [Capulet et Pâris].

LE SERVITEUR

Trouver ceux dont le nom est écrit sur la feuille ! Il est écrit que
le cordonnier doit se servir de son mètre, le tailleur de ses

40 formes, le pêcheur de ses pinceaux et le peintre de ses filets.
Mais on m'envoie chercher des gens dont le nom est écrit sur ce
papier, alors que je suis incapable de lire les noms que celui qui
sait écrire a écrits ici. Il faut que je trouve des gens qui savent et
ces messieurs tombent à pic.

Entrent Benvolio et Roméo.

BENVOLIO

45 Allons, l'ami, comme un feu peut en éteindre un autre,
Une peine peut être atténuée par une autre douleur.
Si tu as le vertige, tourne dans l'autre sens, cela t'aidera.
Un chagrin sans espoir se guérit dans la langueur d'un autre.
Si ton œil brille d'une nouvelle flamme
50 L'ancienne inflammation finira par mourir.

ROMÉO

Dans ce cas, la feuille de plantain[1] est un très bon remède.

BENVOLIO

En quel cas au juste ?

ROMÉO

Si tu te casses la jambe.

BENVOLIO

Enfin, quoi, Roméo, tu délires ?

ROMÉO

Si je délire, je suis fou à lier,
55 En prison, sans rien à manger dans la cellule
Où je suis fouetté, torturé et... Bonsoir, l'ami.

---

1. Feuille dont les vertus médicinales aidaient à cicatriser les plaies.

LE SERVITEUR

Bien le bonsoir. S'il vous plaît, monsieur, est-ce que vous savez
lire ?

ROMÉO

Oui, je sais lire l'avenir dans ma propre infortune.

LE SERVITEUR

60 Pas besoin de livres pour ça ! Mais s'il vous plaît, est-ce que vous
savez lire tout ce qui est écrit là ?

ROMÉO

Oui, si j'en connais l'alphabet et la langue.

LE SERVITEUR

Voilà qui est honnête. Adieu, monsieur.

ROMÉO

Attends, l'ami, oui, je sais lire.

Il lit la lettre.

65 Le Signor Martino, son épouse et ses filles, le Comte Anselme
et ses charmantes sœurs, la Dame veuve d'Utruvio, le Sieur
Placentio et ses aimables nièces, Mercutio et son frère Valentin,
mon oncle Capulet, son épouse et ses filles, ma nièce, la belle
Rosaline, et Livia, le Sieur Valentio et son cousin Tybalt, Lucio
70 et la pétulante Héléna. Voilà une belle assemblée ! Où doivent-
ils se rendre ?

LE SERVITEUR

Là-haut.

ROMÉO

Pour souper ? Chez qui ?

LE SERVITEUR

Chez nous.

ROMÉO

75 Qui ça, nous ?

LE SERVITEUR

Chez mon maître.

ROMÉO

En effet, j'aurais dû te le demander plus tôt.

LE SERVITEUR

Alors je vais vous le dire sans que vous me le demandiez. Mon
maître est le grand, le riche Capulet, et si vous n'êtes pas de la
80 maison des Montaigu, je vous invite à venir vider un verre de
vin. Que Dieu vous garde.

Il sort.

BENVOLIO

À cette fête que Capulet donne chaque année
Tu verras la belle Rosaline que tu aimes tant,
Aux côtés de toutes les jolies filles de Vérone :
85 Laisse tes préjugés, va y jeter un coup d'œil
Et compare son visage à d'autres que je te montrerai.
Tu verras que ton cygne est en fait un corbeau.

ROMÉO

Le jour où la dévote religion de mes yeux
Admettra cette erreur, que mes larmes deviennent feu,
90 Et que ces yeux, que mes pleurs n'ont jamais pu noyer,
Ces flagrants hérétiques, soient brûlés pour avoir menti[1].
Une fille plus belle qu'elle ! Le soleil qui voit tout
N'a pas vu sa pareille depuis que le monde est monde.

---

1. Cette image annonce ironiquement le sonnet de la rencontre de Roméo et
Juliette (I. 5, v. 42 et suiv.) et fait de Roméo un futur hérétique, assimilant ainsi
le coup de foudre de l'amour à une forme de conversion religieuse.

BENVOLIO

Allons ! Elle était belle parce qu'elle était seule,
95 Elle-même avec elle-même pesée dans tes yeux !
Sur la balance de ton cristallin pèse alors
L'amour de ta dame avec quelque autre visage,
Dont je te montrerai l'éclat à cette fête,
Et l'absolu dès lors te paraîtra passable.

ROMÉO

100 J'irai, non pour voir le spectacle annoncé,
Mais pour me délecter des splendeurs de ma belle.

[Ils sortent.]

Scène 3

Entrent Lady Capulet et la Nourrice.

LADY CAPULET

Nourrice, où est ma fille ? Fais-la venir.

LA NOURRICE

Mais par le pucelage que j'avais encore à douze ans,
Je lui ai dit de venir. Hé oh ! mon agnelle. Hé ! ma coccinelle.
Mon Dieu, où est cette fille ? Eh ! Juliette !

Entre Juliette.

JULIETTE

͡h bien, qui m'appelle ainsi ?

LA NOURRICE
Votre mère.

JULIETTE
Madame, je suis ici, que disiez-vous ?

LADY CAPULET
Je vais te le dire. Nourrice, laisse-nous un instant,
Nous avons à parler en secret. Non, Nourrice, reviens.
Je me ravise, tu vas participer à notre entretien.
10   Tu sais que ma fille a bien l'âge maintenant.

LA NOURRICE
Son âge, ma foi, je peux l'indiquer à une heure près.

LADY CAPULET
Elle n'a pas encore quatorze ans.

LA NOURRICE
Je miserais quatorze de mes dents
(Bien qu'à mon grand regret il n'en reste que quatre)
15   Qu'elle n'a pas quatorze ans !
Combien y a-t-il d'ici à la Saint-Pierre-aux-Liens[1] ?

LADY CAPULET
À peu près quinze jours.

LA NOURRICE
De près ou de loin, de tous les jours de l'année,
La veille de la Saint-Pierre elle aura quatorze ans,
20   Suzanne et elle — paix soit aux âmes chrétiennes —
Avaient le même âge. Suzanne, elle, est au ciel.
Elle était trop parfaite pour moi. Mais, comme je disais,
À la Saint-Pierre, la veille au soir, elle aura quatorze ans.

---

1. Située le 1ᵉʳ août, cette fête avait remplacé dans le calendrier chrétien l'ancienne fête celtique de Lugnasadh (*Lammastide* en anglais), la fête des récoltes qui inaugurait le trimestre d'été.

Pour sûr, ça, dame oui, je m'en souviens.
25 Cela fera onze ans, le jour du tremblement de terre,
Qu'elle a été sevrée, ça je l'oublierai jamais
Ce jour-là de tous les jours de l'année.
J'avais mis de l'absinthe sur le bout du téton,
Assise au soleil, au pied du mur du pigeonnier.
30 Monsieur et vous-même étiez allés à Mantoue,
C'est que j'en ai, de la mémoire ! Mais, comme j'ai dit,
Quand elle a senti l'absinthe sur le bout de mon téton,
Avec son goût amer, ah ! la petite coquine,
Fallait voir ses grimaces et comme elle s'en prenait au téton !
35 « Ça suffit », qu'il fait, le pigeonnier. Pas la peine j'vous jure
De me dire deux fois de plier bagage.
Et onze ans ont passé depuis ce jour-là,
Car elle tenait déjà debout toute seule. Même, par la Sainte
                                                                    [Croix,
Qu'elle courait et trottait partout ; car, pas plus tard
40 Que la veille, elle s'était cogné le front en tombant,
De sorte que mon mari (Dieu le garde, c'était un gai luron)
Releva la petite. « Ah bon, qu'il dit, tu tombes sur la figure !
Tu tomberas sur le dos quand tu seras plus maligne !
Pas vrai, Julie ? » Et, par Notre-Dame,
45 La petite arrêta de pleurer et dit « oui ».
On voit bien à présent qu'elle avait raison !
Ah ! j'vous assure, même si je vivais mille ans,
Ça, je l'oublierais pas. « Pas vrai, Julie ? » qu'il dit,
Et la petite friponne arrête et dit « oui ».

LADY CAPULET

50 En voilà assez, je t'en prie, arrête un peu.

LA NOURRICE

Oui, madame, mais je ne peux m'empêcher de rire
En pensant qu'elle cessa de pleurer et dit « oui ».
Pourtant je vous garantis qu'elle avait sur le front
Une bosse aussi grosse qu'une couille de coq.

55 Un mauvais coup ! Et elle pleurait à chaudes larmes,
« Ouais », qu'il dit, mon mari, « tu es tombée sur la figure ?
Tu tomberas sur le dos quand t'auras l'âge,
Pas vrai, Julie ? » Et elle s'arrête et dit « oui ».

JULIETTE

Arrête donc toi aussi, je t'en prie, Nourrice.

LA NOURRICE

60 Bon, j'ai fini. Que Dieu te bénisse !
Tu étais le plus beau bébé que j'aie jamais nourri,
Et si je vis assez longtemps pour te voir mariée,
Je serai comblée.

LADY CAPULET

Vierge Marie ! C'est justement de mari
Que je viens te parler. Dites-moi, Juliette, ma fille
65 Est-ce que vous pensez déjà au mariage ?

JULIETTE

C'est un honneur dont je ne rêve pas encore.

LA NOURRICE

« Un honneur » ! Si je n'avais pas été ton unique nourrice,
Je dirais que la sagesse t'est venue en me tétant le sein.

LADY CAPULET

Eh bien, il est temps de penser au mariage. De plus jeunes
70 Que vous, ici à Vérone, des dames très estimées,
Ont déjà des enfants. Si je compte bien
Je vous avais déjà donné le jour à l'âge
Où vous êtes encore vierge. En un mot
Le vaillant Pâris veut faire de vous sa femme.

LA NOURRICE

75 Un homme, ma jeune dame, madame, un homme
Que le monde entier... un vrai modèle d'homme.

LADY CAPULET

Tout l'été de Vérone n'a pas pareille fleur.

LA NOURRICE

Oui, une fleur, en vérité c'est une fleur.

LADY CAPULET

Que dites-vous, pouvez-vous aimer ce gentilhomme ?
80 Vous l'apercevrez ce soir à notre fête.
Lisez ce livre qu'est le visage du jeune Pâris,
Et trouvez y le plaisir que la beauté a écrit de sa plume.
Examinez l'harmonie qui marie tous ses traits,
Et comme ils se combinent bien entre eux,
85 Et ce qui reste obscur dans ce charmant ouvrage
Vous le trouverez écrit en marge de ses yeux.
À ce précieux livre d'amour, cet amant que rien ne lie,
Ne manque, pour le parfaire, qu'une couverture.
Le poisson vit dans la mer et la beauté extérieure
90 S'enorgueillit aussi de celle qu'elle recouvre.
Aux yeux du monde, l'apparence de l'ouvrage
Vaut la légende dorée qu'il tient en ses fermoirs.
Ainsi vous partagerez tout ce qu'il peut avoir,
Et, avec lui pour mari, vous en serez plus sage.

LA NOURRICE

93 Non pas plus sage, plus ronde, au contact d'un homme.

LADY CAPULET

Dites-moi si oui ou non l'amour de Pâris vous convient ?

JULIETTE

Je verrai à l'aimer, si voir peut faire aimer.
Mais la flèche de mon œil ne volera pas plus loin
Que le permettra la force que vous lui donnerez.

Entre un serviteur.

LE SERVITEUR

100 Madame, les invités sont arrivés, le souper est servi, on vous
réclame, on demande mademoiselle et on maudit la Nourrice à
l'office. On est tous débordés. Je dois aller servir, je vous en
prie, suivez-moi au plus vite.

Il sort

LADY CAPULET

Nous te suivons. Juliette, le comte est là, il attend.

LA NOURRICE

105 Va, ma fille, va pour avoir nuit et jour ton content.

Elles sortent.

Scène 4

*Entrent Roméo, Mercutio, Benvolio, en compagnie de cinq
ou six masques et de porteurs de torches[1].*

ROMÉO

Alors, allons-nous faire ce discours à titre d'excuse,
Ou bien entrer sans autre forme de cérémonie ?

BENVOLIO

La mode n'est plus à tous ces beaux artifices.

---

1. À la Renaissance, il était admis que les masques, à l'occasion des fêtes,
s'invitent dans les demeures de l'aristocratie sous prétexte d'y donner un petit
divertissement.

Point n'est besoin d'un Cupidon aux yeux bandés
5 Portant l'arc en bois peint des Tartares[1],
Effarouchant les dames comme un épouvantail,
Ni de prologue débité d'une voix faible
Avec l'aide d'un souffleur, pour entrer en ces lieux.
Qu'elles nous mesurent comme bon leur semblera,
10 Nous, nous leur mesurerons quelques mesures et voilà.

ROMÉO

Qu'on me donne une torche, pas d'entrechats pour moi ;
Comme je suis d'humeur sombre, je tiendrai la chandelle.

MERCUTIO

Ah non, cher Roméo, on veut que tu danses.

ROMÉO

Pas question. Tu as des souliers de bal
15 Au cuir souple, moi un cœur de plomb
Qui me cloue au sol et entrave mes pieds.

MERCUTIO

Puisque tu es amoureux, emprunte les ailes d'Éros
Et sers-t'en pour voler plus haut que nous tous.

ROMÉO

Amour m'a tant blessé de ses flèches que je ne peux pas
20 M'envoler de ses plumes légères. Ligoté,
Je ne peux pas bondir et fondre sur ce chagrin :
Je m'enfonce sous le lourd fardeau de l'amour.

MERCUTIO

C'est que pour t'enfoncer, c'est toi qui dois peser.
Étreinte trop puissante pour une si tendre chose.

_____
1. Arc en forme de lèvres ou d'accolade.

ROMÉO

25 L'amour, une tendre chose ? Il est trop dur,
Trop brutal et fougueux, il est comme l'épine.

MERCUTIO

Si l'amour est trop dur, sois dur avec l'amour.
Rends coup pour coup, il sera sur le flanc.
Qu'on me passe un écrin où fourrer mon visage,
30 Un masque pour un masque. Car il m'importe peu
Qu'un regard sourcilleux dénombre mes défauts.
Voici d'épais sourcils qui rougiront pour moi.

BENVOLIO

Allez, frappons à la porte, entrons, et sitôt dans la place
Que chacun danse et coure sans ménager ses jambes.

ROMÉO

35 Qu'on me donne une torche. Je laisse les cœurs volages
Taquiner du talon les roseaux insensibles[1].
Un vieux dicton sied très bien à mon cas :
Je tiendrai la chandelle, et je regarderai.
Heureux au jeu, je suis fait comme un rat.

MERCUTIO

40 Comme un chat ! La nuit les chats sont gris, dit le gendarme.
Si tu n'es qu'un manche, on te sortira de la fange,
La fange de l'amour où tu es englué
Jusqu'aux oreilles. Allons-y, nos torches brûlent pour rien.

ROMÉO

Ce n'est pas vrai.

MERCUTIO

45 Je veux dire qu'en s'attardant ainsi, on gaspille

---

1. En Angleterre, le sol des maisons, comme celui des palais, était tapissé de roseaux.

La lumière comme une lanterne allumée en plein jour.
Comprends mon intention, car dans notre bon sens
Il y a cinq fois plus de raison qu'en chacun de nos sens.

ROMÉO

Nos intentions sont bonnes en allant à ce bal
50 Mais cela n'a pourtant aucun sens.

MERCUTIO
                              Et pourquoi donc?

ROMÉO

J'ai fait un rêve cette nuit.

MERCUTIO
                              Moi aussi.

ROMÉO

Ah, de quoi as-tu rêvé?

MERCUTIO
                              De choses à dormir debout.

ROMÉO

C'est en dormant couché que l'on fait de vrais rêves.

MERCUTIO

Alors, je vois que la Reine Mab t'est apparue.
55 C'est l'accoucheuse des fées et elle vient,
Pas plus grosse qu'une agate
Au doigt d'un échevin,
Tirée par un attelage de tout petits atomes,
Se poser sur le nez des hommes endormis.
60 Son carrosse est une coquille de noisette vidée
Par l'écureuil menuisier ou un ver endurci,
Qui sont depuis toujours les carrossiers des fées.
Les rayons de ses roues sont des pattes de faucheux,
La capote est tissée d'ailes de sauterelles,

65 Les rênes sont faites de fins fils de la Vierge,
   Le collier un humide éclat de lune,
   Le fouet une patte de grillon, la lanière un fil d'araignée,
   Le cocher un moucheron vêtu de gris,
   Pas plus gros que le quart du petit poil rond
70 Qu'on tire de la main des filles paresseuses.
   C'est ainsi que nuit après nuit elle galope
   Dans la cervelle des amoureux qui rêvent alors d'amour,
   Sur les genoux des courtisans qui rêvent alors de révérences,
   Sur les doigts des robins qui rêvent aussitôt d'honoraires,
75 Sur les lèvres des dames qui rêvent aussitôt de baisers,
   Ces lèvres que Mab en sa colère afflige
   De boutons parce qu'elles sentent trop les bonbons.
   Tantôt elle galope sur le nez d'un courtisan,
   Et le voilà qui rêve qu'il flaire une requête.
80 Tantôt avec la queue d'un cochon de la dîme[1]
   Elle chatouille les narines d'un chanoine endormi
   Qui rêve alors d'un nouveau bénéfice.
   Tantôt elle s'aventure sur le cou d'un soldat,
   Et le voilà qui rêve d'ennemis égorgés,
85 D'assauts et d'embuscades et d'épées de Tolède,
   De rasades profondes de cinq brasses, et puis, bien vite,
   Elle bat le tambour à son oreille, sur quoi il sursaute et s'éveille,
   Et, ainsi effrayé, lâche une ou deux prières,
   Et puis il se rendort. C'est cette même Mab
90 Qui va la nuit tresser la crinière des chevaux,
   Collant les poils follets en paquets répugnants,
   En nœuds qui, démêlés, annoncent le malheur.
   C'est elle, la sorcière, qui pèse sur les vierges, quand elles sont
                                                    [sur le dos,
   Et leur enseigne à porter leur tout premier fardeau,
95 Faisant d'elles de bonnes bêtes de somme.
   C'est elle...

---

1. Impôt levé par l'Église et que les paysans payaient parfois en nature (en donnant un cochon, par exemple).

ROMÉO

Arrête, Mercutio, tais-toi, ça suffit !
Tu ne penses qu'à la chose.

MERCUTIO

                    C'est vrai, je parle des rêves
Des rejetons d'une cervelle oisive,
Qui ne viennent d'autre chose que de la fantaisie,
100 Dont la substance est fine comme l'air,
Et plus inconstante que le vent qui courtise
À présent le sein glacé du nord, et qui,
Tout dépité, s'en va souffler ailleurs,
Se tournant vers le sud emperlé de rosée.

BENVOLIO

105 Ce vent dont tu nous parles nous fait perdre le nord.
Le souper est fini, nous arriverons en retard.

ROMÉO

Non, trop tôt, j'en ai peur, car mon esprit redoute
Qu'un avenir encore suspendu dans les astres,
N'entame dès ce soir un cours bien funeste
110 Lors de cette fête nocturne et ne marque la fin
De la vie méprisable enclose en ma poitrine
Par l'affreuse échéance d'une mort avant terme.
Mais que le timonier à la barre de ma vie,
Dirige aussi la voile[1]. Allons-y, mes amis !

BENVOLIO

115 Battez, tambours.

---

1. Début d'un réseau d'images associant la vie et la destinée humaines à une barque ballottée sur les flots. Ces images sont, semble-t-il, empruntées au *Canzoniere* de Pétrarque (voir en particulier les sonnets 122 et 177).

Scène 5

Une salle de réception chez Capulet. Des musiciens se préparent.
Entrent les masques, ils font le tour de la salle
et se rangent sur les côtés. Entrent des serviteurs
qui portent des serviettes sur les bras.

PREMIER SERVITEUR

Où est donc passé Lapoëlle ? Pas de risque qu'il aide à desservir !
Lui, porter une assiette ? Lui, la nettoyer ?

DEUXIÈME SERVITEUR

Quand les bonnes manières sont entre les mains d'un ou deux
individus et qu'en plus ils ne se lavent pas les mains, alors c'est
5 moche !

PREMIER SERVITEUR

Débarrassez-moi de ces tabourets, poussez ce dressoir et attention à l'argenterie. Eh vieux, mets-moi de côté une part de
frangipane et, si tu m'aimes, dis au portier qu'il laisse entrer
Susie Lameule et Nelly, Antoine et Lapoëlle.

TROISIÈME SERVITEUR

10 J'arrive !

PREMIER SERVITEUR

On te cherche, on te réclame, on t'appelle, on te demande dans
la grand-salle.

QUATRIÈME SERVITEUR

On ne peut pas être au four et au moulin. Du nerf, les gars !
Remuons-nous un peu, le dernier aura les restes.

Sortent les serviteurs. Entrent Capulet, Lady Capulet, Juliette,
Tybalt et la Nourrice. Tous les invités, accompagnés
des dames, vont accueillir les masques.

CAPULET

15   Bienvenue, messieurs. Les dames qui n'ont pas de cors
Aux pieds seront vos partenaires.
Ah! mes belles, laquelle d'entre vous
Refusera à présent de danser?
Celle qui fait la fine bouche,
20   Elle a des cors aux pieds, j'en mets ma main au feu. J'ai visé juste?
Bienvenue, messieurs. J'ai connu le temps où,
Moi aussi, je portais un masque, et je savais
Susurrer à l'oreille d'une jolie femme
Une histoire à son goût. C'est fini, bien fini.
25   Vous êtes les bienvenus, messieurs. Allez, les musiciens, jouez
Jouez! Place, place, faites de la place! et vous, mesdemoiselles,
ouvrez le bal.

Les musiciens jouent, on danse.

De la lumière! Bande de bons à rien, enlevez ces tréteaux!
Éteignez-moi le feu, il fait trop chaud ici.
Ah! mon cher, ce divertissement imprévu arrive à point.
30   Non, non, restez assis, cher cousin Capulet,
Nous avons tous deux passé l'âge de danser.
Combien de temps cela fait-il que vous et moi
N'avons pas participé à un bal masqué?

LE COUSIN CAPULET

Au moins trente ans, ma foi.

CAPULET

Mais non! mon cher, beaucoup moins que cela!
35   C'était aux noces de Lucentio, à la Pentecôte,
Et qu'elle revienne vite ou pas, cela fera vingt-cinq ans
Qu'on n'a pas eu l'occasion de mettre un masque.

LE COUSIN CAPULET

Ça fait plus, ça fait plus, son fils est déjà plus vieux que ça,
Il a bien trente ans.

CAPULET
Qu'est-ce que vous me racontez?
40 Il y a deux ans il n'était pas encore majeur.

ROMÉO
Quelle est cette dame qui orne le bras
De ce cavalier, là-bas?

LE SERVITEUR
Je ne sais pas, monsieur.

ROMÉO
Oh! pour elle, les torches redoublent leur éclat,
Elle est comme un joyau[1] sur la joue de la nuit,
Un brillant à l'oreille d'une Noire. Beauté
45 Trop riche pour qu'on en jouisse, trop chère pour la terre.
Colombe couleur de neige dans un vol de choucas,
Cette dame là-bas se détache parmi ses compagnes.
La danse terminée, j'irai voir où elle est
Et ma grossière main sera bénie rien qu'en touchant la sienne!
50 Mon cœur a-t-il aimé avant ce jour? Mes yeux, jurez que non.
Jamais avant ce soir je n'avais vu la vraie beauté.

TYBALT
Cet homme, d'après sa voix, doit être un Montaigu.
Va chercher ma rapière, petit. [*Sort le page.*] Quoi! cet esclave ose
Venir ici, sous ce masque grotesque,
55 Pour rire et se moquer de nos cérémonies?
Par le sang et l'honneur de ma race,
Ce n'est pas un péché de le frapper à mort.

---

1. L'image du joyau, qui traduit le mot anglais *jewel*, fait allusion au surnom que la Nourrice a donné à Juliette (*Jule*), ainsi prénommée parce qu'elle est née au mois de juillet (le 31, la veille de *Lammastide*). Contrairement aux artifices de la rhétorique pétrarquisante, l'amour vrai introduit une forme de coïncidence quasi magique entre la chose et le nom.

CAPULET

Allons, allons, neveu, qu'as-tu à maugréer ainsi ?

TYBALT

Mon oncle, cet homme est un Montaigu, notre ennemi,
60 Un gueux venu ici pour nous défier
Et se gausser, ce soir, de nos cérémonies.

CAPULET

N'est-ce pas le jeune Roméo ?

TYBALT

C'est lui, ce gueux de Roméo.

CAPULET

Calme-toi, mon neveu, et laisse le tranquille.
Il se conduit ici en digne gentilhomme,
65 Et, à vrai dire, Vérone vante en lui
Un garçon vertueux, plein de modération.
Je ne souffrirai pas, pour tout l'or de la ville,
Qu'ici, en ma maison, on puisse l'offenser[1].
Alors, sois patient, n'y fais plus attention,
70 Telle est ma volonté et, si tu la respectes,
Fais bonne figure, ne fronce plus le sourcil,
C'est un visage qui ne sied guère à notre fête.

TYBALT

Il sied parfaitement quand un gueux se mêle aux invités,
Je ne le supporterai pas.

CAPULET

Si, tu le supporteras !
75 Mon petit monsieur, il en sera comme je dis. Non mais !
Qui est le maître ici, moi ou toi ? Non mais !
Monsieur ne le supportera pas ! Que Dieu sauve mon âme :

---

1. En vertu du devoir d'hospitalité qui était considéré comme sacré.

Tu veux faire une émeute parmi mes invités !
Monsieur veut faire le coq ! Monsieur veut commander !

TYBALT

80   Mais, mon oncle, c'est une infamie.

CAPULET

                          Ça suffit comme ça, assez !
Tu n'es qu'un insolent. Ah, c'est comme ça ?
Cet esclandre pourrait te coûter cher. Je sais ce que je dis.
Tu veux me contrarier. C'est vraiment le moment !
[*À ses invités.*] Bravo, mes amis ! [*À Tybalt.*] Tu n'es qu'un petit
                                      [coq, allez.
85   Tais-toi, sinon — [*À ses invités.*] De la lumière, de la lumière ! —
                              [[*À Tybalt.*] Quelle honte !
Je saurai te faire taire ! Allons, amusez-vous, mes bons amis !

TYBALT

La patience qu'on m'impose alors que je suis hors de moi
Fait tressaillir ma chair dans cet assaut contraire[1].
Je vais m'en aller, mais une telle intrusion
90   Va voir sa douceur se changer en poison.

ROMÉO

Si de ma main indigne je devais profaner
Ce sanctuaire, voici mon doux péché : mes lèvres,
Ces deux pèlerins rougissants, vont effacer
La rudesse de mon geste dans un tendre baiser.

JULIETTE

95   Bon pèlerin, vous offensez là votre main

---

1. Les sentiments contradictoires se bousculent chez Tybalt comme ils se heurteront chez Roméo et Juliette, chez qui le sentiment amoureux naît sur fond de haine ancestrale. Le déchaînement de la haine de Tybalt à l'encontre de Roméo n'est pas moins fort que le coup de foudre amoureux qui réunit Roméo à Juliette. Celle-ci résumera parfaitement ce paradoxe dans le vers « Mon unique amour né de mon unique haine » (I. 5, v. 135).

Qui offre ainsi l'hommage de sa dévotion,
Car les saintes ont des mains que les pèlerins touchent,
Paume contre paume, c'est là leur pieux baiser.

ROMÉO
Les saintes ont-elles des lèvres comme les pèlerins ?

JULIETTE
100 Oui, pèlerin, des lèvres pour prier.

ROMÉO
Ô chère sainte, que les lèvres imitent tes mains.
Elles prient pour que leur foi ne soit pas désespoir.

JULIETTE
Les saintes restent de marbre en dispensant leurs grâces.

ROMÉO
Ne bouge pas tandis que je recueille le fruit de ma prière[1].
105 [*Il l'embrasse.*] Tes lèvres sur les miennes ont lavé mon péché.

JULIETTE
Alors mes lèvres portent le péché qu'elles t'ont pris.

ROMÉO
Le péché de mes lèvres ? Quelle douce tentation ! [*Il l'embrasse.*]
Rends-moi mon péché.

JULIETTE
Tu embrasses comme il faut.

LA NOURRICE
Madame votre mère voudrait vous dire un mot.

[*Juliette sort.*]

---

1. Ce vers clôt les quatorze vers partagés qui constituent le sonnet de la rencontre.

ROMÉO

110 Et qui donc est sa mère ?

LA NOURRICE
Voyons, jeune homme,
Sa mère est la maîtresse de maison, une dame
Digne, sage et vertueuse. J'ai nourri sa fille,
Celle avec qui vous parliez. Moi je dis que celui qui l'aura
Touchera des écus.

ROMÉO
C'est une Capulet ?
115 Oh ! terrible créance. Ma vie devient la dette de mon ennemi.

BENVOLIO
Assez, va-t'en, la fête bat son plein.

ROMÉO
Eh oui, je le crains, mon trouble est à son comble.

CAPULET
Non, messieurs, ne partez pas déjà,
On vous prépare un buffet et des rafraîchissements.

Les masques lui chuchotent quelque chose à l'oreille.

120 Ah, c'est donc ça ! Eh bien, je vous remercie tous,
Merci messieurs et bonne nuit à tous.
Qu'on apporte des torches, des torches. Allons, au lit.
Ah, mon ami, il se fait tard, je crois,
Et je vais me coucher.

[*Sortent Capulet, Lady Capulet, les dames et les masques.*]

JULIETTE
125 Viens ici, Nourrice. Qui est ce gentilhomme ?

LA NOURRICE

Le fils et l'héritier du vieux Tiberio.

JULIETTE

Et celui qui sort en ce moment ?

LA NOURRICE

Pardi, je crois que c'est le jeune Petruchio.

JULIETTE

Et celui qui suit, là, et qui ne voulait pas danser ?

LA NOURRICE

130 Je ne sais pas.

JULIETTE

Va demander son nom. S'il est déjà marié,
Alors dans la tombe je serai déflorée[1].

LA NOURRICE

Son nom est Roméo et c'est un Montaigu,
Le fils unique de votre grand ennemi.

JULIETTE

135 Mon unique amour né de mon unique haine,
Inconnu vu trop tôt et reconnu trop tard.
Pour moi, l'amour est comme un enfant bâtard
Qui me pousse à aimer la source de ma haine.

LA NOURRICE

Qu'est-ce que tu chantes là ?

JULIETTE
            Un refrain que m'a appris

---

1. Cette image prémonitoire associe le thème macabre et l'érotisme et
rappelle les tableaux où l'on voit la jeune fille que la Mort (au masculin en
anglais) s'apprête à étreindre.

140 L'un de mes cavaliers.

                        On appelle Juliette.

« Juliette ».

                        LA NOURRICE
                Oui, on arrive, on arrive,
Venez, allons-nous-en, tous les invités sont partis à présent.

                        Elles sortent.

ACTE II

Prologue

Le Chœur

Alors le vieux Désir gît sur son lit de mort
Et la jeune Passion brûle d'en hériter.
La belle pour qui l'Amour languissait, se mourait,
N'est plus belle à côté de la douce Juliette.
5 Roméo est aimé et de nouveau il aime.
Tous deux sont sous le charme d'un regard échangé.
Lui doit gémir pour celle qu'il croit son ennemie,
Elle arracher le tendre appât de l'amour à de terribles crocs.
Tenu pour ennemi, il lui est interdit
10 De faire les promesses que les amants se font.
Tout aussi amoureuse, ses moyens sont bien moindres
De pouvoir rencontrer son bel amour naissant.
La passion les conforte, le temps leur est propice,
Tempérant ces rigueurs par d'extrêmes douceurs[1].

---

1. Là encore, le prologue a la forme d'un sonnet.

Scène 1

Entre Roméo, seul.

ROMÉO

Comment aller plus loin quand mon cœur est ici ?
Retourne-toi, sombre glaise, et retrouve ton centre[1].

Roméo se retire, entrent Benvolio et Mercutio.

BENVOLIO

Roméo ! Cousin Roméo ! Roméo !

MERCUTIO
                              Il est sage,
Sur ma vie, il est parti chez lui pour aller se coucher.

BENVOLIO

5 Il a filé par ici et sauté le mur de ce verger.
Appelle-le, bon Mercutio.

MERCUTIO

Mieux, je vais le faire apparaître.
Roméo, es-tu là ? Humeurs ! Folie ! Passion ! Amant !
Apparais sous la forme d'un soupir,
10 Ne dis qu'un seul couplet et je serai satisfait.
Soupire : « Hélas ! hélas ! », fait rimer « amour » avec « toujours »,
Trouve un mot galant pour ma marraine Vénus,
Un petit nom charmant pour son fils héritier,
Le jeune aveugle Abraham Cupidon, lui qui visa si bien
15 Quand le roi Cophétua s'enticha d'une gueuse[2].
Il n'entend pas, ne bouge pas, ne remue pas :
Le singe fait le mort, je dois le faire apparaître.

---

1. Image biblique de l'homme, dont la chair est comparée à de la glaise. 2. Allusion à la ballade grivoise de Cophétua, roi d'Afrique tombé amoureux d'une belle mendiante.

Je te conjure d'apparaître, par l'œil brillant de Rosaline,
Par son grand front, sa lèvre purpurine,
20 Par son pied mignon, sa jambe fine, sa cuisse frémissante,
Et par tous les domaines qui s'étendent alentour,
Sous tes traits familiers apparais devant nous.

BENVOLIO

Mais s'il entend, tu vas le mettre en colère.

MERCUTIO

Non, ce n'est pas possible ; ce qui pourrait l'offenser
25 Serait de faire se dresser quelque étrange démon
Dans le cercle de sa maîtresse et de le laisser planté là
Jusqu'à ce que, par magie, elle le fasse retomber tout pendant[1].
Dans ce cas il pourrait bien se sentir offensé.
Mon invocation est franche et honnête : c'est au nom de sa
                                                        [maîtresse
30 Que je l'invoque, seulement pour qu'il se dresse.

BENVOLIO

Viens, il s'est caché parmi les arbres
Pour mieux se mêler aux humeurs des ténèbres,
Son amour est aveugle et le noir lui va bien.

MERCUTIO

Si l'amour est aveugle, il ne peut viser juste.
35 Alors il va s'asseoir dessous un néflier
Et souhaiter que sa belle soit ce genre de fruit
Que les filles appellent nèfles quand elles rient entre elles.
Oh ! Roméo, si elle était cette nèfle, si elle était
Cette nèfle grande ouverte et toi une queue de poire[2] !

---

1. Le langage de l'incantation magique, qui renvoie au *Docteur Faust* de Marlowe écrit deux ans avant *Roméo et Juliette*, sert de métaphore grivoise pour désigner l'érection et la détumescence qui suit l'orgasme. 2. La nèfle, quand elle est mûre, évoque la vulve féminine. Quant à la « queue de poire » (*poperin pear* en anglais), elle désigne le pénis avec, de surcroît, un jeu de mots sur l'anglais *pop her in* (« pénètre-la ») !

40 Roméo, bonne nuit. Je vais dans mon lit à roulettes,
Ce lit des champs est bien trop froid pour que j'y dorme.
Allez, on s'en va ?

BENVOLIO

Oui, partons ! Inutile de chercher.
Celui qui ne veut pas qu'on le trouve.

[*Sortent Benvolio et Mercutio.*]

Roméo s'avance.

ROMÉO

Il rit des plaies celui qui n'a jamais eu de blessures.

[*Entre Juliette, au balcon.*]

45 Chut ! Quelle est cette lumière qui brille à la fenêtre ?
C'est l'orient, et Juliette est le soleil levant.
Lève-toi beau soleil et tue l'envieuse lune
Qui est déjà malade et pâle de douleur
De voir que sa servante est bien plus jolie qu'elle.
50 Ne sois plus sa servante puisqu'elle est si jalouse,
Sa robe de vestale est d'un vert anémique,
Bonne pour les bouffons, jette-la aux orties[1].
Voici ma dame, ah ! voici mon amour !
Oh, si seulement elle le savait !
55 Elle parle et pourtant ne dit rien : qu'importe ?
Ses yeux sont éloquents et je veux leur répondre.
C'est trop d'audace. Ce n'est pas à moi qu'elle parle.
Deux des plus belles étoiles de tout le firmament
Devant s'absenter un moment, ont supplié ses yeux
60 De briller à leur place jusqu'à ce qu'elles reviennent.
Et si ses yeux prenaient leur place et les étoiles la leur ?

---

1. L'habit de bouffon était traditionnellement fait de jaune et de vert mélangés. Il y a aussi une allusion à la chlorose, ou anémie des jeunes filles.

La splendeur de ses joues ferait honte aux étoiles
Comme le jour éclipse une lanterne. Une telle lumière émanerait
De ses yeux dans le ciel que les oiseaux chanteraient
65   Au royaume des airs, croyant la nuit finie[1].
Voyez comme elle incline sa joue sur sa main.
Oh ! Que ne suis-je un gant enfermant cette main
Pour mieux toucher sa joue !

JULIETTE
Hélas !

ROMÉO
Elle parle.
Oh ! parle encore, archange de lumière.
70   Tu éclaires la nuit au-dessus de ma tête,
Comme un messager ailé, envoyé par le ciel, éblouit
Les yeux écarquillés des mortels
Qui renversent la tête pour mieux le contempler,
Quand il navigue sur les airs et chevauche
75   Les nuages gonflés qui passent nonchalants.

JULIETTE
Ô Roméo, Roméo, pourquoi donc es-tu Roméo ?
Renie ton père et abdique ton nom.
Ou, si tu ne veux pas, jure d'être mon amour,
Et moi je cesserai d'être une Capulet.

ROMÉO
80   Vais-je en entendre plus ou dois-je lui parler ?

JULIETTE
Il n'y a que ton nom qui est mon ennemi :

---

1. L'hyperbole pétrarquiste affirme la supériorité de la beauté de l'être aimé
sur l'éclat des planètes. On peut aussi voir ici une anticipation ironique de la
nuit d'amour de Roméo et Juliette, où les deux époux interprètent différem-
ment le chant des oiseaux au réveil (III. 5, v. 1-35).

Tu es toi, même si tu n'étais pas un Montaigu.
Qu'est-ce qu'un Montaigu ? Ce n'est ni main, ni pied,
Ni bras, ni visage, ni aucune partie
85 Qui font le corps d'un homme. Oh ! sois quelque autre nom.
Qu'y a-t-il dans un nom ? Ce que nous nommons rose
Sentirait aussi bon avec un autre mot.
De même Roméo, s'il n'était Roméo,
Garderait cette chère perfection qu'il possède
90 En dehors de son nom. Roméo, rejette ton nom
Et, en échange de ce nom qui n'a rien de toi,
Prends-moi tout entière.

ROMÉO
Je te prends au mot :
Appelle-moi seulement amour et je serai baptisé à nouveau[1] :
Désormais, plus jamais je ne serai Roméo.

JULIETTE
95 Qui es-tu pour ainsi te cacher derrière l'écran de la nuit
Et surprendre mes secrets ?

ROMÉO
S'il faut donner un nom,
Je ne sais pas comment te dire qui je suis :
Mon nom, ma chère sainte, est pour moi haïssable
Car pour toi c'est le nom d'un ennemi,
100 Et s'il était écrit, je le déchirerais.

JULIETTE
Mes oreilles n'ont pas encore bu cent mots
Prononcés par ta bouche, mais je connais la voix.
N'es-tu pas Roméo, et un Montaigu ?

---

1. Ce second baptême confirme la conversion « hérétique » de Roméo à un nouvel amour.

ROMÉO
Ni l'un ni l'autre, ma belle, si ces noms te déplaisent.

JULIETTE
105 Comment es-tu venu ici, dis-le moi, et pourquoi ?
Les murs de ce verger sont hauts, durs à escalader ;
Tu risques la mort, étant donné qui tu es,
Si l'un de mes parents te trouve en cet endroit.

ROMÉO
Les ailes légères de l'amour m'ont fait franchir ces murs,
110 Car les remparts de pierre n'arrêtent pas l'amour.
Ce que l'amour peut faire, l'amour ose le faire.
Aucun de tes parents ne peut me retenir.

JULIETTE
Mais s'ils te voient, ils vont t'assassiner.

ROMÉO
Hélas ! il y a plus de danger dans tes yeux
115 Que dans vingt de leurs épées[1]. Un doux regard de toi,
Et je suis à l'abri de leur inimitié.

JULIETTE
Pour rien au monde je ne voudrais qu'ils te voient ici.

ROMÉO
Le manteau de la nuit me dérobe à leurs yeux.
Si tu ne m'aimes pas et qu'ils me trouvent ici,
120 Il vaut mieux que leur haine mette un terme à ma vie,
Si surseoir à la mort, c'est vivre sans amour.

JULIETTE
Mais qui donc t'a guidé pour trouver cet endroit ?

---

1. Autre exemple d'hyperbole pétrarquiste.

ROMÉO

C'est l'amour qui d'abord m'a poussé à savoir,
M'a donné son avis, moi j'ai prêté mes yeux.
125 Je ne suis pas pilote, pourtant si tu vivais
Sur de lointains rivages baignés par l'immense océan,
Je tenterais l'aventure pour pareille cargaison.

JULIETTE

Tu sais que le masque de la nuit me cache le visage,
Sinon une rougeur virginale empourprerait ma joue
130 Pour tout ce que tu m'as entendue dire ce soir.
Je voudrais respecter les convenances et vraiment effacer
Tout ce que j'ai dit. Mais au diable les manières !
M'aimes-tu ? Je sais que tu vas dire oui,
Et je veux croire ta parole. Et pourtant si tu jures,
135 Tu peux te parjurer. Jupiter rit, dit-on,
Des serments d'amoureux. Ô gentil Roméo !
Si tu aimes, dis-le avec un cœur sincère,
Ou si tu crois que je suis trop vite séduite,
Je froncerai le sourcil, jouerai les coquettes et ce sera non ;
140 Alors tu me courtiseras, sinon pas question.
En vérité, beau Montaigu, je suis trop amoureuse,
Ce qui peut te faire croire que je suis bien légère ;
Mais, crois-moi, Roméo, je serai plus fidèle
Que celles qui usent d'artifices pour sembler réservées.
145 J'aurais dû mettre un peu plus de distance, je l'avoue,
Mais tu m'as entendue, avant que je le sache,
Déclarer mon amour ; alors pardonne-moi,
Et ne vois nulle frivolité dans cet aveu
Que la nuit noire a ainsi révélé.

ROMÉO

150 Madame, je vous jure par la lune sacrée qui
Argente là-bas les arbres du verger...

JULIETTE

Oh ! ne jure pas par la lune, la lune inconstante,
Qui change tous les mois dans son orbite ronde,
De peur que ton amour s'avère aussi changeant.

ROMÉO

155 Alors par quoi jurer ?

JULIETTE

Ne jure pas du tout,
Ou, si tu y tiens, jure par ta gracieuse personne,
Car c'est bien toi le dieu que j'idolâtre[1],
Et alors je te croirai.

ROMÉO

Si le cher amour de mon cœur...

JULIETTE

Non, ne jure pas. Bien que tu sois toute ma joie,
160 Je n'éprouve aucune joie à sceller ce contrat ce soir :
Il est trop brutal, trop imprévu, trop soudain,
Trop semblable à l'éclair qui a déjà disparu
Avant qu'on puisse dire « Un éclair ! ». Bonne nuit, mon amour.
Cet amour en herbe, levé par les souffles d'été,
165 Sera, qui sait ?, tout en fleur quand on se reverra.
Bonne nuit, bonne nuit ! Qu'un même calme et doux sommeil
Apaise un cœur qui soit au mien pareil.

ROMÉO

Oh, me laisseras-tu ainsi insatisfait ?

JULIETTE

Mais quelle satisfaction peux-tu avoir ce soir ?

---

1. On voit encore, au détour de cette image, que l'amour-passion est
assimilé dans la pièce à une forme d'hérésie religieuse.

ROMÉO

170 Échanger tous les deux des vœux d'amour fidèle.

JULIETTE

Avant même que tu l'aies demandé, je t'ai fait ce serment,
Et pourtant j'aimerais pouvoir le faire encore.

ROMÉO

Tu voudrais le reprendre ? Et pourquoi, mon amour ?

JULIETTE

Pour être généreuse et te le redonner,
175 Même si je ne souhaite rien de plus que ce que j'ai.
Ma munificence est vaste comme la mer,
Et mon amour aussi profond : plus je te donne
Plus je reçois, car l'un et l'autre sont infinis.
J'entends du bruit dans la maison. Cher amour, adieu !

[*La Nourrice appelle en coulisse.*]

180 Tout de suite, bonne Nourrice !... Doux Montaigu, sois fidèle.
Reste encore un peu, je vais revenir.

[*Sort Juliette.*]

ROMÉO

Ô nuit bénie, nuit bénie ! Je crains,
Puisqu'il fait nuit, que ce ne soit là qu'un rêve
Trop flatteur et trop doux pour être vrai.

[*Entre Juliette, au balcon.*]

JULIETTE

185 Trois mots, cher Roméo, et cette fois bonne nuit.
Si ton penchant pour moi est honorable
Ton intention le mariage, fais-moi savoir demain
Par celle que je trouverai le moyen de t'envoyer,
Le lieu et l'heure de la cérémonie.

190 Je mettrai à tes pieds toute ma destinée
     Et jusqu'au bout du monde je suivrai mon seigneur.

                    LA NOURRICE [*En coulisse.*]
Madame !

                         JULIETTE
Tout de suite, j'arrive... Mais si tes intentions ne sont pas
                                          [honnêtes,
Je te supplie...

                    LA NOURRICE [*En coulisse.*]
                    Madame !

                         JULIETTE
                    Voilà, voilà, j'arrive...
195 De ne plus faire d'efforts et de m'abandonner à mon chagrin.
     Demain j'enverrai quelqu'un.

                         ROMÉO
                         Mon âme ne désire rien d'autre...

                         JULIETTE
Mille fois bonne nuit !

                    [*Sort Juliette.*]

                         ROMÉO
     Nuit mille fois plus sombre quand elle perd ta lumière.
     L'amour va à l'amour, comme l'écolier fuit ses cahiers
200 Mais l'amour quitte l'amour, comme l'enfant va au collier[1].

                    [*Entre à nouveau Juliette au balcon.*]

_____

     1. Chassé-croisé complexe de deux mouvements antithétiques : l'élan est
comparé à la fuite (son contraire) tandis que le départ est comparé à un
cheminement fait à contrecœur.

JULIETTE

Pssst ! Roméo ! Psst ! Oh ! que n'ai-je la voix du fauconnier
Pour rappeler à moi ce noble tiercelet[1] !
La captive est enrouée et ne peut parler haut,
Sinon j'envahirai l'antre où Écho sommeille,
205 Pour rendre sa voix plus enrouée que la mienne
À force de crier le nom de Roméo[2].

ROMÉO

C'est mon âme qui appelle mon nom.
La langue des amants, la nuit, a un son argentin[3],
Comme la musique la plus suave pour qui sait y prêter l'oreille.

JULIETTE

210 Roméo !

ROMÉO
Mon tout petit gerfaut[4].

JULIETTE
À quelle heure demain
T'enverrai-je quelqu'un ?

ROMÉO
À neuf heures.

JULIETTE

Je n'y manquerai pas. Cela fait vingt ans à attendre.
Je ne sais plus pourquoi je t'ai rappelé.

---

1. Jeune faucon pèlerin.   2. La nymphe Écho, amoureuse de Narcisse, n'était pas aimée du beau jeune homme qui préférait regarder sa propre image dans le miroir de l'onde. Désespérée, elle se flétrit, son corps disparut et bientôt elle ne fut plus qu'une voix. Voir Ovide, *Métamorphoses*, III. 358-510.   3. Cette image sera rappelée plus loin (IV. 4, v. 126) au cours de la scène burlesque où les musiciens appelés pour le mariage doivent remballer leurs instruments pour cause de deuil inattendu...   4. Jeune faucon encore au nid.

ROMÉO

Alors je reste là jusqu'à ce que tu t'en souviennes.

JULIETTE

215 J'oublierai à nouveau pour que tu restes,
Me rappelant combien j'aime ta compagnie.

ROMÉO

Alors je resterai pour que tu oublies à nouveau
Et j'oublierai où j'habite pour m'installer ici.

JULIETTE

C'est presque le matin, je voudrais que tu partes,
220 Mais pas beaucoup plus loin que l'oiseau qu'un enfant
Capricieux laisse aller quand il ouvre la main,
Tel un pauvre prisonnier entravé dans ses chaînes
Qu'il ramène à lui avec un fil de soie,
Tant il est amoureux et jaloux de sa liberté.

ROMÉO

225 Je voudrais être ton oiseau !

JULIETTE

                    Mon amour, je le voudrais aussi,
Et pourtant je te tuerais à force de te chérir.
Bonne nuit, bonne nuit. Se quitter est un si doux chagrin
Que je pourrais le dire jusqu'au petit matin.

[*Sort Juliette.*]

ROMÉO

Que le sommeil tombe sur tes yeux et que la paix règne sur ton
                                                              [cœur.
230 Je voudrais être le sommeil et la paix pour un si doux repos !
Je vais me rendre à la cellule de mon père confesseur
Pour demander son aide et lui dire mon bonheur.

[*Il sort.*]

Scène 2

[Entre Frère Laurent seul, portant un panier].

FRÈRE LAURENT

Le matin à l'œil gris sourit à la nuit renfrognée
Et strie de sa lumière les nuées de l'orient
Tandis que, tel un ivrogne, les ténèbres jaspées
Quittent le sentier du jour et du char de Titan[1].
5 Avant que le soleil montre son œil brûlant
Pour saluer le jour et sécher la rosée,
Je dois remplir notre panier d'osier
De plantes vénéneuses, de fleurs aux sucs précieux.
La terre, mère de la nature, en est aussi la tombe :
10 La tombe, où tout repose, est le ventre où tout naît[2].
Nous trouvons des enfants d'espèces différentes,
Tous sortis de son ventre et qui sucent son sein.
Nombreux sont ceux qui ont beaucoup de qualités,
Aucun n'en est privé, mais tous sont différents.
15 Grandes sont les vertus curatives des plantes,
Les simples et les pierres et leurs propriétés.
Il n'est rien de si humble existant sur la terre
Qui n'apporte à la terre un bienfait spécifique.
Mais toute perfection détournée de son but
20 Renie son origine et sombre dans le mal.
La vertu se fait vice lorsqu'elle est fourvoyée,
Comme le vice par un geste peut être racheté.

[Entre Roméo.]

Sous la jeune enveloppe de cette fragile fleur

---

1. Allusion au char du soleil conduit par Apollon. Juliette, au début de son épithalame, fera quant à elle allusion à Phaéton. Voir note *infra*, p. 107-108.   2. Juxtaposition des contraires qui renvoie au caractère quasiment interchangeable des cycles de la vie et de la mort dans la pièce.

Le poison comme la guérison s'épanouissent.
25 Lorsqu'on la respire, les sens s'en réjouissent,
Mais si l'on y goûte, elle paralyse les sens et le cœur.
Deux princes ennemis campent ici face à face,
En l'homme comme en ces herbes : la révolte et la grâce ;
Et lorsque c'est la mauvaise qui est prédominante,
30 Bien vite le ver rongeur dévore cette plante.

ROMÉO

Bonjour, mon père.

FRÈRE LAURENT

Benedicite.
Quelle voix matinale me montre tant de suavité ?
Mon enfant, c'est la preuve d'un esprit bien malade
D'être de si bonne heure loin du lit en balade.
35 C'est chez le vieillard que le souci monte la garde,
Et du souci, où qu'il loge, le sommeil se garde ;
Mais, là où la jeunesse insouciante et sans façons
Couche ses membres, là règne un sommeil de plomb.
Alors, dans cette visite matinale, je vois
40 Que de quelque inquiétude tu es devenu la proie,
Ou, si ce n'est pas le cas, j'ai raison si je dis
Que Roméo ne s'est pas couché de la nuit.

ROMÉO

C'est vrai. Mais mon repos n'a été que plus doux.

FRÈRE LAURENT

Dieu pardonne le péché ! C'était Rosaline, avoue !

ROMÉO

Rosaline, mon père ? Non, ce n'est pas du tout ça.
J'ai oublié et ce nom et le chagrin qu'il me causa.

FRÈRE LAURENT

Voilà bien mon bon fils ; mais où donc étais-tu ?

ROMÉO

Je vais te le dire et cela ne sera pas tu.
À la fête de mon ennemi je m'en suis allé
50 Et là, soudain, quelqu'un m'a blessé,
Que j'ai blessé à mon tour. Pour nous le seul remède
Réside dans ta sainte médecine et ton aide.
Je n'ai aucune haine, mon père, car ainsi
Ma requête sert aussi mon ennemi.

FRÈRE LAURENT

55 Sois clair, mon bon fils, et simple dans ta narration.
À confession douteuse, douteuse absolution.

ROMÉO

Alors sache clairement que le tendre amour qui a pris mon cœur
[au filet
N'est autre que la fille ravissante du riche Capulet.
Nous nous aimons tous deux pour le meilleur et pour le pire.
60 Nous avons tout uni sauf ce que tu dois unir
Par le sacrement du mariage. Où, quand, comment
Nous nous sommes rencontrés, courtisés et liés par nos serments,
Je te le raconterai en route. Mais je t'en prie,
Consens à sceller notre union dès aujourd'hui.

FRÈRE LAURENT

65 Bienheureux saint François, quel soudain changement !
Est-ce que Rosaline que tu aimais follement
Est si vite oubliée ? L'amour des jeunes gens
Réside moins dans le cœur que dans les sens.
Jésus ! Marie ! Que de larmes marines
70 Ont coulé sur tes joues pâles au nom de Rosaline !
Que d'eau salée versée en pure perte
Assaisonnant ton amour, une vraie salade verte !
Le soleil n'a même pas chassé du ciel tes soupirs.

Tes plaintes d'antan, je crois encore les ouïr.
75 Regarde sur ta joue, on voit encore la trace
D'une ancienne larme que rien n'efface.
Si tu étais toi-même, si ces souffrances étaient les tiennes,
Il n'y avait alors que Rosaline qui les détienne.
As-tu donc changé ? Alors il faut que tu rabâches
80 Que les femmes peuvent faillir quand les hommes sont lâches.

ROMÉO

Mon amour pour Rosaline, tu l'as souvent blâmé.

FRÈRE LAURENT

Son excès, mon enfant, pas parce que tu aimais.

ROMÉO

Et tu m'as demandé d'enterrer cet amour.

FRÈRE LAURENT

Pas dans un tombeau
Où l'on couche un amour pour en faire naître un nouveau.

ROMÉO

85 Je t'en prie, pas de blâme, celle que j'aime ce jour
Me rend grâce pour grâce, répond à mon amour,
L'autre n'en faisait rien.

FRÈRE LAURENT

Oh ! elle savait parfaitement
Que tu récitais par cœur ton rôle d'amant.
Allez viens, suis-moi, jeune inconstant.
90 Pour une raison au moins à t'aider je consens,
Car ce que cette alliance peut faire venir au jour
C'est de changer la haine en un parfait amour.

ROMÉO

Oh ! Partons d'ici ! Ne perdons pas de temps.

FRÈRE LAURENT
Tout doux ! Qui va trop vite trébuche bien souvent.

Ils sortent.

Scène 3

[Entrent Benvolio et Mercutio.]

MERCUTIO
Où diable ce Roméo peut-il être ? N'est-il pas rentré chez lui la nuit dernière ?

BENVOLIO
Pas chez son père, j'ai parlé à son serviteur.

MERCUTIO
Alors c'est encore cette fille pâle au cœur dur, cette Rosaline,
5 qui le tourmente tant qu'il en deviendra fou.

BENVOLIO
Tybalt, le parent du vieux Capulet, a envoyé une lettre chez son père.

MERCUTIO
Un défi, ma parole !

BENVOLIO
Roméo y répondra.

MERCUTIO

10 Quiconque sait écrire peut répondre à une lettre.

BENVOLIO

Non, c'est l'auteur de la lettre qui aura la réponse : défi contre
défi.

MERCUTIO

Hélas ! pauvre Roméo, il est déjà mort, poignardé par l'œil noir
d'une blanche donzelle, l'oreille percée par une chanson
15 d'amour, le fond du cœur fendu par la flèche du jeune archer
aveugle, le petit Cupidon. Est-il homme à affronter Tybalt ?

BENVOLIO

Pourquoi ? Qu'est-ce donc que Tybalt ?

MERCUTIO

Plus que le prince des Chats[1]. Oh ! c'est le courageux maître de
l'étiquette : il se bat comme on chante, il suit la partition, il
20 garde la mesure, les intervalles et la cadence. Il vous accorde une
demi-pause, prime, seconde et tierce, en plein dans la poitrine :
un vrai boucher pour les boutons de soie, un bretteur, un
bretteur, un gentilhomme de la meilleure académie, le cham-
pion de la première et de la seconde cause. Ah ! L'immortel
25 *passado*, le *punto reverso*, le *haï*[2] !

BENVOLIO

Le quoi ?

MERCUTIO

La peste soit de ces bouffons grotesques, de ces poseurs

---

1. Allusion au fabliau contant les exploits de Tibert le Chat dans *Le Roman
de Renart*, traduit en anglais dès 1481, et donc bien connu du public élisabé-
thain.   2. Termes d'escrime tirés du manuel de l'Italien Vincentio Saviolo
publié en anglais en 1595 sous le titre de *Vincentio Saviolo His Practise* (« La
pratique de l'escrime selon Vincentio Saviolo »). *Passado* désigne l'estocade,
punto reverso le revers, et *haï* la touche.

zézayants, de ces faiseurs d'accents à la mode. Doux Jésus ! c'est
une fine lame, un homme courageux, une parfaite putain !
30 Alors, mon vieux, n'est-il pas lamentable qu'on soit affligés de
ces parasites étrangers, de ces marchands de mode, de ces « pardonnez-moi, très cher » si à cheval sur leur nouveau dada qu'ils
ne peuvent plus s'asseoir à leur aise sur nos bons vieux bancs ?
Oh ! leurs os, leurs os !

[*Entre Roméo.*]

BENVOLIO

35 Voici Roméo, voici Roméo qui arrive !

MERCUTIO

Vidé de sa laitance, aussi sec qu'un hareng. Ô chair, chair,
comme te voilà poissonnifiée[1] ! Le voilà maintenant qui donne
dans les couplets que Pétrarque versait à flots. Comparée à sa
dame, Laure n'était qu'une souillon (elle avait un meilleur
40 amant pour la chanter en vers), Didon un dindon, Cléopâtre
une marâtre, Hélène et Héro, des harpies hétéros, Thisbé, un
petit œil gris ou quelque chose comme ça, mais c'est sans
importance[2]. Signor Roméo, bonjour ! Voilà un salut bien

---

1. Comme les échanges burlesques de Samson et Grégoire au début de la
pièce, ces piques amicales relèvent du thème traditionnel du Combat de
Carnaval et de Carême (illustré par Bruegel dans un célèbre tableau), utilisé ici
comme métaphore de la guerre des sexes (les femmes vident les hommes de leur
laitance pour en faire des poissons secs). En outre, Shakespeare joue sur l'effet
d'écho entre Romeo et *roe* (la laitance).   2. Laure de Noves fut chantée par
Pétrarque dans son *Canzoniere* ; Didon, reine de Carthage, fut aimée et
abandonnée par le Troyen Énée qui la quitta pour aller s'établir en Italie, où
ses descendants devaient fonder Rome ; Cléopâtre, reine d'Égypte, fut successivement aimée par César et Marc Antoine (Shakespeare lui consacrera sa
dernière grande tragédie amoureuse, *Antoine et Cléopâtre*, en 1607). Quant à
Hélène, elle déclencha la guerre de Troie à la suite de son adultère avec le beau
Pâris, tandis que Héro (chantée par Marlowe dans son poème *Héro et Léandre*)
se jeta dans la mer pour aller rejoindre son amant noyé dans l'Hellespont.
Thisbé enfin, l'héroïne tragico-burlesque de la farce finale du *Songe d'une nuit
d'été* (comédie écrite la même année que *Roméo et Juliette*), se tue comme
Juliette, afin d'aller rejoindre dans la mort son amant Pyrame qui dans un

français pour vos culottes à la française. Tu as joué les faux
45 jetons, hier soir !

ROMÉO

Bonjour à tous les deux. Comment ça, j'ai joué les faux jetons ?

MERCUTIO

En te faisant la belle, oui, monsieur, en te faisant la belle. Tu ne
comprends pas ?

ROMÉO

Excuse-moi, bon Mercutio, mon affaire était importante et,
50 dans un cas comme le mien, un homme peut bien faire une
entorse à la courtoisie.

MERCUTIO

Autant dire que, dans un cas comme le tien, un homme risque
fort de se faire un tour de reins à force de faire des courbettes.

ROMÉO

Tu veux dire, pour tirer sa révérence.

MERCUTIO

55 Naturellement, tu touches droit au but.

ROMÉO

C'est une explication des plus courtoises.

MERCUTIO

Mais je suis l'étalon même de la courtoisie.

---

soudain accès de désespoir s'était suicidé juste auparavant. En effet, en trouvant
le manteau ensanglanté de Thisbé lors de leur rendez-vous nocturne près de la
tombe de Ninus, il avait cru que sa bien-aimée avait été dévorée par un lion
(voir aussi Ovide, *Métamorphoses*, IV, 55-169). La liste qui suit n'est guère dans
la note des « belles dames du temps jadis » et relève d'un effet de burlesque qui
joue sur les sons et les allitérations. Notre traduction s'efforce d'en donner une
idée en sacrifiant parfois le sens littéral de l'anglais car l'effet sonore et allitératif
compte autant ici que la signification.

ROMÉO

Tu veux dire la fine fleur.

MERCUTIO

Exact.

ROMÉO

60 Alors je peux dire que les talons de mes escarpins sont de cuir
pleine fleur.

MERCUTIO

Un point pour toi. Maintenant, suis bien cette plaisanterie
jusqu'à ce que tu aies usé tes escarpins, pour que, le jour où
leur unique semelle sera usée, il puisse te rester, après usage, une
65 plaisanterie fine et unique.

ROMÉO

La plaisanterie est un peu plate, uniquement unique par son
unicité.

MERCUTIO

Viens à mon secours, bon Benvolio, mon esprit m'abandonne !

ROMÉO

Fais marcher la cravache et les éperons, fais marcher la cravache
70 et les éperons, ou je déclare que j'ai gagné la manche.

MERCUTIO

D'accord, mais si nos esprits s'en vont à la chasse à la bécasse, je
suis fichu, car ton esprit est plus volatil que mes cinq sens
réunis. Alors, je t'ai cloué le bec ?

ROMÉO

On ne s'est jamais retrouvés ensemble sans que tu te fasses
75 plumer.

MERCUTIO

Je vais te mordre l'oreille pour cette plaisanterie.

ROMÉO

Sois un bon jars, ne me mords pas.

MERCUTIO

Ton esprit est vraiment comme une pomme douceâtre, c'est
une sauce qui pique.

ROMÉO

80   Mais n'est-ce pas là un bon accompagnement pour une oie un
peu fade ?

MERCUTIO

Oh ! ton esprit est comme de la peau de chevreau qui, d'un
pouce de long, s'étire jusqu'à faire une belle verge.

ROMÉO

Alors je l'étire encore pour que cette verge soit belle et, si je
85   l'ajoute au jars que tu es, tu vas enfler pour devenir un gros
dindon salace[1].

MERCUTIO

Eh bien, tout cela n'est-il pas mieux que des gémissements
d'amour ? Maintenant te voilà sociable, te voilà à nouveau
Roméo, non plus tête de lard mais tel que t'ont fait l'art et la
90   nature[2], car cet amour pleurnichard est comme un grand
nigaud qui court partout, la langue pendante, pour fourrer son
joujou dans un trou.

---

1. Le duel verbal qui oppose Roméo et Mercutio est aussi éblouissant
qu'intraduisible. Partis de l'idée de la *wild goose chase*, qui consistait proverbia-
lement à « courir la campagne », les deux amis jouent ensuite sur différents sens
du mot *goose*, à savoir les sens d'idiot, de volaille, de prostituée et de maladie
vénérienne. Ces échanges rappellent la veine, aussi virtuose qu'un peu artificielle et parfois obscure, d'une comédie comme *Peines d'amour perdues* (1594).
Dans la pièce, la grivoiserie qui marque le langage de la Nourrice et de Mercutio
sert de contrepoint à l'idéalisme de la maladie d'amour romantique.   2. L'uti-
lisation de la deuxième personne par Mercutio (*thou art*) prépare en fait un jeu
de mots sur « l'*art* et la nature ».

BENVOLIO

Arrête, ça suffit.

MERCUTIO

Tu veux que j'arrête mon histoire à contre-poil, la queue
95 pendante ?

BENVOLIO

Elle risquait en effet d'être un peu trop longue.

MERCUTIO

Oh ! tu te trompes, je l'aurais raccourcie, car ma petite histoire
avait touché le fond et en fait je ne voulais pas pousser la chose
plus avant.

ROMÉO

100 En voilà une bien bonne[1].

[*Entrent la Nourrice et son serviteur Pierre.*]

Une voile ! une voile !

MERCUTIO

Deux, deux, un pantalon et un jupon.

LA NOURRICE

Pierre !

PIERRE

J'arrive.

LA NOURRICE

105 Pierre, mon éventail.

---

1. Cette fois, les jeux de mots confondent délibérément les deux paronymes
que sont les mots *tale* (l'« histoire ») et *tail* (la « queue »).

MERCUTIO

Bon Pierre, pour cacher son visage, car le plus beau des deux est
encore l'éventail.

LA NOURRICE

Bien le bonjour, messieurs.

MERCUTIO

Bien le bonsoir, belle et gente dame.

LA NOURRICE

110 Comment ça, bonsoir ?

MERCUTIO

Parfaitement, croyez-moi, car le doigt cochon du cadran pointe
à présent sur la fente de midi[1].

LA NOURRICE

Non mais dites donc ! Vous êtes un drôle de lascar !

ROMÉO

Quelqu'un, gente dame, que Dieu a fait pour qu'il se défasse
115 lui-même.

LA NOURRICE

« Qui se défasse lui-même », qu'il a dit. Ma foi, c'est bien
tourné ! Mes seigneurs, l'un de vous peut-il m'indiquer où
trouver le jeune Roméo ?

ROMÉO

Je peux vous le dire, mais le jeune Roméo sera plus vieux quand
120 vous l'aurez trouvé qu'il ne l'était quand vous le cherchiez.
Faute de mieux, je suis le plus jeune de ce nom.

---

1. Jeu sur *hand* qui signifie à la fois la main et l'aiguille du cadran, et sur
prick qui désigne l'encoche, ou la fente, qui indique midi à l'horloge, mais aussi
le pénis.

LA NOURRICE

Vous parlez bien.

MERCUTIO

Alors, est-ce que le pire est bien ? En vérité vous comprenez très bien. Subtil, très subtil !

LA NOURRICE

125 Si vous êtes celui que je cherche, je désirerais vous parler en toute confidence.

BENVOLIO

Elle veut l'inviter à souper.

MERCUTIO

Une maquerelle, une maquerelle, une maquerelle ! Taïaut !

ROMÉO

Quel gibier as-tu débusqué ?

MERCUTIO

130 Ce n'est pas une poule faisane, monsieur, à moins, monsieur, que ce ne soit une cocotte de carême qui moisit avant qu'on l'ait mangée.

[Il fait quelques pas vers eux et chante.]

> *Une vieille poule faisane,*
> *Une vieille poule faisane*
135 > *Est bonne chair en carême.*
> *Mais une poule faisandée*
> *Ne vaut pas quatre deniers*
> *Faisandée avant même*
> *Qu'on ait pu la manger[1].*

---

1. Là encore, il est impossible de traduire littéralement l'anglais qui joue sur les mots *hare* (« lièvre ») et *hoar* (« moisi » mais aussi « putain » par homologie avec *whore*).

140 Roméo, viendras-tu chez ton père ? Nous y allons dîner.

ROMÉO

Je vous suis.

MERCUTIO

Adieu, antique dame, adieu, madame, madame, madame.

LA NOURRICE

Et dites-moi, monsieur, qui est ce margoulin effronté qui a tout d'un gibier d'impotence[1] ?

ROMÉO

145 Un gentilhomme, Nourrice, qui aime s'écouter parler et qui en dit plus en une minute qu'il n'en supporterait en un mois.

LA NOURRICE

S'il dit du mal de moi, je lui rabattrai son caquet, à lui comme à vingt freluquets de son espèce, même s'il était plus costaud qu'il n'est ; et si moi je ne peux pas, je saurai bien trouver ceux qui
150 s'en chargeront. Malotru ! Je ne suis pas l'une de ses gourgandines, je ne suis pas l'un de ses coupe-jarrets. [*S'adressant à Pierre.*] Et toi, il faut que tu restes là sans rien faire. Tu supportes que la première canaille venue abuse de moi pour son plaisir.

PIERRE

Je n'ai jamais vu un homme abuser de vous pour son plaisir. Si
155 je l'avais vu, j'aurais dégainé en vitesse, je vous le garantis ! Je n'hésite pas à dégainer aussi vite qu'un autre si je vois l'occasion d'une bonne querelle et si j'ai la loi pour moi.

LA NOURRICE

Sûr, devant Dieu, je suis si contrariée que je tremble de partout. Ah ! le malotru ! [*S'adressant à Roméo.*] S'il vous plaît, monsieur,

---

1. Dans son indignation, la Nourrice confond les mots *roguery* (« canaillerie ») et *ropery* (« homme de corde » ou « gibier de potence »).

160 un mot... Comme je vous l'ai dit, ma jeune maîtresse m'a
demandé de venir vous trouver. Ce qu'elle m'a demandé de
vous faire savoir, je le garderai pour moi, mais d'abord, laissez-
moi vous avertir que si c'est pour la mener en bateau, comme
on dit, ce serait se conduire en goujat, comme on dit, car la
165 noble demoiselle est jeune. Par conséquent, si c'est pour jouer
double jeu avec elle, ce ne serait vraiment pas joli joli de faire ça
à une noble demoiselle, ce serait une bien malhonnête façon de
se conduire.

ROMÉO

Nourrice, recommande-moi à ta dame et à ta maîtresse. Je te
170 jure...

LA NOURRICE

Brave cœur, en vérité je lui dirai tout. Seigneur Jésus ! Elle va
être une femme heureuse !

ROMÉO

Que lui diras-tu, Nourrice ? Tu ne m'écoutes pas.

LA NOURRICE

Je lui dirai, monsieur, que vous jurez... ce qui, si je comprends
175 bien, est une proposition digne d'un gentilhomme.

ROMÉO

Dis-lui de trouver
Un moyen de se rendre à confesse cet après-midi,
Et là, dans la cellule du Frère Laurent,
Elle sera confessée, absoute et mariée. Voici pour ta peine.

LA NOURRICE

180 Non, vraiment, monsieur, sans façons.

ROMÉO

Allons, prenez ça, je vous dis.

LA NOURRICE

Cet après-midi, monsieur ? Bien, elle y sera.

ROMÉO

Toi, bonne Nourrice, tu attendras derrière le mur de l'abbaye,
Dans moins d'une heure, mon valet te rejoindra
185 Et t'apportera des cordes, nouées comme des haubans,
Qui m'aideront dans le secret de la nuit
À me hisser tout en haut du hunier de ma joie.
Adieu, sois loyale, je récompenserai tes peines.
Adieu, recommande-moi à ta maîtresse.

LA NOURRICE

190 Ah ! Que le Dieu du ciel vous bénisse ! Écoutez, monsieur.

ROMÉO

Que dis-tu, ma chère Nourrice ?

LA NOURRICE

Peut-on se fier à votre valet ? N'avez-vous jamais entendu dire
Que deux personnes peuvent garder un secret à condition d'en
                                                    [retirer une ?

ROMÉO

Je te garantis que mon valet est aussi sûr que l'acier.

LA NOURRICE

195 Bien, monsieur, ma maîtresse est la plus douce des dames.
Mon Dieu, mon Dieu ! quand elle n'était qu'une petite chose
                                                    [babillarde...
Oh ! Il y a un noble seigneur en ville, un dénommé Pâris,
Qui serait trop heureux d'aller à l'abordage ; mais elle, la bonne
                                                    [âme,
Elle aimerait autant voir un crapaud, oui, un crapaud,
Que de voir ce Pâris. Je la mets en colère parfois
Quand je lui dis que c'est là l'homme qu'il lui faut ;
Mais je vous garantis, quand je dis ça, elle devient blanche,

Blanche comme un linge dans le monde à Versailles[1].
Dites-moi, romarin et Roméo commencent bien
205 Par la même lettre, non ?

ROMÉO

Oui, Nourrice, tous deux commencent bien par un « r », et
alors ?

LA NOURRICE

Ah ! tu te moques de moi ! Rrrr... c'est pour les chiens. « R »,
c'est pour le... [derrière][2] ! Non, je sais que ça commence avec
210 une autre lettre car elle brode de si jolies histoires là-dessus, sur
vous et le romarin, que ça vous ferait du bien de les entendre.

ROMÉO

Recommande-moi à ta maîtresse.

[*Sort Roméo.*]

LA NOURRICE

Oui, mille fois... Pierre !

PIERRE

J'arrive.

LA NOURRICE

215 Passe devant et que ça saute !

Ils sortent.

---

1. Traduit la bourde de la Nourrice qui dit « *in the versal* [pour *universal*]
world ». 2. En anglais, la lettre « r », qui se prononce [a:], fait penser au
grognement d'un chien, mais c'est aussi le début du mot *arse*, le « derrière ».
« Roméo » ne peut donc pas commencer par la lettre « r » car, dans la version
romantique de l'amour, le nom de l'aimé ne saurait être mis ainsi devant
derrière !

Scène 4

[Entre Juliette.]

JULIETTE

Neuf heures sonnaient à l'horloge quand j'ai envoyé la Nourrice.
Elle avait promis d'être de retour dans une demi-heure.
Peut-être ne l'a-t-elle pas trouvé. Non, ce n'est pas ça.
Oh! elle traîne la jambe! les messagers de l'amour devraient être
                                                    [des pensées
5   Dix fois plus rapides que les rayons du soleil,
Chassant les ombres sur les collines ténébreuses.
C'est pourquoi ce sont des colombes agiles qui tirent le char de
                                                    [l'Amour,
C'est pourquoi Cupidon, vif comme le vent, a des ailes.
Le soleil est à présent au plus haut
10 De sa course. Aujourd'hui, de neuf à douze,
Il y a trois longues heures et elle n'est toujours pas là.
Si elle avait les passions et le sang bouillant de la jeunesse,
Elle serait aussi rapide que la balle au bond :
Mes mots l'auraient lancée jusqu'à mon doux amour,
15 Et lui me l'aurait renvoyée.
Mais les vieilles gens font souvent les morts,
Ils sont lourds, lents, pesants, pâles comme le plomb.

[Entrent la Nourrice et Pierre.]

Oh! Dieu, la voici. Ô Nourrice chérie, quelles nouvelles ?
L'as-tu trouvé ? Renvoie ton valet.

LA NOURRICE

Pierre, reste à la grille.

[Sort Pierre.]

JULIETTE

Alors, bonne et douce Nourrice, Seigneur Dieu, pourquoi cet
[air triste ?
Même si les nouvelles sont tristes, dis-les d'un air joyeux.
Si elles sont bonnes, tu gâches la musique des douces nouvelles
En la jouant devant moi avec un visage aussi aigre.

LA NOURRICE

25   Je suis éreintée, laissez-moi en paix un moment.
Hélas, mes pauvres os ! Quelle équipée !

JULIETTE

Je voudrais que tu aies mes os et moi tes nouvelles.
Allez, je t'en prie, parle, bonne, bonne Nourrice, parle.

LA NOURRICE

Doux Jésus ! quelle hâte ! Ne pouvez-vous pas attendre un peu ?
30   Vous ne voyez donc pas que je suis à bout de souffle ?

JULIETTE

Comment peux-tu être à bout de souffle, quand tu as assez de
[souffle
Pour me dire que tu es à bout de souffle ?
L'excuse que tu imagines pour ce retard prend plus de temps
Que le récit que tu t'excuses de ne pas faire.
35   Les nouvelles sont-elles bonnes ou mauvaises ? Réponds.
Dis oui ou non. Pour les détails j'attendrai.
Je veux savoir : sont-elles bonnes ou mauvaises ?

LA NOURRICE

Bien. Vous avez fait un choix stupide. Vous ne savez pas choisir
un homme. Votre Roméo ? Non, pas lui, même s'il est plus
40   beau de visage qu'un autre, même s'il a la jambe mieux faite, et
pour ce qui est de la main, du pied et du corps, même s'il est
superflu d'en parler, tout est incomparable. Ce n'est pas la fine
fleur de la courtoisie, mais je jurerais qu'il est doux comme un

agneau. Va ton chemin, ma fille, et sers Dieu. Au fait, avez-vous
45 dîné à la maison ?

JULIETTE

Non, non. Mais je savais déjà tout cela.
Que dit-il de notre mariage, qu'en est-il ?

LA NOURRICE

Seigneur, que j'ai mal à la tête ! Ma pauvre tête !
Elle bat comme si elle allait éclater en mille morceaux.
50 Mon dos, d'un autre côté, oh ! mon dos, mon dos !
Quel petit sacripant que votre cœur de m'avoir envoyée
Attraper la mort en me faisant courir ainsi à droite et à gauche !

JULIETTE

En vérité, je suis navrée que tu ne te sentes pas bien.
Douce, douce, douce Nourrice, réponds-moi, que dit mon
[amour ?

LA NOURRICE

55 Votre amour dit, en gentilhomme honnête qu'il est, et courtois,
aimable, et beau, et, je vous le garantis, vertueux... Où est votre
mère ?

JULIETTE

Où est ma mère ? À la maison, pardi !
Où pourrait-elle bien être ? Quelle curieuse réponse !
60 « Votre amour dit en honnête gentilhomme qu'il est :
Où est votre mère ? »

LA NOURRICE
Oh ! Sainte Mère de Dieu !

Êtes-vous si ardente ? Par Marie, ma foi, remettez-vous !
Est-ce là le cataplasme pour mes os douloureux ?
Une autre fois, faites vos commissions vous-même.

JULIETTE

65 Pas tant de manières. Allez, que dit Roméo ?

LA NOURRICE

Avez-vous la permission d'aller à confesse aujourd'hui ?

JULIETTE

Oui.

LA NOURRICE

Alors allez vite à la cellule du Frère Laurent.
Là, un mari vous attend pour faire de vous sa femme.
70 Voici ce coquin de sang qui vous monte aux joues.
Elles tournent à l'écarlate à la moindre nouvelle.
Allez vite à l'église, moi je dois me rendre ailleurs
Pour chercher une échelle à l'aide de laquelle votre amour
Doit grimper jusqu'au nid d'une oiselle, sitôt qu'il fera nuit.
75 Je suis la bête de somme qui peine pour votre plaisir,
Mais c'est vous ce soir qui aurez ce loisir.
Bon, je vais dîner, et vous, dépêchez-vous !

JULIETTE

Pas de péché, Nourrice, je suis aux anges, grâce à vous[1].

[Elles sortent.]

---

1. *Hie to high fortune* : littéralement, « je cours vers ma bonne fortune ».
Juliette reprend ici l'invitation de la Nourrice (*Hie you*, « Dépêchez-vous ») en
jouant sur la sonorité des mots pour exprimer toute sa jubilation.

Scène 5

[*Entrent le Frère Laurent et Roméo.*]

FRÈRE LAURENT

Puisse le ciel sourire sur ce saint sacrement
Et faire que l'avenir nous épargne toute affliction.

ROMÉO

Amen, amen, mais quelle que soit l'affliction qui me frappe,
Elle ne peut égaler la joie que je reçois
5   De la voir, ne fût-ce qu'une brève minute.
Joins seulement nos mains par des prières,
Et qu'ensuite la mort dévoreuse d'amour en fasse à sa guise[1].
Pour moi c'est assez de dire que Juliette est à moi.

FRÈRE LAURENT

Ces violents plaisirs ont une fin violente :
10   Ils meurent lorsqu'ils triomphent, comme le feu et la poudre
Explosent en s'embrassant. Le miel le plus doux
Semble écœurant par sa douceur même
De sorte que sa saveur sucrée nous ôte l'appétit.
Aime donc avec mesure, pour éviter que l'amour meure.
15   La précipitation est source de retard, comme trop de lenteur[2].

[*Juliette fait irruption dans la cellule et embrasse Roméo.*]

Voici la dame. Oh ! un pied si léger
Ne va pas beaucoup user le silex éternel.
L'amoureux peut chevaucher les fils de la Vierge
Qui s'étirent, nonchalants, dans l'air folâtre de l'été,

---

1. Le thème macabre apparaît en contrepoint, faisant de la Mort envieuse la rivale de Roméo.   2. L'image du baiser de la poudre et du feu est un rappel subliminal de l'image de la torche et du joyau qui décrivait Juliette, avec cette fois une note de danger aussi violent qu'extrême. Frère Laurent poursuit par des proverbes et des dictons dans le cadre de sa rhétorique du conseil.

20 Sans tomber, tant la vanité de l'amour semble légère.

JULIETTE
Bonsoir à mon saint confesseur.

FRÈRE LAURENT
Roméo te remerciera, ma fille, pour nous deux.

JULIETTE
Qu'il soit deux fois remercié, sinon son merci est de trop.

ROMÉO
Ah ! Juliette, si la mesure de ta joie
25 Est aussi comble que la mienne, et si tu es plus habile
Pour la décrire, alors embaume de ton souffle
L'air qui nous entoure et que la riche musique de ta voix
Chante ce bonheur de rêve qui nous est donné
À toi et à moi, par des retrouvailles si précieuses.

JULIETTE
30 La pensée, plus riche en matière qu'en mots,
S'enorgueillit du sens et non de l'ornement.
Il n'y a que les mendiants pour calculer leur richesse,
Mais, pour mon compte, mon amour vrai a tellement grandi
Que je n'arrive pas à connaître la moitié de ma fortune.

FRÈRE LAURENT
35 Venez, venez avec moi, faisons vite.
Si vous me le permettez, je ne vous laisserai pas seuls
Avant que la Sainte Église ait réuni vos deux êtres en un seul.

[*Ils sortent.*]

ACTE III

Scène 1

[Entrent Mercutio, Benvolio et leurs gens.]

BENVOLIO

Je t'en prie, bon Mercutio, retirons-nous,
Il fait chaud, les Capulet sont dans la rue,
Et si nous les rencontrons, nous n'éviterons pas une querelle,
Car, avec cette canicule, le sang s'échauffe vite.

MERCUTIO

5 Tu me fais penser à ces drôles qui, dès qu'ils passent le seuil
d'une taverne, vous flanquent leur épée sur la table en décla-
rant : « Dieu me garde de faire appel à toi » puis, sous l'effet du
deuxième verre d'alcool, la dégainent, sans raison aucune,
contre le serveur.

BENVOLIO

10 Je ressemble à ces drôles ?

MERCUTIO

Allons, allons, tu as l'humeur aussi chaude que quiconque en
Italie, et tu es aussi vite hors de toi pour rien que tu es hors de
toi lorsqu'un rien t'énerve.

BENVOLIO

Et que me sont donc ces riens ?

MERCUTIO

15 S'il y en avait deux comme toi, il n'y aurait bientôt plus personne, car vous vous tueriez l'un l'autre. Toi, tu serais capable
de te quereller avec un homme sous prétexte que sa barbe
compte un poil de plus ou de moins que la tienne. Tu te
querellerais avec un homme qui casse des noisettes pour la
20 seule raison que tes yeux sont noisette. Quel œil autre que le
tien pourrait aller chercher pareil motif de querelle ? Ta tête est
pleine comme un œuf de querelles et pourtant, à force de
coups, ta tête n'est plus que la coquille vide d'un œuf pourri
après toutes sortes de bagarres, tant tu t'es querellé. Tu t'es
25 battu avec un homme qui éternuait dans la rue parce qu'il avait
réveillé ton chien qui dormait au soleil. N'as-tu pas cherché
noise à un tailleur parce qu'il portait son nouveau pourpoint
avant Pâques[1] ? Et à un autre parce qu'il attachait ses souliers
neufs avec de vieux rubans ? Et tu voudrais, malgré tout, me
30 faire la leçon pour m'empêcher de me quereller ?

BENVOLIO

Si j'étais aussi prompt que toi à me quereller, je vendrais la
jouissance pleine et entière de ma vie au premier venu en
espérant pouvoir profiter ainsi d'une heure et quart de répit.

MERCUTIO

La pleine et entière jouissance ! Tu perds le sens !

[*Entrent Tybalt, Petruchio et d'autres.*]

BENVOLIO

35 Sur ma tête, voici venir les Capulet.

MERCUTIO

Par mon talon, je n'en ai cure.

___

1. Il était alors de rigueur de porter des vêtements neufs à Pâques, peut-être
en liaison avec le fait que la nouvelle année (civile) commençait le 25 mars.

TYBALT

Suivez-moi de près, je vais leur parler.
Messieurs, bonsoir, un mot avec l'un de vous deux.

MERCUTIO

Seulement un mot avec l'un d'entre nous ? Ajoutez-y quelque
40 chose ; comme ça, nous aurons des mots entre nous, puis des
mots et des coups.

TYBALT

Vous me trouverez assez disposé à cela, monsieur, si vous m'en
donnez l'occasion.

MERCUTIO

Vous ne pouvez pas saisir une occasion sans qu'on vous la
45 donne ?

TYBALT

Mercutio, tu marches de concert avec Roméo ?

MERCUTIO

De concert ? Quoi, tu nous prends pour des musiciens ? Si tu
nous prends pour des musiciens, attends-toi à n'entendre que
des discordances. Voici mon archet, voici qui vous fera danser.
50 Diantre, de concert !

BENVOLIO

Nous sommes ici à discuter dans un lieu public.
Ou bien vous vous mettez à l'écart en privé,
Pour parler calmement de vos griefs,
Ou bien vous partez. Ici tous les yeux sont braqués sur nous.

MERCUTIO

55 Les yeux des hommes sont faits pour voir ; alors, qu'ils regardent !
Moi, je ne bougerai pas pour plaire à qui que ce soit.

[*Entre Roméo.*]

TYBALT

Allons, que la paix soit avec vous, monsieur, voici venir mon
[homme.

MERCUTIO

Je veux être pendu, monsieur, s'il porte votre livrée.
Que diable, rendez-vous d'abord sur le pré et là il vous suivra,
60 C'est en ce sens que Votre Seigneurie pourra l'appeler « son
[homme ».

TYBALT

Roméo, l'amour que je te porte ne trouve pas
De meilleure expression que celle-ci : tu es un lâche !

ROMÉO

Tybalt, la raison que j'ai de t'aimer excuse
Le fait que je ne réponde pas à ton salut
65 Avec la rage qui convient. Je ne suis pas un lâche.
Alors, adieu ; je vois que tu ne me connais pas.

TYBALT

Morveu, ceci ne saurait excuser l'affront
Que tu m'as fait. Alors, retourne-toi, en garde !

ROMÉO

Je jure que je ne t'ai jamais fait d'affront,
70 Mais que je t'aime plus que ce que tu peux imaginer
Tant que tu ignores la raison de mon amour.
Ainsi, bon Capulet, toi dont j'estime le nom
Tout autant que le mien, n'insiste pas.

MERCUTIO

Ce calme n'est que vile et infamante soumission !
75 C'est *alla stoccata* qui a le dernier mot[1] !

---

1. *Alla stoccata* (« à l'estocade ») désigne ici ironiquement Tybalt.

[Il dégaine.]

Tybalt, chasseur de rats, on va faire un tour ?

TYBALT

Que me veux-tu ?

MERCUTIO

Seulement l'une de tes neuf vies, bon Roi des Chats. J'ai l'intention de commencer par t'en prendre une puis, selon la
80 façon dont tu en useras avec moi, je mettrai la pâtée aux huit autres. Allez-vous tirer l'épée du fourreau par les oreilles ? Dépêchez-vous, sinon la mienne vous sifflera aux oreilles avant que la vôtre soit sortie.

TYBALT

Je suis ton homme.

[Il dégaine à son tour.]

ROMÉO

85 Doux Mercutio, rengaine ta rapière.

MERCUTIO

Allez, monsieur, votre *passado*.

[Ils se battent.]

ROMÉO

Dégaine, Benvolio, désarme-les.
Messieurs, tenez-vous, pas d'outrage à la loi !
Tybalt, Mercutio, le Prince a expressément
90 Interdit ces passes d'armes dans les rues de Vérone.
Tybalt, arrête ! Bon Mercutio !

*[Tybalt blesse Mercutio sous le bras
de Roméo qui s'est interposé.]*

UN AMI DE TYBALT

Partons, Tybalt.

[*Tybalt s'enfuit avec ses amis.*]

MERCUTIO

Je suis blessé.
La peste soit de vos deux maisons. J'ai mon compte.
Lui, il est parti et il n'a rien ?

BENVOLIO

Quoi ! tu es blessé ?

MERCUTIO

95 Oui, oui, une égratignure, une égratignure mais parbleu c'est
[assez.
Où est mon page ? Va, gredin, va chercher un chirurgien.

[*Le page sort.*]

ROMÉO

Courage, ami, la blessure ne peut pas être bien grave.

MERCUTIO

Non, c'est vrai, elle n'est pas aussi profonde qu'un puits, ni
aussi large qu'un porche d'église, mais c'est assez, elle fera
100 l'affaire. Si vous demandez à me voir demain, je serai muet
comme une tombe[1]. Je suis assaisonné pour ce bas monde, je
vous le garantis. La peste soit de vos deux maisons ! Bon
Dieu, un chien, un rat, une souris, un chat, égratigner un
homme à mort ! Un vantard, un gredin, un lâche qui se bat

---

1. Jeu de mots sur *grave* (« *you shall find me a grave man* »), qui signifie à la
fois « grave » (adj.) et « tombe » (subst.). Ainsi Mercutio joue jusqu'au bout
son rôle de bouffon et il meurt au milieu des rires de ses amis qui pensent
qu'il joue la comédie. Mais le rire se fige en un rictus qui annonce la
sarabande de Mort dans la pièce, de sorte que la comédie vire désormais au
tragique.

105 selon les règles de son manuel d'arithmétique... Pourquoi
diable l'as-tu mis entre nous ? C'est sous ton bras que j'ai été
touché.

ROMÉO

Je croyais bien faire.

MERCUTIO

Aide-moi à me réfugier quelque part, Benvolio,
110 Ou je vais m'évanouir. La peste soit de vos deux maisons,
Elles ont fait de moi une charogne pour les vers.
J'ai mon compte et pour de bon. Ah ! vos maisons !

[Il sort, aidé par Benvolio.]

ROMÉO

Ce gentilhomme, proche parent du Prince,
Mon fidèle ami, a été mortellement blessé
115 Par ma faute ; ma réputation est ternie
Par les calomnies de Tybalt, par Tybalt qui, il y a moins d'une
                                                                    [heure,
Est devenu mon cousin. Oh ! douce Juliette,
Ta beauté a fait de moi une femmelette,
Elle a amolli la trempe d'acier de mon caractère.

[Entre Benvolio.]

BENVOLIO

120 Oh ! Roméo, Roméo, le vaillant Mercutio est mort !
Cet esprit courageux a rejoint les nuages,
Lui qui avant son heure a méprisé la terre.

ROMÉO

Le noir destin de ce jour pèsera sur les jours à venir :
Ainsi commencent des malheurs que d'autres doivent finir.

[Entre Tybalt.]

BENVOLIO

125 Voici le furieux Tybalt qui revient à la charge.

ROMÉO

Qui revient triomphant quand Mercutio est mort.
Retournez donc au ciel, charitables pensées,
Et toi, Fureur à l'œil de feu, sois désormais mon guide !
Alors, Tybalt, retire ce nom de lâche
130 Dont tu m'as traité, car l'âme de Mercutio
Est là toute proche au-dessus de nos têtes,
Attendant que la tienne aille en sa compagnie.
Toi ou moi, ou tous les deux, partirons avec lui.

TYBALT

Petit misérable qui étais de concert avec lui,
135 C'est toi qui iras le rejoindre !

ROMÉO

Voilà qui en décidera.

[*Ils se battent, Tybalt tombe.*]

BENVOLIO

Roméo, sauve-toi, va-t'en !
Les citoyens s'attroupent, Tybalt a été tué.
Ne reste pas là, hébété. Le Prince te condamnera à mort
Si tu es pris. Va-t'en, prends la fuite, pars d'ici.

ROMÉO

140 Oh ! Je suis le jouet de la Fortune !

BENVOLIO

Pourquoi restes-tu ?

[*Sort Roméo.*]

Entrent des citoyens.

UN CITOYEN

Par où s'est enfui l'homme qui a tué Mercutio?
Tybalt, cet assassin, par où s'est-il enfui?

BENVOLIO

Tybalt? Le voici qui gît là.

UN CITOYEN
                    Allons, monsieur, suivez-moi.
Au nom du Prince, je vous somme d'obéir.

> [*Entrent le Prince, Montaigu, Capulet
> et leurs épouses, suivis d'autres gens.*]

LE PRINCE

145 Où sont les vils instigateurs de cette rixe?

BENVOLIO

Ô noble Prince, je peux expliquer l'enchaînement
Funeste de cette fatale querelle.
Ici gît, tué par le jeune Roméo, l'homme
Qui a tué ton parent, le vaillant Mercutio.

LADY CAPULET

150 Tybalt, mon neveu, ô l'enfant de mon frère!
Ô Prince, ô mon époux! Oh! voici répandu le sang
De mon cher parent. Prince, si tu es juste,
Verse le sang des Montaigu pour prix de notre sang.
Ô mon neveu, mon neveu!

LE PRINCE

155 Benvolio, qui a commencé cette rixe sanglante?

BENVOLIO

Tybalt, ici, mort, que la main de Roméo a tué.
Roméo, qui lui parlait doucement, l'a prié de réfléchir
À la futilité de cette querelle et invoqua aussi
Votre grand déplaisir, le tout dit d'une voix

160 Douce, sans passion, le genou humblement plié,
    Mais il ne réussit pas à apaiser l'humeur violente
    De Tybalt, sourd à la paix. Celui-ci alors a menacé
    La poitrine du courageux Mercutio de sa pointe d'acier,
    Lequel, tout aussi échauffé, se bat pointe à pointe
165 En un combat mortel et, avec un mépris martial,
    Écarte d'une main la froide mort, de l'autre
    La renvoie à Tybalt dont la dextérité
    La lui retourne. Roméo, lui, s'écrie bien haut :
    « Arrêtez, mes amis ! Amis, séparez-vous ! » Plus vif que sa langue,
170 Son bras agile abaisse leurs lames fatales,
    Et il se précipite entre eux deux ; mais, par-dessous son bras,
    Une méchante botte portée par Tybalt touche à mort
    Le brave Mercutio. Alors Tybalt s'enfuit,
    Mais peu après il vient retrouver Roméo
175 Qui depuis peu nourrissait des pensées de vengeance.
    Et les voilà qui s'affrontent, vifs comme l'éclair : car, avant
    Que je puisse dégainer pour les séparer, l'intrépide Tybalt est tué,
    Et, alors qu'il s'effondre, Roméo se retourne et prend la fuite.
    Voilà la vérité, Benvolio en répond sur sa tête.

LADY CAPULET

180 C'est un parent des Montaigu ;
    L'affection qu'il leur porte le fait mentir. Il ne dit pas la vérité.
    Ils étaient au moins vingt à se battre dans cette noire mêlée
    Et à vingt ils n'ont réussi à prendre qu'une seule vie.
    Je demande la justice que toi, Prince, tu dois rendre.
185 Roméo a tué Tybalt, Roméo doit mourir.

LE PRINCE

Roméo l'a tué, lui qui a tué Mercutio.
Qui, maintenant, va payer pour ce sang précieux ?

MONTAIGU

Pas Roméo, Prince. Il était l'ami de Mercutio,
Sa faute n'a fait qu'exécuter ce que la loi aurait tranché,

190   La tête de Tybalt.

LE PRINCE
Et, pour ce délit,
Nous l'exilons d'ici sur-le-champ.
Je suis moi-même touché par ce déchaînement de haine :
C'est mon sang que vos rixes barbares ont fait couler ici.
Mais je vous punirai d'une amende si forte
195   Que vous regretterez la perte que vous m'avez fait subir.
Je serai sourd à vos plaidoyers comme à vos excuses,
Ni pleurs ni prières ne rachèteront ces crimes.
Ils sont inutiles. Que Roméo parte sur l'heure,
Car, si on le trouve, il subira la loi.
200   Qu'on emporte ce corps, et obéissez-moi ;
La clémence est un crime si elle absout les tueurs.

[*Ils sortent.*]

Scène 2

[*Entre Juliette, seule.*]

JULIETTE
Galopez au plus vite, coursiers aux pieds de feu,
Vers le palais de Phébus. Un cocher
Comme Phaéton vous fouetterait vers l'ouest,
Amenant derrière lui les nuages de la nuit[1].

---

0. Phaéton, fils supposé d'Apollon, avait, en guise de gage de confiance, demandé à son père de le laisser conduire le char du soleil. Malgré les conseils

5   Tire ton épais rideau, nuit où l'on fait l'amour,
     Que le soleil fuyard referme ses paupières, que Roméo
     Se jette dans mes bras, sans être vu ni entendu.
     Les amants, pour accomplir les rites de l'amour,
     S'éclairent à leur propre beauté. Si l'amour est aveugle,
10 Il s'accorde d'autant mieux à la nuit. Viens, austère nuit,
     Matrone sans atours tout habillée de noir,
     Apprends-moi à jouer à qui perd gagne cette partie
     Où se donnent nos deux virginités sans tache.
     Cache ce sang indompté qui bat là dans mes joues
15 Avec ta cape noire, jusqu'à ce que l'amour s'enhardisse,
     Et apprends que l'amour vrai est acte simple et chaste.
     Viens, nuit, viens, Roméo, toi, le jour de ma nuit,
     Car tu reposeras sur les ailes de la nuit
     Plus blanc que neige fraîche sur le dos d'un corbeau.
20 Viens, douce nuit, viens, amoureuse nuit au front noir,
     Donne-moi mon Roméo, et quand je mourrai,
     Enlève-le et découpe-le en petites étoiles,
     Et il rendra si beau le visage des cieux
     Que le monde entier s'éprendra de la nuit
25 Et n'adorera plus le soleil éclatant.
     Oh! j'ai acheté une maison d'amour
     Mais je n'en jouis pas encore et, bien que vendue,
     Personne n'y est encore entré. Ce jour est
     Interminable, autant qu'une veille de fête
30 Aux yeux de l'enfant impatiente de porter
     Sa robe neuve. Oh! voici venir ma nourrice.

       [*Entre la Nourrice avec l'échelle de corde,*
              elle se tord les mains.]

---

du dieu, il ne put longtemps diriger l'attelage qui avait déjà brûlé une partie de la terre dont il s'était trop approché, créant ainsi les déserts et la race noire. Jupiter dut foudroyer l'inconscient pour mettre un terme à sa course folle. Voir Ovide, *Métamorphoses*, II, 1-331.

Elle apporte des nouvelles et toute langue qui prononce
Le nom de Roméo parle avec une céleste éloquence.
Alors, Nourrice, quelles nouvelles ? Qu'as-tu là ? Les cordes
35 Que Roméo t'a demandé d'aller chercher ?

LA NOURRICE

> Oui, oui, les cordes.

JULIETTE

Mon Dieu, quelles nouvelles ? Pourquoi te tordre ainsi les mains ?

LA NOURRICE

Hélas ! jour de malheur, il est mort, il est mort, il est mort !
Nous sommes perdues, madame, nous sommes perdues.
Jour maudit, il n'est plus, on l'a tué, il est mort.

JULIETTE

40 Le ciel peut-il donc être aussi cruel ?

LA NOURRICE

> Roméo, lui, le peut,

Si le ciel ne le peut. Ô Roméo ! Roméo,
Qui aurait jamais pu penser ça ? Roméo !

JULIETTE

Quel démon es-tu donc pour tant me tourmenter ?
C'est là une torture à faire hurler dans le terrible enfer.
45 Roméo s'est-il tué ? Tu n'as qu'à dire « oui »
Et ce simple « oui » sera un poison plus sûr
Que le regard mortel que lance le basilic[1].
Je ne suis plus moi-même si j'entends ce « oui »,
Si ce sont ces yeux clos qui te font dire « oui »[2].
50 S'il est mort, réponds « oui », et s'il vit, réponds « non ».

---

1. Reptile fantastique censé provenir d'un œuf de coq couvé par un serpent
et dont le regard était mortel.   2. Série de jeux de mots sur le son [*ai* :] décliné
successivement comme *I* (je, moi) et *ay* (oui).

Ces sons brefs décideront de mon bonheur ou de mon malheur.

LA NOURRICE

J'ai vu sa blessure, de mes yeux je l'ai vue,
Dieu me pardonne, là, sur sa poitrine d'homme,
Pitoyable cadavre, un cadavre ensanglanté et pitoyable,
55 Pâle, pâle comme la cendre, tout barbouillé de sang,
Couvert de sang coagulé ; en le voyant, je me suis évanouie.

JULIETTE

Oh ! que mon cœur ruiné se brise, se brise sur-le-champ !
En prison mes yeux, ne contemplez plus la liberté.
Vile terre[1], retourne à la terre, que tout mouvement cesse,
60 Et que toi et Roméo sur une même bière lourdement s'affaissent.

LA NOURRICE

Oh ! Tybalt, Tybalt, le meilleur ami que j'avais !
Oh ! très courtois Tybalt, honnête gentilhomme,
Ai-je donc tant vécu pour te voir ainsi mort ?

JULIETTE

Quelle tempête souffle ainsi des vents si contraires ?
65 Roméo a-t-il été tué ? Est-ce que Tybalt est mort ?
Mon très cher cousin et mon mari plus cher encore ?
Alors, terrible trompette, sonne le Jugement dernier,
Car qui peut encore vivre si ces deux-là sont morts ?

LA NOURRICE

Tybalt est mort et Roméo banni.
70 Roméo, lui, l'a tué et il est banni.

JULIETTE

Ô Dieu, la main de Roméo a-t-elle versé le sang de Tybalt ?

---

1. Terme qui, comme la glaise plus haut, sert à désigner le corps mortel.

LA NOURRICE

Hélas ! oui, trois fois hélas ! oui.

JULIETTE

Ô cœur de vipère caché sous un visage en fleur !
Dragon a-t-il jamais gardé une si belle grotte ?
75 Magnifique tyran, angélique démon,
Corbeau aux plumes de colombe, agneau vorace comme un loup,
Méprisable substance de divine apparence !
Tu es le parfait contraire de ce dont tu as l'air,
Un saint damné, un gredin honorable.
80 Ô nature, qu'allais-tu faire en enfer
Lorsque tu as abrité l'esprit d'un démon
Dans le mortel paradis d'une si douce chair ?
Y eut-il jamais livre au contenu plus vil
Avec une reliure aussi belle[1] ? Oh ! pourquoi cette duplicité
85 Dans un palais si merveilleux ?

LA NOURRICE

Il n'y a ni sincérité,
Ni fidélité, ni honnêteté chez les hommes. Tous sont parjures,
Renégats, vauriens et menteurs.
Ah ! où est mon valet ? Donne-moi un peu d'eau-de-vie.
Ces peines, ces malheurs, ces chagrins me font vieillir de dix ans.
90 Honte à ce Roméo !

JULIETTE

Que ta langue se couvre de pustules
Pour faire un vœu pareil ! Il n'est pas né pour la honte.
Sur son front la honte a honte de paraître,
Car c'est un trône où l'honneur peut être couronné
Seul monarque de la terre tout entière.
95 Oh ! comme j'ai eu tort de l'avoir décrié !

---

1. Les oxymores font ici pendant à ceux de Roméo en I. 1 et ils servent à traduire les sentiments contradictoires de Juliette. L'image du livre reprend celle que
Lady Capulet avait utilisée pour vanter les qualités du jeune Pâris (I. 3, v. 85-88).

LA NOURRICE

Allez-vous dire du bien de celui qui a tué votre cousin ?

JULIETTE

Vais-je dire du mal de celui qui est mon mari ?

Ah ! mon pauvre seigneur, quelle langue pourra guérir ton nom

Quand moi, ta femme depuis trois heures, je te mets à mal ?

100   Mais pourquoi, misérable, as-tu tué mon cousin ?

Ce méchant cousin aurait tué mon mari.

Refluez, larmes ridicules, remontez vers votre source première,

L'affluent de ces pleurs appartient au chagrin

Et non à la joie comme vous le faites par erreur.

105   Mon mari est vivant que Tybalt voulait tuer,

Et Tybalt est mort qui voulait tuer mon mari.

Tout ceci me console. Alors pourquoi pleurer ?

Mais il y avait un mot, pire que la mort de Tybalt,

Qui m'a tuée, et ce mot je voudrais l'oublier.

110   Oui, mais il est là, oppressant ma mémoire

Comme les crimes qui pèsent sur l'âme des pécheurs.

« Tybalt est mort et Roméo banni. »

Ah ! Ce mot de « banni », ce seul mot de « banni »

A tué dix mille Tybalt ; car la mort de Tybalt

115   Était une peine suffisante si l'on en était resté là ;

Ou si le malheur amer se plaît en compagnie

Et par nécessité n'arrive jamais seul,

Pourquoi, quand elle a dit : « Tybalt est mort », n'a-t-elle pas
                                                                              [ajouté

« Ton père » ou bien « ta mère » ou même tous les deux,

120   Ce qui eût suscité des lamentations ordinaires ?

Tandis que la mort de Tybalt a pour épilogue

« Roméo est banni ». Ah ! prononcer ce mot,

C'est père, mère, Tybalt, Roméo et Juliette ;

Tous sont morts, tous sont assassinés. « Roméo est banni » ;

125   Il n'y a ni fin, ni limite, ni mesure, ni frontière,

Dans la mort qu'annonce ce mot. Ce malheur est au-delà des
                                                                              [mots.

Où sont mon père et ma mère, Nourrice?

LA NOURRICE

Ils pleurent et se lamentent sur le corps de Tybalt.
Voulez-vous les rejoindre? Je vais vous y conduire.

JULIETTE

130 Lavent-ils ses blessures de leurs larmes? Les miennes couleront,
Quand leurs yeux seront secs, pour l'exil de Roméo.
Ramasse cette échelle. Pauvres cordes, on vous a trompées,
Vous comme moi, car Roméo est banni.
Il avait fait de vous le chemin conduisant à mon lit,
135 Mais moi je mourrai vierge, vierge et veuve à la fois.
Venez, cordes, venez; Nourrice, j'irai à mon lit de noces
Et, si ce n'est pas Roméo, que la mort prenne ma virginité!

LA NOURRICE

Allez vite dans votre chambre. Je trouverai Roméo
Et il vous consolera. Je sais bien où il est.
140 Écoutez-moi, Roméo sera ici ce soir.
Je cours le voir, il se cache dans la cellule de Laurent.

JULIETTE

Oh! trouve-le, donne cet anneau à mon chevalier fidèle
Et dis-lui de venir me voir pour un dernier adieu.

[Elles sortent.]

Scène 3

[Entre le Frère Laurent.]

FRÈRE LAURENT

Approche, Roméo, approche, homme rempli de crainte :
Voilà que l'affliction s'est éprise de tes charmes
Et te voilà marié à la calamité.

[Entre Roméo.]

ROMÉO

Mon père, quelles nouvelles ? Quelle est la sentence du Prince ?
5 Quelles nouvelles afflictions encore inconnues de moi
Cherchent à me serrer la main ?

FRÈRE LAURENT

Tu as trop abusé,
Mon fils, de ces mauvaises fréquentations !
Je viens t'annoncer la sentence du Prince.

ROMÉO

Comment peut-elle être moins rude que le Jugement dernier ?

FRÈRE LAURENT

10 Un verdict plus clément est tombé de ses lèvres,
Non pas la mort du corps, mais son bannissement.

ROMÉO

Ah ! le bannissement ! Non, aie pitié de moi, dis « la mort »,
Car l'exil apparaît beaucoup plus terrifiant,
Bien pire que la mort. Ne dis pas « bannissement » !

FRÈRE LAURENT

15 De ce lieu, de la ville de Vérone, tu as été banni.
Sois patient car le monde est vaste et grand.

ROMÉO

Il n'est pas d'autre monde, hors des murs de Vérone,
Que le purgatoire, la torture, l'enfer lui-même.
Être banni de Vérone, c'est être banni du monde,
20 Et l'exil du monde, c'est la mort. Alors « banni »
N'est qu'un autre nom donné à la « mort » ; en disant « banni »
Au lieu de mort, tu me décapites avec une hache d'or
Et tu souris de voir le coup qui m'assassine ainsi.

FRÈRE LAURENT

Ô péché mortel, ô grossière ingratitude !
25 Ton crime est passible de mort, mais le Prince clément,
En prenant ta défense, a détourné la loi
Et changé en exil ce mot funeste qu'est « la mort ».
C'est une grâce insigne et tu ne le vois pas.

ROMÉO

C'est une torture, non une grâce. Le ciel se trouve
30 Là où vit Juliette, et si un chat, un chien,
Une petite souris, tous les êtres inférieurs,
Vivent ici au ciel et peuvent la regarder,
Roméo, lui, ne le peut pas. Il y a plus d'avantages,
D'honneur et de privilèges pour des mouches
35 Charognardes, que pour Roméo ; elles peuvent se poser
Sur la blanche merveille qu'est la main de la chère Juliette,
Et voler d'immortelles faveurs sur ses lèvres
Qui, telles de chastes et pures vestales, rougissent encore
Du baiser qu'elles se donnent, y voyant un péché[1].
40 Roméo, lui, en est empêché, Roméo est banni.
Les mouches le peuvent et moi je prends la mouche[2].
Ce sont des êtres libres et moi je suis banni.
Et pourtant tu me dis que l'exil n'est pas la mort ?

---

1. Ce vers rappelle en filigrane les images du sonnet échangé par les amoureux pendant le bal (I. 5, v. 92-94). 2. Jeu de mots sur *fly*, la « mouche », et *to fly*, « voler », « s'enfuir ».

N'as-tu pas une boisson empoisonnée, un couteau aiguisé,
45 Quelque moyen rapide, si sordide soit-il ?
    N'as-tu que ce mot de « banni » pour me tuer ? « Banni » ?
    Ô mon Père, c'est le mot des damnés en enfer :
    Il provoque des hurlements. Comment as-tu le cœur,
    Toi, un homme de Dieu, toi, un confesseur qui absous les
                                                        [péchés,
50 Toi qui te dis mon ami, comment as-tu le cœur
    De me déchirer ainsi avec ce mot de « banni » ?

                        FRÈRE LAURENT
    Tu as perdu la tête, écoute-moi deux secondes.

                        ROMÉO
    Oh ! tu vas encore parler de bannissement.

                        FRÈRE LAURENT
    Je vais te fournir une armure pour te protéger de ce mot,
55 Et ce doux lait face à l'adversité, la philosophie,
    T'apportera le réconfort bien que tu sois banni.

                        ROMÉO
    « Banni », encore ce mot ? Au diable la philosophie !
    Si la philosophie n'a pas le pouvoir de créer une Juliette,
    De déplacer une ville, de casser la sentence d'un prince,
60 Elle ne sert à rien, elle n'a aucun pouvoir. Ne dis plus rien.

                        FRÈRE LAURENT
    Oh ! je vois ! les fous n'ont pas d'oreilles.

                        ROMÉO
    Comment en auraient-ils, quand les sages n'ont pas d'yeux ?

                        FRÈRE LAURENT
    Parlons de ta situation, si tu veux bien.

                        ROMÉO
    Tu ne peux pas parler de ce que tu ne ressens pas.

65 Si tu avais mon âge, si tu aimais Juliette,
   Marié depuis une heure, Tybalt assassiné,
   Amoureux comme moi et comme moi banni,
   Alors tu pourrais parler, tu pourrais t'arracher les cheveux,
   Et te jeter à terre comme je fais à présent,
70 Pour prendre les dimensions de la tombe à creuser.

[*On frappe.*]

FRÈRE LAURENT
Relève-toi, on frappe. Bon Roméo, cache-toi.

ROMÉO
Non. Il faudrait que les plaintes de mon cœur meurtri
Dégagent une brume qui me cache aux regards.

[*On frappe.*]

FRÈRE LAURENT
Écoute comme on frappe !... Qui est là ?... Roméo, relève-toi.
75 Tu vas être pris... Attendez un instant... Debout !

[*On frappe fort.*]

Cours jusqu'à mon bureau... Un instant ! Bonté divine,
De quelle stupidité tu fais preuve... J'arrive, j'arrive.
Qui frappe si fort ? D'où venez-vous ? Que voulez-vous ?

[*LA NOURRICE. En coulisse.*]

Faites-moi entrer et vous connaîtrez mon message :
80 Je viens de la part de madame Juliette.

FRÈRE LAURENT
                              Alors, entrez.

[*Entre la Nourrice.*]

LA NOURRICE

Ô saint Frère, oh! dites-moi, saint Frère,
Où est l'époux de ma dame? Où est Roméo?

FRÈRE LAURENT

Là, par terre, ivre de ses propres larmes.

LA NOURRICE

Oh! il est bien dans le même état que ma maîtresse,
85   Exactement pareil. Quelle triste communion!
Quelle situation pitoyable! Elle est couchée comme lui
À sangloter et à pleurnicher, à pleurnicher et à sangloter.
Debout, debout si vous êtes un homme!
Pour l'amour de Juliette, pour elle, relevez-vous!
90   Pourquoi tomber si bas et pousser tous ces « Oh! »[1]?

[*Il se lève.*]

ROMÉO

Nourrice!

LA NOURRICE

Ah! monsieur! Ah! monsieur! la mort est la fin de tout.

ROMÉO

Parlais-tu de Juliette? Comment va-t-elle?
Ne voit-elle pas en moi un tueur endurci,
Maintenant que j'ai souillé l'enfance de notre joie
95   En versant un sang si proche du sien?
Où est-elle, que fait-elle, et que dit
Ma secrète épouse de nos amours proscrites?

---

1. La lettre « O » comme le son [*ou*] sont redondants dans *La Pitoyable Tragédie de Roméo et Juliette*. On en dénombre quelque 180. La lettre « O » est utilisée pour exprimer la lamentation, la douleur, l'indignation. Elle désignait aussi le sexe de la femme, et Shakespeare, dans le premier chœur d'*Henry V*, l'utilise à propos de l'enceinte de bois (*wooden O*, prologue, vers 13) du théâtre du Globe.

LA NOURRICE

Oh ! elle ne dit rien, monsieur, elle pleure et pleure encore.
Elle s'effondre sur son lit, puis d'un coup se redresse,
100 Elle appelle Tybalt, puis elle crie Roméo
Et elle retombe ensuite à nouveau.

ROMÉO

C'est comme si ce nom[1],
Tiré à bout portant de la gueule d'un canon,
La tuait, comme la main maudite qui porte ce nom
A tué son cousin. Oh ! dis-moi, Frère, dis-moi
105 En quel misérable endroit de mon corps
Loge mon nom ? Dis-le-moi, pour que je mette à sac
Cette maison que j'abhorre.

[*Il tente de se tuer et la Nourrice lui arrache son poignard.*]

FRÈRE LAURENT

Retiens ta main désespérée.
Es-tu un homme ? Ton aspect le proclame. Tes pleurs
Sont ceux d'une femme et tes actes forcenés sont
110 Ceux d'une bête enragée, dénuée de raison.
Étrange femme à l'apparence d'un homme,
Bête dénaturée qui mêle ainsi deux natures.
Tu me laisses sans voix. Par ma sainte règle,
Je te croyais d'un caractère mieux trempé.
115 As-tu tué Tybalt ? Veux-tu te tuer toi-même ?
Et tuer ainsi ta femme qui ne vit que par toi
En retournant sur toi une maudite haine ?
Pourquoi t'en prendre à ta naissance, au ciel et à la terre,
Puisque la naissance, le ciel et la terre s'unissent
120 Tous trois en toi, vivant, qui veux les désunir.
Allons ! Tu fais honte à ta beauté, à ton amour, à ton esprit,

1. Voir sur ce point les interrogations de Juliette sur la question de la validité du nom (II. 1, v. 81-92).

Et, tel un usurier, tu regorges de biens
Sans te servir d'aucun pour l'usage légitime
Qui devrait embellir ta forme, ton amour et ton esprit.
125 Ta belle forme humaine n'est qu'une figure de cire
Qui s'éloigne de ce qui fait la valeur d'un homme.
Ton cher serment d'amour n'est qu'un parjure creux
Qui détruit l'amour que tu as juré de chérir.
Ton esprit, ornement de beauté et d'amour,
130 Dévoyé par l'usage que tu fais de l'un comme de l'autre,
Telle la flasque de poudre aux mains d'un soldat gauche,
Est mise à feu par ta propre ignorance,
Te faisant sauter par ton moyen de défense.
Allons, ressaisis-toi, l'ami! Ta Juliette est en vie,
135 Elle pour l'amour de qui tu mourais à l'instant[1].
De quoi te plains-tu? Tybalt voulait te tuer,
Mais tu as tué Tybalt. De quoi te plains-tu?
La loi qui te menaçait de mort devient ton amie
Et la change en exil. De quoi te plains-tu?
140 Les bienfaits du ciel pleuvent sur ta tête,
Le bonheur te courtise dans ses plus beaux atours,
Mais telle une petite fille malapprise et maussade,
Tu boudes ta fortune tout comme ton amour.
Prends garde, prends garde, c'est ainsi qu'on meurt misérable.
145 Allez, va voir ta bien-aimée comme il a été convenu,
Monte jusqu'à sa chambre... Pars et va la consoler.
Mais prends soin de partir avant que le guet soit en poste,
Sinon tu ne pourras pas te rendre à Mantoue,
Où tu dois demeurer jusqu'à ce que l'on puisse
150 Dévoiler votre mariage, réconcilier vos amis,
Implorer le pardon du Prince. Fasse que la liesse
Qui accompagnera ton retour soit joyeuse, mille fois plus
Que tu n'auras versé de larmes lors de ton départ.

---

1. Ironie dramatique soulignant la précipitation de Roméo qui ne pourra pas s'empêcher de répéter la même situation en sombrant à nouveau dans le désespoir à l'acte V.

[*À la Nourrice.*] Passe devant, Nourrice, mes compliments à ta
[maîtresse,
155   Demande-lui d'envoyer bien vite la maisonnée au lit,
Car tous ces lourds chagrins doivent les y inciter.
Roméo ne va pas tarder.

LA NOURRICE

Seigneur Dieu! j'aurais pu passer ici toute la nuit
À entendre de si sages conseils. Ce que c'est que d'être instruit!
160   Mon seigneur, je vais dire à ma dame que vous arrivez.

ROMÉO

Va, dis à ma tendre aimée de préparer ses remontrances.

[*La Nourrice s'apprête à sortir et revient.*]

LA NOURRICE

Voici, monsieur, une bague qu'elle m'a dit de vous donner,
[monsieur.
Hâtez-vous, faites vite, car il est déjà tard.

[*Sort la Nourrice.*]

ROMÉO

Comme ces paroles me redonnent confiance!

FRÈRE LAURENT

165   Allez, bonsoir, va-t'en! Ton cas se résume à ceci :
Ou tu pars avant que le guet soit en poste,
Ou au lever du jour tu t'enfuis déguisé.
Tu t'installes à Mantoue. Je trouverai ton valet
Et il t'informera de façon régulière
De tout ce qui ici peut t'être favorable.
Donne-moi la main. Il est tard. Adieu, bonne nuit.

ROMÉO

Si une joie plus grande que la joie ne m'appelait là-haut,
Je serais vraiment triste de te quitter si tôt.
Adieu.

[*Ils sortent.*]

Scène 4

[*Entrent Capulet, Lady Capulet et Pâris.*]

CAPULET

Les événements, monsieur, ont si mal tourné
Que nous n'avons pas eu le temps de convaincre notre fille.
Voyez-vous, elle aimait tendrement son cousin Tybalt,
Et moi aussi. Enfin, nous sommes nés pour mourir.
5 Il est très tard, elle ne descendra pas ce soir.
Et ça, je vous le jure, n'était votre compagnie
Il y a bien une heure que je serais au lit.

PÂRIS

Le temps de la mort confisque le temps de l'amour.
Madame, bonne nuit, recommandez-moi à votre fille.

LADY CAPULET

10 Je n'y manquerai pas, et dès demain matin je saurai ce qu'elle
[pense.
Ce soir elle est totalement murée dans son chagrin.

[*Pâris se prépare à sortir, Capulet le rappelle.*]

CAPULET

Seigneur Pâris, je vais tout tenter pour vous offrir
L'amour de ma fille. Je pense qu'elle se laissera gouverner
En tous points par moi ; en fait, j'en suis persuadé.
15 Femme, allez la voir avant d'aller vous coucher,
Faites-lui part de l'amour de mon fils Pâris,
Et dites-lui... vous m'entendez... que mercredi prochain...
Mais au fait... quel jour est-on ?

PÂRIS

Lundi, monseigneur.

CAPULET

Lundi ! ah bon ! ah bon ! Mercredi est trop tôt.
20 Allons-y pour jeudi, jeudi dites-lui
Qu'elle épousera ce noble comte.
Serez-vous prêt ? Que dites-vous de cette hâte ?
Ce sera en toute simplicité, un ou deux amis,
Car, voyez-vous, la mort de Tybalt est si récente
25 Qu'on pourrait penser qu'on ne fait pas cas de lui
Comme parent, si l'on faisait les choses en grand.
C'est pourquoi nous n'inviterons que six ou sept amis,
Voilà tout. Alors, que dites-vous de jeudi ?

PÂRIS

Monseigneur, je voudrais que ce jeudi soit demain.

CAPULET

30 Parfait, sauvez-vous, entendu pour jeudi.
Femme, allez voir Juliette avant d'aller au lit,
Préparez-la en vue du mariage qui l'attend.
Adieu, monseigneur. Un flambeau jusqu'à ma chambre, holà !
C'est qu'il est si tard qu'on pourrait
5 Presque dire qu'il est tôt. Bonne nuit.

[*Ils sortent.*]

Scène 5

[*Entrent Roméo et Juliette, dans la chambre au-dessus.*]

JULIETTE

Tu veux déjà partir ? Le jour n'est pas encore levé.
C'était le rossignol et non l'alouette
Qui perçait ainsi ton oreille craintive.
La nuit, il chante là-bas sur ce grenadier.
5 Crois-moi, mon amour, c'était le rossignol.

ROMÉO

C'était l'alouette, la messagère du matin,
Et non le rossignol : vois quelles lueurs envieuses
Festonnent les nues qui là-bas se scindent à l'est.
Les bougies de la nuit sont éteintes et le joyeux matin
10 Avance à petits pas sur les crêtes vaporeuses.
Je dois partir et vivre, ou rester et mourir.

JULIETTE

Cette lumière là-bas, ce n'est pas l'aube, je le sais, moi :
C'est quelque météore que le soleil exhale
Pour être cette nuit ton porteur de flambeau,
15 Et éclairer tes pas sur la route de Mantoue.
Oui, reste encore un peu. Nul besoin de partir.

ROMÉO

Qu'on me prenne et qu'on me mette à mort,
Cela m'est égal si tel est ton désir.
Je dirai que ce gris là-bas n'est pas l'œil du matin,
20 Mais le reflet du croissant de Cynthia au front pâle.
Et je ne dirai pas que c'est une alouette dont les notes frappent
La voûte du ciel là-haut au-dessus de nos têtes.
Je préfère rester, je ne veux plus partir.
Mort, sois la bienvenue ! c'est le vœu de Juliette.
25 Comment vas-tu, mon âme ? Parlons, il ne fait pas encore jour.

JULIETTE

Si, si, le jour se lève, pars, va-t'en, disparais !
Oui, c'est bien l'alouette qui chante aussi faux
Avec ses trilles rauques et ses aigus discordants.
On dit que l'alouette sait faire de doux accords,
30   Ce n'est pas vrai car elle sépare nos corps.
On dit que l'alouette et l'affreux crapaud ont échangé leurs yeux ;
Oh ! que n'ont-ils aussi échangé leurs voix, puisque cette voix
Qui nous alarme nous arrache aux bras l'un de l'autre
Et te chasse d'ici avec cette fanfare pour chasseurs[1].
35   Il fait de plus en plus clair, va-t'en à présent.

ROMÉO

Plus le jour apparaît, plus notre peine semble noire.

Entre la Nourrice.

LA NOURRICE

Madame.

JULIETTE

Nourrice.

LA NOURRICE

Madame votre mère vient dans votre chambre.
40   Le jour s'est levé, soyez prudents, prenez garde.

Elle sort.

JULIETTE

Alors, fenêtre, laisse entrer le jour et fais sortir la vie !

ROMÉO

Adieu, adieu ! un baiser, je descends.

---

1. Shakespeare superpose ici deux traditions, celle des sonneries de cors au début de la chasse et l'aubade traditionnellement offerte aux jeunes mariés au matin de leurs noces (*hunt's up*).

[Il descend.]

JULIETTE

Tu t'en vas donc, amour, seigneur, mari, ami ?
Je veux de tes nouvelles chaque jour de chaque heure
45 Car dans une minute il y a bien des jours.
Oh ! selon ce calcul je vais être bien vieille
Avant de revoir un jour mon Roméo.

ROMÉO

Adieu.
Je ne manquerai aucune occasion
50 De t'envoyer un message, mon amour.

JULIETTE

Oh ! crois-tu que nous nous reverrons un jour ?

ROMÉO

Je n'en doute pas et tous ces malheurs inspireront
De tendres propos dans les temps à venir.

JULIETTE

Ô Dieu, mon âme entrevoit quelque mauvais présage.
55 Maintenant que tu es en bas, il me semble
Que tu es comme un mort au fond d'une tombe.
Ou mon regard se trouble, ou tu as l'air bien pâle.

ROMÉO

Crois-moi, mon amour, toi aussi tu as l'air très pâle.
Le chagrin assoiffé boit notre sang. Adieu, adieu.

Il sort.

JULIETTE

60 Ô Fortune, Fortune, tous les hommes te disent inconstante.
Si tu es inconstante, que fais-tu avec lui
Qui est renommé pour sa fidélité ? Sois inconstante, Fortune,
Et alors, je l'espère, tu ne le garderas pas longtemps

Mais tu me le renverras.

Entre Lady Capulet.

LADY CAPULET

65 Holà! ma fille, êtes-vous levée?

JULIETTE

Qui m'appelle? C'est madame ma mère.
S'est-elle couchée si tard ou bien levée si tôt?
Quelle étrange raison la fait venir ici?

Elle revient de la fenêtre.

LADY CAPULET

Alors, comment vas-tu, Juliette?

JULIETTE

Madame, pas très bien.

LADY CAPULET

70 Tu pleures toujours la mort de ton cousin?
Qu'espères-tu? Que le flot de tes larmes le sorte de la tombe?
Même si tu le pouvais, tu ne lui rendrais pas la vie.
Allons, finissons-en. Un peu de peine montre beaucoup
[d'amour,
Mais beaucoup de peine révèle peu de force d'âme.

JULIETTE

75 Permettez pourtant que je pleure : la perte est si grande.

LADY CAPULET

Vous ressentirez la perte mais cela ne vous rendra pas l'ami
Que vous pleurez.

JULIETTE

Ressentant si fort la perte,
Je ne peux que pleurer à jamais cet ami.

LADY CAPULET

Crois-moi, ma fille, tu pleures moins sa mort
80 Que le fait de savoir que le scélérat qui l'a tué est en vie.

JULIETTE

Quel est ce scélérat, madame?

LADY CAPULET
                    Ce scélérat de Roméo.

JULIETTE

Ce scélérat et lui sont à des milles l'un de l'autre.
Dieu lui pardonne, c'est ce que je fais du fond du cœur.
Pourtant, aucun autre homme ne me fend plus le cœur.

LADY CAPULET

85 C'est parce que ce traître, cet assassin est en vie.

JULIETTE

Oui, madame, il se trouve hors d'atteinte de ces mains.
Je voudrais que nul autre que moi venge la mort de mon cousin.

LADY CAPULET

Nous le vengerons, tu peux en être sûre.
Allons, ne pleure plus. J'enverrai quelqu'un à Mantoue,
90 La ville où ce fuyard banni s'est réfugié,
Et il lui offrira un breuvage si étrange
Qu'il ira prestement tenir compagnie à Tybalt.
J'espère bien qu'alors tu seras satisfaite.

JULIETTE

Non, jamais je ne serai satisfaite avec ce Roméo
95 Tant que je ne le verrai pas... mort...
Est mon pauvre cœur d'avoir perdu un proche[1].

_____

1. Juliette a désormais appris à déguiser ses sentiments sous le masque d'un double langage, où elle feint de s'affliger pour Tybalt en exprimant son amour pour Roméo.

Madame, si vous pouviez seulement trouver quelqu'un
Pour porter le poison, je le préparerais...
De telle sorte que Roméo, lorsqu'il le boira,
100 S'endormira vite en paix. Oh! comme mon cœur répugne
À entendre son nom, quand je ne peux aller jusqu'à lui
Pour assouvir l'amour que je portais à mon cousin Tybalt
Sur le corps de celui qui l'a assassiné!

LADY CAPULET

Trouve le moyen et je trouverai l'homme.
105 Mais à présent, ma fille, je t'apporte de joyeuses nouvelles.

JULIETTE

La joie arrive à point quand on en a grand besoin.
De quoi s'agit-il, madame, je vous prie?

LADY CAPULET

Voilà! eh bien, ma fille, tu as un père attentionné,
Un père qui, pour t'arracher à ton chagrin,
110 A prévu pour toi un jour de joie imminent
Que tu n'attendais pas, que je n'espérais pas.

JULIETTE

Madame, à la bonne heure, et quel est donc ce jour?

LADY CAPULET

Eh bien, ma fille, jeudi matin de bonne heure,
Le vaillant, le jeune, le noble gentilhomme,
115 Le comte Pâris, en l'église Saint-Pierre,
Aura le bonheur de faire de toi une joyeuse épouse.

JULIETTE

Par l'église Saint-Pierre et par saint Pierre aussi,
Il ne fera pas de moi une joyeuse épouse.
Je m'étonne d'une hâte qui me force au mariage
0 Avant qu'un fiancé vienne me faire sa cour.
Je vous supplie de dire à mon seigneur et père, madame,

Que je refuse de me marier si vite ; et quand je le ferai, je jure
Que ce sera avec Roméo, que je hais, comme vous le savez,
Et non avec Pâris. En voilà des nouvelles !

LADY CAPULET

125 Voici votre père qui vient, dites-le-lui vous-même,
Et voyez comment il réagira face à vous.

Entrent Capulet et la Nourrice.

CAPULET

Quand le soleil se couche, la terre s'irise de rosée,
Mais quand il s'agit du coucher de soleil de mon neveu,
Alors, il pleut à verse.
130 Eh bien, ma fille, une fontaine ? Quoi ! toujours en pleurs ?
Des averses de larmes ? Dans un si petit corps
Tu es une barque, la mer et le vent.
Ces yeux, que je peux appeler la mer, sont envahis par
Une marée de larmes. Ton corps est une barque
135 Voguant sur l'eau salée, les vents sont tes soupirs
Qui, se déchaînant avec tes larmes et elles avec eux,
À moins d'une soudaine accalmie, risquent de faire sombrer
Ton corps battu par la tempête[1]. Eh bien, femme ?
Lui avez-vous fait part de notre décision ?

LADY CAPULET

140 Oui, monsieur, mais elle refuse, elle vous remercie.
Je voudrais que cette sotte soit mariée à sa tombe.

CAPULET

Tout doux, expliquez-vous, expliquez-vous, femme.
Comment ça ? elle refuse ? Est-ce qu'elle ne nous remercie pas ?

---

1. Capulet s'adonne, lui aussi, à des *conceits* pétrarquisants. Ces vers
apportent en outre une pointe d'ironie dramatique, car Roméo avait déjà
comparé son destin d'amoureux contrarié à une barque ballottée par les flots
déchaînés. Voir aussi l'acte V, scène 3, v. 118, où cette même image sert à
conclure son monologue avant sa mort.

N'est-elle pas fière ? Ne s'estime-t-elle pas honorée,
145 Tout indigne qu'elle est, quand nous faisons en sorte
Qu'un si digne gentilhomme puisse être son mari ?

JULIETTE

Fière, non, mais reconnaissante de ce que vous avez fait.
Je ne peux pas être fière de ce qui me révolte,
Mais je vous sais gré de cette haine qui se veut de l'amour.

CAPULET

150 De quoi, de quoi, de quoi, de quoi ? Qu'est-ce que cette ergoteuse ?
« Fière », « je vous sais gré » et « je ne vous remercie pas »,
Et cependant « pas fière », petite mijaurée ?
Reprenez vos mercis, épargnez-moi votre fierté,
Et préparez vos gambettes pour le jeudi qui vient
155 Afin d'accompagner Pâris en l'église Saint-Pierre,
Sinon, je t'y traînerai comme un condamné à l'échafaud.
Allez, ouste, charogne livide ! Assez, petite garce !
Face de carême !

LADY CAPULET
Allons, allons, vous avez perdu la tête ?

JULIETTE
Mon cher père, je vous supplie à genoux.

Elle s'agenouille.

160 Ayez la patience de m'écouter, un mot, un seul.

CAPULET

Va te faire pendre, petite garce, jeune insolente !
Je vais te dire, moi : va à l'église jeudi,
Sinon, ne me regarde jamais plus en face.
Tais-toi, ne réplique pas, ne réponds pas.
165 Mes doigts me démangent. Femme, on se croyait mal lotis
Que Dieu ne nous ait donné que cet unique enfant,

Mais maintenant je vois que c'en est une de trop,
Que c'est malédiction de l'avoir eue pour fille.
Hors d'ici, traînée !

LA NOURRICE
Que le Dieu du ciel la bénisse !
170 Vous avez tort, monseigneur, de la traiter ainsi.

CAPULET
Et pourquoi, madame Sagesse ? Tenez votre langue,
Mère Prudence, allez donc cancaner avec vos commères.

LA NOURRICE
Je ne dis rien de mal.

CAPULET
Eh bien alors, bonsoir !

LA NOURRICE
On n'a plus le droit de parler ?

CAPULET
Taisez-vous, espèce de radoteuse !
175 Allez donc abreuver vos commères de conseils,
Ici, on n'en a rien à faire.

LADY CAPULET
Vous êtes trop échauffé.

CAPULET
Par la sainte hostie, ça me rend fou ! De jour, de nuit,
À toute heure, en toute saison, au travail, au repos,
Seul ou en compagnie, mon souci a toujours été
180 De la voir mariée, et le jour où je lui trouve
Un gentilhomme de bonne famille,
Propriétaire de beaux domaines, jeune, de haut lignage,
Bourré, comme on dit, de toutes les qualités,
Aussi bien fait de sa personne qu'on peut l'être pour un homme...

185 Et j'ai devant moi une pauvre idiote qui pleurniche,
Un pantin qui geint quand la Fortune lui sourit,
Qui vous répond « Je ne veux pas me marier, je ne peux pas aimer,
Je suis trop jeune, veuillez me pardonner ! »
On refuse le mariage et il faut pardonner !
190 Allez paître où vous voulez, mais pas dans ma maison.
Prenez garde, réfléchissez, je n'ai pas l'habitude de plaisanter.
Jeudi est proche. Décidez en votre âme et conscience.
Si vous êtes ma fille, je vous donnerai à mon ami ;
Sinon, vous pouvez vous faire pendre, mendier, mourir de faim,
195 Crever dans la rue ! Car, sur mon âme, je ne te connais plus,
Jamais tu ne jouiras des biens qui m'appartiennent.
Croyez-m'en, réfléchissez, car je tiendrai parole.

JULIETTE

N'y a-t-il pas de pitié là-haut dans les nuages,
Pour voir combien ma douleur est profonde ?
200 Ô vous, ma tendre mère, ne me rejetez pas !
Différez ce mariage d'un mois, d'une semaine.
Ou, sinon, faites dresser le lit de mes noces
Dans le sombre tombeau où repose Tybalt.

LADY CAPULET

Ne me parle pas, car je ne dirai rien.
205 Fais comme tu voudras, c'est fini entre nous.

Elle sort.

JULIETTE

Ô mon Dieu ! Ô Nourrice, comment empêcher ça ?
Mon époux est sur terre et ma foi est au ciel.
Comment cette foi reviendra-t-elle sur terre
À moins que mon mari, ayant quitté cette terre,
10 Ne m'en délie au ciel ? Console-moi, conseille-moi.
Hélas ! Hélas ! pourquoi faut-il que le ciel use de tels stratagèmes
Contre une créature aussi faible que moi ?
Que dis-tu ? N'as-tu pas une parole de joie ?

Un peu de réconfort, Nourrice.

LA NOURRICE
                    Ma foi, si, écoute :
215 Roméo est banni et il y a fort à parier
Que jamais il n'osera venir vous reprendre.
Ou, s'il le fait, ce ne pourra être qu'en cachette.
Alors, puisque les choses en sont venues là,
Je pense que le mieux pour vous est d'épouser le comte.
220 Oh ! c'est un charmant gentilhomme !
Roméo, à côté, n'est qu'une lavette. Un aigle, madame,
N'a pas l'œil plus vert, plus vif, plus beau
Que Pâris. Que mon cœur soit maudit
Si cette seconde union ne vous rend pas heureuse,
225 Car elle surpasse la première ; ou, si ce n'était pas le cas,
Votre premier mari est mort, ou ce serait tout comme,
Si, vivant près d'ici, vous ne pouviez en jouir.

JULIETTE
Parles-tu avec ton cœur ?

LA NOURRICE
Et avec mon âme aussi, sinon, que le diable les emporte !

JULIETTE
230 Amen.

LA NOURRICE
Comment ?

JULIETTE
Eh bien, c'est là un merveilleux réconfort !
Rentre et dis à ma mère qu'ayant contrarié mon père,
Je suis allée à la cellule de Laurent,
235 Pour me confesser et recevoir l'absolution.

LA NOURRICE
Sainte Vierge, j'y vais ; voilà une sage décision.

[*Elle sort.*]

JULIETTE
Vieille sorcière ! démon perfide !
Quel est le plus grand péché ? Me vouloir ainsi parjure,
Ou calomnier mon seigneur avec la même langue
Qui l'a porté aux nues, disant mille et mille fois
Qu'il était sans pareil ? C'en est fini, conseillère !
Entre mon cœur et toi il y a un fossé.
Je me rends chez le Frère savoir comment guérir ;
Si tout le reste échoue, je peux au moins mourir.

Elle sort.

ACTE IV

Scène 1

Entrent le Frère Laurent et Pâris.

FRÈRE LAURENT

Jeudi, monsieur ? Cela laisse peu de temps.

PÂRIS

Mon beau-père Capulet veut qu'il en soit ainsi
Et je n'ai pas envie de freiner cette hâte.

FRÈRE LAURENT

Vous dites ignorer les pensées de la dame ?
5   Cela n'est pas régulier et je n'aime pas ça.

PÂRIS

Elle n'arrête pas de pleurer la mort de Tybalt,
Et je ne lui ai donc que peu parlé d'amour,
Car Vénus ne sourit pas dans une maison de larmes[1].
Or son père, monsieur, estime dangereux
10 Qu'elle donne prise à un si grand chagrin.

---

1. Dans cette pièce, où l'amour-passion naît de la conjonction d'étoiles contraires, l'astrologie joue un rôle clé. Elle divisait le ciel en douze maisons correspondant aux signes du zodiaque. L'influence bénéfique d'une planète telle que Vénus pouvait effectivement se voir contrariée par la maison où elle se trouvait. Ici, le caractère néfaste de la maison est symbolisé par le deuil et les larmes de Juliette.

Dans sa sagesse il veut hâter notre mariage
Pour arrêter cette inondation de larmes
Qui est aggravée par la solitude
Et qu'une vie à deux va peut-être endiguer.
15 Vous connaissez à présent la cause de cette hâte.

FRÈRE LAURENT
Je préfèrerais ne pas savoir pourquoi il faut la freiner...
Regardez, monsieur, la dame vient vers ma cellule.

Entre Juliette.

PÂRIS
Heureuse rencontre, madame, ma chère épouse.

JULIETTE
Vous ne pourrez le dire que quand je pourrai être une épouse.

PÂRIS
20 Cela pourra et devra être dès jeudi, mon amour.

JULIETTE
Ce qui doit être sera.

FRÈRE LAURENT
Ça, c'est sûr.

PÂRIS
Venez-vous vous confesser à ce bon père ?

JULIETTE
Vous répondre serait me confesser à vous.

PÂRIS
25 Ne lui cachez pas que vous m'aimez.

JULIETTE
Je vous confesserai que je l'aime.

PÂRIS

Vous lui direz, j'en suis sûr, que vous m'aimez aussi.

JULIETTE

Si c'est le cas, cet aveu aura plus de prix
S'il est fait dans votre dos plutôt que devant vous.

PÂRIS

30 Pauvre âme, les larmes ont bien abîmé ton visage.

JULIETTE

Les larmes ont remporté une piètre victoire,
Car, avant leurs ravages, il n'avait guère de charme.

PÂRIS

Tu lui fais plus de tort que tes larmes en le traitant ainsi.

JULIETTE

Ce n'est pas calomnier, monsieur, si c'est la vérité,
35 Et tout ce que j'ai dit, je me le dis en face[1].

PÂRIS

Ton visage est à moi et tu l'as calomnié.

JULIETTE

C'est possible, car il ne m'appartient plus.
Êtes-vous libre maintenant, mon père,
Ou dois-je revenir plus tard pour les vêpres?

FRÈRE LAURENT

40 Oui, je suis libre à présent. Tu es bien pensive, mon enfant...
Monseigneur, merci de bien vouloir nous laisser seuls.

---

1. Jeu de mots sur l'expression *to my face*, qui signifie à la fois «à mon visage» et «en face».

PÂRIS

Dieu me garde de perturber vos dévotions !
Juliette, je vous réveillerai tôt jeudi matin.
D'ici là, en guise d'adieu, voici un pieux baiser.

Il sort.

JULIETTE

45 Oh ! ferme la porte et, quand ce sera fait, viens
Pleurer avec moi : il n'y a ni espoir, ni remède, ni secours !

FRÈRE LAURENT

Ô Juliette, je connais déjà ton chagrin,
Et je ne sais plus à quel saint me vouer.
J'apprends que jeudi prochain, sans qu'on puisse rien
50 Pour différer cela, tu dois être mariée à ce comte.

JULIETTE

Ne me dis pas, Frère, que tu es au courant de ce projet
Sans me dire comment empêcher cela.
Si, dans ta sagesse, tu ne peux pas m'aider,
Alors dis seulement que ma décision est sage,

Elle sort un couteau.

55 Et ce couteau la confirmera aussitôt.
Dieu a uni nos cœurs et toi tu as joint nos mains :
Et cette main, unie par toi à celle de Roméo,
Accepterait de signer un nouveau contrat,
Et mon cœur fidèle, tel un traître rebelle,
60 Se tournerait vers un nouvel amour ? Voilà qui les tuera tous deux !
Alors, avec la longue expérience de tes années,
Donne-moi vite un conseil ; sinon, vois comment,
Entre ma détresse et moi, ce couteau viendra
Servir d'arbitre et trancher dans le sang un litige

65 Que ni ton art ni l'autorité de ton âge
    N'auront pu conduire à une issue honorable[1].
    Hâte-toi de parler, j'ai hâte de mourir
    Si tes paroles ne me parlent pas de remède.

FRÈRE LAURENT
    Arrête, ma fille, j'entrevois une lueur d'espoir
70 Qui exige une action aussi désespérée
    Que l'acte désespéré que nous voulons empêcher.
    Si, plutôt que d'épouser le comte Pâris,
    Tu as la ferme volonté de te donner la mort,
    Alors il est probable que tu devras te prêter
75 À un simulacre de mort pour écarter la honte,
    Et affronter la mort pour mieux y échapper.
    Si tu as ce courage, il y a un remède.

JULIETTE
    Oh ! plutôt que d'épouser Pâris, dis-moi
    De sauter du haut des créneaux d'une tour,
80 D'errer sur des routes infestées de voleurs, d'être là
    Où grouillent des serpents ; enchaîne-moi avec
    Des ours hurlants ou cache-moi la nuit dans la fosse commune,
    Là où craquent les os des squelettes entassés,
    Les tibias puants et les crânes jaunis dépourvus de mâchoires ;
85 Dis-moi d'aller au fond d'une tombe fraîchement creusée
    Et de m'y enfermer avec un mort roulé dans son linceul.
    Tout cela, lorsqu'on me le racontait, me faisait très peur,
    Mais je le ferai sans crainte et sans hésitation,
    Pour rester l'épouse sans tache de mon doux bien-aimé.

---

1. Image juridique. L'expérience et le savoir sont présentés en termes de *common law* comme le médiateur (*commission*) qui était nommé en cas de litige entre deux parties afin d'essayer de trouver une issue honorable et équitable. L'idée d'appliquer le vocabulaire légal au suicide, acte au moins contraire à la loi de Dieu, est paradoxale, mais elle est aussi prémonitoire dans la mesure où elle annonce la façon dont Juliette mettra fin à ses jours avec l'« heureux poignard » de Roméo (V. 3, v. 168).

FRÈRE LAURENT

90 Alors, attends, rentre chez toi, fais bonne figure,
Accepte d'épouser Pâris. Demain, c'est mercredi,
Demain soir, veille à te coucher seule.
Ne laisse pas la Nourrice dormir dans ta chambre.
Prends cette fiole et, une fois dans ton lit,
95 Bois jusqu'au bout cette liqueur distillée.
Aussitôt dans tes veines tu sentiras couler
Une humeur léthargique et glaciale : ton pouls
Suspendra sa cadence naturelle. Il ne battra plus
Et il s'arrêtera. Ni chaleur ni souffle, aucun signe de vie ;
100 Les roses de tes lèvres et de tes joues deviendront
Cendres livides et les fenêtres de tes yeux se fermeront
Comme lorsque la mort clôt le jour de la vie.
Chaque partie de ton corps privée de sa souplesse
Sera raide, dure et froide ainsi que dans la mort
105 Et, avec l'apparence d'un cadavre rigide,
Tu passeras quarante-deux heures d'affilée
Avant de t'éveiller comme d'un plaisant sommeil.
Alors, quand ton fiancé viendra demain matin
Te sortir de ton lit, tu seras étendue morte.
110 Puis, selon la coutume de notre pays, on te mettra
Dans tes plus beaux atours et, le cercueil ouvert,
On te transportera dans cet ancien tombeau
Où tous les Capulet gisent pour l'éternité.
Entre-temps, en attendant que tu te réveilles,
115 Roméo, par une lettre, connaîtra notre plan.
Il accourra ici, et lui et moi guetterons
L'heure de ton réveil, et cette même nuit
Roméo t'enlève loin d'ici vers Mantoue.
Voilà qui t'arrachera au déshonneur actuel,
120 Si nul revirement, aucune frayeur de femme
N'abattent ton courage en menant cette action.

JULIETTE

Donne, donne ! Oh ! ne me parle pas de peur !

FRÈRE LAURENT

Tiens, va-t'en, sois forte et résolue
Dans ton entreprise ; j'envoie en toute hâte un frère
125 À Mantoue porter ma lettre à ton mari.

JULIETTE

Amour, donne-moi la force et cette force m'aidera.
Adieu, bon père.

Ils sortent.

Scène 2

*Entrent Capulet, Lady Capulet, la Nourrice
et deux ou trois serviteurs.*

CAPULET

Va inviter tous ceux dont le nom est écrit ici.
Petit, va m'engager vingt bons cuisiniers.

UN AUTRE SERVITEUR

Vous n'en aurez pas de mauvais, monsieur, car je verrai bien
s'ils se lèchent les doigts.

CAPULET

5 Ah bon ! tu peux les juger là-dessus ?

UN AUTRE SERVITEUR

Pardi, monsieur, seul un mauvais cuisinier ne se lèche pas les
doigts ; par conséquent, je n'engagerai pas ceux qui refusent de
se lécher les doigts.

CAPULET

Allez, va-t'en.

Sort l'autre serviteur.

10 Cette fois on est loin d'être dans les temps.
Eh bien, est-ce que ma fille est allée chez le Frère Laurent ?

LA NOURRICE

Ma foi, oui.

CAPULET

Bon ! Il aura peut-être une bonne influence sur elle,
C'est une petite garce grincheuse et entêtée.

LA NOURRICE

15 Voyez comme elle revient l'air joyeux de confesse.

Entre Juliette.

CAPULET

Alors, tête de mule, où êtes-vous allée traîner ?

JULIETTE

Là où j'ai appris à me repentir du péché
De désobéissance et d'insoumission
À vous-même et à vos demandes, avec l'ordre
20 Du vénérable Laurent de me jeter à vos pieds
Pour implorer votre pardon.

Elle s'agenouille.

Je vous demande pardon.
Dorénavant je me laisserai toujours guider par vous.

CAPULET

Qu'on aille chercher le comte et qu'on l'informe de ceci.
Je veux que dès demain matin ce nœud soit noué.

JULIETTE

25 J'ai rencontré ce jeune seigneur dans la cellule de Laurent.
Je lui ai témoigné ce que peut accorder un amour bienséant,
Sans dépasser les bornes de la pudeur.

CAPULET

Alors j'en suis heureux. C'est bien, relève-toi.
C'est ce qu'il fallait faire. Il me faut voir le comte.
30 Oui, ma foi, allez, dis-je, faites-le venir ici.
Dieu m'en est témoin, ce saint et révérent Frère
Fait vraiment beaucoup pour toute notre ville.

JULIETTE

Nourrice, viendrez-vous avec moi dans ma chambre
Pour m'aider à choisir la parure qu'il convient
35 Que je porte pour la journée de demain ?

LADY CAPULET

Non, pas avant jeudi, nous avons tout le temps.

CAPULET

Va, Nourrice, va avec elle. Demain nous irons à l'église.

Sortent Juliette et la Nourrice.

LADY CAPULET

Nous allons être à court de victuailles
Et il fait presque nuit maintenant.

CAPULET

                                    Bah ! Je vais me remuer
40 Femme, tout ira bien, je te le garantis.
Toi, va voir Juliette, aide-la à se faire belle.
Je n'irai pas au lit cette nuit, laissez-moi seul :
Pour une fois je vais faire la maîtresse de maison. Holà, ho !

Ils sont tous partis. Bon, j'irai moi-même à pied
45 Chercher le comte Pâris afin de l'avertir
Pour demain. Je suis terriblement soulagé,
Que cette petite rebelle ait entendu raison.

Ils sortent.

Scène 3

Entrent Juliette et la Nourrice.

JULIETTE

Oui, cette tenue est la mieux. Mais, je t'en prie,
Bonne Nourrice, laisse-moi seule cette nuit car il me faut
Beaucoup prier afin de pouvoir obtenir
Que le ciel me sourie, car tu sais à quel point
5 J'ai commis de péchés par ma mauvaise humeur.

Entre Lady Capulet.

LADY CAPULET

Ah! vous êtes occupées? Vous avez besoin de moi?

JULIETTE

Non, madame, nous avons choisi ce qui est nécessaire
Et tout ce qui convient pour la journée de demain.
S'il vous plaît, laissez-moi seule à présent
10 Et que la Nourrice veille avec vous cette nuit
Car je suis sûre que vous avez beaucoup à faire
Avec toute cette précipitation.

LADY CAPULET
Bonne nuit.
Mets-toi au lit et repose-toi, tu en as besoin.

Sortent Lady Capulet et la Nourrice.

JULIETTE
Adieu! Dieu seul sait quand nous nous reverrons.
15 Je sens des sueurs froides, la peur envahit mes veines
Et mon sang chaud en est presque glacé.
Je vais les rappeler pour reprendre courage.
Nourrice! Que ferait-elle ici?
Cette scène lugubre, je dois la jouer seule.
20 Voilà le breuvage! Et si cette potion n'agissait pas du tout?
Il me faudrait alors me marier demain matin?
Non, non! ceci l'empêchera.

[Elle prend un poignard.]

Toi, reste là.

[Elle pose le poignard à côté d'elle.]

Et si c'était un poison que le Frère
Voulait m'administrer pour que je disparaisse
25 De peur que ce mariage ne cause son déshonneur,
Étant donné qu'il m'a déjà unie à Roméo?
Je le crains. Et pourtant il me semble que non,
Car il a su prouver qu'il était un saint homme.
Et si, quand je serai déposée au tombeau,
30 Je m'éveillais avant que Roméo
Vienne me libérer? Je frémis à cette idée!
Ne vais-je pas suffoquer au fond de ce caveau,
Dont la gueule puante n'aspire jamais d'air pur,
Et mourir étouffée avant que Roméo n'arrive?
Ou, si je survis, n'est-il pas imaginable
Que d'affreuses visions de mort et de nuit

S'ajoutant à l'effroi d'un lieu comme celui-là,
Ce caveau, cet ancien réceptacle,
Où, pendant tant de siècles, les os
40 De tous mes ancêtres se sont accumulés,
Où Tybalt ensanglanté, fraîchement mis en terre,
Gît et pourrit dans son suaire ; c'est là, dit-on,
Qu'à certaines heures de la nuit les esprits se rassemblent...
Hélas ! hélas ! n'est-il pas probable que si
45 Je me réveille trop tôt au milieu de ces miasmes
Et de ces cris à rendre fou n'importe quel mortel
Comme celui qui entend la mandragore arrachée à la terre[1] ?
Oh ! si je me réveille, ne vais-je pas perdre la tête,
Entourée de toutes parts par ces frayeurs hideuses,
50 Et, dans ma folie, ne vais-je pas jouer avec les os de mes aïeux,
Tirer de son suaire le corps mutilé de Tybalt ?
Ne vais-je pas, ainsi enragée, me faire sauter la cervelle
En prenant pour massue le tibia d'un ancêtre ?
Oh ! regarde ! Il me semble apercevoir le spectre de mon cousin,
55 Lancé à la poursuite de Roméo qui l'a embroché
À la pointe de sa rapière. Arrête, Tybalt, arrête !
Roméo, Roméo, Roméo ! Vois ! C'est à toi que je bois.

Elle s'effondre sur son lit, cachée par les rideaux.

---

1. La mandragore est une plante (utilisée à l'époque comme opiacée mais aussi pour certaines pratiques magiques) dont les racines fourchues évoquent une petite forme humaine. On la ramassait au pied des gibets où elle naissait, dit-on, de la semence des pendus et, lorsqu'on l'arrachait, elle poussait un cri affreux, capable de faire perdre la raison à ceux qui l'entendaient.

Scène 4

Entrent Lady Capulet et la Nourrice.

LADY CAPULET

Tiens, Nourrice, prends ces clés et va chercher d'autres épices.

LA NOURRICE

On demande des dattes et des coings pour la pâtisserie.

Entre Capulet.

CAPULET

Allez, du nerf, du nerf, du nerf! Le second coq a chanté!
La cloche du couvre-feu a sonné, il est trois heures.
5   Surveillez les pâtés, ma bonne Angélique,
Ne lésinez sur rien.

LA NOURRICE

                Allez, monsieur le marmiton, allez,
Allez donc vous coucher. Demain, ma foi, vous serez malade
D'avoir ainsi veillé toute la nuit.

CAPULET

Non, pas du tout. Non mais! J'ai, pour moins que ça,
10   Passé bien des nuits blanches sans être malade.

LADY CAPULET

Oui, vous avez chassé la souris en votre temps,
Mais désormais je veille à vous épargner cette veille.

Sortent Lady Capulet et la Nourrice.

CAPULET

Jalousie, jalousie!

Entrent trois ou quatre serviteurs avec des broches,
des bûches et des paniers.

Alors, mon garçon, qu'est-ce que tu portes là ?

LE PREMIER SERVITEUR
Des choses pour le cuisinier, monsieur, mais je ne sais pas quoi.

CAPULET
15   Dépêche-toi, dépêche-toi !

[*Sort le Premier Serviteur.*]

Petit, va chercher des bûches plus sèches !
Appelle Pierre, il te montrera où elles se trouvent.

LE DEUXIÈME SERVITEUR
J'ai assez de cervelle, monsieur, pour trouver des bûches tout seul
Et je ne vais pas déranger Pierre pour ça.

CAPULET
20   Par la messe ! Voilà qui est bien dit. Ah ! Le joyeux fils de garce !
C'est toi qui seras une bûche.

[*Sort le Deuxième Serviteur.*]

... Ma foi, il fait jour !

On joue de la musique.

Le comte sera ici d'une minute à l'autre avec les musiciens,
C'est ce qu'il a dit. Je l'entends, il est tout près.
Nourrice ! Femme ! Holà ! Eh bien, Nourrice, je t'appelle.

Entre la Nourrice.

25 Va réveiller Juliette, va, aide-la à se préparer.
Je vais bavarder avec Pâris. File, dépêche-toi,
Dépêche-toi! Le futur marié est déjà arrivé.
Dépêche-toi, te dis-je.

[*Sort Capulet.*]

Scène 5

La chambre de Juliette. La Nourrice avance jusqu'au lit.

LA NOURRICE

Maîtresse! allons, maîtresse! Juliette! un vrai loir, je vous
[jure!
Mon agnelle! Eh bien! madame! Hou la paresseuse!
Ma chérie! madame! mon petit cœur! Eh! la mariée!
Quoi! pas un mot? Vous prenez un acompte aujourd'hui.
5   Du sommeil pour la semaine, car la nuit prochaine, je vous jure
Que le comte Pâris va jouer son va-tout pour que
Vous ne dormiez pas du tout! Dieu me pardonne!
Sainte Vierge, amen! comme elle dort bien!
Je dois la réveiller. Madame, madame, madame!
10 C'est que si vous voulez que le comte vous prenne
Au saut du lit, ma foi, il vous fera sursauter, pas vrai?
Quoi! Tout habillée, en robe de mariée, puis recouchée?
Je dois absolument vous réveiller. Madame, madame, madame!
Hélas! Hélas! Au secours, au secours! ma maîtresse est morte!
Oh! maudit soit le jour où je suis née!
Holà, de l'eau-de-vie! monseigneur, madame!

Entre Lady Capulet.

LADY CAPULET

Quel est ce bruit ?

LA NOURRICE
Ô jour de malheur !

LADY CAPULET

Qu'y a-t-il ?

LA NOURRICE
Regardez, regardez ! Oh ! quel jour de malheur !

LADY CAPULET

Mon Dieu, mon Dieu, mon enfant, toute ma vie.
20 Reviens, lève les yeux ou je vais mourir avec toi.
Au secours, au secours ! Appelez du secours !

Entre Capulet.

CAPULET

Faites venir Juliette, que diable, son époux est arrivé.

LA NOURRICE

Elle est morte ! décédée ! elle est morte ! hélas ! jour de malheur !

LADY CAPULET

Jour de malheur, elle est morte, elle est morte, elle est morte !

CAPULET

25 Ah ! laissez-moi la voir. Tout est fini, hélas ! Elle est froide,
Son sang s'est figé et ses membres sont raides.
La vie depuis longtemps a déserté ses lèvres,
Et la mort s'étend sur elle comme la gelée précoce
Recouvre la plus douce fleur de toute la prairie.

LA NOURRICE

30 Quel jour de malheur!

LADY CAPULET

Oh! quelle heure douloureuse!

CAPULET

La mort qui me l'a prise pour me faire pleurer
Paralyse ma langue, m'empêche de parler.

Entrent Frère Laurent, Pâris et des musiciens.

FRÈRE LAURENT

Allons! La mariée est-elle prête à se rendre à l'église?

CAPULET

Prête à partir pour ne plus revenir.
35 Oh! mon fils, la veille de ton mariage,
La Mort a couché avec ta femme. Elle est étendue là,
Fleur qu'elle était, déflorée par la Mort.
La Mort est mon gendre, la Mort est mon héritière.
Elle a épousé ma fille. Je veux mourir
40 Et tout lui laisser: ma vie, mes biens, tout est à la Mort[1].

PÂRIS

Ai-je si longtemps rêvé de voir ce jour en face
Pour qu'il m'offre aujourd'hui un si triste spectacle?

LADY CAPULET

Jour maudit, malheureux, misérable et haïssable!
C'est l'heure la plus noire que le temps ait connu
45 Au cours de son long et pénible pèlerinage[2].
Je n'avais qu'une seule enfant, une pauvre fille si aimante,
Elle était toute ma joie et tout mon réconfort,

---

1. La mort en anglais est du genre masculin. Voir note *supra*,
p. 59.   2. L'image du pèlerinage rappelle ironiquement le motif du pèlerin
lié à Roméo (voir I. 5, v. 95-100).

Et la Mort cruelle l'a arrachée à ma vue !

La Nourrice

Quel malheur ! Ô jour malheureux, malheureux, malheureux
[jour !

50 Jour funeste ! Oh ! jour de profond malheur !
Fallait-il que je voie une chose pareille !
Ô jour détestable, ô jour, ô jour détestable !
Jamais on n'a vu jour plus noir qu'aujourd'hui.
Ô jour de malheur, ô malheureux jour !

Pâris

55 Trompé, divorcé, outragé, bafoué, assassiné !
Trompé par toi, Mort abominable, cruelle
Entre les cruelles, Mort, tu m'as anéanti !
Ô mon amour, ô ma vie, non plus vie mais amour dans la Mort !

Capulet

Méprisé, désespéré, haï, martyrisé, assassiné !
60 Temps implacable, pourquoi es-tu venu
Massacrer, massacrer notre cérémonie ?
Mon enfant, mon enfant, mon âme et non plus mon enfant,
Tu es morte. Hélas ! ma fille est morte,
Et avec mon enfant mes joies sont enterrées.

Frère Laurent

65 Paix, de grâce ! un peu de retenue. Le remède au désespoir
N'est pas dans ces déchaînements. Le ciel et vous
Aviez cette belle jeune fille en partage. Elle est au ciel,
Ce n'en est que mieux pour elle. Ce qu'elle avait de vous,
Vous ne pouviez le soustraire à la mort et le ciel
70 Conserve sa part dans la vie éternelle.
Vous vouliez qu'elle s'élève dans le monde,
Votre ciel était de la voir s'élever,
Et maintenant vous pleurez qu'elle se soit élevée
Au-dessus des nuages, aussi haut que le ciel ?
75 En l'aimant de la sorte, vous l'aimiez si mal

Que vous devenez fous de la voir aussi bien.
Femme longtemps mariée n'est jamais bien mariée,
La mieux lotie est celle qui meurt jeune mariée.
Séchez vos larmes et déposez ce romarin
80 Sur cette belle dépouille et, selon la coutume,
Dans ses plus beaux atours portez-la à l'église.
Bien que notre faible nature nous pousse à la douleur,
La raison, elle, se réjouit de ces pleurs.

CAPULET

Que tous ces préparatifs de fête
85 Se changent en sombres funérailles,
La musique en glas mélancolique,
Le banquet de noce en triste repas d'enterrement,
Les hymnes solennels en mornes chants funèbres,
Les bouquets de noce en couronnes mortuaires,
90 Et que tout dès lors se change en son contraire[1].

FRÈRE LAURENT

Monsieur, retirez-vous et vous, madame, suivez-le,
Et vous aussi, seigneur Pâris. Que chacun se prépare
À escorter cette belle dépouille jusqu'à sa tombe.
Vous avez dû pécher. Le ciel fait les gros yeux,
95 N'allez pas l'irriter en fâchant le bon Dieu.

Tous sortent, sauf la Nourrice et les musiciens.
Ils déposent du romarin sur le corps
de Juliette et tirent les rideaux.

LE PREMIER MUSICIEN

Ma foi, on peut remballer nos flûtes et partir.

---

1. Ces vers donnent l'une des clés de la structure de la pièce, véritable
tragédie du retournement, où l'on passe sans cesse d'un extrême à l'autre, de la
haine à l'amour, de l'amour à la mort, du rire à la douleur et vice versa.

LA NOURRICE

Ah ! mes bons amis, remballez, remballez,
Vous voyez bien qu'on est dans un triste état.

LE PREMIER MUSICIEN

Ma foi oui, c'est là un triste étui[1].

Sort la Nourrice.

Entre Pierre.

PIERRE

100 Musiciens, ho ! les musiciens ! « Le cœur en joie », « Le cœur en
joie ». Oh ! si vous voulez que je vive, jouez-moi « Le cœur en
joie ».

LE PREMIER MUSICIEN

Pourquoi « Le cœur en joie » ?

PIERRE

Ô musiciens, parce que mon cœur joue « J'ai le cœur brisé ». Oh !
105 jouez-moi une joyeuse complainte pour me consoler.

LE PREMIER MUSICIEN

Non, pas une complainte ! Ce n'est pas le moment de jouer cela
maintenant.

PIERRE

Alors, vous ne voulez pas ?

LE PREMIER MUSICIEN

Non.

---

1. Jeu de mots sur *case* qui signifie à la fois « l'état, la situation » et « l'étui »
où l'on range les instruments de musique.

Pierre

110   Alors, je vais vous en donner, moi, vous allez m'entendre !

Le Premier Musicien

Qu'allez-vous nous donner ?

Pierre

Pas d'sous, ça non, mais des clous !
Je vais vous en donner, moi, du violoneux !

Le Premier Musicien

Et moi je vais vous en donner du larbin !

Pierre

115   Je vais vous chatouiller la caboche avec ma dague de larbin. Pas
d'anicroches avec moi. Gare à votre dos ! gare au sol. Vous
prenez bien note ?

Le Premier Musicien

Si vous nous plaquez le dos au sol, nous sommes à votre
portée[1].

Le Deuxième Musicien

120   S'il vous plaît, rengainez cette dague et dégainez votre esprit.

Pierre

Alors, en garde, gardez-vous de mes pointes. Je vais vous battre
à plate couture à coups de pointes d'esprit et rengainer ma
pointe d'acier. Répondez-moi en hommes.

Quand le chagrin vous étreint,

---

1. Calembours formés à partir du lexique musical. *Crotchet* signifie à la fois
« croche » et « caprice », tandis que *I'll re you* et *I'll fa you. Do you note me ?*
envoient aux notes du solfège.

125   *Quand l'esprit est accablé de lourdes peines,*
       La musique alors, avec un son argentin...

Pourquoi « son argentin » ? Pourquoi une musique au son
argentin ? Que répondez-vous, Simon Mandoline ?

LE PREMIER MUSICIEN

Ma foi, monsieur, c'est parce que l'argent sonne juste à l'oreille.

PIERRE

130   Balivernes. Que dites-vous, Hugues Crincrin ?

LE DEUXIÈME MUSICIEN

Je dis « son argentin » parce que les musiciens jouent pour de
l'argent.

PIERRE

Balivernes aussi. Que dites-vous, Jacques Larchet ?

LE TROISIÈME MUSICIEN

Ma foi, je ne sais pas quoi dire.

PIERRE

135   Ah ! mille pardons, monsieur ne parle pas, il chante ! Je répon-
drai pour vous. C'est « une musique au son argentin » parce que
les musiciens n'ont jamais d'or pour la musique.

       Alors la musique au son argentin
       Leur garantit le pain quotidien.

              Il sort.

LE PREMIER MUSICIEN

140   Quelle infâme crapule que cet individu !

LE DEUXIÈME MUSICIEN

Qu'il aille se faire pendre, ce jean-foutre. Venez, entrons là en attendant le retour du cortège et de rester pour dîner.

Ils sortent.

ACTE V

Scène 1

Entre Roméo.

ROMÉO

Si j'en crois la flatteuse vérité du sommeil,
Mes rêves présagent l'arrivée de joyeuses nouvelles.
L'amour, roi de mon cœur, est léger sur son trône,
Et toute la journée une étrange allégresse
5 M'a rendu si heureux que je ne touche plus terre.
J'ai rêvé que ma dame venait et qu'elle me trouvait mort
(Rêve singulier qui permet à un mort de penser)
Et que ses baisers sur mes lèvres m'insufflaient tant de vie
Que je ressuscitais et devenais empereur.
10 Dieu ! que la jouissance de l'amour est douce
Pour que son ombre donne déjà tant de joies !

Entre Balthazar, le valet de Roméo, chaussé de bottes.

Des nouvelles de Vérone ! Eh bien, Balthazar ?
M'apportes-tu des lettres de Frère Laurent ?
Comment va mon aimée ? Et mon père, va-t-il bien ?
15 Comment va ma Juliette ? J'insiste pour savoir,
Car rien ne peut aller mal si elle se porte bien.

BALTHAZAR

Alors, elle va bien et rien ne peut aller mal.

Son corps repose dans le tombeau des Capulet
Et son âme immortelle vit avec les anges.
20 Je l'ai vue enterrée au caveau de ses pères,
Je me suis hâté aussitôt pour venir vous le dire.
Oh ! pardonnez-moi de porter de mauvaises nouvelles
Mais c'est vous, monsieur, qui l'avez demandé.

ROMÉO

Ah ! c'est donc ça ? Alors je vous défie, étoiles !
25 Tu sais où j'habite, va me chercher de l'encre et du papier,
Loue des chevaux de poste. Je pars d'ici ce soir.

BALTHAZAR

Je vous en prie, monsieur, prenez patience.
Votre visage est blême, vous avez l'air hagard,
Et je redoute quelque malheur.

ROMÉO

Il n'en est rien, tu te trompes.
30 Laisse-moi et fais ce que je te dis de faire.
Le Frère ne t'a pas donné de lettre pour moi ?

BALTHAZAR

Non, mon bon seigneur.

ROMÉO

Peu importe. Va-t'en,
Et loue ces chevaux. Je te rejoins tout de suite.

Sort Balthazar.

Eh bien, Juliette, ce soir je dormirai à tes côtés.
35 Voyons ce qu'il faut faire. Ô mal, que tu es prompt
À pénétrer l'esprit des hommes désespérés.
Je me souviens de cet apothicaire
(Il habite près d'ici), je l'ai vu l'autre jour,
En haillons, le sourcil broussailleux,

40   Il récoltait des plantes. Il semblait famélique,
      La misère ne lui avait laissé que la peau et les os.
      Dans sa pauvre officine pendaient une tortue,
      Un crocodile empaillé et des peaux de poissons
      Aux formes inquiétantes, et sur ses étagères
45   Une misérable série de boîtes vides, des pots
      De faïence verte, des vessies, des graines moisies,
      Des bouts de ficelle et de vieux pains de pétales
      De roses, le tout sur un étalage clairsemé.
      Voyant cette misère, je me suis dit que
50   « Si quelqu'un à cette heure avait besoin d'un poison,
      Dont la vente est passible de mort à Mantoue,
      Il y avait là un pauvre hère qui le lui vendrait bien. »
      Oh ! cette pensée n'a fait qu'anticiper le besoin que j'en ai,
      Et c'est à moi que ce miséreux doit le vendre[1].
55   Si j'ai bonne mémoire, c'est ici sa maison.
      Comme c'est jour férié, la boutique est fermée.
      Holà ! Apothicaire !

                        Entre l'Apothicaire.

                        L'APOTHICAIRE
                      Qui appelle si fort ?

                            ROMÉO
      Approche-toi, l'ami. Je vois que tu es pauvre.
      Tiens, voilà quarante ducats. Donne-moi
60   Une dose de poison, quelque chose de foudroyant
      Qui se répande dans toutes les veines, de sorte que celui
      Qui, las de la vie, en prend, tombe raide mort
      Et expulse ainsi son souffle hors de sa poitrine
      En une explosion aussi violente que la poudre

---

1. Après les prémonitions de son rêve, Roméo s'invente ici un destin en
décrivant une coïncidence dans laquelle il voit après coup un signe de la
Nécessité.

65 Qui crache le feu du ventre du canon meurtrier[1].

L'APOTHICAIRE

J'ai de ces drogues mortelles, mais la loi de Mantoue
Punit de mort quiconque en fait commerce.

ROMÉO

Toi, qui es si démuni, dans une telle misère,
Tu as peur de mourir ? La faim creuse tes joues,
70 Le besoin et les privations crient famine dans tes yeux.
La misère abjecte te fait courber l'échine.
Ni le monde, ni les lois de ce monde ne sont tes amis,
Le monde n'a pas de loi qui puisse t'enrichir,
Alors ne sois plus pauvre, enfreins la loi, prends cet argent.

L'APOTHICAIRE

75 C'est ma pauvreté qui dit oui, non ma volonté.

ROMÉO

Je paie ta pauvreté, non pas ta volonté.

L'APOTHICAIRE

Vous n'aurez qu'à verser ceci dans un liquide,
Le boire d'un trait et, même si vous étiez aussi fort
Que vingt hommes, ce poison vous expédierait sur-le-champ.

-----

1. Le texte anglais dit *Doth hurry form the fatal cannon's womb*, ce qui appelle
une double remarque. Le mot *womb*, c'est-à-dire l'utérus, la matrice, se
substitue ici à l'image plus familière de la gueule du canon (*cannon's mouth*)
qu'on attendrait dans ce contexte. Cette image est, par ailleurs, à rapprocher de
celle des vers 5-6 du premier prologue *From forth the fatal loins of these two foes/
A pair of star-crossed lovers take their life* (« Des fatales entrailles de ces races
rivales/Sont nés deux amants sous une mauvaise étoile »). L'ambiguïté de
l'expression *take their life*, qui dans le contexte signifie à la fois « naître » et « se
suicider », montre déjà le caractère quasi interchangeable d'Éros et de Thanatos,
dans la mesure où la source même de la vie (*loins* ou *womb*) est associée à la
mort (*fatal*, *take their life*).

ROMÉO

80 Voici ton or, le pire des poisons pour l'âme humaine,
    Car il commet plus de meurtres en ce monde odieux
    Que les pauvres mixtures qu'on t'interdit de vendre.
    C'est moi qui te vends du poison, pas toi.
    Adieu, achète à manger et va te remplumer.
85 Quant à toi, cordial et non poison, viens avec moi
    Au tombeau de Juliette, c'est là qu'est ton emploi.

Ils sortent.

Scène 2

Entre le Frère Jean.

FRÈRE JEAN

Saint moine franciscain, holà, mon frère !

FRÈRE LAURENT

Cette voix doit être celle du Frère Jean.
Bienvenue à toi qui arrives de Mantoue. Que dit Roméo ?
Ou bien, s'il a mis son message par écrit, donne-moi sa lettre.

FRÈRE JEAN

5   J'étais allé chercher un frère mendiant,
    Un moine de notre ordre qui visite les malades
    Dans cette cité, afin qu'il m'accompagne.
    Je l'ai trouvé, mais les officiers de santé,
    Pensant que nous étions tous deux entrés
10 Dans une maison infectée par la peste,

Mirent les scellés sur la porte et refusèrent qu'on sorte,
Si bien que mon voyage à Mantoue s'est arrêté là.

FRÈRE LAURENT
Qui donc a porté ma lettre à Roméo ?

FRÈRE JEAN
Je n'ai pas pu la faire parvenir — la voici —
15 Ni trouver un messager pour te la rapporter,
Tant ils craignaient la contamination.

FRÈRE LAURENT
Quelle malchance ! Par mon saint ordre, ce n'était pas là
Un message ordinaire, mais une lettre d'importance,
Lourde de conséquences, et toute négligence
20 Peut faire courir un grand danger. Cours, Frère Jean,
Va me chercher une barre de fer et apporte-la tout de suite
À ma cellule.

FRÈRE JEAN
Frère, je pars et je te l'apporte.

Il sort.

FRÈRE LAURENT
Maintenant je dois aller seul à ce tombeau.
Dans trois heures la belle Juliette va s'éveiller
25 Et elle me maudira parce que Roméo
N'a pas été prévenu de ce qui s'est passé,
Mais je m'en vais écrire de nouveau à Mantoue
Et la garder dans ma cellule jusqu'au retour de Roméo,
Pauvre morte vivante enfermée avec les morts.

Il sort.

Scène 3

*Entrent Pâris et son page, portant des fleurs
et de l'eau parfumée.*

PÂRIS

Donne-moi ta torche, petit. Va et reste à l'écart.
Non, éteins-la plutôt, car je crains d'être vu.
Couche-toi de tout ton long sous les cyprès là-bas,
Colle bien ton oreille sur la terre caverneuse,
5   Pour que pas un pied ne foule le cimetière,
Dont le sol instable est meuble à force d'être creusé,
Sans que tu l'entendes. Tu n'auras qu'à siffler
Afin de m'avertir si tu entends qu'on vient.
Donne-moi ces fleurs, va, fais comme je dis.

LE PAGE

10   J'ai presque peur de rester seul en cet endroit,
Ici au cimetière, mais j'en prends le risque.

Il sort. Pâris jette les fleurs sur la tombe.

PÂRIS

Douce fleur, reçois ces fleurs sur le lit de tes noces
Dont le dais n'est, hélas, que poussière et que pierre.
Chaque jour je viendrai l'arroser de gouttes d'eau musquée
15   Ou, à défaut, de larmes distillées par mes plaintes.
Et le deuil que pour toi je désire observer
Sera de venir chaque soir, fleurir ta tombe et pleurer.

Le page siffle.

Le page m'avertit que l'on vient par ici.
Quels pas maudits se risquent au milieu de la nuit
Pour contrarier mon deuil et les rites d'amour?
Quoi, on vient avec une torche! Nuit, cache-moi un instant!

[Pâris se cache.]

*Entrent Roméo et Balthazar portant une torche,
une pioche et une barre de fer.*

ROMÉO

Donne-moi cette pioche et cette barre de fer.
Tiens, prends cette lettre. Tôt demain matin,
Veille à bien la remettre à mon seigneur et père.
25 Donne-moi cette torche. Sur ta vie je t'ordonne,
Quoi que tu puisses entendre ou voir, de rester à l'écart
Et de ne pas m'interrompre dans mon entreprise.
La raison pour laquelle je descends dans cet antre de mort,
C'est en partie pour voir le visage de ma femme
30 Mais surtout pour reprendre un précieux anneau
À son doigt mort, un anneau dont je veux
Faire un usage très cher. Alors pars d'ici, va-t'en.
Mais si tu te méfies et reviens pour épier
Ce que j'ai ensuite l'intention de faire,
35 Par le Ciel, je t'arracherai les membres un à un,
Et joncherai ce cimetière affamé de tes restes.
À cette heure je me sens comme une bête sauvage,
Mon humeur est plus féroce et plus inexorable
Qu'un tigre au ventre creux ou la mer qui rugit.

BALTHAZAR

40 Je m'en vais, monsieur, je ne vous gênerai pas.

ROMÉO

Ainsi tu me témoigneras ton amitié, prends cela.
Vis et sois heureux, adieu, bon compagnon.

BALTHAZAR

Malgré tout, je vais me cacher là derrière.
Son regard me fait peur, je crains ce qu'il veut faire.

[Balthazar se retire.]

ROMÉO

45 Ô détestable panse, ô ventre de la mort,
Tu t'es repu de ce qu'il y a de plus cher sur terre,
Voilà comment je force tes mâchoires pourries
Avant de te gaver de plus de chair encore.

Roméo force l'entrée du tombeau.

PÂRIS

Mais c'est là l'insolent, l'orgueilleux Montaigu, le banni,
50 L'assassin du cousin de mon amour ; on pense
Que c'est ce chagrin qui a causé sa mort,
Et il vient jusqu'ici bassement profaner
Ces corps ensevelis. Je m'en vais l'arrêter.

[Il dégaine son épée.]

Cesse ta besogne sacrilège, vil Montaigu,
55 La vengeance peut-elle se poursuivre après la mort ?
Criminel condamné, c'est moi qui t'appréhende.
Obéis et suis-moi car tu dois mourir.

ROMÉO

C'est vrai, je dois mourir, et c'est pourquoi je suis ici.
Bon et noble jeune homme, ne tente pas un homme au désespoir.
60 Quitte ces lieux et laisse-moi. Pense à ces disparus,
C'est à eux de te faire peur. Je t'en supplie, jeune homme,
Ne charge pas ma tête d'un nouveau péché
En déchaînant ma fureur. Oh ! va-t'en,
Dieu m'est témoin que je t'aime plus que moi-même,
65 Car je suis venu ici armé contre moi-même,
Ne reste pas, va-t'en. Vis, et tu diras ensuite
Que la pitié d'un fou a ordonné ta fuite.

PÂRIS

Je me moque bien de tes adjurations
Et je t'arrête ici pour crime de félonie.

ROMÉO

70 Tu tiens à me provoquer ? Alors, en garde, petit !

Ils se battent.

LE PAGE

Oh ! Seigneur, ils se battent ! je vais prévenir le guet.

[*Sort le page.*]

PÂRIS

Ah ! je suis touché à mort ! Sois miséricordieux :
Ouvre la tombe et étends-moi à côté de Juliette.

ROMÉO

Par ma foi, c'est promis.

[*Pâris meurt.*]

Mais voyons ce visage.
75 Le parent de Mercutio, le noble comte Pâris !
Que disait donc mon valet lorsque nous chevauchions
Et que l'âme tourmentée je l'écoutais à peine ? Il me disait,
Je crois, que le comte Pâris devait épouser Juliette.
N'est-ce pas ce qu'il a dit ? Ou bien ai-je rêvé ?
80 Ou suis-je fou à ce point que, l'entendant parler de Juliette,
J'ai inventé cela ? Oh ! donne-moi ta main,
Qui, comme la mienne, a signé le livre de l'amère infortune.
Je vais t'ensevelir dans un glorieux tombeau,
Un tombeau ? oh non ! une lanterne[1], jeune homme assassiné,
85 Car Juliette repose ici, et sa beauté fait
De ce tombeau un palais inondé de lumière.
Défunt, repose ici, enseveli par un défunt.
Il arrive souvent que, sur le point de mourir,

---

1. Au sens d'édifice lumineux. On trouve encore en Charente-Maritime,
dans la région de Saintes, des « lanternes des morts ».

Les hommes se sentent tout heureux. Ceux qui les veillent
90   Appellent cela l'éclair d'avant la mort[1]. Oh! comment puis-je
Dire que c'est un éclair? Oh! mon amour, ma femme,
La mort qui a sucé le miel de ton haleine
N'étend pas son empire sur ta beauté.
Tu n'es pas conquise! L'étendard de la beauté
95   Est encore écarlate sur tes lèvres et tes joues,
Et la blême bannière de la mort n'a pas été hissée.
Tybalt, tu gis donc là dans ton sanglant linceul;
Quelle plus grande faveur puis-je te faire
Que d'user de la main qui faucha ta jeunesse
100 Pour trancher à son tour celle de ton ennemi?
Pardonne-moi, cousin. Ah! Juliette chérie,
Pourquoi es-tu si belle encore? Faut-il croire
Que la mort immatérielle est amoureuse,
Et que l'odieux monstre décharné te garde
105 Ici dans la nuit noire pour être ton amant?
Pour éviter cela, je vais rester toujours avec toi
Et jamais de ce palais d'obscure nuit
Je ne repartirai. Ici, ici, je veux rester
En compagnie des vers qui sont tes serviteurs.
110 Ici je veux fixer mon éternelle demeure
Et arracher au joug des étoiles ennemies
Ma chair lasse de ce monde. Mes yeux, un dernier regard,
Mes bras, une dernière étreinte, et vous, mes lèvres,
Vous, les portes du souffle, scellez d'un pieux baiser
115 Un contrat éternel avec la mort rapace.
Viens, guide amer, viens, répugnant nocher,
Pilote désespéré, précipite à présent
Sur les rocs écumants ta barque fatiguée, malade de la mer.
Je bois à mon amour! *[Il boit.]* Honnête apothicaire,

---

1. Jeu de mots sur *lightning*, qui signifie l'«éclair», et sur *lightening*, le
«soulagement», l'«allègement». La croyance selon laquelle les mourants entre-
voyaient une dernière lueur de joie avant de disparaître était alors très
répandue.

120 Ta drogue est foudroyante. Ainsi, dans un baiser, je meurs.

[*Il s'effondre.*]

Entre le Frère Laurent avec une lanterne,
une barre de fer et une bêche.

FRÈRE LAURENT

Saint François, aidez-moi ! Que de fois cette nuit,
Mes vieux pieds ont trébuché sur les tombes ! Qui va là ?

BALTHAZAR

Un ami, quelqu'un qui vous connaît bien.

FRÈRE LAURENT

Que Dieu vous bénisse. Dites-moi, mon bon ami,
125 Quelle est cette torche là-bas qui prête en vain
Sa lumière aux vers et à ces crânes aux yeux vides ?
Si je vois bien, elle brûle dans le tombeau des Capulet.

BALTHAZAR

Oui, saint homme, et c'est là qu'est mon maître,
Celui que vous aimez.

FRÈRE LAURENT
Qui donc ?

BALTHAZAR
Roméo.

FRÈRE LAURENT

130 Depuis combien de temps est-il là ?

BALTHAZAR
Une bonne demi-heure.

FRÈRE LAURENT

Suis-moi jusqu'au tombeau.

BALTHAZAR
Je n'ose pas, monsieur.
Mon maître ne sait pas que je ne suis pas parti d'ici
Et il a proféré d'horribles menaces de mort
Si je restais pour espionner ce qu'il faisait.

FRÈRE LAURENT
135 Eh bien, reste, j'irai seul. La peur m'envahit,
Oh! j'appréhende quelque coup du sort.

BALTHAZAR
Comme je dormais ici sous cet if,
J'ai rêvé que mon maître se battait en duel contre un homme
Et que mon maître le tuait.

FRÈRE LAURENT
Roméo!

Le Frère se penche et voit le sang et les armes.

140 Hélas! hélas! quel est ce sang qui souille
Les dalles de pierre menant à ce tombeau?
Que signifient ces épées sanglantes délaissées par leur maître,
Rougies et gisant là dans cet endroit de paix?
Roméo! qu'il est pâle! qui encore, quoi, Pâris aussi!
145 Et baignant dans son sang? Quelle heure cruelle
Est la cause de ce pitoyable malheur?

Juliette se relève.

La dame bouge.

JULIETTE
Oh! Secourable Frère, où est mon époux?
Je me rappelle bien le lieu où je dois être
Et c'est là que je suis. Où est mon Roméo?

FRÈRE LAURENT

J'entends du bruit. Madame, quittons ce lieu
De mort, d'infection et de sommeil contre nature.
Une force beaucoup trop puissante pour nous
A contrarié nos plans. Viens, sortons d'ici.
155 Ton mari, le voici là étendu sur ton sein,
Et Pâris aussi est mort. Viens, je te ferai entrer
Dans une communauté de saintes nonnes.
Ne perds pas de temps en questions, le guet arrive.
Viens, partons, bonne Juliette. Je n'ose rester plus longtemps.

JULIETTE

160 Pars, va-t'en, moi je ne partirai pas.

Sort Frère Laurent.

Qu'est-ce que je vois ? Une coupe serrée dans la main de mon
[fidèle amour ?
C'est du poison, je le vois, qui a causé sa fin prématurée.
Oh ! l'avare a tout bu sans me laisser une seule goutte amicale
Pour m'aider à le suivre ? Je vais baiser tes lèvres,
165 Peut-être y reste-t-il encore du poison,
Ce doux cordial qui me ferait mourir ?

[*Elle l'embrasse.*]

Tes lèvres sont chaudes.

UN GARDE [*Dans les coulisses.*]
Conduis-moi, mon petit. De quel côté ?

JULIETTE

Ah ! du bruit ? Alors, faisons vite. Ô heureux poignard,
Voici ton fourreau. Rouille en ce sein et donne-moi la mort.

[*Elle se poignarde et s'effondre, morte,*
sur le corps de Roméo.]

Entrent le page et les gardes.

LE PAGE

170 Voici l'endroit. Là où brûle la torche.

LE PREMIER GARDE

Le sol est couvert de sang. Fouillez le cimetière.
Vous et vous, allez : arrêtez tous ceux que vous trouverez.

[Sortent quelques gardes.]

Quel triste spectacle ! Ici gît le comte assassiné,
Et Juliette en sang, encore chaude, vient de rendre l'âme,
175 Elle qui pendant deux jours est restée couchée là dans ce
                                                    [tombeau.
Allez prévenir le Prince. Courez chez Capulet,
Réveillez Montaigu. Que d'autres continuent à chercher.

[Sortent quelques gardes.]

Nous voyons bien l'endroit où gisent ces malheureux,
Mais pourquoi ont eu lieu tous ces tristes malheurs,
180 Nous ne pouvons le savoir sans connaître les détails.

Entre Balthazar [accompagné de plusieurs gardes].

LE DEUXIÈME GARDE

Voici le valet de Roméo. Nous l'avons trouvé dans le cimetière.

LE PREMIER GARDE

Tenez-le sous bonne garde jusqu'à ce que le Prince arrive ici.

Entre un autre garde accompagné de Frère Laurent.

LE TROISIÈME GARDE

Voici un moine qui tremble, soupire et pleure.
Nous lui avons confisqué sa pioche et sa bêche
Comme il sortait de ce côté-ci du cimetière.

LE PREMIER GARDE
Grave présomption. Arrêtez aussi le Frère.

Entre le Prince [Escalus accompagné de sa suite].

LE PRINCE
Quel est donc ce malheur qui arrive si tôt
Et nous arrache ainsi au repos matinal ?

Entrent Capulet et Lady Capulet
[accompagnés de serviteurs].

CAPULET
Qu'est-il donc arrivé pour qu'on hurle ainsi partout ?

LADY CAPULET
190 Oh ! les gens dans la rue crient « Roméo »,
D'autres crient « Juliette » et d'autres crient « Pâris », tous
[accourent
Dans une grande clameur vers notre tombeau.

LE PRINCE
Quelle est cette peur qui frappe nos oreilles ?

LE PREMIER GARDE
Mon souverain, ici gisent le comte Pâris assassiné,
195 Roméo mort, Juliette morte avant lui,
Encore chaude et de nouveau tuée.

LE PRINCE
Fouillez, cherchez, trouvez la cause de cet horrible meurtre.

LE PREMIER GARDE
Voici un moine et le valet du défunt Roméo,
Ils portaient avec eux des outils pour ouvrir
200 La tombe de ces morts.

CAPULET

Ô cieux ! ô femme, voyez le sang versé de notre fille !
Ce poignard s'est fourvoyé car, voyez, son étui
Est vide au flanc de Montaigu,
Et du sein de ma fille il a fait son fourreau.

LADY CAPULET

205 Quel malheur ! ce spectacle de mort est comme un glas
Qui sonne pour dire qu'à mon âge le sépulcre m'attend.

Entre Montaigu [accompagné de serviteurs].

LE PRINCE

Approche, Montaigu, car tu t'es levé à l'aube
Pour voir ton fils, ton héritier, trop tôt couché.

MONTAIGU

Hélas ! mon suzerain, ma femme est morte cette nuit,
210 L'exil de son fils a arrêté son souffle.
Quel nouveau malheur conspire contre mon âge ?

LE PRINCE

Regarde et tu verras.

MONTAIGU

Ô jeune malappris, quelle est cette façon hâtive
Que tu as de précéder ton père dans la tombe ?

LE PRINCE

215 Fermez un instant vos bouches à la douleur,
Jusqu'à ce que nous puissions éclaircir ces mystères,
Connaître leur source, leur responsable et leur vraie filiation,
Et je serai alors le général de votre deuil
Pour vous mener à la mort, s'il le faut. D'ici là, restez calmes
Et que l'infortune soit l'esclave de la patience.
Faites comparaître les suspects.

FRÈRE LAURENT

C'est moi le principal, moi le moins apte au crime,
Suspect numéro un, puisque l'heure et le lieu
Témoignent contre moi de cet horrible meurtre.
225 Je suis ici à la fois accusateur et défenseur,
Moi-même condamné, moi-même innocenté.

LE PRINCE

Alors, dis sur-le-champ tout ce que tu sais.

FRÈRE LAURENT

Je serai bref car le temps qui me reste à vivre
N'est pas aussi long qu'une ennuyeuse histoire.
230 Roméo, ici mort, était le mari de Juliette,
Et elle, ici morte, son épouse fidèle.
Je les ai unis en secret et leur mariage a eu lieu
Le jour où Tybalt a perdu la vie ; sa mort prématurée
Bannissait de la ville le jeune marié ;
235 C'est pour lui, non pour Tybalt, que Juliette pleurait.
Pour détourner la source de son chagrin
Vous l'aviez promise au comte Pâris et vouliez la marier
Contre sa volonté. Alors elle vient me voir
Et, le regard affolé, me supplie de trouver un moyen
240 De la délivrer de ce second mariage,
Sans quoi dans ma cellule elle se donnait la mort.
Je lui ai donc fourni un puissant somnifère
Que j'avais mis au point et qui produisit l'effet
Que j'avais espéré, moulant sur son visage
245 Le masque de la mort. J'écrivis à Roméo
Qu'il revienne à Vérone en cette horrible nuit
Pour l'aider à quitter cette tombe usurpée,
À l'heure où la potion cesserait ses effets.
Mais le Frère Jean, le porteur de ma lettre,
250 Fut retenu par accident et hier soir
Il me la rapporta. Alors, tout seul,
À l'heure prévue pour son réveil,

Je suis venu la tirer du caveau ancestral
Pour la garder en secret dans ma cellule
255 Jusqu'à ce que je puisse avertir Roméo.
Mais lorsque j'arrivai, quelques minutes avant
L'heure de son réveil, ici, morts prématurément,
Gisaient le noble Pâris et le fidèle Roméo.
Elle s'éveille, je la supplie de sortir de ce lieu
260 Et de supporter patiemment la volonté du ciel,
Quand, effrayé par un bruit, je sors du caveau.
Mais elle, désemparée, refuse de me suivre,
Préférant, semble-t-il, se faire elle-même violence.
Voilà ce que je sais et, pour ce qui est du mariage,
265 La Nourrice est au courant. Si, dans cette affaire, les choses
Ont mal tourné par ma faute, que ma vieille vie
Soit sacrifiée quelques heures avant terme
Aux rigueurs de la loi la plus impitoyable.

LE PRINCE

Nous avons toujours vu en toi un saint homme.
270 Où est le valet de Roméo ? Que peut-il ajouter à cela ?

BALTHAZAR

J'ai porté à mon maître la nouvelle de la mort de Juliette.
Alors, en toute hâte, il a quitté Mantoue
Pour venir ici même, jusqu'à ce tombeau.
Avant, il m'a ordonné de remettre à son père cette lettre.
275 Puis il a pénétré dans le caveau, menaçant
De me tuer si je ne le laissais pas seul.

LE PRINCE

Donne-moi cette lettre, je veux la voir. [*Il prend la lettre.*]
Où est le page du comte qui a alerté le guet ?
Petit, que faisait donc ton maître à cet endroit ?

LE PAGE

Il était venu fleurir la tombe de sa dame.
'l m'a ordonné de me tenir à l'écart et c'est ce que j'ai fait.

Peu après quelqu'un vient, une torche à la main, pour ouvrir le
[tombeau.

Mon maître alors tira son épée contre lui
Et puis moi j'ai couru pour avertir le guet.

LE PRINCE

285 Cette lettre confirme les paroles du Frère :
L'histoire de leurs amours, l'annonce de sa mort.
Et il écrit ici qu'un pauvre apothicaire
Lui a vendu du poison et qu'ensuite il vint à ce tombeau
Pour s'y donner la mort à côté de Juliette.
290 Où sont ces ennemis ? Capulet ! Montaigu !
Voyez donc quel fléau vient châtier votre haine.
Le ciel a tué vos joies en tuant leur amour
Et moi, qui ai fermé les yeux sur vos discordes,
J'ai perdu deux parents. Tout le monde est puni.

CAPULET

295 Montaigu, ô mon frère, donne-moi la main.
C'est la seule dot à laquelle je peux prétendre
Pour ma fille.

MONTAIGU

            Moi, je peux te donner davantage,
Car je veux lui élever une statue d'or pur,
Et, tant qu'on connaîtra le nom de Vérone,
300 Nulle effigie ne sera plus honorée qu'elle
Car Juliette eut un cœur très sincère et fidèle.

CAPULET

Celle de Roméo ne sera pas moins belle à côté,
Pauvres enfants victimes de notre inimitié.

LE PRINCE

Sombre est la paix qu'apporte ce matin.
305 Le soleil endeuillé ne montre pas son front.
On reparlera de ces choses si tristes : partons !

Certains seront punis, d'autres seront pardonnés,
Car jamais il n'y eut pire cortège de maux
Que dans l'histoire de Juliette et de Roméo.

Ils sortent.

BIBLIOGRAPHIE

Sources primaires

Éditions de *Roméo et Juliette*

BONNEFOY, Yves, *Roméo et Juliette*, Paris, Gallimard, « Folio Théâtre », 2001.

BOURGY, Victor, *Roméo et Juliette*, in GRIVELET, Michel, et MONTSARRAT, Gilles, éd., *William Shakespeare. Œuvres complètes. Tragédies I*, Paris, Robert Laffont, « Bouquins », 1995.

DÉPRATS, Jean-Michel, et VENET, Gisèle, éd., *Roméo et Juliette*, in *Shakespeare. Tragédies I*, Paris, Gallimard, « Bibliothèque de la Pléiade », 2002.

Critiques

CALLAGHAN, Dypna, éd., *William Shakespeare*. Romeo and Juliet. *Texts and Contexts*, Boston et New York, Bedford/St Martin's, 2003.

HALIO, Jay L., éd., *Shakespeare's* Romeo and Juliet. *Texts, Contexts, and Interpretation*, Associated University Press, Cranbury, Londres et Mississauga, 1995.

KRISTEVA, Julia, « Roméo et Juliette : le couple d'amour-haine», in *Histoires d'amour*, Paris, Denoël, 1983 ; rééd. Gallimard, « Folio Essais », 1988, p. 264-284.

–, « *Roméo et Juliette* ou l'amour hors la loi », in *Shakespeare et la France* (actes du congrès 2000 de la Société française Shakespeare), éd. Patricia Dorval, Montpellier, 2000.

LAROQUE, François, « Les configurations symboliques du désir dans *Roméo et Juliette*», in *Shakespeare. Roméo et Juliette. La passion amoureuse*, Paris, Ellipses, 1991, p. 47-53.

–, *Shakespeare comme il vous plaira*, Paris, Gallimard, « Découvertes », 1991 ; nouvelle édition, 2004.

MAGUIN, Jean-Marie, et WHITWORTH, Charles, éd., Roméo et Juliette. *Nouvelles perspectives critiques*, Montpellier, coll. « Astraea », n°5, 1986.

MAGUIN, Jean-Marie et Angela, *William Shakespeare*, Paris, Fayard, 1996.

WELLS, Stanley, éd., Romeo and Juliet *and its Afterlife*, *Shakespeare Survey* 49, Cambridge, Cambridge University Press, 1996.

CHRONOLOGIE

1564 – Naissance de William Shakespeare le 23 avril (date probable), baptisé le 26 avril à Stratford-upon-Avon.

1567 – Naissance de Claudio Monteverdi.

1570 – La reine Élisabeth Ire (montée sur le trône en 1558 à la mort de sa demi-sœur Marie Tudor) est excommuniée par le pape Pie V.

1571 – Bataille de Lépante qui voit la victoire de la flotte chrétienne, armée par Venise et le pape, sur les Turcs.

1572 – 24-29 août. Massacre de la Saint-Barthélemy.

1574 – Shakespeare entre à la *grammar school* de Stratford où il est initié aux auteurs latins, notamment aux *Métamorphoses* d'Ovide.

1580 – Première édition des *Essais* de Montaigne. Ils seront traduits en anglais par John Florio en 1603.

1582 – Réforme du calendrier dit « grégorien » par le pape Grégoire XIII. La réforme ne sera adoptée en Angleterre qu'en 1752. Le 28 novembre, Shakespeare épouse Anne Hathaway, de huit ans son aînée.

1587 – Exécution de Marie Stuart, veuve de François II et ancienne reine de France, au château de Fotheringay.

1592-1594 – Épidémie de peste à Londres, qui entraîne la fermeture des théâtres. Shakespeare écrit *Vénus et Adonis* et *Le Viol de Lucrèce,* et commence à composer des sonnets.

1593 – Mort de Christopher Marlowe, l'auteur du *Juif de Malte* et du *Docteur Faust,* assassiné dans une taverne près de Londres à l'âge de 28 ans.

1595-1596 – Shakespeare écrit et dirige au théâtre *Richard II, Roméo et Juliette* et *Le Songe d'une nuit d'été.*

1597 – Publication du premier in-quarto de *Roméo et Juliette.*

1599 – Construction du théâtre du Globe au sud de la Tamise.

1600 – Le philosophe Giordano Bruno est brûlé vif sur le *Campo dei Fiori* à Rome.

1603 – Mort de la reine Élisabeth Ire. Son cousin Jacques VI d'Écosse est couronné roi d'Angleterre sous le titre de Jacques Ier.

1606 – Naissance de Pierre Corneille.

1609 – Publication des *Sonnets* de Shakespeare par l'éditeur Thomas Thorpe.

1613 – Incendie du Globe pendant une représentation d'*Henry VIII*. Shakespeare achète la maison de New Place à Stratford, où il se retire.

1616 – Mort de Shakespeare le 23 avril.

1623 – Publication par les acteurs Henry Hemminges et Richard Condell de l'in-folio du théâtre complet de Shakespeare.

Table

Composition réalisée par IGS

Achevé d'imprimer en avril 2006 en France sur Presse Offset par

BRODARD & TAUPIN

GROUPE CPI

La Flèche (Sarthe).
N° d'imprimeur : 34634 - N° d'éditeur : 71315
Dépôt légal 1ère publication : août 2005
Édition 02 - avril 2006
LIBRAIRIE GÉNÉRALE FRANÇAISE – 31, rue de Fleurus – 75278 Paris cedex 06

THE SINGLE DAD'S FAMILY RECIPE

RACHAEL JOHNS

MILLS & BOON

® and ™ are trademarks owned and used by the trademark owner and/or its licensee. Trademarks marked with ® are registered with the United Kingdom Patent Office and/or the Office for Harmonisation in the Internal Market and in other countries.

First Published in Great Britain 2018
by Mills & Boon, an imprint of HarperCollins*Publishers*
1 London Bridge Street, London, SE1 9GF

The Single Dad's Family Recipe © 2018 Rachael Johns

ISBN: 978-0-263-26472-2

38-0218

MIX
Paper from
responsible sources
FSC™ C007454

FSC
www.fsc.org

This book is produced from independently certified FSC™ paper to ensure responsible forest management.

For more information visit: www.harpercollins.co.uk/green

Printed and bound in Spain
by CPI, Barcelona

To Ann Leslie Tuttle—for making writing
The McKinnels of Jewell Rock a joy!

Chapter One

As Eliza Coleman stared at the door of the new restaurant at McKinnel's Distillery, she forced a smile to her lips. The action ached a little because her facial muscles were rusty from neglect. But today she needed to put the last couple of years in a box and at least feign a little positivity. No way Lachlan McKinnel would want to employ a sad sack as head hostess for his "exciting new venture," the phrase he'd used to describe his new restaurant in the online advertisement she'd read.

She hadn't actually been looking for employment in Oregon but she hadn't *not* been looking either. Living on her grandmother's couch in her tiny apartment in New York wasn't terrible—she adored Grammy Louise—but lately Grammy had been trying to coax her up off the couch and out of the house. She'd even suggested coming along to her salsa class or signing up for online dating.

Eliza shuddered at the thought of both. The last time she'd been on a date was almost six years ago and she'd married that guy. Did people even go on dates anymore? From what her girlfriends told her, hookups were the name of the game now. And she wasn't interested in *them* either.

At first, getting a job had appealed only marginally more than Grammy's other suggestions—at work, Eliza would have to interact with people—but the more she'd thought about it, the more it seemed like a not-too-bad idea. Work would at least help pass the long hours during the day and she couldn't live on her savings forever. On a whim, she'd decided to look far and wide because the idea of getting away from everything—going someplace where no one knew her—held a certain appeal.

And that search had brought her to a little mountain town called Jewell Rock. Her plane had touched down only hours ago in nearby Bend and she'd rented a car and driven straight here, not even pausing to find breakfast, despite the loud complaints of her stomach.

She stood in front of the door, her hand trembling as she lifted it to the handle. Her last actual job interview had been almost as long ago as her last date and the whole concept of selling herself terrified her, but then again, what did she have to lose? After everything she'd already lost, a job in a place she'd never heard of a week ago wasn't the be-all and end-all.

Trying to ignore the debate going on inside her head, she checked her smile was still in place and then pushed open the door. As she stepped inside, her jaw almost touched the polished wooden floorboards. She wasn't sure what she'd been expecting but it wasn't mahogany paneling, flocked wallpaper and Gothic-type mirrors that made her feel as if she'd just stepped back in time.

It felt strangely warm and welcoming, like nowhere had felt for a very long time.

Behind the brass-railed bar were floor-to-ceiling whiskey bottles as if someone had traveled the world and returned with a bottle from each city. If Eliza didn't know for a fact this building was a recent addition to the boutique distillery, she'd have been fooled into believing it was circa 1950s—like the rest of the establishment.

As the door thumped shut behind her, she stepped further into the restaurant and inhaled deeply. The scent of bourbon filled the air but there was also a hint of something sweet that made her empty stomach rumble. Placing a hand against it, she silently willed it to settle, as the last thing she needed was loud gurgling noises emanating from her stomach while Lachlan McKinnel interviewed her.

"Hello!"

It took a second for her to realize the deep-voiced greeting was coming from off to her right. She turned to see a man with thick golden-blond hair, wearing black trousers and a chef's white shirt, standing in the doorway to what was clearly the kitchen part of the restaurant. A very good-looking man. The thought took her by surprise and she blinked as he smiled warmly and walked forward to close the gap between them.

"Eliza?" he asked as he paused in front of her and offered his hand.

She realized she'd been standing there frozen and mute, just staring at him. There was a reason for this— he was much taller and better-looking in person than he'd appeared from the images she'd found online—but it wasn't a *good* reason. She wasn't here to gawk and drool over her potential boss, she was here to impress him. Here to nab herself a job and a new life about as far from New York City and her past life as she could get without leaving the country.

"Um, yes, hi." She shook his hand and silently cursed herself for sounding so staccato. "You must be Lachlan."

"I am." His handshake was firm and she felt a surprising little jolt inside her. Eliza put it down to the fact she hadn't so much as touched a man in almost a year. "It's a pleasure to meet you."

She nodded as he let go of her hand. *Smile. Act happy. Pretend to be someone else if you have to.* "You, too," she answered chirpily, hoping her tone didn't sound as awkward to his ears as it did to hers. "And this place is gorgeous. I can already imagine it full of people. Did you design it?"

His lips quirked a little at one side and she realized he was the one supposed to be asking the questions, but hey, she tended to talk when she was nervous. "The concept was mine but I had a lot of help from my brothers and my sisters. Mac, specifically, handled the construction side and Sophie and Annabel had a lot of input on the interior."

"Obviously a talented family," she said and then immediately regretted the words. He probably thought she was sucking up or, worse, flirting with him. A cold sweat washed over her at the thought.

But he chuckled. "Don't tell them that, or they'll get big heads. Now, shall we get started?"

"Yes, good idea." The sooner they got down to business, the less likely she was to say something stupid.

He led her over to one of the tables—she noticed her résumé waiting there—and held out a chair for her to sit down. As she lowered herself onto the seat, her breath caught a waft of his sweet-and-spicy scent. She couldn't tell if it was an actual aftershave or if he'd been cooking and the delicious aromas of his creations lingered on him.

"Can I get you a drink? Coffee? Whiskey?" He winked as he said this last word, yet at the same time she didn't think he was entirely kidding. It might not be afternoon yet, but this *was* a whiskey distillery.

She played it safe. "Surprise me."

He nodded once and then retreated behind the bar. The urge to turn her head and watch him was almost unbearable but she resisted, choosing instead to take in more of her surroundings. Her eyes were drawn to an old grandfather clock that stood between the doors leading to the bathrooms. It was beautiful and fit right in with the rest of the decor. She could just imagine glancing at it to check the time when she was working.

"It's a beauty, isn't it?"

Eliza snapped her head to the bar at the sound of Lachlan's voice and saw him, too, admiring the old clock.

"My grandfather bought it out from Scotland. It was his father's, and it's over a hundred years old. Never misses a beat."

"It's gorgeous," she agreed as he turned back to what he was doing.

A few moments later, he returned to the table and set a glass mug in front of her with what looked (and smelled) like coffee in the bottom and cream on the top. "You told me to surprise you, so I thought I might as well try you out on what I hope will be our signature drink."

She drew the mug toward her, picked it up and inhaled deeply, the strong concoction rushing to her head and making her mouth water. "This isn't just coffee, is it?"

Lachlan grinned, shook his head and placed a second mug down on the table. Then he discarded the tray on the table beside them, pulled out the chair opposite her and sat. "I don't plan to offer our patrons *just* anything here. Go on, taste it!"

She felt his intense gaze boring into her as she took a sip and relished the quick burn of whiskey as she swallowed. It likely wasn't a good idea to drink on an empty stomach, but she welcomed the little bit of Dutch courage right now. Something about him set her on edge—she told herself it was simply that she needed this job, so she wanted to impress him, but that wasn't the full story.

She'd been around so many chefs in her life she thought herself immune to the uniform, but the way her pulse sped up around Lachlan McKinnel said otherwise. And he wasn't even wearing the whole kit and caboodle. *Not good.* Her hormones needed to calm their farm because whatever ideas they might suddenly have, she wasn't planning on acting on *any* attraction, but especially not with someone she worked for.

"It's good," she said as she set the mug down on the table again.

"Just good?" The smile he'd been wearing since she arrived drooped a little, making her feel as if she'd kicked a puppy.

"No. Of course not." She rushed to reassure him. "It's fantastic. The best coffee I've ever tasted. I could get addicted to this stuff."

As if to prove her point, she lifted the mug again and took another sip.

He threw back his head and laughed long and loud.

"It's okay, I was just kidding. I'm not that pathetic that I need constant reassurance, but I'm glad you like it."

Eliza hadn't laughed in what felt like forever and appeared to have lost the ability to recognize a joke or playful banter. She summoned that smile back as she lowered the coffee to the table again, not wanting him to think her some straitlaced grump who wouldn't be able to sweet-talk the customers.

"Anyway." Lachlan folded his hands together on the table between them, his expression suddenly serious. "You've got quite an impressive résumé. The list of restaurants you've worked for reads like the Michelin Guide."

"Thank you." Her cheeks flushed a little but her stomach tightened as she anticipated his next question: *Why did you leave your last job?* She'd already decided only to tell him the bare basics and hope he didn't scrounge around too much online, but miraculously he went much further back than that.

"Can you tell me how you got into the restaurant business?"

She nodded, knowing he'd eventually ask the inevitable but happy to put it off a little longer. "My father was a restaurant critic and my parents were divorced. On the weekends I spent with my dad, he often took me along when he dined for a review. I guess his passion for good food rubbed off on me. I've wanted to work in restaurants for as long as I can remember."

He quirked an eyebrow. "If you loved food so much, why not become a chef?"

Although she willed them not to, she felt her cheeks turn an even brighter shade of red. She dreaded this question almost as much as the other one. A tiny voice inside her head told her to lie, but she knew from experience that doing so could get her into very hot water. Besides, with Lachlan's big brown eyes trained so intently on her, she didn't think she'd be able to tell even the smallest fib.

"Because I can't cook," she confessed.

When his expression remained blank, she went on. "I've tried. Lord knows, Dad paid for every cooking school he could get me into when I was a teenager, but after the fire department had to be called when I burned down the kitchen, word got around."

A small smile broke on his face. "Seriously? You burned down a kitchen?"

She hung her head in shame and mentally kicked herself. *Probably not the best way to sell yourself, Eliza.* "It was not my finest moment, and after that my grandmother tried to convince me to go into medicine or journalism or law, anything that kept me away from food, but I just couldn't give up, so I got a job as a waitress instead. Finally, I found something I was good at. Talking about food, serving food and customer service. I haven't looked back."

"Well, usually at this point, I'd ask what your favorite dish to cook is, but I'm predicting microwave popcorn or something, and that's not really what I had in mind."

She grimaced. "Good. Because I burn that, as well."

"At least you're honest. Lucky I'm not interviewing for the kitchen. So tell me your favorite dish to *eat* instead."

Millions of foods whirled through her head—it was like asking someone to pick their favorite child, not that she would ever know how that felt. "That really depends on the situation," she said, mentally shaking her head at the dark thoughts that threatened. "If I'm dining out somewhere classy, you can't go wrong with duck confit or a good pan-seared salmon fillet, but if I want comfort food, it's mac'n'cheese every time."

Her heart squeezed a little at the thought of Grammy Louise's mac'n'cheese—the food she'd practically lived on the last couple of months.

"Then you'll be pleased to know I actually plan on having a mac'n'cheese on our menu—not just any old mac'n'cheese, of course. You haven't lived until you've tasted my whiskey-and-bacon take on the old favorite."

Her mouth watered. "That sounds amazing. What else are you planning for the menu?"

Obviously pleased by this question, Lachlan began to speak animatedly about the dishes he'd been experimenting with. "I want hearty food with a unique flair, showcasing McKinnel's whiskey as much as possible. Every table will get a complimentary basket of whiskey soda bread, and for starters, we'll offer things like smoked turkey Reuben sliders, scotch deviled eggs and a whiskey-cheese fondue to share. The mains will be even more whiskey focused, featuring slow-cooked bourbon-glazed ribs, a blue cheese burger in which I mix whiskey into the ground beef..."

He went on and on—listing more delicious dishes, including a steak sandwich with bourbon-sauteed mushrooms and a vegetarian option of butternut squash gnocchi with whiskey cream sauce. Eliza made a conscious effort not to drool.

"I love the sound of all of that," she said, genuine excitement pumping through her body. "You're making me very hungry."

"Really?" He grinned, clearly pleased by her response. "And I haven't even started on dessert yet."

"I can hardly wait," she replied. Food was something she could talk about till the cows came home and talking about it with Lachlan made her realize how much she'd missed it.

"How does caramel-and-whiskey sauce with steamed sponge pudding sound?"

"Oh. My. God." She couldn't help moaning at the thought.

"Or are pumpkin pancakes with bourbon-vanilla maple syrup more your style? Perhaps you like the sound of blueberry-bourbon-cream-cheese pie or maple-bourbon ice cream."

The way he spoke about the food sounded almost seductive and she felt goose bumps sprout on her arms.

"Please stop!" She begged, an alien bubble of laughter escaping her throat. "I didn't eat breakfast and I can't take this anymore."

His lips twisted with amusement. "Why didn't you say so? I just happened to have been playing with my recipe for an Irish apple crisp. How about you taste test for me while we finish the interview?"

Lachlan pushed back his chair to stand before she could reply, and as he did so, the door to the restaurant flung open and they both turned to look. A tall, skinny woman with immaculate makeup and peroxide-blond hair stood there, a girl with a sullen expression at her side.

"Linda! Hallie! What are you guys doing here?" He rushed toward them, stooping to give the girl a hug. "Why aren't you at school? Is something wrong?"

"I need you to look after Hallie for a while," said the woman Eliza presumed must be Linda. "I'm going to LA to look after my sick aunt. She's got cancer."

Eliza's heart went out to the woman and her aunt, but when she looked to Lachlan, the smile he'd been wearing seconds earlier had vanished from his face.

"You don't have an aunt!" he exclaimed.

Linda narrowed her eyes at him. "You don't know everything about me, Lachlan. Maybe if you'd paid more attention, our marriage wouldn't have ended in tatters."

"What the...?" Lachlan's eyes bulged, but he took one look at Hallie and didn't finish his question. When he spoke again, it was clear he was trying to control his annoyance. "Aunt or no aunt, you can't just take Hallie to LA. And if you think you can..."

"Re-lax." Linda's tone was condescending. "Of course, I can't take Hallie with me. That's why she's staying with you for a while."

"What?"

Ignoring Lachlan's one-word question, Linda bent and drew the little girl into her arms, kissing her on her golden pigtailed head. "Be good for Daddy. I'll call you from LA."

She straightened again and took a step toward the door as if that was that, but Lachlan's words halted her in her tracks. "Oh, no, you don't, Linda. We need to talk. Kitchen. Now."

Linda glanced at her watch, let out a dramatic sigh and then flicked her long hair over her shoulder. "Fine, but I don't have long. My plane leaves in two hours."

Lachlan looked to his daughter and smiled warmly. "Hallie, you wait here. Mom and I will be out in a moment." Then, dragging the woman by the arm, he led her into the kitchen and slammed the door shut, leaving Eliza alone with the little girl.

She stared at the child. Lately, she couldn't even handle being around her best friend's children, never mind strangers' offspring.

"Hello," she said after a few moments of silence. Despite her own discomfort at finding herself in the middle of a family drama, Eliza felt for the girl. Although she didn't know the ins and outs of the situation, it was clear this child was Lachlan's daughter, that her mother was dumping her here unexpectedly and her father didn't seem pleased with the news.

However dire her own life was, this was a stark reminder that she wasn't the only one with problems. And a kid as cute as this one should not have to deal with such rejection. It made her blood boil.

"Who are *you*?" the little girl replied.

"I'm Eliza," she said with what she hoped was a friendly smile. "Your dad is interviewing me to work in his new restaurant. Did I hear your name was Hallie?"

"Yep." The girl shuffled forward and flopped into the chair Lachlan had just vacated. The sigh that slipped from her lips sounded far too heavy for someone who could only be about eight years old, nine max.

Before either of them could say another word, raised voices sounded from the kitchen.

"Do you not *want* her?" Linda shouted.

"Do you want to play a game?" Eliza asked loudly. She'd borne witness to a number of screaming matches between her own parents before they divorced and she didn't believe any child should have to hear such things. Especially not their mom questioning their dad's love for them.

Hallie rolled her eyes. "It's okay. I'm used to my parents fighting and I've been waiting for this day for as long as I can remember."

"What do you mean?" Eliza found herself asking. "Has your mom's aunt been sick for a while?"

Hallie laughed. "I've never even met my mom's aunt. I meant I've been waiting for her to get rid of me like she did my brother." Before Eliza could ask what she meant,

Hallie added, "My twin brother has got a condition called cerebral palsy that made Mommy not want him."

The little girl's words shocked Eliza and she found herself unsure of what to say, but Hallie continued on in a matter-of-fact way, "Oh, that's not the story she or Daddy will tell you. They say they grew apart like grown-ups sometimes do and took a child each, but I'm not stupid. I go to Daddy's house every second weekend but Mommy never takes Hamish. That's my brother by the way."

"I see." Eliza's heart hurt—in her research for the interview, she'd read an article on the internet saying that Lachlan had sole custody of a son with special needs, but she'd never imagined the reason why.

"And if Mommy can give up Hamish, then I always knew that one day she might also give up me."

"But she's not giving you up," Eliza rushed to reassure the child. "She's going to look after your sick relative."

Hallie shrugged. "I'm actually glad. Daddy and Hamish live with Grandma Nora, and now I will, too. She's the best. And I already have my own bedroom there."

Despite the child's attempt at bravado, Eliza saw her lower lip wobble and knew the girl was close to tears. Poor precious little thing. Eliza didn't blame her. But she *did* blame her parents. Fighting within earshot of her and both carrying on as if looking after her was a hassle. Some people didn't know how lucky they were.

The voices in the kitchen grew louder, more irate, and no matter Hallie's declaration that she was used to this kind of thing, Eliza couldn't just stand by and do nothing. She got to her feet and held her hand out to the little girl. "Will you show me round the distillery gardens?" *While we wait for your parents to finish*, she added silently. "I loved what I saw when I drove in."

Hallie raised an eyebrow and took a moment to reply as if she knew this was a ploy to get her away from the firing line, but then she pushed her own seat back and stood. "Okay," she said. "If you insist. Come on."

As Eliza followed Lachlan's daughter to the door, she glanced in the direction of the kitchen... This interview was not at *all* going how she'd hoped.

Chapter Two

"Tell me this is some kind of sick joke, Linda!"

Holding her chin high, she folded her skinny arms over her surgery-enhanced chest and glared at him. "Joke? Looking after my ailing aunt is not a joke."

He raised an eyebrow. "Cut the crap. There is no aunt." Her father had never been on the scene, and as far as he knew, Linda's mother was an only child.

Linda let out a long, deep, clearly irritated sigh. "She's my mom's estranged sister if you must know."

"So why isn't Carol trekking across the country to look after her, then?"

"What part of the word *estranged* don't you understand?" she said, speaking slowly as if he were five years old. "Besides Carol has just started a new job in Bend, she can't just take time off when she feels like it."

"But you can, because you have never worked a day in your life." He was about to ask her if she had any idea what it was like to look after someone with a terminal illness—Linda had never been the nurturing type—but he figured she'd work that out pretty quickly.

"There's no need to be such an ass about this." She blew air between her lips, flicking her platinum blonde bangs upward as she did so. "You'd think I'd asked you to sail around the world naked, not look after your *own* daughter."

"Keep your voice down," he growled, glancing toward the shut door. He'd been in such a good mood five minutes ago—thinking that he might have finally found the perfect person to lead his waitstaff—but now he could almost feel the steam hissing from his ears. "You've got some nerve. You know I want her. I've always wanted her *and* our son, but your timing couldn't be worse. I'm trying to open a new restaurant here, and you interrupted me in the middle of an interview."

Linda smirked. "Oh, that makes sense—for a moment there, I thought you were on a date."

He hated himself for it but he took the bait. "And why would that be so amusing? You don't think I date?" She'd be right. He couldn't remember the last time he'd been on a date—between having permanent custody of their son, every second weekend with both kids and work, he didn't have the time—but he wasn't about to admit that. Not to her.

"Keep your pants on," she said, obviously highly amused. "I just meant that woman isn't your type. She's a little too... How should I put it? Rounded?"

His hackles rose even further. He didn't have a type—not anymore—but he didn't like the way Linda spoke about Eliza. She might not look anorexic like his ex-wife, but she had womanly curves in all the right places and he thought that was a hell of a lot more sexy than someone who was afraid to eat carbs.

"So how long do you think you'll be?" he asked, his voice louder than he'd meant. Already he was mentally calculating the extra things he'd have to do now that he had Hallie full-time. He loved his daughter—and his son—more than life itself, but he also understood that kids required time as well as love. Hallie had dance and singing classes and she went to school in Bend, not Jewell Rock, which would mean an hour round-trip twice a day. All this on top of Hamish's therapy appointments and his extracurricular activities. Had Linda thought any of this through?

Again, his ex-wife rolled her eyes as if she were talking with a plank of wood. "She has cancer, Lachlan, I can't give you an exact time and date when she's going to breathe her last breath."

"Isn't there anyone else who can look after her? I'm opening the restaurant in a month!"

"You want me to dump our daughter on strangers?"

"Shh," he hissed again. Then he firmly added, "I *meant* your aunt."

She shook her head. "Can't you show a little compassion? Besides, your mom and your family will help you look after Hallie. It's not like one extra person in your massive family is going to make much of a difference."

They stood there for a few moments, glaring at each other like two opponents in a boxing ring. How dare she assume his mom could help? Although he knew she would do her best, he didn't like asking her to do any more than she already did. And with two family weddings imminent and his two future sisters-in-law pregnant, Lachlan's mom had enough on her hands already. He wasn't a violent man and he would never hit a woman, but the frustration coursing through his body right now made him want to pick something up and throw it against the wall.

Only the thought of his daughter and Eliza in the next room held him back.

Eliza. What must she be making of all this? Would she still be there when he went back out? It was definitely not the first impression he wanted to make on a potential new employee.

Feeling resigned and realizing they'd left their daughter with a stranger, Lachlan let out a long breath. "I take it you've packed Hallie's school uniform?" Linda might have seen fit to take her out of class to bring her to him, but he didn't want her missing any more because of this.

"Of course."

"And can you give me a list of all her extracurricular activities?"

Linda smiled like a child who'd just been told they could stay up past their bedtime and eat junk food. "I'll text everything to you while I'm waiting to board my plane. You're a good man, Lachlan McKinnel."

She moved forward as if to throw her arms around him but he held up a hand, warning her off. If she thought him so good, why had she looked elsewhere for excitement when they were married? Maybe he wasn't good, maybe he was just a pushover. A pushover who had been blinded by Linda's looks and the fun they'd had together when they'd first met but had been paying the price ever since.

"Go say goodbye to Hallie," he said instead and then turned and opened the door for her to go through.

"She's not here!" Linda exclaimed, then turned to him in horror. "Who *was* that woman? What has she done with our daughter?"

"Will you stop being so dramatic?" Lachlan snapped. "They're probably just outside." Although inside, his heart clenched as if someone had wrapped string around it and was tightening quickly. Where *were* Hallie and Eliza?

He strode quickly to the door and breathed a sigh of relief when he opened it and spotted Hallie and Eliza a few yards away, seemingly deep in conversation in the garden. Eliza glanced up as if sensing his presence and the look she gave him told him exactly why they'd moved outside.

Shame washed over him and he felt heat creeping into his cheeks that a stranger had thought it best to intervene so his daughter didn't hear the raised and bickering voices of her parents. At the same time, he was thankful that she had. However many times he told himself not to let Linda rile him up, he always failed miserably in this resolve.

"She's out here," he told his ex-wife.

The possible-kidnapping drama forgotten, Linda rushed over to Hallie and made an elaborate show of bidding her farewell. "I'll miss you, my darling. Be good for Daddy and Grandma Nora. I'll call you every night." She clung to her a few more moments, then kissed her on both cheeks and stepped back.

"Au revoir, folks," she said with an irritating wave of her fingers, before turning and tottering away in her ridiculously high heels to her car. She seemed more like someone off on a beachside vacation than someone off to play nurse.

As Linda sped off down the long drive, Lachlan turned to Eliza. *This is awkward*, he thought, wondering what she must make of arriving in the middle of his family drama. "I'm sorry about that," he said. "That was my ex-wife."

"I guessed." She nodded and her shoulder-length, chocolate-brown hair bobbed a little.

"I had no idea she was going to come over like that or I wouldn't have scheduled the interview."

"I guessed that, too," Eliza replied, but her lips didn't even offer a hint of a smile.

"Daddy." He felt Hallie tugging at the side of his shirt. "Dad-dy. I'm hungry."

"Wait a moment. Can't you see I'm talking?" The moment his words were out, he realized how snappy they sounded.

"Sorry, Daddy," she said, a quiver in her voice and her eyes glistening.

He swallowed the frustration at his daughter—none of this was her fault—and took her small hand in hers. He squeezed it gently three times, which was their secret, silent way of saying *I love you.* "It's okay, glitter-pie. Everything's going to be okay. Can you just give me a moment and then we'll go get some lunch?"

She nodded solemnly and squeezed his hand three times in reply. His heart flooded with warmth. No matter how angry he was at her mother and however untimely this new arrangement was, he never wanted to make Hallie feel like she were a burden.

He looked back to Eliza and offered her a conciliatory smile. He could tell she wasn't impressed with his and Linda's behavior. Although it really wasn't any of her business, he wanted to stick up for himself, wanted to give her a little history of the last tumultuous decade with his ex-wife. But he would never speak badly of Linda in front of Hallie. And besides, there were still so many questions he wanted to ask Eliza about herself and her own professional experience.

Sadly, conducting an interview with his eight-year-old daughter in tow was also not ideal. He was about to ask her if she'd mind if they rescheduled the interview for later in the day or even tomorrow but decided he didn't really have the time. Opening night was four weeks away and so far he'd interviewed ten people for the job and none of them had been suitable.

Yet from the moment Eliza had walked in the door, he'd thought she was the one. There was just something about her that made her look like she belonged in the restaurant—he could already imagine her weaving between the tables on a busy night, chatting to the customers, directing the waitstaff, helping make McKinnel's the place where people wanted to be.

His older brother, Callum, would probably berate him for hiring someone without calling their references or finishing a proper interview but this was *Lachlan's* restaurant and sometimes you had to go with your gut. He ignored the voice in his head that told him how wrong his gut had been about Linda—there'd been adolescent hormones involved there, so it didn't count.

As far as he could see, the only thing against Eliza was that she couldn't cook—but considering he wasn't hiring her for the kitchen, that didn't actually matter. It was her personal skills that counted and the way she'd taken Hallie away from the drama impressed him. Not that Hallie was difficult but he believed Eliza would be able to handle difficult customers, leaving him to focus on the restaurant, which was his area of expertise.

"When can you start?" he asked her.

"What?" She blinked. "You're offering me the job?

Don't you want to ask me more questions? Check my references?"

"I'll call your references later but they won't change my mind, will they?"

"They better not," she said. "Wow. Okay."

"Is that a yes?"

She deliberated so long, he thought she was about to reject his offer, but finally she said, "Will Monday be okay? I have a few things I need to organize first."

As today was Friday, that seemed reasonable. "That would be fine, but if you need a little longer, that's okay, too. And let me know if there's anything I can do to help. Now, my daughter here is hungry and I think I recall you saying you were, as well. Would you like to have an early lunch with us?"

Again she deliberated, but not quite so long this time. "If it's not an imposition?"

"Not at all. It will give us a chance to talk a little more and you can start to try some of the dishes I'll be putting on the menu. Come on, let's head back inside."

"Can we have mac'n'cheese, Dad?" Hallie asked as they started toward the restaurant.

"Of course," he replied.

"That's my favorite food, too," Eliza said, smiling down at his little girl and Lachlan felt the tension that had built inside him with Linda's arrival start to dissolve again.

They went inside and Hallie and Eliza sat at one of the tables while Lachlan went back into the kitchen to make lunch.

He made two separate dishes—one for his daughter sans the whiskey and one for his newest employee with *all* the trimmings. As he worked, he kept one ear to the door, smiling as he heard Hallie chattering away to Eliza, telling her about school, the distillery and the fact her two new aunties were both having babies very soon. It didn't sound like she was too affected by her mother's sudden departure and for that he was grateful. Although Eliza didn't say much, her replies were soft and encouraging and the belief he'd made the right decision in hiring her solidified inside him.

"This smells delicious," she said a few minutes later when he emerged from the kitchen, carrying three bowls of steaming pasta.

"Thanks, Daddy," Hallie said before picking up her fork and diving in as if this were the first meal she'd had in months. He had to wonder if Linda had given her breakfast but again he bit his tongue.

"Let's hope it tastes as good as it looks." Lachlan sat down beside the girls and waited in anticipation as Eliza tasted her first mouthful. He was a good chef but he knew from her résumé that she'd worked in restaurants with some of the best chefs in America and he found he really wanted to impress her.

"Wow," came her one-word reply after a few moments. It wasn't the word but the way she said it and her almost-black eyes that lit up as she did so that made his heart soar.

"It's okay?"

She smiled. "*Okay* is an understatement."

He let out a breath he hadn't even known he'd been holding and picked up his own fork. But before he'd even loaded it with macaroni, the door of the restaurant burst open again and in came half his siblings.

"What's for lunch?" Mac said, before he, Blair and Sophie—his youngest sister by two and a half minutes—halted in their tracks.

"Sorry," Blair said.

"We didn't know you had company," Sophie added.

Lachlan stood and gestured to Eliza. "This is Eliza. I've just offered her the position of head hostess. Eliza, these are three of my siblings, Sophie, Mac and Blair." He pointed to each of them as he spoke.

"Wow. Cool. Hi. Nice to meet you." Sophie rushed forward, offered her hand to shake Eliza's and then pulled out a seat at the table.

Mac and Blair also followed with handshakes and Lachlan couldn't help noticing the way his younger brothers looked appreciatively over his new employee. Mac's appreciation wasn't surprising—he might not date much since splitting with his longtime girlfriend a year ago, but he wasn't dead. And Lachlan had to concede you'd *have* to be dead not to notice how easy on the eye Eliza was.

But Blair's interest surprised him—granted, he was divorced but most of the time he and his ex-wife, Claire, acted like newlyweds. It was very confusing for everyone.

Whatever, he made a mental note to warn them both off Eliza later—he didn't want any flings with his brothers getting in the way of her doing her job.

"Hi, Auntie Sophie, Uncle Mac and Uncle Blair," Hallie said through a mouthful of macaroni.

"Hey, short stuff." Sophie ruffled Hallie's hair. "What are you doing here? Shouldn't you be in school?"

Sophie half looked at Lachlan as she said this and he mouthed back, *Linda*.

Sophie nodded—he'd fill her in later—then she leaned in and sniffed Hallie's lunch. "Mmm, that smell's to die for."

"Okay, okay." Lachlan shook his head as his brothers

also pulled up seats. "I'll go get you all a serving." He knew he wouldn't get rid of them until he did so.

"So where are you from?" Sophie asked when they all had steaming bowls of the best mac'n'cheese in Oregon in front of them.

"New York," Eliza replied.

"Long way from home," Blair commented.

Eliza shrugged. "I'm looking for a change of scenery and a new adventure."

Mac nodded. "I can relate. So where are you living?"

"Um…I actually came straight here from the airport," she admitted, glancing over and meeting Lachlan's gaze. "That's one of those few things I need to organize."

"Hey, why don't you check out the apartment next door to us?" Sophie suggested. "The old tenants moved out last month, and the landlord is still looking for a new one. It's nothing flashy, but it's cozy and not far from here."

"Us?" Eliza asked.

Sophie grinned. "Me and my twin sister, Annabel. She's a firefighter, but I'm sure you'll meet her soon enough. If you're interested, I could call the landlord and see if she can show you round this afternoon."

"That would be wonderful. Thank you. And then I'll need to deliver my rental car back to the airport and work out more permanent transport."

"We can probably help you with that, as well," Blair said.

"I can draw some pictures to go on your new walls," Hallie—never one to be left out—offered.

Everyone laughed.

"Thank you," Eliza said, "that will be wonderful."

Then she looked to Mac. "So are you the genius behind this building?"

"Sure am." As Mac's face glowed with pride, Lachlan felt a pinch of something like jealousy inside him. It might have been Mac's handiwork but much of the concept was Lachlan's and he'd got his hands dirty a few times during the construction. But he bit down on the impulse to state these facts as he knew how uncharitable it would sound—besides, even when they egged him on, he'd never been the type to compete with his brothers, so the feeling was weird. Perhaps he was still unsettled after Linda's dramatic arrival and departure.

Lachlan refilled his brother's bowls and poured Hallie a glass of milk while conversation continued around him. Eliza got along well with his siblings, she showed lots of interest and asked lots of questions about the history of the distillery and the café that had been open until recently.

"We closed it a month ago—in April—so we could finish the construction and decorate the restaurant," Lachlan explained. "It's ideal to have somewhere to eat on the premises as customers tend to buy more whiskey when they can linger for a snack, hence why I want to open up as soon as possible."

"Fantastic," Eliza said, wiping a tiny smudge of cheese-and-whiskey sauce off her bottom lip. "I'm excited to be here at the ground level."

Mac chuckled. "I hope you're prepared to work hard because I can attest to the fact that Lachlan here is a slave driver. I've barely slept in a month."

Lachlan glared at him but Eliza didn't seem perturbed.

"Bring it on," she said as she met his gaze. "*Workaholic* is my middle name."

And something inside him fizzed at this declaration. Someone who wasn't afraid of a little hard work was exactly who he needed in this position. Eliza's good looks had absolutely no bearing on his decision whatsoever.

Chapter Three

Everything was happening so fast, Eliza thought as she flopped back onto her bed in a cute little boutique hotel in Jewell Rock. Unlike the neighboring town of Bend, whose popularity was rising by the second, Jewell Rock was still a national secret and therefore there wasn't an abundance of places to choose from to stay. The few options were all high-quality, rustic, mountain-lodge-type places. Lachlan's sister Sophie was so very friendly that she'd offered Eliza the couch in her and Annabel's apartment for the night, but Eliza had politely declined the generous invitation.

Once upon a time, she'd have accepted such an offer from near strangers—thought of it as an adventure— but things had changed and now she preferred to keep to herself and take new friendships slowly.

Her cell phone beeped and despite the fact that her limbs felt heavy from exhaustion, she rolled over and reached to grab it from the bedside table. Speaking of friends...a message from Lilly, her best one, popped up on the screen.

Just checking in. How was your day? Any news on the job yet? xx

While part of her felt too tired for a conversation, calling was easier than typing out what would inevitably be a long message. She pressed Dial and less than two seconds later, Lilly picked up.

"Tell me the interview was a disaster and you're not moving halfway across the world."

Eliza almost smiled as she snuggled back into the pillows. That was classic Lilly—no time for greetings and a tendency for theatrics. "Oregon is *not* halfway across the world."

Lilly groaned. "Oh, no. You got the job, didn't you?"

"Yes. I start on Monday."

"Monday?" Lilly exclaimed. "How on earth are you going to come home and pack all your things and get back there in that time? Where are you going to live?"

"I'm not coming back to New York." She couldn't bring herself to call it home—without Jack and Tyler, nothing felt like home anymore. "Not yet anyway. The restaurant is opening in a month, so there isn't really time. I don't need much. I'll have a uniform for work and I'll buy whatever else I need locally. And I've already found a place to live. It's an apartment, only a five-minute drive from the restaurant—I might not even need a car. I'm thinking of buying a bicycle and getting fit."

Lord knew after all the comfort eating she'd done

over the last eighteen months, it wouldn't be a bad thing if she lost a few pounds.

"Getting fit?" Lilly sounded horrified. She was married to a chef, wrote food reviews for a popular mommy blog and believed life was too short to waste time exercising.

"It's an idea," Eliza said.

"A crazy one if you ask me," Lilly replied, "but moving on. Where are you living? What was Lachlan McKinnel like? Will you get free whiskey as part of the package because…in your situation, I'm not sure if that's a good thing."

Lilly always asked more than one question at once.

"Don't worry—I'm not going to become an alcoholic," Eliza promised. "This fresh start will be good for me, I can feel it in my bones. In answer to your other questions, I'm moving into an apartment next door to Lachlan's twin sisters. I met one of them this afternoon and she just happened to mention the place next door was vacant. She set me up with the landlord and I checked it out this afternoon. It's perfect, so tomorrow I'm going to buy a bed, a fridge and maybe a couch, a microwave and a TV. That should do me for starters. And as for Lachlan, I'm not sure what to think of him."

"Whoa. There's a lot to unpack here. What do you mean, you're not sure about him? Didn't you like him?"

Eliza pondered her response a few moments before she told her friend about Lachlan's ex. "They're a close-knit family," she added. "Anyway, my opinion of him personally doesn't matter—he's definitely a good chef and he's serious about making the restaurant a success. Since he's going to be my boss and not my friend, I guess that's the main thing."

"Yes, I suppose that true. But are his sisters at least

nice?" Lilly asked. "Perhaps you'll become friends with them. I don't like to think of you all alone across the other side of the *country*."

"They seem nice. A bit younger than us, though— different zone. Sophie asked me if I wanted to join Tindor. Apparently they've both signed up."

Lilly snorted. "Tinder! Jeez, I'm so glad I met Matthew before the dating scene changed so dramatically."

"Mom-my!"

Before Eliza could say anything to that, Lilly's two-year-old daughter, Britt, hollered in the background.

"Mom-my, I did poos in the potty."

Eliza felt torn between laughing and crying at the excited little voice. Jack and Britt had been born only three months apart and every milestone Britt crossed felt like a knife twisting in Eliza's gut. She wanted to be happy for her friend but all she could think about was the fact Jack would never do any of the things Britt was doing.

"I'll let you go," she said, choking up. "Tell Britt I said well done, and I'll send you some photos of my new place tomorrow night when I've furnished it a little."

"All right, my love," Lilly replied. "Chat soon."

Eliza had barely disconnected from her friend when the phone started ringing again.

"Grammy," she said as she answered.

"Hello, my darling," came her grandmother's sing-songy voice down the line. "I've just got in from salsa and I'm dead on my feet, but I couldn't go to bed without checking in on my favorite granddaughter."

"I'm your only granddaughter."

"Even if I had a hundred grandchildren, you'd be my favorite," Grammy said. "Now, tell me, did you get the job?"

"Yes." Eliza filled her grandmother in on her day.

"Wow—that's quite a jam-packed day. But tell me, is Lachlan McKinnel as good-looking in person as he is in his photos?"

Eliza frowned. "How do you know what he looks like?" Although he'd appeared on a local TV show cooking segment, until she'd seen the advertisement for the job and searched online, she'd never heard of him and she was pretty sure her grandmother hadn't either.

"You don't think I'd let my favorite granddaughter fly all the way to Tombouctou without doing a little research." As far as Grammy was concerned, anywhere outside of Manhattan was the end of the earth. "Well, *is* he good-looking?"

Something quivered low in Eliza's belly—indicating that she wasn't as numb as she'd thought. It was quickly followed by guilt that she could be feeling anything so frivolous. "It doesn't matter what he looks like. What matters is that he's passionate about food and has offered me the fresh start I need."

"So he *is* good-looking." Grammy sounded victorious. "I might have to jump on a plane and come and check him out myself if there's potential for a romance."

"I think he's about forty years too young for you."

Grammy laughed. "I meant for you, my dear."

That's what Eliza had been afraid of.

"I'm not looking for love," she said, trying to put her grandmother straight. Her heart had been so full of love once and she'd lost it all in the most tragic of circumstances. Even thinking about loving another left her feeling chilled.

"Did I say anything about love?" Grammy tsked. "Not all relationships have to be serious you know? Fun and mutual pleasure are just as important. I should know."

Eliza blushed. She should be used to her grandma's frankness about sex by now, but it still made her want to cover her ears.

"Even if that's true," she said, "getting involved with my boss would be asking for all sorts of trouble. Been there, done that before, and you know how it ended."

"What happened with Jack was not because Tyler was your boss," Grammy said almost tersely.

But as much as she loved her grandmother, Eliza really didn't want to get into all that—again—right now. "It's a moot point anyway," she said, equally as terse. "I'm not ready for another man in my life yet."

Deep down, she didn't think she'd ever be ready but if Grammy thought there was a slight chance, maybe she'd stop pushing.

"Okay," Grammy relented. "Tell me about Jewell Rock instead, then."

And despite the tiredness she felt from getting up at the crack of dawn, flying across America, getting a job and house hunting all in one day, this was something she could give her grandmother.

"It's beautiful. The complete opposite of New York, but I think you'd love it. There's a big gorgeous lake near where I'm going to live and I'll wake up every day to a view of the mountains. I'm going shopping tomorrow to buy stuff for my apartment, but over the weekend, I hope to have some time to play tourist. I'll email you some photos."

"I'd rather you send me a bottle of McKinnel's whiskey!"

Eliza puffed out a breath of amusement. "I think that can probably be arranged. Now, as much as I love talking to you, I'm exhausted and I've got a big few days ahead so I need to try to get some sleep."

Try being the operative word—sleep hadn't been something she'd easily achieved for a long while.

"It's not even midnight here," Grammy proclaimed. "You young things these days have no stamina. But you're probably right. I need my beauty sleep." Then her tone turned serious. "I love you, cherub. Look after yourself and remember I'm always here—any time of the day or night—to talk if you need it. I might not have suffered a loss like yours, but I'm an old woman and I've experienced enough in my long life to know that when you're hurting you shouldn't bottle it all up inside. Promise me you'll call when you're feeling low."

Eliza tried to swallow the lump that rose in her throat and blink away the tears that came at her grandmother's loving concern. "I promise," she whispered and then quickly disconnected the call before she lost it.

No matter how far she ran from the scene of her heartbreak, she knew she'd never escape the pain but, somehow, she had to learn to live with it. And maybe McKinnels' Restaurant was exactly what she needed to help her do so!

Chapter Four

Lachlan hated to be late on Eliza's first day but getting two kids ready and off to school in the morning took *three* times longer than one kid. And Hallie's hair was responsible for almost half an hour of that time. Thankfully, his mom had offered to take Hamish, so he could drive Hallie into Bend and talk to her teacher to make sure everyone knew that he was the first point of contact for the foreseeable future. Hallie seemed to be taking the change in stride but he'd wanted to spend a little one-on-one time with her just to be sure.

When he finally arrived back at the distillery, his new head hostess was sitting on the restaurant's front step, her elbows resting on her knees, waiting for him. A bicycle was off to one side, leaning against the building. Even though he'd told her she could wear casual clothes until they'd sorted out the uniforms—one of the many jobs on his to-do list for the next few days—Eliza looked professional in smart black trousers, a short-sleeved pink blouse and her hair held back off her face with some kind of pink clip. Pink looked good on her, he thought as he approached—a color he'd never seen the benefits of before now.

"Good morning," he said as she stood to greet him. "Sorry I'm late."

"Isn't that usually the employee's line?"

He grinned, feeling some of the tension dispersing that had built up inside him since Hamish woke at 6:00 a.m. "Perhaps, but I don't like being tardy and I am genuinely sorry you had to wait. Can I get you a coffee to make up for it?"

"Sounds good. Thank you." She hitched her purse against her shoulder as they headed toward the door.

He slipped the key into the lock, pushed the door open and then held it as Eliza went through. The scent of caramel wafted by as she passed him and he wondered if it was perfume or if she'd had something sweet for breakfast. He'd never smelled such a scent on a woman before—his mom, sisters and ex-wife all preferred floral aromas—and he liked it. A lot.

"How was your weekend?" he asked, pushing the thought of caramel to the back of his mind as he flicked the switch so light flooded the restaurant. "Sophie told me you took the apartment. Are you all settled in?"

"Yes," she said, putting her purse down on one of the tables. "Everything seems to have fallen into place. Your sisters are wonderful."

"They have their moments," he said, secretly in complete agreement. His younger sisters were pretty fantastic and the best aunts he could want for his kids, always helping out whenever they could. They'd both make great moms one day, but so far, neither of them had been lucky in the love department.

"What about you?" she asked. "How was your weekend?"

"Busy," he replied as he went behind the bar and turned on the coffee machine. "I played cabdriver to Hallie and my son, Hamish—they have better social lives than me—and then in the evenings I came in here and experimented with a few more dishes."

He yawned at the thought, his body in dire need of a caffeine injection. He'd already had one cup of coffee this morning but it wasn't enough, not at the moment when he was burning the candle at both ends.

"Anyway, how do you like your coffee? Cream? Half-and-half? Sugar?"

Eliza came across to join him, pulling out a stool on the other side of the bar. "Half-and-half and no sugar, please."

"Sweet enough already, hey?" It was supposed to be a joke, but she looked horrified and he mentally kicked himself in the shins. He didn't want her to think he was flirting with her, because he hadn't meant it that way and he got the impression she already didn't have the highest opinion of him. He blamed Linda for that. Eliza had seen him at his worst before she had the chance to find out that he was really a pretty nice, fair and level-headed guy.

"I'm sorry, I didn't mean to make you uncomfortable," he said. "It was just a stupid joke."

"It's okay."

Awkward silence lingered while he finished making the coffee and by the time he placed the mug on the bar in front of her, he decided he needed to clear the air before they got down to business.

"Look, I wanted to apologize properly for the way your interview unfolded the other day. I'm not proud of what you witnessed between me and my ex-wife," he said. "And I want to thank you for taking Hallie outside so she didn't hear our discussion."

Eliza's lip quirked upward at one edge. "Is that what you'd call it?"

"Okay. A *heated* discussion. What you heard may not have given you the best impression of me and that's probably because Linda tends to bring out the worst in me. To be honest, I can barely stand to look at her and if it wasn't for Hallie, I wouldn't have anything to do with her."

"Your personal business isn't any concern of mine." She wrapped her fingers round her mug and drew it up to her lips.

"Still, I'd like to explain. Linda and I got married fairly young—we thought attraction was enough to build a marriage on, and I won't lie, things were good for a while. But then we had twins and everything changed. Our son was born with cerebral palsy and she couldn't handle it. She gave all her attention to Hallie and refused to even hold Hamish. It broke my heart but I hoped in time, she would learn to love him."

He paused a moment, emotion swamping him.

"Hamish is the most lovable kid on the planet, but Linda never came to feel this way. Instead she drew away from me, too—she came to resent the love and attention I gave Hamish—and so she had an affair. I wanted custody of both the kids but she fought in court to keep Hallie and has never so much as acknowledged Hamish again since. So when she came barging in here the other day and said she was off to take care of some sick relative I've never even heard of, the anger I usually manage to contain exploded. How can she give herself to look after a near stranger when she's never given any of herself to her son?"

"I don't know." Eliza twirled a few strands of her hair between her fingers. "But that's really sad. How do you explain that to Hamish?"

Lachlan let out a heavy breath. "So far I've just skirted around the issue. He gets lots of love and attention from me and my family and I hope that we give him everything he lacks not having a mother. I guess because it's always been this way, he's never questioned it. Hamish isn't a dumb kid but his condition has left him with a moderate intellectual disability—he amazes me. He can play things like chess almost as well as an adult, but he takes longer to catch on with things like schoolwork than most kids, and perhaps this has been an advantage when it comes to the absence of his mother."

Eliza smiled sadly. "He sounds like a great kid. I can't imagine how any mother could just abandon their child."

"He is." Lachlan nodded. "And I'll never understand Linda either. Hallie's always been great with Hamish, though, and it may not have sounded like it the other day, but I'm glad to have her with me, too. I'd have appreciated Linda giving me a little more notice, though, so I could organize everything better."

"That's understandable." Eliza took another sip of her coffee and he found himself wondering and wanting to ask about her background. He knew from her résumé when she'd graduated college, which put her in her early thirties, about the same as him—she couldn't have got to that age without some kind of serious relationship. Did she have a crazy ex in her past, as well? Was that why she'd chosen to leave a perfectly good job in a fancy restaurant in New York to come here? She'd told his siblings she was looking for a change of scenery and a new adventure, but people didn't usually look for such things unless something or other had gone wrong.

These were questions he might have been able to ask at the interview, but he felt like the chance had passed him by and that if he asked them now, it might sound like he was prying. Lachlan told himself that Eliza's personal life wasn't any of his business anyway, that as long as she worked hard and did the job he needed her to do, then he didn't care, but he couldn't help being curious.

Pushing that thought aside, he also took a sip of his coffee. Man, that tasted good. Just what he needed, and hopefully with caffeine in his system, he would focus on what mattered—getting the restaurant ready for the grand opening.

He put down his mug. "I thought I could give you the grand tour of the distillery first and introduce you to everyone who works here and then we can come back and go through the list of everything we need to achieve over the next few weeks."

"Sounds good." She downed her last bit of coffee and stood.

Although he still had almost a full mug to drink, Lachlan decided it would be better to get the tour started. Things felt weird between them and he wanted to get back to the easy conversation they'd been having before Linda rudely interrupted the interview.

"I grew up here," he said as they started out of the restaurant, "and, like my brothers and sisters, I'm very passionate about the whiskey and the distillery, even though until now I haven't worked here. What I'm try-ing to say is all of us can tend to go on a bit about the history of the place, and so if we start boring you to tears, let us know."

Eliza let out a sound that was almost a laugh, but not quite. "I'm sure I'll be fascinated."

Was she nervous? What would it take to get this woman to relax? He hoped to God he hadn't made a bad decision in hiring her. He wanted a head hostess who was chatty and friendly, happy to flirt a little if necessary and laugh with the clientele. For a moment, he wondered if he—like Mac and Blair—had been bamboozled by her looks.

"The gardens are beautiful," she said, jolting his thoughts.

And he grabbed hold of the topic, happy that she'd initiated something. "Thanks. My mother is the family green thumb and she does a lot of the work herself, although she does have help these days. We've got a full-time gardener on staff."

"I read that your mom lives here at the distillery, and that your father died recently. I'm sorry," she offered.

"Thank you." It was good to see she'd done her research. "Yes, we lost Dad to a heart attack just over a year ago and a lot has changed around here since then. My older brother has taken over as head of the distillery and where Dad was all about tradition, Callum wants to take the distillery to the next level. In addition to opening the restaurant, he's branching out in the types of whiskey we make. We're now selling McKinnel's touristy merchandise as well, and he's hoping to buy some land next door and actually start growing our own grains."

"Sounds like a lot going on."

"There is, but you don't need to worry about any of that. Our prime concern is the restaurant." He gestured to the building they were approaching. "We'll start in here. You met Blair the other day—he's our head distiller. If you've got any questions about the making of whiskey, he's the one to ask."

Both Blair and Lachlan's other brother Quinn were in the distillery and they stopped talking to welcome Eliza to the distillery family.

"Quinn's in charge of our warehouse," Lachlan explained. "And he recently got engaged."

"Congratulations," Eliza said.

"Thanks heaps." Quinn smiled broadly and the goofy expression that crossed his face whenever he spoke about his fiancée, Bailey, appeared. "We're also expecting twins."

"Quinn and Bailey are going to get married at the distillery and we'll do the catering in the restaurant. Bailey's an event coordinator and we're hoping that with her on board, we'll get to host a lot more weddings here. The first one is actually going to be our oldest brother, Callum, and his fiancée, Chelsea, in two months' time."

"I hope you like weddings," Blair said with a chuckle.

"Who doesn't like weddings?" Eliza asked, but again she didn't smile.

Lachlan let Blair show her round the actual distillery, which—whether she liked it or not—included a brief lesson in whiskey making and then Quinn took them into the warehouse for a quick look. From there, Lachlan took Eliza to the shop and office building. Sophie was busy with customers doing a tasting, so although she offered them a quick wave, they headed down the corridor to Callum's office to find him and Chelsea locked in a passionate embrace.

Lachlan cleared his throat and rolled his eyes at Eliza

as he rapped on the open door. "You two should get a room!"

Chelsea sprang out of Callum's arms and her cheeks turned pink as her gaze fell on Lachlan and Eliza. Callum seemed less embarrassed—in fact, his smug, satisfied smile as his gaze met with Lachlan's made Lachlan try to recall the last time he'd kissed a woman.

He pushed that thought aside. "This is Eliza," he said. "And these two are my brother Callum and his fiancée, Chelsea."

"It's so great to meet you," Chelsea gushed as she rushed around Callum's desk and offered her hand.

"And you, too," Eliza replied with a smile.

Callum also shook her hand. "Welcome to Mc-Kinnel's—Lachlan showed me your impressive résumé. Sounds like we're very lucky to have you here."

"Thanks. I'm excited to be here."

"If you ever need anything or have any questions, my door is always open."

"Maybe you should shut it more often," Lachlan quipped.

Callum gave him the finger and Chelsea reprimanded him. "Don't mind these two," she said. "They're very professional most of the time."

The four of them chatted for a few more moments until Chelsea excused herself. "I'm really sorry," she said, placing her hand on her small bump. "I have to get to a prenatal appointment."

"It's fine." Lachlan smiled at his future sister-in-law. "We should be getting back to the restaurant anyway."

"It was lovely to meet you both," Eliza said.

Callum nodded as he wrapped an arm around Chelsea and pulled her close. "You, too, we'll see you around."

Leaving his brother and Chelsea to no doubt partake in a passionate goodbye, Lachlan led Eliza back down the corridor.

"Oh, do you mind if I buy a bottle of whiskey for my grandma?" she asked, glancing across to where Sophie was just wrapping up a sale.

"Of course." He took her over to the polished wood tasting bar, but neither he nor Sophie would hear of Eliza paying for her bottle.

"Call it a welcome-to-the-team gift," Sophie said as she placed the bottle in a special case for mailing.

"You're close to your grandmother, then?" Lachlan asked as he and Eliza finally headed back to the restaurant.

"Yes. I've been living with her the past few months and she was kind of like a surrogate mom for me in my teens."

"Oh?" Lachlan didn't know if he sounded nosy but he couldn't help asking, "Was your own mom not around?" He remembered her saying her parents were divorced.

"She died when I was thirteen, in a helicopter crash."

It was his turn to say, "I'm sorry," but he couldn't help being happy that she'd shared a little of herself.

"Thank you." Her reply was almost a whisper. "Until then she had full-time custody and I stayed with Dad every second weekend, but after her death I went to live with him and Grammy moved in until I was old enough to take care of myself. We became very close."

"Do you have any brothers or sisters?"

"No. And sometimes I'm not sure if that's a blessing or a curse. Did you like growing up in a big family?"

He chuckled. "Sometimes I loved it and sometimes I hated it. My siblings can be my worst enemies or my best friends. Speaking of family..." He slowed his steps.

"I just remembered, I'd better take you to the house to meet Mom before we head back, or my life won't be worth living. Although she's not involved in the day-to-day running of the distillery anymore, she likes to be kept in the loop."

"Hallie told me you lived with your mom," she said.

"Yes, when Linda and I split up, I moved in with my parents, so Mom could help me with Hamish. It was only supposed to be temporary," he admitted, "but nine years later and we're still there. Sounds pretty pathetic, doesn't it? A thirty-three-year-old man still living with his mom."

There was a hint of a smile on her lips as she met his gaze. "Hallie also told me how much she adores your mom, I can't wait to meet her."

"Come on, then. And let me hold that." He took the box with the whiskey from her grasp before she could refuse and gestured for her to follow him toward the main house, pointing out the smaller cottage on the property as they passed it. "Callum and Chelsea live there—it used to be our grandparents' place. It was the original house they built when they moved over from Scotland in the 1950s."

"It's quaint."

"Yeah, I suppose it is," Lachlan said as they continued. "Blair also lives at the main house with Hamish, Mom and I."

"He's not married?" she asked.

Lachlan tried to detect if there was interest in her question or if she was simply making conversation. "He's divorced, too. But more recently. And it's kinda complicated."

"What divorce isn't?"

He chanced a glance at her as they walked but

couldn't read anything from her expression. "You sound like you speak from experience."

Her forehead crinkled and then she nodded. "I'm smack-bang in the middle of one myself."

"I'm sorry." Suddenly her move across the country made complete sense.

"Thanks. Don't really want to talk about it, though."

"Fair enough." His divorce was ancient history now and still not his favorite topic of conversation, but he couldn't help wondering about hers. Who was the party at fault? Had Eliza and her husband simply drifted apart? Had he been abusive? Was that why she was trying to get as far away as possible from him? Or was she still in love with him?

Lachlan pondered these questions as they walked in silence the rest of the way to his mom's place. The list of things he'd like to know about Eliza was growing longer by the second.

Chapter Five

After meeting Nora McKinnel, who was as friendly and welcoming as the rest of her family, Eliza sat down with Lachlan and started going through his to-do list. As he shared his dream and ideas for the restaurant, she listened intently and couldn't help catching some of his enthusiasm. He asked her questions, valued her experience and was eager to listen to her opinions and suggestions for going forward. It felt good to have a project—something to focus on other than her own woes—and once again, she found herself relaxing in his company. The uncomfortable awareness of earlier in the day had made her tongue tie every time she tried to speak.

As he talked her through the menu, business matters and his vision, she decided her initial opinion of Lachlan as a good guy was more accurate than the one she'd started to form when his ex was there.

Besides, really, who *was* at their best when interacting with their ex-partners anyway?

She'd surprised herself by telling Lachlan about Tyler—well, not *exactly* Tyler, she hadn't mentioned any names or details—but, after he'd been so open and honest about his family situation, it hadn't seemed such a big deal to share that tiny bit of herself. She was glad he hadn't pried and for a moment, she'd wondered if she shouldn't tell him the whole sorry story but she'd bitten her tongue, reminding herself why a move across the country had been so appealing.

In Jewell Rock, she wasn't met with sympathetic looks and awkward conversation because people didn't know what the right thing to say to her was. Over the past couple of days, she'd met the whole McKinnel clan, her landlord and a number of other people as she purchased things for and set up her apartment. None of them had treated her like a leper as many of her friends in New York seemed to now.

"Are you all right?" Lachlan's concerned question drew her out of her musing. "Shall we take a break? I feel like I've been overloading you with information."

She blinked and shook her head. "No. I'm fine. Was just thinking how exciting all this is. I might have worked in lots of restaurants, but I've never been part of the grand opening of any of them."

A smile crept onto his lips. "Me either. Sometimes I have to pinch myself that this is actually happening. And other times, I wonder if I'm crazy, trying to do all this while looking after two kids."

"I don't mean to pry, but how exactly do you plan on running a restaurant while being a full-time single dad?"

"I'm not under the illusion it's going to be easy," he said, "but in some ways, being my own boss will mean

I can be more flexible with my working hours. I've hired another very experienced chef to work with me. The dishes will all be mine to start with, but I'll take the lunch roster most days and he'll take the nights. That way, I can be around for my children in the afternoons, put them to bed and then come across here to help close."

"I see." It sounded like a lot to take on but it wasn't her place to question her boss. And plenty of women managed to work full-time while also being single moms. Why shouldn't a guy be able to do the same? "Did you want me to start making phone calls to set up interviews?"

They'd just finished going through the pile of résumés from people applying for waitstaff jobs. Lachlan had explained they had a few people staying on from the café but as that had only been open a few hours during the day for the lunch period and given the restaurant's expanded hours of operation, they needed to employ quite a few new people. He'd already hired a team of kitchen staff who were due to start soon, but as the waitstaff would be under Eliza's supervision and management, he wanted her to be involved in choosing them ASAP.

"Yes, that would be awesome. I've got a few things I need to do in the kitchen, but how about I make you a cup of coffee before I get to that?"

"Thanks. That sounds good." She smiled to show her appreciation. A boss who made coffee as well as he did was definitely a keeper.

Lachlan stood and headed into the bar area. As she heard the coffee machine whir to life, Eliza looked down at the short list of names they'd drafted together and then picked up the restaurant's cordless phone to call the first one.

She'd made two interview appointments by the time he returned with a steaming mug of coffee and a plate of something that looked and smelled sinful.

"You never ended up trying my apple crisp the other day and I'm eager to hear what you think," he said.

Her mouth watered just looking at it and she knew if it tasted half as good as the hamburger he'd made her for lunch, she'd lick her plate clean. Thank God she'd invested in that bicycle over the weekend.

"I'm sure I'll love it," she said as she picked up her fork and dug it into the dessert. He watched in anticipation as she lifted it to her mouth, which was slightly unnerving, but the taste that exploded in her mouth was worth it.

"That," she proclaimed, "is like no other apple crisp I've ever tasted. And trust me, I've had my fair share."

He grinned smugly. "That'll be my secret ingredient."

"What is it?" she asked, mentally going through the flavors she could taste and trying to work it out. Of course, there was the whiskey, but there was also something else she couldn't quite put her finger on.

He wriggled his eyebrows up and down. "That would be telling. And the only people who will know will be my kitchen staff and they'll be sworn to secrecy."

"That's not fair. You know I can't cook."

He shrugged one shoulder. "I could teach you."

The way he said it sent a ripple of heat through her body and she imagined the two of them working together intimately for lessons. Pushing that thought aside, she laughed it off. "What makes you think you'd be better at teaching me to cook than any of those who have tried and failed before you?"

"You can't be *that* bad," he said, leaning back against one of the other tables and crossing his feet at the ankles.

"No. You're right. I'm worse, but thanks for the offer."

He flashed her a smile of encouragement. "I meant it. Anytime you'd like to learn a few new skills, I'd be happy to teach you a few tricks. I'm actually a pretty patient guy."

"Thanks. I'll give it some thought," she lied and then turned her attentions to finishing the apple crisp.

While she ate, Lachlan talked about setting up a Facebook page and an Instagram account for the restaurant. "Sophie reckons we need one," he said, but the expression on his face made it clear he didn't relish the task. "And some catchy hashtags or something."

Eliza cocked her head to one side and winked playfully. "Hashtag—happy to help with that." She'd recently closed down her own social media accounts because watching everyone else's updates about their children had been too depressing, but a business account would be different. And it would also give her something else to occupy her free time.

Lachlan laughed. "Thanks. That would be awesome." And then with another one of his endearing smiles, he collected her plate and disappeared into the kitchen to do whatever it was he needed to do.

Feeling full and totally satisfied, Eliza continued making her phone calls and then typed up an interview schedule on Lachlan's laptop. Sorting through the applicants and hiring staff would take up the best part of a few days but they both agreed that getting the right people for the job was the most important thing. It felt so good to be busy, being productive again. The time flew by, so that when the door of the restaurant opened and Annabel walked in with Hallie and a little boy that had to be Hamish in tow, Eliza couldn't believe it was almost four o'clock.

"Hi, Eliza." Hallie skipped over to her, peeled her little backpack off her back and dumped it on a chair. "I'm glad you're here. I wanted to give you these." She pulled some hand-drawn pictures out of her bag and laid them on the table in front of Eliza. "I hope you like them."

"Wow. They're gorgeous. Thank you," Eliza said as she gazed down at rainbows and cats. "I can't wait to get home and stick them on my fridge."

Hallie beamed proudly, then turned around and beckoned the little boy who was hanging close to Annabel and holding on to two crutches. "Hamish, come meet Eliza."

As Annabel said, "Hi," and lifted her hand in a wave, the boy stepped forward, the crutches supporting his body as he walked toward them unevenly. But it was his smile that squeezed Eliza's heart—it lit up his whole face as he said, "Hel-lo. I'm Ham-ish."

"Hi, Hamish." Eliza pulled out a chair. "It's nice to meet you. Would you like to sit down?"

He nodded and expertly put the crutches to one side as he lowered himself onto the seat. "Do you…play ch-ess?" he asked, his words slightly slurred.

She wished she could say yes because, although part of her didn't want to get close to anyone else's children, knowing that this poor boy's mom had rejected him made her see red. It made her want to say yes to anything he asked her. "Sadly, I don't," she admitted.

"I could te-ach y-you," Hamish said, his voice buzzing with excitement and reminding her of his dad's offer to teach her to cook. Even before she could reply, he added, "There's a set over there at the bar."

"That sounds like fun," she replied, "but I'd have to check with your dad. I'm supposed to be working, you know?"

"I hope my brother hasn't been working you too hard." Annabel, dressed in her firefighting uniform, pulled out a seat and sat at the table.

"Mostly he's been feeding me," Eliza confessed, patting her stomach.

Annabel bowed her head. "He's a good cook. I'll give him that."

"I thought I heard voices." Lachlan emerged from the kitchen with a tray full of milk shakes and some massive chocolate chip cookies. "How are my two favorite people this afternoon?"

"Don't you mean 'three favorite'?" Annabel asked with a chuckle as she reached forward and picked up one of the milk shakes.

Lachlan rolled his eyes as he stooped down and placed a kiss on each child's head.

Eliza's heart twinged at his obvious affection for his children, whom he'd mentioned frequently throughout the day. His love and desire to put Hallie and Hamish above all else confirmed her decision that he was a good guy.

"We're good, Dad," Hallie and Hamish said together. Then Hamish added, "Can I te-ach 'liza to play ch-ess? She s-said I had to ask you 'cause she's wo-working."

Lachlan reached out and ruffled Hamish's hair. "Not now, she's not. It's knock-off time. But Eliza might want to get home to do other things."

Strangely, Eliza found herself in no hurry to escape. Today had been the best day she'd had in a long while.

Work had done what she'd hoped it would, and the prospect of a night home alone in her new apartment left an emptiness in the pit of her stomach. It was when she was alone that her thoughts turned dark and a loneliness that was impossible to ignore engulfed her.

"It's fine. If you guys have the time, I'd love to learn to play."

"We have all the time in the world, don't we, Dad?" Hallie said, then took a slurp of her milk shake.

Lachlan laughed and pulled up a seat. "Today we do, glitter-pie, as it's the one day you don't have any after-school activities." He looked up at Annabel. "Thanks so much for picking these guys up from school. I owe you one."

"It's always a pleasure hanging out with them. I'm on the same shift tomorrow if you need me to get Hallie from school again."

"Thanks. I'll let you know," Lachlan said as Annabel pushed to a stand.

She looked at Eliza. "Sophie and I are ordering in pizza tonight if you want to come have dinner with us. No pressure, but I thought you might not be in the mood to cook after your first day at work."

"I'm not sure I could eat another bite after today," she said, "but thanks for the offer, I'll think about it." The lie came easily. As much as she liked the twins, she didn't plan to accept. Making friends meant getting close to people, and getting close to people meant sharing things, which she didn't want to do here in her new town.

"Okay. We might see you later, then." With those words, Annabel hugged Hallie and Hamish goodbye and then left.

Lachlan retrieved the chess set from behind the bar

and mouthed *thank you* to her. Hamish took out the pieces and laid them on the board, his tongue sticking out in concentration as he did so.

"Go easy on her." Lachlan winked at Eliza as he said this.

Eliza felt heat rush to her cheeks as he did so. She didn't think he was flirting with her, but her stupid body reacted as if he were and that made her feel uncomfortable.

She dropped her gaze from him and focused on his son as Hamish began to explain what the pieces were called and what moves they could and couldn't make. Hamish's skill and passion toward the game impressed her. And although she tried hard to concentrate, the most she could hope to remember was the name of the pieces. First game, he beat her in three moves, and the second one, with Lachlan leaning close and trying to give her tips, she did only fractionally better.

"I think I'm going to need a few more lessons," she said, "but I'm afraid that's all I'm up for today. I'm suddenly feeling rather tired."

Hamish's lips collapsed into a frown but she had to get out of here. While Annabel was sitting chatting with them, it hadn't felt so awkward. Now that she was left alone with Lachlan and his two kids, it felt too much like they were playing happy families. That thought brought tears rushing to the surface of her eyes.

She shouldn't have stayed so long.

Eliza stood fast, needing to escape before the tears broke free and her new boss thought her a sore loser, crying because a small boy had beaten her at chess.

"Thanks for everything," he said as he also stood. "Get a good night's sleep and don't rush in tomorrow morning as I have to do the school run again before work."

"Okay," she managed. Then she collected her purse from where it still sat on one of the tables by the door and hurried outside. She was just throwing her leg over her bicycle, the first tear sneaking down her cheek, when a little voice called out to her.

"Eliza. You forgot these."

Wincing, she wiped the tear quickly from her cheek and turned her head to see Hallie rushing toward her, waving the rainbows and cat drawings in the air.

"Thank you," she whispered, before opening her bag and depositing the pictures inside.

"Have a good night." Hallie waved, seemingly oblivious to Eliza's torment.

"You, too," Eliza called as she started peddling down the long driveway as hard and fast as her legs would allow. Her lungs struggled to keep up and her thighs began to burn. Maybe if she peddled fast enough, her legs would ache so badly that they would distract her from the pain in her heart.

But it didn't work. When she arrived at the apartment, she simply had sore limbs to go along with her sore heart and was pleased to see no sign of Sophie and Annabel or anyone else, thank God. She was in no mood to pause and make small talk with strangers.

Inside, she dumped her handbag on the counter and pulled out Hallie's drawings. She'd promised to hang them in pride of place on her fridge but as beautiful as they were, she couldn't bring herself to do so. Hanging up another child's art would feel like a betrayal to Jack.

So instead, she opened a bottom drawer and stashed the pages there as tears cascaded down her cheeks.

Chapter Six

"Daddy, do you think Eliza liked my drawings?" Hallie asked as Lachlan stooped to tuck her into bed.

Since getting home hours ago, she and Hamish had waxed lyrical about the virtues of Eliza Coleman. He himself still wasn't 100 percent convinced. While she'd relaxed a bit as the day went by—they'd even enjoyed a little fun banter about the secret ingredient—and had been friendly and engaged with his kids, her sudden departure had him unsure all over again.

One minute, she'd been happily trying to hold her own in a game of chess, the next minute, she'd been rushing out the door as if her chair had caught fire.

What had happened that had made her so skittish?

He wasn't questioning her expertise to do the job he'd hired her for—her résumé was more than impressive, her references had all gushed about her and it was clear to see she knew the restaurant business as well as, if not better, than he did. But he needed her to charm customers and to manage staff without being so awkward. Since the interrupted interview, she'd rarely smiled and he wanted a head hostess who never *stopped* smiling.

"Dad?" Hallie reached up and palmed her hand against his cheek. "I *said*, do you think Eliza liked my drawings?"

"Of course, she did. How could anyone not love your drawings?" he asked, stifling a yawn as he leaned over to kiss her good-night. "Now, you need to get some sleep. School tomorrow and dance after school."

"Okay. I'll try," Hallie promised, although her eyes sparkled as if she wasn't tired in the slightest. Hamish had been the same when he'd put him to bed five minutes earlier. Where did kids get their energy from? If only there was some way he could transfer their energy over to himself, because right now he felt like he could sleep for a month and he knew things were only going to get worse as the opening day loomed.

He needed more hours in the day.

With a final, "Good night, sleep tight, don't let the bed bugs bite," he switched Hallie's light off and then headed down the hallway with a wistful glance into his own bedroom. His bed looked very welcoming but he knew, despite his exhaustion, he wouldn't be able to sleep until he'd ticked a few more things off his to-do list.

Although he'd pretty much finalized the menu—they were off to the printers next week—he still wasn't satisfied with all of the dishes. He wanted each item on the menu to be a unique take on the traditional, which required a little more experimentation before he felt ready to introduce them to the rest of his kitchen team. The team that was due to start a few hours a day next week.

"Would you like to join Blair and me for a nightcap?" His mom held up a bottle of McKinnel's finest as he entered the living room to ask if she could keep an ear out for Hamish and Hallie.

"No, thanks. I was hoping to head back to the restaurant to do a few things. Do you mind listening out for the twins?"

As Blair aimed the remote at the TV and flicked through the channels, his mom frowned. "Of course, I don't, but you're working too hard, honey. Why don't you take a night off?"

While he appreciated her concern, it also frustrated him. He could slow down once the restaurant was open and running smoothly but you only got one opening night. And he wanted to wow the town and do his family proud. He might not be a success when it came to relationships but this he *could* control.

"I'm fine, Mom," he said, stifling another yawn. "Please, don't fuss. The twins should be asleep soon, but buzz me if there are any problems."

"Okay, sweetheart." She relented with a sigh. "Don't stay out too late."

"I won't," he said, having no intention of coming home before he was good and ready. That was the problem with still living at home in your thirties—your mom sometimes forgot you were an adult. Maybe it was time to get a place nearby for him and the kids and hire a nanny to help him out, rather than always rely on his family. Then again, he wasn't sure he could trust anyone else to look after Hamish the way he deserved.

Blair lifted the remote to wave goodbye. "Catch you later, bro."

And Lachlan decided opening the restaurant was enough for now, that the other stuff could wait a little longer. Without another word, he headed out of the house and across the property to the restaurant.

Over the next few days, some of his anxiety about Eliza started to abate again. Every day, she arrived punctually (often before him), dressed to impress and proceeded to work hard for all the hours they were in the restaurant together. She still didn't give much insight into herself but then again, with back-to-back interviews, there wasn't really much time for deep and meaningful conversation.

She shone in the interviews, asking all the right questions, posing scenarios of difficult customers that the applicants had to role-play their way out of. He had to admit her businesslike manner was rather attractive and a number of times he found himself staring at her when he should have been concentrating on the task at hand. Thankfully, he didn't think she'd caught him out.

In the rare moments between interviews, she showed him the progress she'd made on the social media accounts and he fed her to show her his appreciation. Watching anyone enjoy food that he'd thrown his heart and soul into gave him a buzz, but watching Eliza eat, he sometimes found himself harboring rather *un*professional thoughts. The way her lush red lips closed around her fork and her long eyelashes fluttered as she closed her eyes in satisfaction made him wonder if that was the expression she'd have during hot sex.

"Oh, my God, this is amazing." Eliza almost moaned as she finished her first mouthful of butternut squash gnocchi with whiskey cream sauce, and he felt his trousers get a little tight. He loved a woman with a healthy appetite. Thank God there was a table between them hiding the evidence.

"Thanks," he said —secretly pleased at her words—— as he picked up his own fork to start on his lunch.

"Is there anything you can't cook?"

"I'm not that good at scrambling eggs," he admitted. Silently adding that he wasn't *bad* either.

She laughed. She actually laughed—and he felt as if he'd won a gold medal in the freaking Olympics. Although their interactions had grown easier the more time they spent together, a smile from Eliza was as rare as a red banana. And it made him want to tell her all his best jokes, simply for the reward of another upward flicker of her lips.

"But when on earth are you finding the time to make all this delicious food?" she asked. "There's been no time to cook between interviews."

As if her question reminded his body of its fatigue, he had to stifle another yawn. "I usually come over here and play in the kitchen for a few hours after the twins have gone to bed."

"No wonder you drink so much coffee," she said, nodding toward the mug in front of him.

He shrugged. "It's a necessary evil right now but I know it won't be forever. I just want to make sure the recipes are right before the kitchen staff starts."

She rubbed her lips together. "Well, this one tastes pretty much perfect."

"Thanks." He couldn't help beaming at the compliment—late nights and eyes that felt like they needed to be kept open with matches would all be worth it if it got McKinnel's on the map.

"Where did you learn to cook?" she asked. "And more to the point, why?"

"I always liked cooking. It used to drive Dad wild that I'd rather cook with Mom than watch soccer with him and my brothers—he was very traditional like that. Don't get me wrong, I don't mind soccer—you kinda have to when you have a brother like Mac, who is so good he makes the state team and then goes on to play with the bigwigs."

"Mac, who built this restaurant?" she asked, wide-eyed. "He plays professionally?"

"Uh-huh." Lachlan nodded, forgetting that not everyone knew Mac's history. "Well, he did until recently but he retired a year ago." There was a lot more to that story—more he suspected than Mac had admitted even to them—but it wasn't his story to tell.

"I'm sorry," she said. "I'm not really very sporty."

He laughed. "It's fine. Anyway, as I was saying, I used to cook a lot with Mom and my grandma when she was alive, but I never really considered doing it for a career until I went to Scotland. I always just assumed I'd follow in my father's and grandfather's footsteps and become a distiller. There's kind of this rite of passage in our family where we all go back to the county in Scotland where my dad is from and spend some time working at a distillery there.

"Only the year I went, the distillery had a fire and their operations had to close while they rebuilt. I still had six months left on my ticket and didn't want to come home early, so I got a job in a hotel in Inverness, working in the kitchen. I loved it so much more than I had working at the distillery and I knew then that this is what I wanted to do more than anything. Dad wasn't very impressed, but luckily Callum was already working at the distillery and Blair had his sights set on a career as a distiller as well, so he got over it."

"I guess that's one of the benefits of having so many siblings," she said. "It takes the parental pressure off you."

He wanted to ask her then what her childhood had been like—aside from the divorce and the tragic helicopter crash—and whether her mom and dad had certain expectations for her, but she got in with another question first.

"Did you have any formal training?" she asked.

"Yes. When I came back from Scotland, I went to the Oregon Culinary Institute." He went on to give her a brief rundown of his career to date and then asked her about the places she'd worked and the ones she liked the best while they finished their lunch.

She'd worked with some quite-famous chefs and he laughed as she told him some not-so-favorable stories about some of them.

When she'd scraped her plate clean, she stood and went to pick up both their plates. "I guess we should be getting back to work," she said.

But strangely, he was in no hurry to do so. He'd enjoyed sitting, eating and chatting with her far too much—he felt as if they were finally getting to know each other a little better—and he didn't want it to end just yet.

"Leave that," he said, standing and gesturing to the empty plates. "I'll deal with them. And can I get you some steamed sponge pudding with caramel-and-whiskey sauce to finish? It won't be quite as good heated up as it is fresh out of the oven but…"

When he'd been working on perfecting the sauce last night, the caramel component kept reminding him of Eliza and that alluring scent she wore. It had almost driven him to distraction and for the first time in his life, he'd nearly burned the sauce.

"Are you kidding?" She placed her free hand on her tummy. "That sounds amazing and I already know not to expect anything less from you, but if you keep feeding me like this, I'm going to end up the size of a house. Not even a week of working with you and already my clothes are getting tight."

It wasn't an invitation to rake his gaze over her body but he couldn't help himself. And what he saw—delicious curves in all the right places—had all the blood in his head shooting south.

"I think you're perfect just the way you are," he admitted, his voice low.

Her cheeks grew pink but their eyes met and held for a few long moments. He held his breath, wondering if he'd overstepped the mark by voicing such thoughts. It was hardly professional to be making eyes at the staff and the last thing he wanted to do was make her feel uncomfortable, but the words had just slipped out.

Lachlan was about to apologize when she said, "Thank you," and smiled. "Maybe I will have a taste of that pudding after all. I mean, I can't tell our customers how wonderful it is if I haven't tasted it myself, now, can I?"

"Definitely not." Silently, he let out a breath of relief as he headed into the kitchen to plate it up.

Following dessert, they discussed all the applicants they'd interviewed and made a short list of who they wanted to offer jobs to. While Eliza spent the next hour making phone calls to the lucky candidates, Lachlan sat at his computer and did some book work, which included finalizing an advert for the local paper. They passed the next few hours in companionable silence until Annabel arrived with his kids and any hope of silence flew out the open door as they rushed in.

Hamish and Hallie exploded with news about what they'd been up to that day, both talking over the top of each other. He laughed at their enthusiasm as he tried to direct the chatter and although he was glad to see them, he also couldn't help feeling disappointed that his time with Eliza had ended for another day.

Chapter Seven

Late Thursday night, a week after Eliza had arrived in Jewell Rock, she lay in bed staring at her ceiling, wondering if she would ever sleep again. Working alongside Lachlan made the days almost bearable but they went far too fast and the nights dragged on like decades. She'd started taking an extralong detour on her way home from work, not only to take photos of Jewell Rock to send to Grammy, Lilly and Dad and to kill some of the calories she'd consumed at work, but also because it helped shorten the hours between getting home and going to bed.

Every time she closed her eyes, an image of Jack's sweet little face popped into her head, quickly followed by his lifeless one—the latter of which she'd never be able to eradicate from her head.

Almost eighteen months after the day she'd lost her son, that afternoon still haunted her.

If only she'd decided to do something else that day. If only Jack had slept longer, then they wouldn't have had time to visit her friend Kiana and her new baby. If only Kiana didn't have a fishpond. If only...

Eliza tried to read books and watch a series that Lilly raved about on Netflix to distract herself from the "if only" game, but her concentration for such normal things—things she used to love doing to relax—was shot. For about five minutes, she'd considered getting a pet—imagined that it might be nice to have a cat to come home to and snuggle with or a dog she could take on walks—but then a little voice reminded her that if she couldn't keep a child alive, what made her possibly think she was responsible enough to look after an animal?

She understood why Tyler couldn't forgive her, because she could never forgive herself either.

And thoughts like that brought on the tears that she worked hard each and every day to keep away.

At ten o'clock, feeling as if she'd go insane if she lay there any longer, Eliza flung the covers off and jumped out of bed. She pulled on her comfiest jeans, a T-shirt, a light sweater, her sneakers and then tucked her cell in her pocket and headed outside. As she climbed onto her bike, a little voice in her head warned her that it was late and dark out and possibly not the smartest move for a woman (or anyone) to be out alone. But aside from the streetlights, the whole of Jewell Rock seemed to be asleep, and she figured if she stayed on the roads where there were plenty of houses, she'd be safe from wildlife.

An even darker voice wondered if it would truly be the end of the world if something bad did happen to her, but she pushed that aside. She peddled hard but kind of aimlessly, listening out for traffic and any other dangers as she circled around town hoping to finally exhaust herself enough for slumber.

After about twenty minutes, she found herself slowing in front of the entrance to McKinnel's Distillery and guessed her legs had come here on autopilot. She paused, pushing herself high up on the pedals and balancing as she looked over the bridge and into the distance. The lake glistened beautifully in the moonlight and most of the buildings were in near darkness but light shone from the restaurant. She thought about Lachlan's confession earlier that day that he was working late most nights.

Not really sure what she was doing—but knowing that when she was at the restaurant she felt better than when she was anywhere else—she dropped back to the seat and started over the bridge. Thankfully, she didn't need to go near the residential buildings to get to the restaurant as the last thing she wanted to do was wake Lachlan's family. She dismounted the bike and leaned it up against a post, then slowly made her way up the couple of steps onto the restaurant's porch.

As wood creaked beneath her feet, she froze. What the hell was she doing here this late at night? What if Lachlan got the wrong idea? She didn't know exactly what that would be but she knew she didn't want him to get it. Working in the restaurant was the only thing she had to live for at the moment and she didn't want to do anything to mess that up.

She'd all but made the decision to retreat when the door opened and Lachlan's silhouette appeared. "Eliza? Is that you?"

He wore faded jeans and a long-sleeved black T-shirt pushed up to the elbows, giving her a lovely view of his nicely sculpted forearms.

"Hi," she said, feeling like someone who'd been caught trespassing.

He frowned and stepped into the porch light. "Did you forget something today?"

She deliberated a second, racking her mind for a logical excuse for her late-night appearance, then opted for the truth. "I'm not really sleeping well at the moment, so I decided to go for a bike ride. I didn't really think about where I was going and my bike brought me here."

"I'm glad," he said, stepping back and holding the door as he gestured for her to go through. "I wouldn't mind some company and a second opinion on a syrup I've been experimenting with. Want to come in?"

"Okay. If I'm not gonna get in the way?"

"Not at all." He smiled warmly as she stepped past him and then shut the door behind them.

As they headed into the kitchen, he asked, "Why can't you sleep?"

"Probably all the coffee we've been drinking during the day," she said. Not wanting to tell him the truth, she quickly changed the subject. "So what exactly are you making?"

He crossed to the commercial-sized stove and turned the heat on under a pan. She guessed he'd turned it off when he'd trekked outside to investigate the noise. "Bourbon-vanilla maple syrup. It's going to go with pumpkin pancakes, but I'm still trying to get the quantities right. Here, try it for me and see what you think."

Then he took a teaspoon, dipped it into the saucepan and held it out for her. She took the spoon, brought it up to her lips and almost orgasmed on the spot as the flavors melted on her tongue. "I don't think it needs any more experimentation," she said. "The balance between bourbon, vanilla and maple is exquisite. It will go perfectly with pancakes."

"Then let's make some and see."

She raised an eyebrow at him. "I hope by *let's*, you mean you."

He chuckled. "Pancakes are easy."

She snorted. "Easy for you maybe."

He grabbed an apron off a hook on the wall and held it out toward her. "Put this on. I'll show you. We'll keep it simple and just make the plain variety."

"You're going to regret this," Eliza said, but she found herself reaching out and taking the apron from him. Their hands brushed against each other in the process and she tried to distract herself from the little jolt inside her as they did so. The late hour and lack of sleep was obviously messing with her head.

"How come *you* don't have to wear one of these?" she asked as she lowered it over her head and began to knot the ties behind her back.

"Because I don't care about my clothes, whereas yours look nice."

She felt his gaze on her as he spoke and awareness spread across her skin, but once again, she tried to ignore it. Probably she was imagining the heat in his eyes anyway. His ex-wife looked like a supermodel, so he'd hardly find someone like her attractive.

"What? These old things?" She injected a lightness she didn't feel into her voice. But they *were* old—if she'd known her legs were going to lead her to her boss, she might have made more of an effort choosing a nicer outfit.

He shrugged one shoulder and gestured to his clothes, which she saw were covered in splashes of various ingredients. "Either way, I think for me the horse has bolted. Now, shall we get started?"

"Yes." She averted her gaze from his fitted T-shirt. "But only if you promise not to fire me if I burn down your kitchen."

He laughed and shook his head. "I think you're going to surprise yourself."

Together they collected the ingredients from the pantry and got out a frying pan. She was hoping his lessons would be more watch and learn, but he talked her through every step of the process—making her sift the flour three times, add pinches of salt and baking powder, a spoonful of sugar, and then mix milk, egg and a "dash of vanilla" together before whisking the combo into the flour.

"My arm is killing me. Are you sure this isn't whisked enough yet?" After two minutes, her muscles throbbed with the unexpected exertion.

"The secret to fluffy pancakes is in the whisking—no one ever does it as long as they should."

"You're a slave driver." She pouted as she continued, secretly enjoying the task.

He grinned as if pleased by this description. "Okay, that's probably enough," he said a few moments later. "Now taste the batter to ensure it doesn't require any more sugar or salt."

He passed her a teaspoon, which she dipped into the mixture and then brought to her mouth.

"Well?"

She licked her lips. "I think it tastes good, but I'm no expert."

"Yet." He winked as he took the spoon from her. "Now it's time to cook them."

She swallowed. Making batter was one thing, but

her hands shook as he instructed her through placing a dab of butter in the pan and then pouring a measure of batter on top. It sizzled as the batter spread out to the edges of the pan.

"You're doing really well," Lachlan said, his voice low as he stood right next to her and encouraged her like he might a child learning to ride a bike. Only she didn't *feel* like a child when she was around him. Anything but.

"Thanks," she whispered as they both gazed down at their efforts.

"There, see those bubbles? That's how we tell it's time to flip."

Thankfully, he didn't expect her to do some snazzy trick with the pan but handed her a flipper instead.

She barely breathed as she slid the flipper under the pancake and lifted it, but as she tried to turn it, the whole thing fell into a heap in the pan. She let out a shriek of annoyance. "See, I'm hopeless."

"You're not going to give up that easily, are you? Come on, we'll do this next one together."

He expertly cleaned the pan of her mess, then tossed another drop of butter in. "Try again."

And despite feeling as if this was a lost cause and she was wasting his ingredients, Eliza poured another measure into the sizzling pan.

Neither of them spoke, watching until it began to bubble, then Lachlan said, "Grab the flipper again."

But this time when she picked it up, he placed his hand over hers, then gently guided the utensil under the half-cooked pancake and helped her turn it over properly.

"There, that wasn't too hard, was it?" As he spoke, his warm breath tickled her ear and undeniable attraction rippled through her. It had been so long since she'd been this close to a man and it left her feeling a little unsteady on her feet.

Somehow she managed to reply, "But you did that, not me."

"Seriously, Eliza," he said, turning his head to look at her. "It's not that hard. You just need to have a little faith in yourself."

And somehow—under Lachlan's kind and patient instruction—she lifted this first pancake out of the pan and onto a plate and then continued on to make a more than passable batch.

She grinned as she stared at the pile sitting there, begging to be eaten, unable to recall such a sense of achievement in quite some time. Maybe she really had just never had the right teacher before.

They didn't bother going out into the restaurant to eat them but piled two plates high, poured his special syrup over the top and then ate them right there, leaning back against the countertop.

"This is the best midnight snack I've ever had," she said after swallowing the first bite.

"And you didn't burn the kitchen down. Next time, we'll try something a little trickier, like mac'n'cheese. If a girl can cook pancakes and mac'n'cheese, I reckon she's set for life."

She laughed and realized that in the last week working with Lachlan, she'd started to laugh a lot more. She'd started to *feel* a lot more again— emotions other than sadness and grief. Part of her felt guilty about this fact but another part of her wanted to enjoy it.

"I was thinking," she said, "about opening night…"

But he shook his finger at her. "No talking about

work tonight. You're not on the clock now. I want to know about you."

She swallowed, nerves suddenly rushing up her throat. "What do you want to know?" There was only one thing that came to her mind and she didn't want to talk about that with him. Or anyone.

A pensive expression lingered on his face a few moments. "Let's start with the basics. What's your favorite color?"

"Pink," she said with an apologetic shrug. "I guess I never grew out of it."

"No wonder you and Hallie get on so well. Mine's brown."

"Brown?" Eliza couldn't help but scoff. "Whose favorite color is brown?"

"Mine," he said defensively. "It's the color of all my favorite things—chocolate, coffee and...caramel."

"Fair enough." She stifled a smile. "I'm not going to judge you on that. What's your favorite movie?"

He took a moment, rubbing his chin between his thumb and forefinger as if this was a difficult question.

"Let me guess. *The Sound of Music?*"

He laughed. "No, but close. *Mary Poppins.*"

"Seriously?" She raised an eyebrow. "Now you're pulling my leg."

He shook his head. "Uh-uh. I swear. The bank scene where all the grumpy old men are floating up near the ceiling, laughing their heads off—sometimes I watch that if I'm in a bad mood or sad about something, and it never fails to brighten my day."

She frowned, trying to remember the plot—it had been a long time. "But didn't someone die in that scene?"

"Yes, but he died laughing. What better way to go?"

A lump formed in her throat at the notion of there being any good kind of death—she felt tears welling—but thankfully, Lachlan didn't seem to notice. "My turn."

"What?"

"It's my turn to ask a question," he clarified. "Could your ex-husband cook?"

She blinked, startled that he'd gone from impersonal, almost-silly questions to something immensely personal.

"If you can't cook—or couldn't," he added, "because I'm pretty certain I could teach you—I just wondered if he could. Or did you guys mostly eat out?"

Eliza tried to ignore the tightening in her chest that the conversation was heading to a place she didn't want it to go. "He was a chef, so yes, he cooked —or we ate out at work. As we were both in the restaurant industry, that's generally what we did."

"Did you work at the same restaurant?" he asked.

"Yes." She hoped her one-word answer told him that she didn't want to talk about her ex. She'd come out to try to escape dwelling on the past and up until now it had done the trick. "Most embarrassing thing that's ever happened to you?"

He took the bait and within moments, she was laughing. "The night I lost my virginity, I walked my girlfriend back to her parents' place. We were supposed to have been at the movies but instead we made out in the distillery warehouse. Her mom and dad asked me in for cocoa when we got back and then afterward, as I stood up to leave, the used condom fell from my pocket onto their kitchen floor."

"Oh, my Lord, no!" Her hand rushed up to slap her

mouth. "Why hadn't you got rid of it? You weren't keeping it as some kind of trophy, were you?"

He screwed up his face. "What kind of sick freak
do you think I am?" But he was laughing, too. "No, I
didn't want to dispose of it in the distillery in case my
parents found it, so I stuffed it in my pocket, wrapped
in tissues, to get rid of later."

"What did her parents say?" Eliza almost couldn't
ask the question, she was laughing so hard.

"I thought her dad was going to shoot me, so I
feigned shock as if it was the first time I'd ever seen a
condom in my life. I said it must have been on the bus
and stuck to my butt when I sat on the seat or something."

She snorted. "And they bought that?"

"No. Her dad turned and left the room and I thought
he might be off to get his gun, so I hightailed it out of
there."

"Was the girl Linda?" she asked, knowing they'd
got together young.

"Nope. Her name was Rose. Sweet girl, gorgeous inside
and out. But after that episode, her parents sent her away
to boarding school. Pity… Perhaps if we'd stuck together,
I wouldn't have met Linda."

"But then you wouldn't have Hamish and Hallie."

His expression turned serious. "Yeah, that's true.
And I wouldn't swap them for the world. What's your
most embarrassing moment, then?"

"I don't think I want to tell you."

He chuckled. "Come on… It can't be worse than
mine."

"Oh, it's not." She found herself smiling again at the
thought of his. "I don't know if much could top that,

but mine involves a restaurant faux pas and I'm worried you might regret hiring me if I tell you."

He leaned back in his seat and rubbed his hands together. "Fair's fair. I told you mine, now you have to tell me yours. Besides, I like nothing better than a restaurant faux pas—as long as it's not mine."

She sighed. "Okay, then. I threw up on a customer."

His lovely green eyes widened. "You mean, like... vomited?"

She nodded slowly.

"Hey, that's not so bad. You can't help being sick. What was it? Gastro or food poisoning? If it was food poisoning, it's more an embarrassment for the chef."

Pregnancy, she almost said, but couldn't quite bring herself to do so. They were having such a lovely time and if she told him she'd been pregnant, he would ask her what happened to the baby and that answer would end all easy conversation between them from here on in. She liked that he could talk and even joke a bit with her without worrying that he might put his foot in it.

It's amazing how many common, everyday phrases related to dying. She'd found that out soon after Jack died. Friends and family would be chatting away and suddenly say something like "I'd kill for a coffee right now" or "it scared me half to death" and then they'd get all flustered and apologize to her for putting their feet in it, when she wouldn't actually have noticed if they hadn't pointed it out.

"Some kind of twenty-four-hour bug," she said, hoping Lachlan hadn't noticed her hesitation.

"Hardly your fault, but yes, embarrassing." And then, he started to yawn. He tried to cover it but the action made her realize how late it was.

"I should be getting home," she said, pushing back

her seat and starting to collect their plates. "We've got a busy day tomorrow."

For a moment, he looked as if he might try to convince her to stay a little longer, but then he, too, stood. "Leave the plates. We can do them in the morning. I'll drive you home."

"No." The word came out harsher than she meant it to. "I've got my bike and I don't want to put you out."

"Your bike will fit in my truck, or you can leave it here and I can come get you in the morning after school drop-off, but there is no way I'm letting you ride home alone at this time at night."

"No bogeymen got me on the way over," she said.

But he wasn't taking no for an answer. "You were lucky. But my mom would never forgive me if I didn't drive you, and more important, I wouldn't forgive myself. And I'd expect any respectable guy to do the same for my sisters or for Hallie when she's old enough to sneak out late at night. Now, are we going to stand here arguing about it, or are you going to let me give you a lift, so we can all go home and try to get some rest?"

"Okay." She relented. If he was putting her in the same realm as his sister and his daughter, it wasn't like he'd expect her to ask him in for "coffee." Part of her actually felt a little disappointed by this fact, but she told herself it was a good thing. She needed a friend and a job more than she needed to complicate her life any more than it already was. Besides, her surprising physical feelings for him were probably simply because he was the first guy (aside from her dad) she'd spent any time with since Tyler.

"Great. Let me just switch off the lights."

Eliza waited by the door as Lachlan turned everything except the security lights off and then they went outside. It was only as he was locking up that she realized his truck was a few hundred yards away at the house.

"I don't want to wake your family," she said as he gestured for her to follow him that way.

"The kids and Blair sleep like the dead and Mom's probably still up watching the late-night movie. No more excuses."

And although it was dark and he couldn't see, she smiled. If she'd told him about Jack, he'd now be berating himself and apologizing to her for that sentence. Instead, they walked easily across the gravel to the main house, like two people who had just enjoyed a pleasant evening in each other's company. And *that* felt good. Her heart pinched a little with guilt at this, but she told herself to ignore it—this was why she'd moved to Jewell Rock, to learn to live again.

"Thanks for keeping me company tonight," Lachlan said ten minutes later as he lifted her bike out of the bed of his truck and set it down on the ground in front of her apartment block.

"Thank *you*," she replied. "It sure beat counting sheep."

He laughed. "I'm making chocolate, whiskey and bacon chili tomorrow night if you have trouble sleeping again."

"What *is* that?" she asked, unsure whether to grimace or rub her lips together in anticipation.

He cocked his head to one side and winked. "I guess if you really want to know, I'll see you tomorrow night."

And with that, he turned, swaggered around to the driver's side and climbed back into the truck. Smiling, she lifted her hand and waved good-night as she started to wheel her bike toward the building. She secured it out front and then turned back to see him still sitting there, watching her. Only when she went inside and closed the door behind her did she hear him finally drive off down the road.

Chapter Eight

"You guys all set in here?"

Lachlan looked up to see Eliza peering her head around the door to the kitchen. Alongside him worked his assistant chef and three of their new kitchen hands ready for the first ever dinner service. They weren't open yet—the big day was still two weeks away—but Eliza had had the brilliant idea to have a couple of rehearsals. So tonight and next Friday, he'd invited members of his family and the family of his staff to have dinner at the restaurant on him.

"Yep. We sure are." He smiled, loving the sight of her in their new uniforms, the McKinnel's logo in pride of place on her breast pocket.

"Good. Because our first customers have just walked in the door." She winked at him and then turned and hurried into the restaurant to welcome them.

Lachlan gave his kitchen team a quick pep talk and

then took a moment to peek out and watch Eliza and the waitstaff welcoming people and leading them over to tables. Behind the bar, their mixologist was ready and waiting to make magic with the drinks. Everyone and everything was exactly as it should be and Lachlan felt a buzz of pride fill his lungs as he looked on. Granted, they still had a few hours and many dishes of food to get through before they could celebrate their night as a success, but with himself in the kitchen and Eliza making sure everything went smoothly in the dining area, he felt as if he could conquer the world, so a simple restaurant should be a piece of cake.

Eliza looked up from where she'd just seated his mom, her best friend, Marcia, and the twins. As their eyes met, she gave him a slow smile that he felt right down to his toes.

"Daddy!" Hallie spotted him, rushed out of her seat and threw her arms around his waist. "Can I have some french fries, please? Hamish wants french fries, too. Don't you?" she said, glancing back to her brother as if daring him to disagree.

Lachlan smiled as he carried his daughter back to the table. "I was hoping you'd be a little more adventurous than that," he said, lowering her down into her seat, "but if you choose something from the menu, we might be able to do some fries on the side."

"Yay." The twins punched the air in unison.

He chuckled and glanced to his mom and Marcia, who would soon be Quinn's mother-in-law. "Welcome, ladies, so glad you could join us tonight."

"Thanks for inviting me," Marcia said, gazing around. "This place looks fantastic and I feel so privileged to get to try it out before the rest of the town."

"We wouldn't miss this for the world," Nora said,

standing to give him a hug. "I'm so proud of everything you and Eliza have achieved so far."

Lachlan liked the way his mom spoke as if he and Eliza were a partnership and wondered if somehow she could tell that his feelings for the head hostess were growing into something a little more than professional. He'd pretty much finished experimenting with the dishes now—the menu had already gone to print—but their nightly rendezvous hadn't stopped.

And he found himself looking forward to them more and more.

During the day, his conversations with Eliza were strictly professional—revolving almost entirely around what needed to be achieved in the lead up to opening the restaurant—but at night, he forbade them to talk about work. At night, while he taught her to cook, they made easy conversation, which got a little bit more personal with every passing day. He hadn't enjoyed a woman's company this much in as long as he could remember.

"I can't take any of the credit." Eliza scoffed but her cheeks flushed.

"That's not the way my son tells it," Nora said. "He told me these preopening dinners were all your idea. But I do worry the two of you are working far too hard. I hope Lachlan is leaving you some time to relax and settle into your new apartment. How are you finding life in Jewell Rock?"

"Oh, I love it." Eliza smiled. "Everyone is so friendly. I've never lived in a small town before—so it's a little weird that the people at the supermarket already know me by name—but aside from that, I like the slower pace of life. In New York, everyone is always in a rush, but here, no one seems to be in such a hurry they can't stop and say hello."

"Splendid. Now, what are you doing on Sunday?"

Eliza's brow furrowed slightly. "Um, nothing. I'll probably end up cleaning my apartment."

"Nonsense. Sundays are supposed to be days of rest. Housework is strictly forbidden." His mom clapped her hands together. "You'll come to lunch at my place instead."

Eliza looked a little flustered.

"Mom," Lachlan said. "It's customary to *ask* people, not *tell* them when you invite them over for a bite to eat. Eliza might have had enough of us McKinnels during the week and prefer to spend her weekends by herself."

Although secretly he loved the idea of hanging out with her on Sunday, as well.

His mom rolled her eyes. "I'm sorry, Eliza. If you don't have a *better* offer, would you *like* to come have Sunday lunch with me and my ever-growing tribe?"

Eliza laughed. "That would be lovely, thank you. Now, can I get you some drinks to start with?"

That was his cue to head back into the kitchen, and with one last lingering look at Eliza, he did so. He needed to ignore his errant thoughts and focus on cooking.

The next few hours flew by. The kitchen was a hive of activity with Lachlan and his team working seamlessly together, creating dishes he was proud of. There were only two mishaps—a batch of bourbon-glazed brussels sprouts slightly overcooked and one broken plate—but nothing that could be classified a calamity.

Once the desserts had been served, he took a few moments to go out into the dining room and chat to his friends and siblings, who all raved about their dinners.

"We did it," he said to Eliza, meeting her as she was halfway back to the kitchen with an armful of dirty plates. He took them from her, their hands brushing against each other in the process. Her skin was silky smooth and he wanted to reach out and touch it again.

"Did you ever have any doubt?" she asked, her eyes radiant as she grinned at him. "We make a good team."

But she turned and went back to keep clearing tables before he could agree.

Although the cooking and serving part of the evening went fast, the next couple of hours dragged. No one seemed in a hurry to leave and conversation lingered over mugs of Spanish coffee. When the kitchen was sparkling clean, he and Eliza dismissed the rest of the staff, saying that they could handle any last drinks and the locking up of the restaurant. He sent each of his new employees home with leftovers, and when his friends and family finally called it a night, he was overjoyed to be left alone with Eliza.

"You hungry?"

"Famished," she said with a sigh, reaching up to pull her hair free from its ponytail. "But what a night. That went even better than we hoped."

"I agree." He tried not to stare at her gorgeous brown locks, but all he could think about was how silky smooth they would feel if he reached out and ran his fingers through them. "How about we raid the leftovers for our own dinner and I crack open a bottle of wine to celebrate?"

She raised an eyebrow. "While that sounds just about perfect, how am I going to ride home or you drive me home if we drink a bottle of wine between us?"

"Hmm." He rubbed his jaw as he pondered this problem. *Dammit.* "How about a glass, then?"

She chuckled. "A glass sounds like a good idea. Any

more and I might fall asleep anyway. Why don't I grab the wine while you get the food?"

"Good idea. What do you want?"

She shrugged one shoulder. "What's left?" Before he could answer, she added, "Actually, surprise me."

While Eliza poured the wine, Lachlan went into the kitchen and retrieved two bowls of chili. When he returned, they sat down at a table together and talked over the evening. Although everything had gone even better than they'd hoped for, they agreed on a couple of things to finesse in this week's training before the second rehearsal next Friday. When Eliza yawned, Lachlan realized that they'd both been working pretty much nonstop since early that morning.

"Come on," he said, pushing to a stand. "I'll drive you home."

He didn't want to—although physically exhausted, he could happily spend all night talking to her—but she didn't object and together they loaded their plates into the dishwasher, then locked up and headed out into the night.

"What should I bring to your mom's place on Sunday?" she asked as they climbed out of his truck at her apartment block and headed around to the truck's bed to retrieve her bike. This had become a nightly ritual but he suddenly realized that once the restaurant was properly opened, their late-night cooking lessons would likely come to an end and he didn't want them to.

"Just yourself," he said as he held the bike toward her. "There's always enough food to feed a small country."

She chuckled as she reached out to take the bike and once again their hands touched in the interaction. Their gazes collided—her dark eyes glittered in the moonlight, her lips parted slightly and he felt the connection like a physical jolt.

"Thank you," she said, her voice low. "For bringing me and my bike home again."

"Any time," he replied and then, before he could think the ramifications through, he leaned forward and touched his lips to hers. What started as a tentative brush across her mouth, what could have almost been a platonic kiss good-night between friends, turned serious very quickly when she kissed him back. As her tongue slipped into his mouth, muscles all over his body tightened and his heart went into overdrive.

He took his hands off the bike and lifted them to her face, cradling her cheeks in his palms as he deepened the kiss. Eliza let out a little moan of pleasure and it was the most beautiful sound in the world.

A little voice in his head told him that they should take this inside, that at any moment either of his sisters might glance out the window and become an unwitting spectator. It seemed that Eliza was thinking the same thing, for she pulled back and looked up into his eyes.

His heart halted as he waited for her to speak. Had he misread the signs? Perhaps she hadn't enjoyed that kiss as much as he did?

But then she opened those beautiful lips again and whispered, "Do you want to come inside?" Her tone and the expression on her face made it crystal clear what she was offering.

It was all he could do not to shriek for joy. That pesky little voice from earlier tried telling him that maybe he should decline—that sleeping with an employee was quite possibly the worst thing he could do—but his desire for Eliza was stronger than anything else. For two weeks, he'd barely been able to think about anything but kissing her and now that he had, there was nothing he wanted more than to do so again.

"I'd love to," he said, reluctantly dropping his hands from her face so he could take the bike from her grasp and lean it up against the wall.

After that, no more words were necessary. Eliza offered him her hand and he took it happily, his pulse racing as she led him into the building. They grinned conspiratorially at each other as they tiptoed past his sisters' apartment and he felt like a kid about to do something very, very naughty.

But he couldn't wait and thanked the Lord for the just-in-case condom in his wallet.

Chapter Nine

Eliza knew she'd been playing with fire all these late nights she'd been spending with Lachlan but until he'd kissed her, she'd deluded herself into believing that the attraction she felt was one-sided. She'd ignored the way he sometimes looked at her and the way such a look spread heat from her core right down to her toes, telling herself it was all in her imagination. She'd even deluded herself that if such attraction *were* mutual and *if* he ever made a move, she'd be able to resist him on the grounds that they worked together and it wasn't a good idea.

But the moment she'd felt his lips on hers, she'd known she was a lost cause. She couldn't push him away if her life depended on it and neither did she want to.

Adrenaline raced through her body now as she fumbled to find her key in her purse. She shoved it in the lock and pushed open the door. The moment they were inside, Lachlan kicked it shut behind them. Eliza managed to switch on the hall light before her purse and key dropped from her grasp.

They reached for each other again, his hands drawing her face to his, and hers finding their way around his back and sliding up under his shirt. His bare skin was hot and smooth beneath her touch and her mouth watered at the thought of licking it.

She honestly didn't know what had come over her but standing here in her tiny hallway kissing him wasn't nearly enough. As if Lachlan could feel her desperation in her kiss, his hands started to wander. As one thumb teased the skin at her décolletage, the other went lower, gently and teasingly skimming over her breasts.

Fire lit within her—she felt as if she might combust if she didn't feel his hands on her skin. More daring than she'd ever been before, she ripped her hands from beneath his shirt and started undoing the buttons of her own.

She wanted everything and anything he could give her.

As if encouraged by her wantonness, Lachlan's lips followed in the path of his hands, dropping tiny kisses along her neckline that caused her skin to gooseflesh. Heat pooled between her legs and her heart rate went crazy as he expertly unclasped her bra and replaced it with his hands instead.

"You're incredible, so beautiful," he whispered, teasing her nipples with his thumbs. His words made her feel alive, and when he took one nipple into his mouth, she cried out. The pleasure shot through her, right to her core and her knees buckled.

Lachlan was right there to catch her, one arm sliding around her back and holding her close to his lovely, hard chest.

"Which way to the bedroom?" he asked, his voice low and gravelly, exactly as she imagined sex would sound if it spoke.

Unable to speak, she thrust her head in the right direction and squealed as he scooped her up into his arms and carried her into her bedroom like she weighed nothing more than a silk scarf. Her curtains still open from that morning, the moonlight sneaked in and fell across the bed, giving them enough light to make their way to it without switching one on.

They tumbled onto the bed together, legs tangling as their lips sought each other once again. Her hands scrambled for his shirt, but chef's whites weren't the easiest to remove in the near dark while on the brink of sexual satisfaction.

"Help me," she moaned. "I want to feel your skin."

Lachlan sat up, his knees on either side of her hips, his body hovering just above her as he whipped off his upper layers.

Had she ever seen anything so intoxicating as this gorgeous man doing as she'd begged?

She reached out her hand to touch him. More slowly, enjoying the anticipation now that what she wanted was within reach. She felt his quick intake of breath as her fingers glided down his chest, following the arrow of hair to the top of his trousers. Her hand covered the bulge beneath and her insides tingled as she touched him through the material. He felt so good and she could only imagine how much better he would feel inside her.

"Take them off," she demanded.

Slightly groaning as if trying to control himself, Lachlan lifted her hand from his groin and shook his head. "You first," he said. Then, he sat up, ripped off her shoes and yanked her trousers and panties down her legs in one swift move.

Self-consciousness about being fully naked in front of him lasted only seconds, because then he was back, his body stretched out over the top of hers like a warm blanket she wanted to enfold herself in. She could feel his erection against the apex of her thighs and she pressed herself upward, instinct taking over as she rocked herself against him.

He pushed himself up on his arms and swore as he gazed down at her. "Eliza, you do any more of that and this will be over in seconds. Let me take care of you first."

And take care of her he did.

With those words, he claimed her mouth again with his, but this time, his fingers trekked far lower than they had before, sliding between her legs and touching her where it mattered most. He stroked her gently at first, but then the intensity increased as he pushed his finger deeper and circled her bud.

She felt her core tightening, her whole body going still as the pleasure built within her. As if that wasn't maddening enough, he tore his lips from hers and dipped his head, once again twirling his tongue around her nipple and then sucking it right into his mouth. It was almost embarrassing how quickly her first orgasm rolled through her, her body shaking and her inner muscles shuddering against his touch.

It had been so long since she'd felt such intense physical relief. The man had magic fingers but she needed, she *wanted* more. Barely able to move due to the sensations flooding her body, somehow she voiced her desire.

"Lachlan. You're killing me. Please, take off your trousers. I need you."

He looked up from where he'd been pleasuring her breasts and grinned around her nipple. It was the most erotic thing she'd ever seen.

"Just a sec."

And then he pushed up from her again and treated her to a one-man revue as he unbuckled his belt, then shucked his shoes, socks, trousers and underwear in what had to be world-record time. He was a good-looking man fully clothed, but standing at the edge of her bed, moonlight dappling over his bare skin, he was simply glorious.

Lachlan seemed far too busy to go to the gym, so she wondered what he did to get such lovely muscles. She couldn't help gaping at his impressive erection, but she didn't have time to stare or wonder for long.

He stooped and picked his trousers up off the floor. For one horrifying moment, she thought he'd changed his mind and was going to put them back on, but relief flooded her when he pulled out his wallet and conjured a little square foil packet instead. As he ripped it open with his teeth and sheathed himself quickly, she silently thanked the Lord that Lachlan had the forethought to think about it, when she'd almost lost her head.

And then he was back on the bed beside her, taking her in his arms, kissing her like their lives depended on it and making her hot all over again. This time, it was Eliza who slipped her hand between them, moved it lower and wrapped it around his long, hard shaft. She squeezed a little, tentatively at first, but when it grew even more beneath her touch, her own desire took over.

She lifted her hips a little, nudged her entrance with his erection and then hooked her legs up around his back. He plunged inside, not needing any more en-couragement, driving deep into her, his hands pressed against the mattress, their eyes glued on each other as he brought them both quickly to release.

It might only have been missionary sex—boring sex, as Tyler used to say—but nothing felt ordinary about this connection. Banishing Tyler from her head, she cried out as her second orgasm in what felt like a matter of minutes rocked through her, the pleasure so strong she thought she might combust.

Lachlan grinned down at her, then covered her mouth with his, silencing her as he kissed her hard once again. Afterward, they lay there, so still, so quiet, she could feel his heart pumping against her own chest.

What the hell have I just done?

But with him still deliciously inside her, she found she couldn't summon one iota of remorse. A little guilt perhaps that she could feel so wonderful, so alive, but with the aftershocks of pleasure still doing their stuff, definitely no remorse. Sex that good could never have been regretted, no matter what came next.

After what felt like ages but was probably only a minute or so, he pushed up again and looked down at her. "I'm going to go deal with the condom," he said and then slid out of bed. "Back in a sec."

She admired his cute butt as he walked naked to the en suite and then stretched out in bed wondering if that was his only condom. She'd stopped taking the Pill months ago when it became obvious that sex with her husband wasn't on the agenda anymore, but she wouldn't mind if more sex was on tonight's agenda. Now that she'd broken her pact with herself not to get involved with anyone, it seemed silly not to indulge herself with such a willing partner.

As she rolled over, her heart halted in her chest as she came face-to-face with the photo frame with her

little boy's smiling face sitting next to her on the bedside table. She sat up so quickly, her head spun as she
snatched up the frame, then yanked open the bedside
drawer and shoved it inside.

The lightness that had filled her body vanished as
she realized how close she'd come to Lachlan seeing it.
What on earth had she been thinking, sleeping with her
boss of all people? The last thing she wanted was for
him to start asking questions she didn't want to answer
and now that they'd slept together, he might think he had
the right to pry further into her personal life.

What else would he expect? Would he hope tonight
was a prelude to something more? Fear turned her heart
to ice at the thought. If she'd needed sex, she could have
gone to a bar and picked up some stranger or joined that
silly app that Sophie and Annabel were obsessed with.

But her boss? *Oh, Eliza, you stupid, stupid girl.*

She heard the toilet flush and then the door clicked
open and Lachlan stood there, still in all his naked
glory. She froze like a deer in headlights.

He took a step back into the bedroom and then
paused, frowning as he met her gaze. "Are you okay?"
He sounded uncertain. That would make two of them.
"You look like you've seen a ghost."

She rubbed her lips together. "What did we just do?"

His brows furrowed a little more. "We just had incredible sex. At least I thought we did."

Incredible didn't even come close to describing what
they'd just done. Her cheeks flushed at his directness
and she quickly pulled the blankets over her, feeling
suddenly self-conscious. "But you're my boss."

His lips flicked up at the edges and he took a step
closer to the bed. "I could be your boss with benefits."

As he peeled the covers back and lay down next to

her again, heat ripped through Eliza's body at his suggestive tone.

Yes, please, shouted her hormones. Boss with benefits? How freaking fantastic did that sound? Forever was a long time to go without sex simply because she didn't want the intimacy and commitment she'd always thought went hand in hand with making love. She thought of Grammy Louise's advice that sex didn't always have to be serious and hope flared in her heart.

She smiled up at him. "Are you serious? You'd be happy with that kind of arrangement?"

Lachlan blinked, his hands pausing on their way to her body. When he'd suggested "benefits," he'd been joking. For one, he didn't think Eliza was that kind of girl; two, he respected her too much to use her for her body; and three, he also liked her, which meant for the first time in a long while, he wanted more than just sex from a woman. But the smile on her face and the tone of her voice gave him pause.

It sounded almost as if she liked his indecent proposition.

"Um…I… What do *you* want?" he asked, looking directly up into her dark eyes.

"Well." She rubbed her lips together and her chest rose and fell with a heavy breath. "I really like you, Lachlan. You're the first guy I've slept with since my marriage ended and it was amazing. I've really loved spending time with you these last few weeks—during the day and especially at night. Your passion for food is contagious and thanks to you, I've smiled more in the last few weeks than I have in the last year. But I'm still incredibly hurt and raw from my separation, my divorce isn't even final yet and my head isn't in the right place to start another relationship."

"I see. Of course." He nodded fast and summoned a smile, trying to cover over his shock and disappointment. Wasn't it usually the guy quoting such lines? And since when had he wanted a relationship anyway? His kids came first and considering Linda's rejection of Hamish, he'd never allowed himself to dream about finding a woman who might want him *and* his children.

Still, he couldn't help being curious about Eliza's reticence. "Do you think there's a chance you and your ex might get back together?"

His heart squeezed at the prospect and he couldn't help the rush of relief as she shook her head. "No. I loved him with all my heart but he hurt me too badly to ever recover from that."

"He abused you?" His own feelings forgotten, Lachlan clenched his fists as he harbored violent thoughts about a man he'd never met.

"Oh, no, nothing like that. He didn't hurt me physically. Tyler…" She sighed deeply and paused as if considering how much to tell him.

Was she holding back because she didn't want him to think badly of her ex? Obviously she still had feelings for the guy, no matter how much she professed otherwise, and Lachlan couldn't help feeling a tad jealous.

"It's all right," he said encouragingly, trying to ignore his own discomfort. "You can tell me anything, but if you don't want to…I understand."

"Tyler had a drug problem," she said after another few long moments. "When he was young, he dabbled in recreational stuff, but he swore he'd stopped by the time we started going out. I believed him but eighteen months ago, he started up again. Instead of turning to me when…when things got tough, he turned to drugs and his usage quickly started affecting his work. Eventually, with the assistance of his family, I convinced him to get some help. He sought counseling and it appeared to be doing him good. So good it turns out that he decided he liked his counselor more than he liked me."

Eliza sniffed and a tear slid down her cheek. She brushed it away as if embarrassed by it and went on. "Three months ago, he told me he'd been sleeping with her and asked me to move out of our apartment. That's when I moved in with my grandmother again."

His heart went out to this gorgeous woman lying beside him and he stupidly blurted, "Isn't sleeping with a patient breaking some kind of professional rule?"

Something between a scoff and a laugh escaped her lips as she met his eyes. "I think adultery goes against the rules of marriage, too, but you know as well as I do that rules don't always hinder people."

"That's true." He put his hand over hers and squeezed it in a show of support. "But it still sucks. And for what it's worth, I think your ex-husband must be a damn fool, choosing someone else over you."

In fact, Tyler had to be stupid *and* blind because right now, Lachlan couldn't imagine another woman that could give Eliza a run for her money on any level. She was pretty close to perfect.

"Thank you," she whispered, linking her fingers through his and staring down at their joined hands. "That means a lot."

Part of him wanted to hunt this Tyler dude down but another part of him wanted to thank the asshole because while Eliza might not be ready for another relationship right now, at least she was a free agent. Their chemistry was impossible to deny, so perhaps in time, if he was patient, if he played his cards right, he might stand a chance for more than just sex with her.

There hadn't been a woman he *wanted* to stand a chance with in a very long time.

"I mean it," he said, "and if you ever want to talk about any of it, then I'm all ears. It might have been a while ago, but when Linda cheated on me, she taught me a few important life lessons and I've come out the other side relatively unscathed. I believe you will, too."

"Let's hope so," she said with a slow smile. "I feel like moving here, getting away from my past and helping you open the restaurant is a very good step in the right direction. I should probably have mentioned this in my interview, but my last job was working in Tyler's family restaurant. I changed my name back to my maiden name so the connection wouldn't be obvious on my résumé, but when our relationship exploded, I basically lost my job, as well."

Lachlan couldn't believe what he was hearing. "They fired you for *his* indiscretions?" He thought back to the call he'd made to her last employer for a reference—they'd been over-the-top gushy but now he wondered if that wasn't simply because she was good at her job, but also because they didn't want her to cause a fuss about being let go.

"Oh, no, not exactly. His parents were very upset by his behavior and they didn't actually fire me, but I couldn't be comfortable continuing to work there after everything that had gone down. I've had firsthand experience with how dangerous mixing business with pleasure can be and that's why *this*—" she bit her lip and pointed her finger back and forth between them "—scares me. I like being in Jewell Rock. I like my new apartment, living next to your sisters. I like working with you. I didn't want to mess all that up for…"

Her voice trailed off and he finished the sentence for her. "For a bit of fun between the sheets?"

Her lips twisted and her cheeks flushed that beautiful pink color again. Her long dark lashes fluttered as she looked down, not meeting his eyes when she said, "Exactly. But perhaps that's too late. If things are going to be awkward now that we've slept together and you'd rather I quit, then…I understand."

"Quit?" His heart shuddered. The thought of Eliza handing in her notice made his insides turn almost as much as the thought of never *being* inside her again. "Don't talk such blasphemy," he said, turning and finally pulling her into his arms again. "I do *not* want you to quit. I do not want to talk about your ex-husband. But I do want to kiss you again."

And then, before she could say another word, he did exactly that, taking her beautiful face once again between his hands and claiming her mouth with his. Man, she tasted good, no food could ever possibly compare. And if sex was all she was offering, then he'd be an idiot to turn her down. It wasn't like he had a lot of time for anything more right now either.

A moan slipped from her mouth into his, their bodies smashing together as her silky smooth legs entwined with his. They kissed like a couple of crazed teens, their hands wandering, exploring and driving each other to distraction.

Eventually, Eliza tore her lips from his and rolled over so that she was straddling him. Her hair swished from side to side as she smiled seductively down at him with her hips rocking torturously against his growing erection.

"Do you have another condom?" she panted as her hand once again closed around his penis.

Every muscle in his body tensed at her touch. "No. Hot damn. That was my only one. I don't suppose you have any?"

She shook her head.

He groaned. "I'll take a trip to the drugstore tomorrow and stock up."

"Yes. You do that," she said, "but in the meantime..."

And then she smiled suggestively, wriggled down his body and dropped her head to his groin. Seconds later, she had him in her mouth. And a minute later, he'd lost the ability to think straight.

A boss with benefits? Yeah, maybe he could get used to that title.

Chapter Ten

Eliza's phone rang as she was getting herself ready for Sunday lunch and her heart kicked up a notch. Could it be Lachlan? Her body buzzed in anticipation at the thought of seeing him again. But more likely, the caller would be one of three people—Grammy Louise, Lilly or Dad. Sometimes she wondered if they'd set up some kind of roster among them because hardly a day went by when at least one of them didn't call her.

As much as she loved all three, she didn't always feel like talking to them. It was draining to have to re-assure them that she wasn't about to jump off a cliff or drown herself in a lake.

But today, still on a high from Friday night, she wouldn't have to put on too much of an act. She scooped up the phone and swiped to answer. "Hi, Grammy."

"Hel-lo, my gorgeous girl. Happy Sunday."

"You sound out of breath," Eliza said. She carried

the phone back into the bathroom, put her phone on the vanity and her grandmother on speaker so she could continue her hair and makeup as she listened to her grandmother talk about her new beau.

"I'm actually going out to lunch in a moment," Eliza said. She knew for a fact this would make Grammy very happy. "Nora McKinnel, my boss's mom, asked me over for Sunday lunch with their family."

"Ooh, that's lovely. It's so kind of his mom to try to make you feel welcome."

"It's not just Nora," Eliza admitted. "All of the McKinnels have been very friendly and welcoming. I think you'd like them."

"If they are looking after my girl, I already adore them," Grammy said.

"Oh, they are." Eliza blushed, thinking of exactly how well Lachlan had looked after her on Friday night. "In fact, Lachlan's sisters, Sophie and Annabel, will be arriving any minute to give me a lift to the distillery because my bike was stolen."

"What?" Grammy sounded horrified. "Are you okay? What happened to your old one? You'd barely had it five minutes."

"I didn't lock it up properly on Friday night and someone stole it."

"That would never happen in New York, but it's not like you to be so careless either. What happened?"

While smirking at the New York comment, Eliza wondered if she should tell her that she'd been in such a haste to go inside after Lachlan kissed her so they could rip each other's clothes off that she hadn't been thinking straight. Grammy would probably rejoice at such news but something stopped her from being forthright.

She worried if she told her grandmother, Louise might make more of it than it actually was.

"Eliza? Are you still there?"

"Sorry, Grammy. Yes, I was just tired the other night, I think, and I forgot about securing the bike."

"Lachlan's not working you too hard, is he?" There was a hint of if-he-is-I'll-give-him-what-for to her tone.

Eliza bit her lip. Being with Lachlan never felt like work at all. "No, Grammy. I'm loving getting ready for the opening of the restaurant and I'm actually learning to cook a little, as well."

This news was met by silence on the other end of the line. Eliza could not recall another moment in her life where Grammy had been stunned silent.

"I think my hearing's failing me, sweetheart," she said after a few long moments. "I thought you just said you were learning to cook?"

"I am," Eliza replied, pride zapping through her. "Not anything too complicated, but Lachlan has taught me to make pancakes, mac'n'cheese and how to grill a steak."

"My Lord, wonders never cease. This new boss of yours must be some kind of miracle worker."

Eliza thought of the way he listened when she told him her woes, of the way his fingers played her body like she was a violin and him a member of the symphony orchestra. "I think he might be," she said.

"Have you told your father?" Grammy asked.

"What? About me learning to cook?"

Before her grandmother could reply, the intercom buzzed. "Sorry," Eliza said, "but my ride's here. I'm gonna have to go."

"That's okay. Jonathon and I are heading out for an

early dinner and then a Broadway show. You have a lovely lunch."

"I will. You, too, Grammy, but don't do anything I wouldn't do," she teased.

The older woman chuckled. "That, my dear, would make for a very boring date." And then she disconnected.

"You ready?" Sophie's voice sounded through the front door—or was it Annabel's? Eliza couldn't tell the difference unless she saw them in the flesh. And even then it wasn't easy.

"Yes," she shouted so her voice would carry out of her bedroom and down the hallway as she grabbed her purse and the box of chocolates she'd bought for Nora.

A few moments later, she opened the door to find both Sophie *and* Annabel standing there.

"Hi," she said chirpily.

"Wow, you look lovely," the twins said in unison by way of a greeting.

They were both in jeans and casual T-shirts, whereas Eliza had gone for a floral jumpsuit and strappy, heeled sandals. She'd also spent a ridiculously long time blow-drying and straightening her hair.

"Thanks," she said, feeling her cheeks flush. She suddenly felt vastly overdressed and hoped the twins couldn't guess that she'd gone to all this effort for their brother. Although this was a family lunch at his mom's and there wouldn't be any opportunity for shenanigans, her body buzzed in anticipation of seeing him again and she couldn't help wanting to look good for him. She wanted him to be *thinking* about having sex with her, even if he wasn't able to. Her cheeks heated even more at the thought and she wondered what kind of person she'd become. That familiar tug of guilt pulled at her heart.

"And thanks so much for the ride," she added, silently telling her guilt to take a hike—this had *nothing* to do with Jack.

"It's not a problem." Sophie waved a hand in front of her face. "I still can't believe someone stole your bike! I thought this was a safe neighborhood."

Eliza pulled her door shut behind her, then tested the handle to make sure it had locked. "It was my own fault for being careless."

"Have you reported it to the police?" Annabel asked and for a moment, Eliza thought she was talking about the sex.

"What?" A flutter ran through her and her lips tingled traitorously as if Lachlan's had been there only moments ago. Then, once again, her brain caught up. "*Oh*, the bike." She shook her head as they walked together down the corridor to the building's exit. "Not yet. Do you think I should? I figured whoever took it will be long gone by now."

"Maybe, but you should definitely report it," Sophie said, "because if the culprit is caught later for another crime, and they find your bike in his or her possession, then they'll be able to charge them for that, as well."

"I'll think about it."

Seemingly satisfied with this, Lachlan's sisters led her to Sophie's new model orange Mini Cooper and Annabel folded herself into the back seat.

"I don't mind sitting in the back," Eliza offered, but the twins wouldn't hear of it.

"You're our guest today," Sophie said as she settled into the driver's seat.

On the short drive to McKinnel's Distillery, the twins

kept the conversation rolling, talking about a trip Sophie was planning to Scotland the following summer and Eliza did her best to listen—hopefully making the right noises in the right places —when all she could think about was the fact that within minutes she'd be seeing their brother again. The closer they got to the distill-ery, the more the butterflies in her stomach kicked up.

She was really excited about seeing him but also a little nervous, fearful that despite the arrangement they'd decided on, things would get weird or awkward between them. Today would be a test and she desper-ately wanted them to pass it.

"I hope you're hungry," Sophie said as she slowed the car to a stop in front of Nora McKinnel's impres-sive stone-built house.

"Starving," Eliza said, although the truth was there was only one thing she felt very hungry for right now How the heck was she going to sit through a civilized lunch with Lachlan and his family when all she could think about was sleeping with him again?

"Good, because Mom's cooking is not to be missed," Annabel added.

After that, Eliza got out of the car and held the door as Annabel climbed out behind her. Together the three of them headed for the house but even before they'd gone a few feet, the front door opened and Hallie burst out, waving and screaming, "Hello, hello, hello," as she ran toward them. Eliza assumed she was excited to see her aunts, so she couldn't hide her surprise when Hallie threw her little arms around Eliza's waist.

"I was so happy when Granny Nora said you were coming for lunch. Can you sit next to me?"

She laughed and patted the child on the back as she extracted herself. It was lovely to feel wanted but she also couldn't bring herself to get too close. "Hi, Hallie. Let's see where your grandmother wants to put me."

And then she looked up again to the house and saw Lachlan appear in the doorway. He looked absolutely edible in faded jeans and a tight black T-shirt that highlighted all the muscles she'd become intimately acquainted with the other night. Her mouth went dry.

"Hey there." He lifted a hand to wave and any worries she'd been harboring evaporated as he hit her with a smile that made her pulse tingle. It wasn't the only part of her that tingled and she decided that perhaps sitting next to Hallie would be safer than sitting next to him. The way she felt right now, she wasn't sure she'd be able to keep her hands off him if they got so close.

"Hi." She smiled back at him, desire curling low in her tummy.

"You okay?" Annabel asked, turning back and looking quizzically from a few steps ahead.

Eliza felt Hallie tugging on her hand and realized she'd stopped dead in her tracks and was gawking at Lachlan as if he were the first good-looking man she'd ever laid eyes on.

"Oh, yes, sorry..." She tore her eyes from his, summoned a smile for his sister and squeezed the little hand in hers. "Coming."

As she took the few steps onto the porch, Lachlan stepped out of the way and held the door open, gesturing for the four of them to go through.

"It's good to see you again, Eliza," he said as his sisters followed the din into the kitchen. "I hope you had a good Saturday and got to relax a little after Friday night."

Heat flared within her at his words. As far as anyone who could hear their conversation would assume, Lachlan was referring to their busy rehearsal at the restaurant, but that's not what his words conjured in her head.

"Yes," she replied. "I did, thank you. I chilled out on the couch, watching Netflix."

"Sounds blissful," he said.

"And what about you?" she asked.

"I spent most of the day at a dance concert for Hallie." He looked down and grinned at his little girl, who was still clutching tightly onto Eliza's hand. "And then the three of us had a movie night, so yes, it was relaxing enough."

"Ooh, what movie?" She attempted small talk for the sake of Hallie still attached to her hand, when all she wanted to do was press her lips against Lachlan's and take what she needed. *Down, girl.*

"*Beauty and the Beast,*" the little girl replied, seemingly (and thankfully) oblivious to the sparks flying above her head.

"The recent one? Weren't you scared?" Eliza asked. "I've heard it's quite terrifying in places."

Hallie held her chin high. "I'm really brave."

"You most certainly are," Lachlan said. "But why don't you run ahead and see if Granny Nora needs any help? I just need to talk restaurant business with Eliza for a few moments."

Hallie sighed deeply and pouted her outrage but did as she was told nonetheless, leaving Eliza and Lachlan as alone as they could be in a house full of people.

He stepped a little closer and spoke quietly. "It's *really* good to see you." And although he didn't touch her, the way his gaze skimmed down her body sent a familiar current through her.

"You already said that," she whispered, breathing

in his unique male smell, which sent a potent rush to her head.

"It was worth saying again. Although I'd much prefer it if we were alone," he added with a suggestive wriggle of his eyebrows.

"Me, too."

"What are you up to ton—"

But before he could continue, Nora appeared down the hallway and Lachlan cleared his throat. "I'd like you to come in early tomorrow to help me sort through the uniforms before we hand them out to the staff," he said, as if they'd been talking business all along.

"Not a problem. Of course." Eliza hoped his mom didn't click that the staff had already been wearing their uniforms on Friday night at the rehearsal.

"Lachlan, the poor girl has come to lunch. She's not on your clock now. Leave her alone." Shaking her head at her son, Nora reached out and pulled Eliza into a hug. "Welcome. I'm so glad you made it."

"Thanks," Eliza managed.

"Sophie told me your bike was stolen," Nora said as she released Eliza from her embrace. That's shocking—if I ever find out who took it, I'll skin them alive."

"Someone took your bike?" Lachlan asked, concern creasing his brow.

She nodded. They'd exchanged a couple of brief messages yesterday, but she hadn't mentioned the bike as she didn't want him to feel responsible. "I must have forgotten to lock it up Friday night."

His eyes widened as realization dawned.

"I've just remembered," Nora continued, "I have an old bike in storage if you'd like to borrow it. It's nothing flashy but I think it still does the trick."

"Thank you. If you're sure. That would be wonderful," Eliza replied.

"Of course, I'm sure. I can't remember the last time I used it—I think the twins might still have been in high school." She laughed. "I'll get one of the boys to dig it out for you after lunch."

"Thank you. Oh, and by the way, these are for you." Eliza handed the older woman the box of chocolates.

Nora grinned. "Ooh, these are my favorites, although you didn't need to give me anything. It's a pleasure to have you here. Now, come on through and say hi to everyone."

She turned and started back where she'd come from, gesturing for Eliza to follow behind.

Eliza looked to Lachlan. "After you," he said, and then he reached out his hand and placed it on the small of her back to guide her. It was like he'd flicked a match against the cotton of her jumpsuit, but somehow she managed to put one foot in front of the other and head into the country-style kitchen.

It had felt enormous when Lachlan had brought her to meet his mom a couple of weeks ago, but now, with so many people crowded around the table, it didn't feel so big. There was a buzz of noise as all Lachlan's family chatted amicably.

"Everyone!" Nora exclaimed loudly. The chatter immediately died out as all eyes turned to them. "Eliza's here."

"Hi, Eliza," everyone around the table chorused.

Nora turned back to look at Eliza. "Is there anyone you haven't met yet?"

Before Eliza could answer, a tall, slender woman with long red hair down to her butt lifted a hand and waved.

"Hey there. I'm Claire, Blair's ex-wife—everyone's been telling me so much about you, so it's nice to finally meet."

Claire was sitting next to Blair and Eliza vaguely remembered Lachlan mentioning something about Blair's divorce being complicated. She tried not to show her surprise as she said, "Hi. Lovely to meet you, too."

"Take a seat," Nora said, nudging Eliza toward the table.

"Is there anything I can do to help you?" she asked Nora instead.

The older woman tsk-tsked. "Don't be silly. I didn't invite you here to work—you've been doing enough of that lately. There are plenty of others here to help. Now, make yourself comfortable and I'll get you a drink. What do you fancy? Tea, coffee, orange juice or something stronger?"

"Can I have some water, please?" Eliza asked as she sat down at one of the few empty seats. She needed something to cool her down.

"I hear you're from New York," Claire said from across the table. "I love New York so much. Do you miss it?"

Eliza smiled and made small talk about her hometown for a few moments, but all the while she spoke she was conscious of Lachlan's gaze. Before long, the casserole dishes were delivered to the table and once everyone was served, they all seemed to talk again at once. Eliza found it hard to keep track of any one conversation—she wasn't used to such big family gatherings but Lachlan playing footsie with her under the table didn't help either.

At first, it was just his shoe, gently nudging hers, but then he slipped it off and as his foot trekked slowly up her calf, it was all she could do to stop moaning and squirming in her seat.

"Are either of you off to another one of your Tinder dates tonight?" Mac asked his sisters, a smirk on his face telling them exactly what he thought of the hookup app.

Sophie stuck out her tongue at him. "Don't mock it until you've tried it, bro. You should sign up —might get you out of that permanent funk. You used to be fun, you know."

Trying to ignore Lachlan's wandering foot, Eliza looked between the siblings, enjoying their banter. There was only herself, her dad and her grandma in her family and although Tyler had two siblings, none of them spoke to each other so she'd never experienced anything like the fun and warmth that filled this room. Even when the McKinnels teased each other, it was done in love and Eliza could see why Claire would be so loathe to lose her place here.

"Oh, darlings." Nora frowned at the Tinder chat. "I've heard all about that app. All the men on there are only looking for one thing."

Quinn snorted. "Most men are only looking for one thing." His fiancée, Bailey, elbowed him. "Ouch!"

"Wh-at one thing?" Hamish asked. Everyone pretended not to hear him.

Annabel chuckled. "Mom, I thought you wanted Sophie and me to find Mr. Right and give you more grandbabies."

Nora's expression remained serious as she reached beside her and squeezed Annabel's hand. "I just want you to be happy again, sweetheart."

Annabel took a few seconds before she smiled and Eliza recognized a sadness there—similar to the one she saw in the mirror everyday. During their late-night sessions in the restaurant, Lachlan had shared stories about his siblings and Annabel's was the saddest of all.

Her high-school sweetheart was in the military and a few years ago went missing in action, presumed dead after an explosion.

"I know, Mommy," Annabel said, "and this is the first step. I've actually met some really nice guys. Not everyone on Tinder is only looking for hookups. In fact, I'm seeing a really nice man—he lives in Bend—and I think it could get serious."

Nora's eyes sparkled and she clapped her hands together. "Oh, that's simply marvelous."

"Chill, Mom," Mac said, "she said it *could* get serious. There aren't any wedding bells yet."

Everyone laughed, then Callum said, "Probably a good thing. I think two weddings and three babies in a year are enough, even for our family."

Nora then looked to Eliza. "What about you, dear? Are you single?"

Lachlan's wandering foot pressed into the junction at Eliza's thigh. They exchanged a look of two people who shared an illicit secret and it was all she could do not to squeak. Instead, she squeezed her knees together and managed to say, "Yes. I am."

"You should join Tinder, too," Sophie suggested and then laughed. "I've been exchanging horror stories with Annabel but it sounds like she might not need the app much longer, so I'll need another partner in crime."

Eliza saw Annabel blush and bite her lower lip as if to stifle a smile. Yep, she looked like a girl who was falling in love, something that Eliza herself didn't think she'd ever have the capacity to do again. Love could be amazing but then there was the flip side. "I'm not really looking for a relationship right now," she said.

With her words, Lachlan pushed back his seat and

the chair legs scraped loudly against the tiled floor. Everyone looked at him.

"Eliza, come with me. I'll get that bike for you now."

"There's no rush to do that now, sweetheart," Nora said to Lachlan. "Plenty of time to—" She stopped mid-sentence as she and Annabel exchanged a pointed look. "*Oh*. Take your time, dears."

"Can I come, Da-ad?" Hamish asked, starting to get up from his seat.

"Dad won't be long," Annabel said to her nephew. "And I need you and Hallie to help me clear the table."

Eliza felt heat rushing from her core, painting her neck and body red. What was Lachlan playing at? It was obvious Annabel at least suspected he was summoning her to scratch an itch and she could already imagine the gossip that might ignite once they left. Yet, despite this and the fact they'd agreed to keep their liaison a secret, she couldn't stand up fast enough.

He didn't say one word to her as they hurried out of the house, her following behind like some lovesick puppy dog at his heels, but the moment they were out of sight, he took hold of her hand. With the jolt that shot through her at the connection, the last of her scruples or embarrassment evaporated. Her panties were already wet with desire and the knowledge that he was equally desperate for her only compounded that desire.

"This way," he said as he led her round the back to the garage and let them in through a side door. He shut it behind them and then slid the lock across to hinder interruption. The sound of the lock clicking into place sent a shiver of lust down her spine and when Lachlan turned back around to look at her, she saw the heat she felt reflected in his eyes.

"You were very naughty back there," she whispered, feeling very naughty herself.

He shrugged one shoulder lazily but didn't sound very apologetic when he said, "It's your fault. You drive me to distraction."

And then the conversation ceased as he dragged her toward him. As their lips met, Eliza's hands went straight for his belt buckle. After their interactions under the table, they were way past foreplay and she wanted him inside her without delay.

"You got a condom?" she panted.

In reply, he slipped a tiny foil packet from his pocket and held it up in front of her face. "I stocked up."

Those three words were perhaps the sexiest ones anyone had ever spoken.

"Good," she said as she conquered the buckle and pushed his jeans and underwear down his legs. She took the condom from him, ripped it open and he groaned as she slid it down his deliciously hard length.

But when Lachlan tried to rid her of her clothing, he struggled.

"What in the world is this thing?" he asked as he pulled his head back to gaze at her outfit.

Eliza silently cursed her choice of attire, but when she'd chosen it that morning, the last thing she'd thought was that she'd end up in a garage having sex. This was so out of character for her, but also so invigorating. The illicitness of their situation only spurred her on more.

She undid the jumpsuit and let it—along with her panties—slither to the floor, feeling sexier and more alive than she had in a long while as she stepped out of it and stood before him in nothing but heels and her bra.

Lachlan sucked in a breath as his gaze raked down her body. His eyes widened at exactly the moment she realized her mistake. When they'd slept together at her house, she'd made sure not to turn on the lights and figured that somehow when they slept together again, she'd manage a similar trick.

But it was light in here and, in the heat of the moment, she'd felt as if she were a different person and had completely forgotten about her scar.

"What's this?" he asked, his voice soft as he reached out and touched it.

Although her stomach fluttered as his finger ran a line along her skin, her body went ice-cold. How could she have been so careless?

"Um." She swallowed. Her mouth parched, she was all of a sudden aware of her nakedness. A voice in her head told her to ignore his question, to simply kiss him till he forgot it, but she couldn't.

She scrambled for her jumpsuit—this was no conversation to have sans clothes—and tried to collect her thoughts as she hurried to put it on again. She could lie. What other reasons were there for such a scar across her abdomen? But although there must be a zillion, her brain came up with not one.

"Have you got a child?" he asked, his voice a little rough but his gaze trained on hers so she couldn't look anywhere else.

She shook her head and felt tears spring to her eyeballs. "Not anymore."

Chapter Eleven

Not anymore. What on earth did that mean? For a moment, Lachlan wondered if, like Linda, Eliza had abandoned a kid to her ex, but he found himself unable to believe such a thing of her. His heart rate slowed as a number of other possible scenarios ran through his head.

"What happened?"

"I lost him," she whispered as a tear snaked down her cheek.

Lost? "You had a stillbirth?" he prodded gently.

Again she shook her head and another tear followed the first. "His name was Jack. He was fourteen months old and he was beautiful."

Every bone in Lachlan's body turned to ice. Fourteen months wasn't a stillbirth. That would have been bad enough, but this…this was so much worse than he'd imagined. He had no words, but in his head, he swore.

"One day I took Jack to visit a friend and her new baby. I was cuddling the newborn, talking to my friend…" She sniffed again, but it didn't stop the flood of tears down her checks.

He grabbed his jeans off the floor and dug in his pocket for the handkerchief his mom had made him carry from an early age. He held it out to her and when she took it, their fingers touched, but the current that usually flowed beneath them was different now

"Thanks." As she wiped her eyes, Lachlan quickly pulled on his jeans, not wanting his nakedness to make her uncomfortable.

"Jack was playing quietly with some toy cars on the floor behind us and we didn't hear him wander off. As it was my friend's first child, their house wasn't fitted with all the usual child-safety devices yet, and somehow Jack let himself out the back door and into their yard." She took a long breath. "They had a fishpond."

Shit. He could see where this was heading and almost could not bear to listen. He wanted to put his hands over his ears but if *he* couldn't bear listening, how much worse must it be for her to be relating this nightmare to him? Instinctively, he reached out again and took her into his arms.

As he pulled her close, her tears already soaking into his shirt, he whispered, "It's okay. You don't have to tell me any more."

But she did.

She pulled her head back and looked up at him, her dark eyes wide with anguish. "I should have been watching him. If I'd been paying attention, I would have seen him leave the room and I would have followed him outside. He loved water… He was just being curious." Again, her face crumpled. "I don't know how long he was there, his little face under the ripples. Did he know what was happening? Did he wonder where I was? Why I wasn't helping him?"

Although she kept talking, her words blended together in her distress, becoming almost impossible to decipher. But he knew the gist. She blamed herself for the death of her child and he honestly couldn't comprehend how anyone could ever get over that.

He felt compelled to say, "It was a terrible accident. It's not your fault. You can't think like that."

But she countered quickly, "Tyler thinks it was. He can never forgive me, but what he doesn't see is that I understand that, because I can never forgive myself either. I don't blame him for finding solace in someone else."

Again, Lachlan wanted to tell her that Tyler was a fool, but deep down he understood where they were both coming from. He already didn't like the man, but he understood that grief caused people to do terrible things, to make unwarranted statements. There were no winners in this game of blame and he didn't think many marriages could recover from something like this.

But what would be the point in saying that? His words couldn't change the past.

Feeling utterly helpless, he held her tighter, wishing he could do something to take away her pain. Yet he knew that was impossible.

How could you ever get over the death of a child?

His mind went to Hamish and Hallie, and his chest tightened at the thought of anything ever happening to either of them. Due to Hamish's condition, he was more susceptible than most kids to illness. There'd been times when he'd been so sick Lachlan had feared the worst might come, but his son was a fighter and had always bounced back. As Hamish's cerebral palsy was mild, the doctors believed he had a good chance of living a reasonably long life.

But Lachlan had to wonder how he'd cope if the prognosis was different, if Hamish were taken from them. He wasn't honestly sure he'd be able to.

Perhaps having Hallie to live for would help, but Eliza didn't have that.

And the person who should have stood by her through all of it had turned against her. Somehow, despite everything, she'd managed to get out of bed day after day, to come into work, to paste a smile on her face when smiling was probably the last thing she felt like doing. Somehow, despite experiencing two of life's most traumatic things—the death of a child and the breakup of a marriage—she'd attempted to continue living. And that only made him admire and respect her more.

"I'm sorry." She suddenly pulled back. "You don't need me falling apart on you like this. I just…"

"Don't apologize," he said, perhaps more forcefully than needed, but the last thing he wanted was for Eliza to feel like opening up to him had been a burden. They may have known each other less than a month, but he already cared deeply for her. All those sleepless nights suddenly made a lot of sense and he wished she'd told him earlier, so he could have supported her. "Let me be here for you. If you ever want to talk about Jack, I'm happy to listen. I can't even imagine what such loss would feel like, but…"

Anger flashed across her face. She fisted the handkerchief into a tight ball in her hand. "I don't *want* to talk about it! Talking doesn't help, it only makes the ache worse. That's why I moved here—to start afresh— and the only hope I have of achieving that is if people don't see me as the woman with the dead baby. That's why I didn't tell you before, because I didn't want you to look at me the way you are now."

He opened his mouth to object, to tell her that he would never think of her in such terms, but then he felt the pity etched in his face and he knew she was right.

Eliza cast her gaze around the garage and thrust her finger at the old bicycle leaning against the wall off to one side. "Is that the bike your mother said I could have?"

"Yes."

"Tell her I'm sorry but I'm not feeling well and I had to go home," she said as she crossed the garage to retrieve it.

"Eliza, please. Don't go. I'm sorry, I…" he called after her, but she waved a hand at him.

As she unlocked the door, she turned back and Lachlan's heart squeezed with hope. "Can you promise me one thing?" she asked.

He nodded. "Of course. Anything." After the conversation they'd just had, she could tell him to run a marathon on hot coals and he'd give it his best darn shot.

"Can you not mention this conversation or…my… Jack to anyone? It's not that I want to forget him," she said, as if he would ever think anything of the sort, "but it's easier this way."

He took some comfort from her request as it made it sound as if she didn't plan on quitting and leaving Jewell Rock or anything like that. Perhaps he hadn't just lost the best employee he had. But no matter how much he loved and wanted the restaurant to succeed, it wasn't the restaurant worrying him now.

"I won't," he promised.

"Thank you," she said, before opening the door and disappearing with the bike.

Lachlan wanted to go after her, to make sure she was okay, but he didn't want to risk making things even worse than they already were. And if he didn't head back to the house soon, they'd probably send out a search party. The last thing he felt like doing was going inside and playing happy families.

Leaning back against a workbench, he dropped his head into his hands and sighed. Talk about complicated. When Eliza had leaped at the chance to enjoy some no-strings-attached sex, he should have wondered what the catch was.

After a few moments, he straightened his clothes and forced himself to go back to the house. His mom was just serving her famous marionberry pie for dessert when he returned, and all his family looked past him quizzically.

"What have you done with Eliza?" Blair asked, amusement in his voice.

"She wasn't feeling well," Lachlan said, crossing over to his seat and ruffling Hamish's hair as he said back down beside him. He had a sudden urge to hug both his kids. "She had a really bad migraine."

When Sophie raised her eyebrows, he elaborated, not meeting his sister's or anyone else's eye. "It came on really quick and she just needed to get home and lie down."

Lachlan knew he'd never been a good liar and this falsehood was probably written all over his face, but he was hardly going to tell his family the truth—whether there were kids present or not.

"But she left her stuff behind." Hallie stooped down

and picked up Eliza's purse from where it had been sitting on the floor by her feet.

Lachlan cursed silently. He guessed her cell and house key were in the bag and the fact she hadn't even thought about this proved just how upset she was. Although he didn't think she wanted him to go after her, part of him was glad for an excuse to do so. He pushed to a stand. "I'll take them to her," he said, reaching across the table to take the purse from Hallie.

Before anyone could say anything else, he was out of there. He grabbed his keys from the hallway table as he rushed out of the house and headed for his truck. Eliza hadn't made it far and he saw her on the road just past the entrance to the distillery. He slowed the vehicle and jumped out. "Eliza!"

She looked up and her eyes widened as she held up her hand to halt him. "Please, Lachlan, I can't. I just… don't want to. Not now."

Her cheeks were red and blotchy, her eyes bloodshot and her mascara was running down her cheeks, mingling with her tears. To him, she still looked gorgeous and it took all his willpower not to rush at her and hold her close. He longed to help, to offer her comfort.

Instead he took a tentative step toward her and held out her purse as if he were holding out a treat to a wild animal. "It's okay. We don't need to talk, but you left these behind."

Horror flashed across her face. "Oh, Lord, what must your family think of me?"

"Don't worry about them. I told them you had a migraine and I'm a pretty convincing liar."

"Thank you. I didn't even realize."

He nodded. "You're welcome." And then as much as

it pained him to do so, he turned and went back to the truck because that's what she wanted him to do.

His cell started ringing in his pocket as he parked back in front of his house. Could it be her? Hope lit in his heart as he yanked the phone out. If she needed him, he would turn right back around. But the hope was short-lived when he glanced down at the screen and saw Linda's name staring back at him.

Damn. He wanted to speak to his ex-wife even less than he wanted to go inside, but he knew that if he didn't answer, she'd keep calling until he did. Better to get it over with. With a resentful sigh, he slid his finger across the screen to answer and lifted the phone to his ear. "Linda."

"And a good afternoon to you, too, Lachlan."

"What can I do for you?" he asked, ignoring her obvious dig. He was in no mood to deal with her antics.

"I've got some good news!"

"Your aunt has had a miraculous recovery?" Although he hoped that was the case for the sake of this woman he'd never met, his stomach clenched at the thought that he would have to give Hallie back. It might have been crazy and exhausting trying to juggle her activities with Hamish's and the restaurant preparation, but they'd managed and he'd loved having both his kids with him, where he'd always wanted them to be.

"What?" She sounded as if she didn't know what he was talking about. "*Oh*, um…yes actually, she seems to be doing much better, but the really good news is I've scored an acting role in a new sitcom. I'm going to be famous!"

"Excuse me?" He shook his head, wondering if he'd heard right. Linda had always proclaimed she'd one day make it big as an actress but, as far as he knew, she'd never taken any steps toward this so-called dream.

She repeated herself. "Isn't it exciting?" When he didn't say anything, she added, "Oh, Lachlan, can't you just be happy for me for once?"

"I knew there was never an aunt!"

Her irritating giggle sounded through the phone line. "Actually there was. The role I'm playing is a woman looking after her dying aunt. Apparently I nailed the audition and they might actually make this woman's character bigger than it was originally going to be."

His body filled with loathing. He didn't give a damn about any of that. "What about our daughter? Where does she fit in this new life of yours?"

"Well, that's why I'm calling. To let you know I'm going to be busy for a while focusing on work, but once I've set myself up in an apartment, I guess she can come live with me in LA."

"You *guess*?" Lachlan's grip tightened on the phone. This day was going from bad to worse. He thought of Eliza, of the tragic conversation they'd just had and how she would do anything to get her child back. And here was his ex, so blasé about their children. "What about the fact her family and friends are here?"

"She'll make new friends and there are such things as airplanes, you know."

"Over my dead body will she be moving to LA," he growled. "If you go through with this, that's it. I'll file for full custody again and this time, I'll make sure I get it."

"Don't take that tone with me, Lachlan. I'm not your wife now. But," she added, "perhaps you have a point. I don't really think I'm cut out for motherhood. I need some time to find who I really am, so maybe it would be better for Hallie if she lives with you permanently and comes to visit me for holidays."

Not cut out for motherhood? His ex-wife was damn lucky they were having this conversation over the phone because he'd never been more angry in his life. Linda didn't give two hoots about what was best for Hallie, she was only thinking of herself. His heart ached for his daughter, who deserved more than a mother so willing to pass her on to someone else to look after. He wanted his daughter's mom to fight for her, to want her.

Hallie, *and* Hamish, warranted so much more than a mother who was more invested in her own life than she was in her children's. He couldn't remember what he'd ever seen in Linda. The less she had to do with his kids the better. Heaven forbid Hallie would grow up to be anything like her narcissistic mother.

"Good. It's settled, then," he said. "I'll have my lawyer draw up the papers and send them to you." Then before she could say another word, he disconnected the call.

He stared at the phone in his hand, feeling totally conflicted. A big part of him wanted to celebrate the fact that he'd soon have full custody of both his kids— although he wouldn't put it past Linda to make things difficult just for the sake of it—but there was another part at a loss.

What would he say to Hallie? She'd seemed nonplussed about Linda going off for a while, but how could he tell her that her mother wasn't coming back? Abandoning Hallie to look after a sick relative was one thing, but choosing to star in some stupid sitcom over her daughter was quite another.

And celebrating anything after the conversation he'd just had with Eliza didn't sit right.

Lachlan felt like he'd been put through the emotional wringer—in less than an hour, he'd gone from highly aroused to the depths of sadness, then raging anger and now desolation again. But as much as he cared for Eliza, his focus needed to be on Hallie and making sure she was protected in all this. He'd need to think carefully about what to tell her and how to tread from here on in.

With that thought, he let out a heavy sigh, shoved his cell back into his pocket and went inside to face the music.

Chapter Twelve

Eliza couldn't get back to her apartment fast enough. Her legs and lungs burned with the exertion and her eyes stung almost as bad. Not wanting to have another bike stolen, she took the bike into the building and then hurried into her apartment where she went straight into the bedroom and pulled out the photo of Jack. She flopped onto the bed, looked down at his perfect little face and then clutched it desperately to her chest.

Her whole body ached at the knowledge this was as close as she would ever get to holding him again.

After all the tears she'd sobbed, she didn't think there would be any left, but she knew that tears didn't have a limit. Only right now, she wasn't sure whether she was crying about her loss or the fact she'd done what she'd promised not to do and told Lachlan about her son.

Probably a combination of both.

Jewell Rock had felt like a safe haven when no one

knew her dark secret—even her apartment had begun to feel like a home—but now as she looked around, she felt like a stranger in her own place again and was terrified she'd blown everything.

It was one thing, Lachlan knowing about Tyler's betrayal. Lots of people could relate to a cheating ex; Lachlan himself even had experience in that department. But it was quite something else when they knew you'd lost a child.

She would never forget Jack—that would be impossible—but in New York, she'd almost come to wish that other people would. There, where everyone knew what had happened, her grief had become like a prison. It was the elephant in every conversation, the first thing people thought of when they thought of her. Her loss had consumed her, the sadness becoming who she was, suffocating.

In Jewell Rock she'd started to breathe again. She'd started to notice the beauty in her surroundings when, for eighteen months, she hadn't been able to see anything but sorrow. In Jewell Rock, she got to be someone else, even if only for a few hours a day, and allowing herself to be that other person was the only way she could cope.

But the one person whom she spent the most time with now knew about Jack.

She swallowed as her hand subconsciously went to her pocket, closing around the handkerchief Lachlan had given her when she'd become teary, and recalled the horror on his face when she'd told him. Horror that quickly turned to sympathy.

She drew the small square of cotton from her pocket and stared down at it. Crisp and white when he'd given it to her, it was now streaked with black lines from her mascara. She shuddered to think about what her face looked like now. Would Lachlan ever find her attractive again after seeing her snot-cry like that?

He'd been so kind, so gentle in his endeavors to comfort her, but it wasn't comfort she wanted from his hands. She wanted the release, distraction and oblivion that came when his lips touched hers.

Eliza drew the handkerchief up to her nose, hoping to smell him on it, but all she could smell was her own heartache and anger. Shame and mortification washed over her when she thought of how she'd treated him. Rejecting his offer to talk, pushing him away, running as fast as she could and leaving him to explain her sudden departure to his family. Hopefully they'd bought his excuse that she had a migraine, but she'd put him in a terrible position and the thought of facing him tomorrow made her nauseous.

But she also couldn't keep running from her problems forever.

Besides, how could she run out on Lachlan so close to the opening of the restaurant?

As scary as the prospect was, she needed to face him again and to apologize for today's behavior. It was probably a pipe dream but she hoped they could at least try to go back to the easy way things were between them. She didn't want to give up sleeping with him but even more important, she didn't want to lose her new job. Work had given her purpose again, a reason to get out of bed every morning.

With a deep sigh, she put Jack's photo back on the bedside table and twisted the handkerchief between her fingers. She should wash it and give it back to him.

She also recognized that if she wanted to recover from today, she needed to reach out. To apologize for her meltdown this afternoon and for rushing out like that. Her Grammy always said you shouldn't let the sun go down on an argument and although this wasn't an argument as such, she wouldn't be able to attempt sleep if she didn't at least try to make amends.

With that thought, she reached for her purse, which she'd dumped on the bed, and retrieved her cell. Then, her fingers shaking a little, she typed out a quick message to Lachlan.

I'm sorry I freaked out today. Thanks for covering for me. I'll pop in to see your mother tomorrow and say thank you. xx

Just before she pressed Send, she deleted the two kisses, horrified that she'd almost sent them to her boss. Granted, they'd become a little more than chef and hostess but kisses in messages were definitely *not* part of their arrangement. And she didn't want to muddy the waters.

Perhaps she should send Nora some flowers, she thought, as she waited for a reply. She felt as if she should do something to make up for her behavior today, but maybe flowers were a little over-the-top. They might make more of a big deal about this than she wanted it to be. *And* she'd already given Nora chocolates. Feeling at a loss, she glanced again at the framed photo of Jack.

What do you think I should do, little man?

And then the most ridiculous idea entered her head—so ridiculous she almost believed it had come from her little boy. Children believed anything was possible.

I should make Nora cookies!

She let out a little laugh of disbelief. *Her*, cook for someone with the expertise of Nora McKinnel? A few cooking lessons did not make her an expert and the idea that she could cook anything on her own was farcical. All the same, the idea refused to be silenced and Eliza found herself pushing off the bed and heading into the kitchen, wondering what would be the worst that could happen. She'd be very careful, but if she *did* set the kitchen on fire…well, Annabel would probably be home soon and had the skills to save them all.

And if the cookies were a disaster, no one would ever have to know that she'd attempted them, but how many people did she know who found comfort in baking? Perhaps she could find some, too.

Decision made, she flung open her food cupboard and immediately came across a problem. Like Mother Hubbard, her cupboard was bare, but this only deterred her for a few moments.

You're not going to give up that easily, are you?

There was a supermarket down the road and, thanks to Nora, she had a new bike to take her there. The prospect of heading out now—when her head hurt and her whole body ached from sobbing—had her heart filling once again with despair, but a little voice told her she needed to be brave. She needed to step out of her comfort zone and try new things, or she would be the opposite of brave and flounder.

The next morning Eliza arrived at the restaurant before anyone else and, carrying her purse under one arm and a plastic container in the other, let herself inside with the key Lachlan had entrusted her with. Although they were still only training staff and preparing for their grand opening, she felt as if she'd been here a lot longer than a few weeks. She'd spent as much—if not more—time in this beautifully designed space than she had in her apartment and many of the happy memories she was starting to collect had taken place here.

She only hoped they would continue.

With that thought, she went around, pulling back blinds and turning on lights, rousing the coffee machine to life and trying to ignore the nerves that fluttered in her stomach at the knowledge Lachlan would be here any moment.

In the middle of her baking efforts yesterday afternoon, he'd sent her a short response to her message: It's all good. See you tomorrow.

But until they were face-to-face and acting normal again, she wouldn't be able to completely relax.

Trying to distract herself, she peeled back the lid on the container of cookies and took a sniff before popping them in a safe spot behind the bar. Even though she'd had breakfast not long ago, her mouth watered at the sugary aroma that teased her nostrils. Triple chocolate chip cookies. If her kitchen hadn't looked like a disaster zone after her efforts, she might not be able to believe that she'd actually succeeded in making them. Without any assistance.

She'd followed the recipe she found on the internet to a T and had set up a chair in front of the oven and watched as the cookies had been baking, terrified she'd leave them too long and burn the lot.

The sound of the front door opening jolted her thoughts and she looked up to see Lachlan coming in.

"Coffee. I need it now." He grunted as he stalked toward her and came around the bar to stand alongside her.

She blinked, unsure what to make of his brusque tone, and then registered how terrible he looked. Well,

as terrible as it was possible for one of the best-looking
guys she'd ever laid eyes on to look. His hair was way
more disheveled than usual, dark circles hung beneath
his eyes and there was a shadow along his jaw as if he
hadn't had the time or inclination to shave that morning. Usually she didn't mind a little sexy stubble on
a man but his whole demeanor erased such an effect.

His ashen appearance couldn't possibly be because of
what had happened between them yesterday. Could it?

"I'll make you some," she said and immediately set
to work to do exactly that. He was much better at making coffee than she was but in the state he was in, she
guessed he wouldn't be fussy.

"Thanks." He lifted a hand to his mouth to try to
cover over a yawn. Then he said, "Are you okay? After
yesterday?"

She pursed her lips and nodded, still not wanting to
talk about Jack but comforted by the fact he didn't seem
to be angry at her.

He smiled sadly, then leaned back against the bar. Almost immediately, he frowned and stepped forward. Eliza
realized the container of cookies on the shelf beneath the
bar hadn't quite been pushed in far enough and he'd felt it.

"What are these?" he asked as he peered beneath the
counter and picked up the box.

Her heart did a ridiculous flip as she watched him
peel back the lid. It felt as if he were doing so in slow
motion. *Oh, Lord.* What had she been thinking, bringing them in here? They might have tasted okay to her
but maybe that had been wishful thinking. Her fingers
trembled around the metal jug as she said, "I had a bi-
zarre urge to bake yesterday afternoon."

"*You* cooked these?"

She nodded. And then before she could snatch them

away from him, he plucked one out and took a bite. Every part of her froze as she waited for his verdict. But instead of saying anything, he took another bite and then another, devouring the cookie entirely.

"Man, these are excellent," he said finally, grabbing another. "And I really needed that sugar boost."

"You really like them?" she asked, entirely distracted from her task of making coffee.

"I do," he said, his gorgeous lips twisting up at the edges. "I knew you could cook if only you believed in yourself. But if these are for anything special, then you'd better take them off me before I ingest the lot of them."

She shook her head. "They're all yours." It seemed silly now to say she'd made them for his mom to apologize for her weird behavior yesterday—she didn't want to bring all that up again—but she was glad he appeared to be enjoying them. She doubted he'd eat them all, but if he did, she'd think of something else to give his mother.

"In that case." He took another. "I'm comfort eating."

She almost laughed, having never heard the phrase "comfort eating" come from a man before, but he didn't appear to be in a laughing mood.

"Why?" she asked instead. "What's the problem?" Again, her heart hitched a little as she silently prayed it wasn't her. He'd been nice about the cookies but after yesterday, did her presence here now make him uncomfortable? She didn't want to leave but perhaps he'd prefer her to.

"Kid trouble." He let out a deep sigh. "Between Hallie and Hamish, I think I got maybe two hours of sleep max."

"Oh, no. Are they sick?" Both of them had seemed

happy and in good health yesterday—well, as in good health as Hamish ever was with his condition —but she remembered clearly how a child could go from rosy cheeked to feverish in a matter of hours.

Lachlan deliberated a moment as if contemplating how much to share, but when she handed him his coffee, he wrapped his fingers around it and said, "Thanks. Hallie was upset because I gave her some bad news last night. Linda called and told me she's not coming back and that she thinks it would be better if Hallie lives full-time with me now."

"Linda's staying with the sick aunt indefinitely?"

"There was no sick aunt," he said and then went on to inform her that Linda's real purpose for heading to LA was to audition for acting roles.

Eliza felt her eyes boggle as he told her the whole story. She could not imagine a woman so easily deserting her children, but then again, Linda had done it once before with Hamish. Anger burned within her at the thought.

"Hallie had such a fabulous day yesterday, and I thought it was better to tell her the truth and get it over with. I tried to make it sound like her mother loved and wanted her to move to LA but believed that Hallie would be happier staying here with me and Hamish, but…" He sighed and ran a hand through his hair, obviously distressed. "She's a smart kid and she saw right through my attempt to soften the blow. For all she acts tough, she was heartbroken. She bawled her little eyes out into my chest until she finally fell asleep, still shuddering."

"Oh, the poor sweet girl." Eliza tried to swallow the lump in her throat. The last thing Lachlan needed was another crying female on his hands, but her heart broke for Hallie.

He nodded and took a sip of his coffee. "Then I'd just climbed into bed myself when Hamish woke up with really bad muscle spasms."

Eliza thought of the little boy who had physical disabilities but always seemed so chirpy and optimistic. She was relieved to hear that she was not responsible for Lachlan's lack of sleep but deeply saddened by his explanation. "Does he get them a lot?"

"We're really lucky in that he doesn't have as many debilitating symptoms as some CP kids do, but he goes through patches where the pain is pretty bad and sleep is always the first thing to be affected."

"What can you do for him?"

"I do a little bit of massage, offer him pain relief, sit with him and make stupid dad jokes to try to distract him…" His voice trailed off as if she wasn't the only one trying not to cry.

"It must be heart wrenching watching him go through that."

"It kills me," Lachlan said simply. No wonder he looked like he'd been hit by a bus.

She didn't know what to say. What could she say? He spoke again before she had to.

"And it makes me question all of this." He made a sweeping gesture with his arm, indicating the restaurant.

She frowned. "What do you mean?"

He laughed, but it wasn't an amused kind of chuckle. "How the hell do I think I can cope opening a restaurant, *running* a restaurant and being the father I need to be at the same time? I must have been delusional!"

"No. You're not." Without thinking, she reached out

to touch his arm. His skin was warm beneath her fingers and it was on the tip of her tongue to offer to help with the kids, but she reminded herself he had family for that. "And you are not on your own doing any of those things. Don't worry about the restaurant—we've got it covered, it's going to be awesome—and Hallie and Hamish are going to be so proud of their dad."

He glanced down at her hand on his arm and then looked back up into her gaze. It was wrong to feel such attraction during such a conversation, but she couldn't ignore the way her insides bubbled. And the way his pupils dilated told her he felt it, too.

Her tongue darted out to try to moisten her suddenly parched lips, but it wasn't her own mouth she craved. Almost of its own accord, her hand traveled up his arm, across his broad shoulder to rest at the back of his neck.

She might not be able to fix his kid and ex-wife problems, but she could attempt to take his mind off them for a few moments, to give him some of the relief his touch had given her. And with this goal in mind, she stepped up close, pulled his head toward her and stretched up to kiss him.

Within seconds, Lachlan's hands landed on her back, sliding upward and into her hair as he deepened their kiss. Her body melted as her breasts pressed against his hard chest and his knee slid between her legs. Her heart rate went berserk and all thoughts of propriety left her head as she reached between them for her prize.

Lachlan groaned as her hand slid into his trousers and closed around his hot, getting-harder-by-the-second penis. Then he tore his mouth from hers and muttered, "Are you sure you want this?"

"Uh-huh." She nodded, knowing he was referring to yesterday. "Do you?"

"Stupid question. Come on, we don't have long." Grabbing her hand, he led her over to the door, which he quickly locked, before all but dragging her into the kitchen and kicking that door closed behind them.

As it shut, they came together like magnets, kissing and touching as if it were an Olympic race and they were going for gold. The knowledge that their staff would be arriving any minute meant they didn't have long for fondling and caressing. But that didn't matter. The moment Eliza had touched his arm, the moment he'd looked hungrily into her eyes, she'd been ready for this.

Her body mourned the loss of his touch as he retrieved a condom from his wallet, undid his belt buckle, freed and sheathed himself in a matter of seconds. Then he lifted her up against one of the counters, pushing her skirt up around her hips as he did so. No time to take off her panties, he pushed that scrap of lace aside as well, and two seconds later, he was inside her.

She cried out in bliss as he thrust hard and she wrapped her legs around his waist, urging him deeper. The pleasure that ripped through her was so intense she had to hold on tight to his shoulders to anchor herself. His orgasm followed quickly on the heels of hers and they held each other, their foreheads pressed together as they waited for their heart rates to return to something like normal.

He was still inside her when they heard knocking on the front door. She snapped her head back and looked into his eyes, horrified that her fellow colleagues might guess what they'd been up to. But when she saw his smile and the color once again in his cheeks, she thought such a discovery was worth it.

"You are amazing," he said, then claimed her lips in

another quick kiss before drawing out of her. "I need to go to the bathroom. Do you think you could unlock the door and let in the troops?"

"Sure." She smiled as he turned away and then she slid off the counter and straightened her skirt and panties. As she walked out of the kitchen, she pulled her hair out of its now-messy ponytail and redid it with her fingers.

"Sorry," she said to the group gathered, faking a frown. "The lock must be playing up. But come on in. Ready for a big day?"

A couple of the female staff looked at her quizzically as if they didn't quite believe her faulty-lock excuse, but she turned away and set off to begin the working day. They still had much to prepare for the grand opening next week.

Chapter Thirteen

"Good morning," Nora said as Lachlan wandered into the kitchen. "Can I pour you some coffee?"

"Yes, please." He summoned a smile for her as he sat at the table and then ran a hand through his still-wet hair. He'd been up at the crack of dawn to have a shower in peace before the kids woke up. "Have you heard anything from Hallie or Hamish yet?"

She shook her head. "Not a murmur, but I've just popped some blueberry muffins in the oven for their breakfast."

"Thanks," he managed, still too tired for too many words but grateful for all his mom's help where his children were concerned. She'd been especially good with Hallie, making sure they did girlie things together to try to distract her from Linda's absence.

"So, one week until the big day!" Nora said brightly as she placed a mug of steaming caffeine in front of him. "Excited much?"

He made some sort of grunt in response and then took a big gulp of coffee. This was his *dream*. Since he'd first decided to become a chef, he'd harbored the secret (and then not-so-secret) fantasy of opening his own restaurant. The fact that he was also helping expand the family business should have made it even more exciting, but with everything else going on in his head right now, he just couldn't drum up the enthusiasm he'd once felt.

Or maybe he was just nervous, anxious that everything would go right on the opening night. Eliza and Sophie had been working hard together to drum up some media attention and the pressure was on to impress those who'd promised to turn up next Friday night.

"Did you hear Annabel's bringing her new beau?" Nora asked, seemingly oblivious to his disenchantment or putting his almost-monosyllabic responses down to him still being half-asleep. She continued without waiting for him to reply, "I can't wait to meet him. Has she told you anything about him? She's been very cagey with me. I'm sure Sophie knows more than she's letting on as well, but you know how vault-like those two are with each other's secrets."

She finally paused and looked at him expectantly. "Well?"

He shrugged. "Well, what?"

"I was asking you about Annabel and her new man."

"Sorry. If anyone has said anything—and I don't think they have—it's gone in one ear and out the other. Between the kids and the restaurant—" *and my sneaky sessions with Eliza*, he added silently "—I don't have room in my head to focus on anything else right now."

"Hmm." Nora frowned and then leaned back against the counter. She stared at him long and hard, making him squirm a little. "I'm very proud of all you've done so far with the restaurant but I am worried that you're overworking yourself what with the restaurant and the kids, and I don't want you to burn out. That wouldn't be good for anyone, especially those gorgeous grandchildren of mine."

"I'm fine, Mom. Things will calm down in a few months when we've been open for a bit. Don't stress."

"It's not my stress I'm worried about. Look," she said, with a tone that said she meant business, "I was thinking, why don't I look after the twins tonight and maybe you and Eliza could go out and get dinner together, have someone else cook for you for a change? And as it's Saturday, there's no reason to rush up in the morning, so you can stay out as late as you like! You both deserve a last hurrah before the restaurant opens."

His mom grinned from ear to ear as if immensely pleased with herself for presenting this offer, but getting a babysitter wasn't the issue. He had plenty of family always ready and willing to help with the kids if asked, but he and Eliza simply didn't have the kind of arrangement where dinner was involved.

In theory, things had been good since that awful afternoon in the garage. The next morning, they'd had mind-blowing sex in the restaurant kitchen and had been at it almost every day since, finding moments before the staff arrived or after they'd left for the day.

But he missed hanging out with her like they used to do when he'd been giving her cooking lessons late at night. Most nights, he ended up with Hallie in bed with him and as much as he adored his daughter, she was like an octopus, her arms and legs flying all over the place while he was trying to dodge them. On the rare occasions he found himself alone, he fantasized about what it would be like to have a woman in bed with him instead.

But not just any woman.

Still with Hallie's nighttime neediness, he couldn't risk sneaking out of the house and having her wake up to find him gone. He didn't begrudge his daughter his time and attention, but he missed talking and laughing with Eliza.

During the day while they worked, moments for conversation were few and far between and there was always another person within earshot. At night, instead of being with Eliza where he longed to be, he lay in bed, thinking about her and flicking through the books on grief he'd borrowed from the local library. He knew he was a fool to get involved with a woman who had shut off her heart to anything more than sex but he couldn't help himself.

"Don't you think asking my employees out for dinner is overstepping the line?" Lachlan said.

His mom blinked, looking genuinely confused. "Well, I…I thought Eliza had become a little more than an employee to you. She came to lunch with us and—"

"*You* invited her to lunch," he interrupted, not wanting to be reminded about that afternoon. Since then, things had changed between them. And he didn't think it was because of him like Eliza had predicted. Although his heart hurt every time he thought about what she'd lost, he'd done his best not to treat Eliza any differently, but she'd retreated again into herself. Only when they were in the throes of passion did he really feel as if he had any chance of getting close to her.

"Yes, but we all saw the way you two were with each other when you were here. It was clear to all of us you were attracted to each other. And then you went out to get the bike together and—"

Again Lachlan interrupted but didn't meet his mom's gaze as he said, "There's nothing between Eliza and I."

"Really?" Nora raised an eyebrow. She'd always had the annoying knack of being able to read him and his siblings like picture books.

And he'd never been able to lie to her face.

He sighed. "Okay, you're right. I do like her. How could I not? And, I admit, there have been a few moments, but..." He paused, considering how much to tell her. "She's not ready for a romantic relationship right now. She and her husband have only recently separated and she's still hurting from his betrayal."

"Ah..." His mom nodded. "So that's it."

Now it was his turn to look confused. "What's what?"

"The first time I saw her, I thought there was something troubling her. She has a lost look in her eyes and I thought maybe she was grieving the death of somebody close."

A chill prickled his skin as once again he considered telling her about Jack. He longed to ask her opinion about whether she thought Eliza could ever recover from losing her son. Although Nora had never lost a child herself, she was a mother and could probably put herself in such a position to give him advice. She'd also lost her husband only recently so she understood grief. The question was on the tip of his tongue, but he swallowed it, not wanting to break Eliza's confidence.

He'd have to make do with the books.

"Don't think so," he said, staring into his coffee so again he didn't have to look her in the eye. "Her mom's dead but she died a long time ago."

"But she's grieving the loss of her husband. Someone doesn't actually have to die for you to go through the stages of grief." She smiled encouragingly at him. "Give her time, honey. And be patient. I've got a good feeling about this one."

He had to laugh, because she said "this one," like Eliza was one in a long line of women he'd been interested in, when the truth was she was the first. He hadn't been a complete monk and had enjoyed a few flings over the years, but no one had ever occupied his headspace the way Eliza did.

She was special. And she was broken.

"Anyway," he said, pushed back his chair indicating this conversation was over and tried to shake her from his thoughts, "I don't have time for a relationship right now. The kids need me."

And as if to prove his point, Hallie wandered into the kitchen at that moment. Her hair was fuzzy from sleep and she had her favorite teddy bear in a headlock. Since his conversation with her about Linda, she'd started carrying the bear everywhere, where previously she only snuggled it at nighttime.

"Hey, glitter-pie," he said, forcing chirpiness into his voice as he went across and scooped her up into his arms. "How's my favorite girl this morning?"

She buried her head into his chest and he heard a muffled, "Hungry."

"That's good because Grandma's made you some delicious blueberry muffins."

"I want cereal," she demanded.

Usually Lachlan would insist she ate something healthy for breakfast, but today he didn't have the energy to object to the sugary cereal she requested and besides, he'd do practically anything to see his little girl smile again. "Okay, just this once I don't think Uncle Blair will mind if we raid his secret cereal stash."

She looked up into his eyes and almost smiled. "Thanks, Daddy."

His heart leaping at these two words, he lowered her onto a chair and set about getting her what she wanted.

His mom again raised her eyebrows from where she stood against the counter. "Don't start," he said, under his breath. "She's allowed to eat sugar occasionally."

"I agree. I wasn't thinking about Hallie's breakfast and I promise this is the last thing I'll say on this, but whether Eliza will go out to dinner with you or not, maybe you should call some friends and take a night off. Lord knows I've had to tell Callum this before, but all work and no play…"

"D-a-ad!" Hamish's voice carried down the corridor from his bedroom, saving Lachlan from hearing the rest of his mom's lecture. He looked at the door.

"I'll get Hallie's cereal," Nora said, her tone resigned. "You go get our boy."

"D-a-ad!" Hamish called again just as Lachlan got to his bedroom door. Once again, he summoned a smile for the benefit of his son and silently told himself to stop being so pathetic.

"Hey, champ. How are you feeling this morning?"

Hamish screwed up his face and stretched his arms over my head. "A little sore, but it's not too bad. Can I smell Grandma's blueberry muffins?"

"You sure can. Let's get you out of bed so you can have some." He reached for Hamish's crutches. "Do you need to go to the bathroom before breakfast?"

"Not yet," Hamish said. "My tummy is more loud than my bladder right now."

Lachlan laughed as he helped his son to stand.

Hamish never failed to help him put things in perspective. If anyone had any reason to grumble about the lot they were given in life, it was his son, but Hamish rarely complained or dwelled on his disabilities.

"Are you going to work today?" Hamish asked as they slowly made their way toward the kitchen.

"No," Lachlan said, making the decision at that moment. "I'm going to spend every minute with you and Hallie."

After weeks and weeks of experimentation, he was as happy with the menu as he was ever going to be—even his kitchen staff could cook it almost as well as he could—so there wasn't any need to go into work today.

"Really?"

"Really," Lachlan said, feeling guilty that Hamish sounded surprised by this. He thought he'd been doing a good job of spending time with his kids and working, but perhaps not. "What say we take a picnic to the river and maybe even go for a swim?"

"Yippee." Hamish punched the air in excitement. "Can we take our bikes?"

"Hallie! Slow down," Lachlan called as the three of them peddled along the path by the Deschutes River. It was a beautiful day and the riverbanks were busy with locals riding bikes and walking dogs and tourists taking photo after photo of the gorgeous scenery, which Lachlan had to admit he took for granted, having grown up on the river.

"Why can't *you* hurry up?" Hallie shot back and Lachlan chanced a glance sideways at Hamish, who was doing his best, peddling hard on his adaptive bike. Usually Hallie was very caring and considerate of her brother, but occasionally she got frustrated at him not being able to do everything as quickly or efficiently as she could. Since Lachlan had told her about Linda, these episodes of frustration seemed to be coming more frequently.

"Sorry." Hamish's shoulders slumped and he stopped peddling altogether.

"You're doing great," Lachlan said, "but I'm ready for a break. Hallie," he called ahead again, "let's stop for lunch."

"O-kay." She reluctantly turned around and came back to join them.

"How about under that big tree over there?" Lachlan pointed to a spot not far from the playground.

The three of them peddled over and once their bikes were secure, Lachlan pulled the picnic blanket out of his backpack and started to unload the feast.

"Hallie, can you pour everyone a drink of juice?" he asked, handing her the carton and pointing to the plastic cups he'd just unloaded.

She made a noise of annoyance with her tongue but did as she was told.

"Thank you, Hallie," Lachlan said when the drinks were poured and he'd laid the containers of food down on the rug between them. "Now, eat up."

When the kids filled their plates and started to eat, Lachlan became aware of the silence between them. Usually when the three of them were together, Hallie chattered endlessly, and he and Hamish were hard pressed to get a word in, but today she barely said anything.

"How're things at school?" he asked, trying to draw her out of her shell.

She shrugged one shoulder. "Okay."

He tried a different tack. "Are you looking forward to

the summer break?" Hallie was booked into a dance and drama camp and Hamish would also attend a summer camp to enable Lachlan to continue to work. He pushed aside the smidgen of guilt that sneaked into his heart at this, but he knew the kids would have a ball, much more fun than if they were stuck at home or the restaurant with him.

"Maybe."

Feeling defeated, Lachlan looked to his son. "What about you? Ready for vacation?"

But rather than answering the question, Hamish pointed his finger toward the river and shrieked, "Hey. Isn't that 'liza?"

Hallie spun around and her face lit up for the first time that day. Before Lachlan could stop her, she'd scrambled to her feet and was racing off toward the riverbank in the direction of a woman who was, if not Eliza, then her doppelgänger. A tingle pulsed beneath his rib cage as he registered her sitting on the grass, her knees against her chest and her arms wrapped around them as she looked longingly into the distance.

He hadn't expected to see her today and his body reacted predictably at the sight of Eliza in denim cutoff shorts that highlighted her tanned, shapely legs, a pink fitted T-shirt and a cap that held her gorgeous brown hair captive, but the jolt of attraction waned as he followed her gaze to the playground. The playground full of toddlers with their smiley parents helping them navigate equipment they weren't quite ready for.

Did any of those children look like Jack?

He didn't know, because Eliza hadn't told him anything else about her son. He'd tried to bring him up a couple of times when they were alone, but they were alone so infrequently and when they were, she usually brushed him off, using sex to distract him.

The sex was off the charts—better than any sex he'd ever had, which is why he was so easily distracted—but you didn't need a psychology degree to know she was using it to try to ease her pain. He was happy to help her in any way he could, but all the books he'd read about grief indicated that this was an avoidance tactic and that what people who suffered such a tragic loss really needed was to talk about it. To talk about the person who had passed.

He wondered if she'd ever had counseling or if she talked about Jack back in New York. He hoped so. The books encouraged friends of the bereaved to speak about their dead loved one, but he didn't even know if Eliza classified him as a friend.

And that hurt, because he wanted to be her friend.

"Are you coming to see 'liza?" Hamish asked, and Lachlan realized that while he'd been pontificating on grief, his son had pulled himself up with his crutches. Hamish started off after Hallie before Lachlan had a chance to reply.

He stood, thinking that he'd better rescue Eliza from his excitable offspring. They didn't know about Jack so they were liable to say something to upset her. As he thought this, he suddenly realized that he was doing exactly what she said people did—second-guessing her feelings. But he'd seen the sad expression on her face as she'd watched the kids playing and he couldn't help wanting to protect her.

As he got closer, Eliza looked up and waved. Her lips curved into one of her punch-him-in-the-chest smiles. Relief mixed with joy that she seemed happy to see him and his kids.

Welcome to Streatham Library
Tel: 020 7926 6768
www.lambeth.gov.uk/libraries

Borrowed Items 23/08/2018 10:28
XXXX4988

Item Title	Due Date
* kiss, a dance a diamond	13/09/2018
* single dad's family recipe	13/09/2018

* Indicates items borrowed today
Thankyou for using self service
Download ebooks
audiobooks:lambeth.oneclickdigital.eu
Download magazines:
www.rbdigital.com/lambeth

He tried for a casual smile as he slowed in front of her. "Fancy meeting you here," he said.

She laughed. "It's such a beautiful day, I thought I should get outside and make the most of it. I still feel like I'm walking through a postcard when I come down here. Jewell Rock really is pretty, as pretty as any place I've ever been."

Not as pretty as you. But he managed not to voice this thought. "It really is," he said instead, "but I have to admit, growing up here kinda makes you take it for granted."

"I can understand that. Did you and your brothers and sisters spend a lot of time down here?"

He nodded. "Mom and Dad used to send us off in the morning with a packed lunch and we'd spend the day climbing the trees and swimming here. It wasn't as touristy back then and the playground was much more basic."

"Sounds blissful," she said.

"D-dad." Hamish tugged his hand. "Can we get an ice cream?"

"Yes. *Please!*" Hallie jumped up and down, her moodiness from earlier seemingly forgotten now that she had her hand in Eliza's. Eliza chuckled and smiled down at her.

The sight of them together made his heart squeeze— a little girl who desperately wanted a mother who cared, a woman who had lost her child and her way.

"Would you like to get an ice cream with us?" he asked Eliza.

"Ooh, yes, please do," Hallie said, another little jiggle accompanying her words.

Lachlan predicted Eliza would say no, offer some ex- cuse because hanging out with his family was definitely outside of their arrangement, so he almost couldn't believe his ears when she said yes. Maybe she simply didn't want to disappoint his kids, but whatever the reason, he was happy for the chance to spend some time with her outside the restaurant and with their clothes *on*.

"Right this way, then," he said.

The ice-cream truck was parked in the lot and close enough that he could see the picnic blanket and their bikes, so they walked over without packing up.

Hamish went for his usual choice of triple chocolate and peanut butter, but Hallie deliberated for what felt like hours, until Eliza asked for a caramel ice cream and Hallie decided she'd have the same. Lachlan didn't get anything, explaining that he usually had to finish one if not both of the kids' cones, and then the four of them walked back to the picnic blanket and sat down to eat.

It was surprising Hallie managed to eat hers at all because she spoke incessantly, which at least meant there were no awkward pauses in conversation.

Eliza listened earnestly as she licked her ice cream and Lachlan had to admit he liked watching her do so. Occasionally she'd ask Hamish a question, but before long, Hallie always took control of the discussion again. Lachlan tried to contribute as well, but he kept trying to work out if Eliza was really enjoying hanging out with them or biding time until she could retreat.

"Can you braid?" Hallie asked Eliza as she handed Lachlan her half-eaten cone.

Eliza blinked. "You mean braid hair?"

Hallie nodded excitedly. "Yes. Stacey at school always has pretty braids and Daddy only ever does bunches for me. Can you braid my hair now?"

Holding his daughter's ice cream, Lachlan was about

to tell Hallie to leave Eliza alone, but Eliza popped the last bit of her cone in her mouth and nodded.

"Sure I can," she said, repositioning herself onto her knees and patting the space in front of her. "Come, sit here."

Hallie didn't need to be asked twice and as Eliza did his daughter's hair, Lachlan and Hamish ate the rest of the ice creams and watched.

"You make that look easy," he said with a chuckle when she'd finished.

She shrugged. "I find doing hair quite therapeutic. Happy to do it whenever you want me to, Hallie."

"Thank you." Hallie gave Eliza a big hug, then looked to Lachlan. "Can I go play now, Daddy?"

"Sure, but wait for your brother," he said, reaching across for Hamish's crutches. Not only did Hallie wait, but she gave her brother her hand to help him up and then kept close to him as they headed off to conquer the playground together. It warmed his heart to see her happy and caring again.

"She sure can talk, can't she?" Eliza said with a chuckle.

"That's an understatement," he replied. "But actually she's been uncharacteristically quiet since I told her about Linda. I'd hoped bringing her out today would help her out of her shell again."

"And it looks like it has."

He nodded, choosing not to tell Eliza that this hadn't been the case until she'd shown up. He didn't want to put that kind of pressure on her but he couldn't help noticing how his little girl adored his employee. And he couldn't blame her—Eliza was easy to like and actually listened when Hallie talked, unlike her own mother.

Perhaps Eliza was simply a good actress but she genuinely seemed to be enjoying hanging out with them.

He couldn't help imagining how different their lives could be if Hallie and Hamish had a mother like Eliza instead.

But the moment that thought entered his head, he berated himself for it. Was that why he liked her so much? Because secretly he was looking for a substitute mother for his children? He didn't *think* that was the case, but even so, fantasies like that were asking for trouble because, even before she'd told him about Jack, Eliza had made her position crystal clear.

"She's really good with Hamish, too, isn't she?"

Eliza's observation broke Lachlan's thoughts and he followed her gaze to see Hallie staying close to her brother as he climbed one of the structures. "Most of the time, yeah."

"He's pretty amazing, though," she continued. "He doesn't seem to let his condition keep him back. You should be really proud of your kids."

"I am."

They spent a few more minutes talking easily about Hallie and Hamish and as they chatted, Eliza planted her hands on the blanket and leaned back as if she was settling in for the long haul. Not wanting to monopolize the conversation with his kids, he asked after her grandmother and her father, whom she'd spoken a little about during their stolen moments together.

Her eyes lit up when talking about her grandmother in a way he'd only ever seen them do on rare occasions. "Grammy's such a character," she said and he laughed as she told him about her dating escapades.

And then a little boy toddled toward them, chasing a bright blue plastic ball that had got away from him and

Eliza's relaxed expression vanished as the ball rolled onto the blanket. As the toddler got closer, she picked up the ball and held it out to him.

His chubby little fingers closed around it just as his dad arrived beside them. "Sorry," he said, slightly breathless. "This little guy has suddenly got fast. Thanks."

Eliza seemed lost for words, so Lachlan smiled back and said, "You're welcome. Have a great day."

"Thanks." As the man scooped up the kid and jogged away again, Lachlan looked back to Eliza. She'd gone pale, as if she'd seen a ghost.

"Did Jack liking playing with balls?" he asked. His heart pounded in his chest as he did so but he believed here in the park with his kids only a short distance away, she couldn't change the subject in the manner she usually did.

Seconds ticked by. Eliza's mouth opened as if she were about to open up to him, but then she glanced at her watch and sprang to her feet. "I've just remembered something I have to do. Thanks for the ice cream. Say goodbye to Hallie and Hamish for me."

And then she turned and fled in the opposite direction of the playground. As Lachlan watched her run, he cursed under his breath and punched his fist into the ground. He'd pushed her too far. Hadn't she told him she didn't want to talk about her son? Why couldn't he just respect those boundaries and be patient like his mom had advised him?

Chapter Fourteen

"Oh, my goodness! What are you guys doing here?" Eliza shrieked in a most unprofessional manner as she looked up and saw her dad and Grammy Louise coming through the restaurant entrance. She almost tripped over her feet in her rush to get to them and she didn't know who to embrace first. So she threw her arms around both of them and pulled them into a group hug.

"Careful, dear, you'll ruin my hair," Grammy said.

She laughed and let them go to take a good, hard look at them. It was only a month since she'd last seen them but it felt like years. "Your hair looks fabulous, Grammy. And you look great, too, Dad. Nice shirt." She reached a finger out to touch it and found herself grinning uncontrollably. "I've missed you guys."

"We've missed you, too, sugar," her dad replied.

Grammy grabbed hold of Eliza's hands. "You're looking gorgeous, darling. This mountain air obviously agrees with you."

"Thanks," she said, thinking that it wasn't the mountains that had put the glow in her cheeks. "I still can't believe you're both here." Tears sprang to her eyes as the emotion of seeing them again got to her.

Her father reached out and brushed his thumb over her cheek. "You didn't think we'd miss this, did you?" he asked, glancing around at the rapidly filling restaurant.

There was a local band playing in the corner and the drinks were already flowing as her waitstaff seated and welcomed the patrons. She wanted this night to be perfect for Lachlan. At that thought, her heart squeezed and she asked her father, "Are you here in a professional or personal capacity?"

"Can't I be both?" he joked.

As more people came in the door behind them, Eliza decided she didn't have time to worry about the prospect of him writing a bad review. Besides, she had a more pressing issue. Like where to seat her family? Her mind scrambled as she searched for a solution. The restaurant was fully booked for opening night but she couldn't possibly turn them away when they'd come all this way.

As if reading her mind, her grandmother leaned closer and whispered, "We're booked under a false name. Your lovely boss called me last weekend and asked if we would like to come and we cooked up the aliases Mr. and Mrs. Brown so you wouldn't find out."

Lachlan had arranged for her dad and grandmother to come? Her heart bumped against her ribs at this news. How did he even get Grammy's number? Immediately she remembered that she'd listed her grandmother as next of kin on her employment forms because her father was always so hard to pin down. Grammy wasn't much better but at least she stayed in New York and had a landline to contact her on.

Although she'd changed her name back to her maiden one, long before that her mother had changed both of theirs back to *her* maiden name, so she and her father didn't share the same surname and Eliza realized she'd never actually told Lachlan exactly *who* her father was. A restaurant reviewer, yes, but not *the* restaurant reviewer with his own column in the *New York Times*. Which meant Lachlan had no idea that he'd invited one of America's most famous restaurant reviewers into his world.

"Splendid," she said, telling her nerves to take a hike. Unless something went terribly wrong in the kitchen, it was much more likely her father would write a glowing review as Lachlan's food was unlike anything she'd ever tasted before. And *that* would put McKinnel's on the map. "Come right this way, then."

Eliza led them to a table by the window, which looked out onto a gorgeous view of the lake at dusk. And just happened to be next door to the long table crowded with McKinnels. Nora was there with her children, their partners and her grandchildren, including Annabel's hunky new man, whom she'd introduced on the way in. Apparently he was a colleague at the fire station who'd swiped right on Annabel when he came across her on the infamous dating app.

"Grammy, Dad, I'd like you to meet the McKinnels," she said and then quickly introduced them individually. They all shook hands and Eliza couldn't help but notice her dad held Nora's hand a fraction longer than necessary. He had a bit of a reputation as a Casanova and she hoped he'd behave but she didn't have time to worry about that either as more patrons arrived.

"Stella, your waitress for the night, will be with you in moment," she said before kissing Grammy on the cheek, then turning and heading back to do her job.

The rest of the evening passed in a blur. Eliza didn't get the chance to talk to her family, but at one stage, she glanced across to see that the McKinnels had made room for Grammy and Dad at their table. Grammy was in her element, sipping whiskey and holding court, everyone looked to be hanging on to her every word, all except her father and Nora McKinnel, who appeared lost in a conversation of their own.

She was happy her family was being looked after and couldn't wait to spend some time with them herself. Couldn't wait to sit down and slip off her heels once most of the patrons had gone home. Her feet were aching from overuse but the only time she got five seconds' reprieve was when Lachlan came out of the kitchen when all the entrées had been served.

The musicians quieted as he borrowed the singer's microphone and Eliza leaned back against the bar to listen. Even before Lachlan spoke, the crowd erupted in applause, which wasn't surprising, considering the compliments to the chef she and the waiters had been receiving all night.

"Welcome, everyone," he said, grinning out at the patrons. "I want to thank you all for joining us tonight for the grand opening of McKinnel's. It's good to see some new faces and also some familiar ones, people who have been friends and supporters of the distillery since my father and his brother first opened. I wish Dad was here today to see us working hard to expand his legacy and I want to thank my brother Callum for believing in me to open a restaurant to complement the amazing things he, Blair, Quinn and Sophie are already doing with the distillery."

He smiled in the direction of his family table and then lifted an arm and gestured around him. "And thanks to Mac and his craftsmanship for taking my and Callum's ideas and creating this amazing building. To Mom, for keeping us all from killing each other as we continue to grow the distillery and to Annabel, who is always on hand in case of an emergency."

Everyone laughed and Lachlan continued, his voice getting a little choked, "McKinnel's truly is a family affair and there are two other people who also deserve a special mention. Thank you, Hallie and Hamish, for putting up with me working ridiculous hours. One day, you'll know that everything I do is for you guys."

Eliza sniffed as a tear slid down her cheek. If Lachlan went on much longer like this, she didn't think there'd be a dry eye in the house. As she listened to him thank his assistant chef, their talented kitchen hands and the enthusiastic front-of-house team, she felt so proud and happy for his success. Not only was he a very good-looking man and a generous lover, but he was a hard-working, kind man and a dedicated father. He'd told her he thought Tyler a fool for leaving her. Well, she thought exactly the same about his ex-wife.

Lost in these thoughts, it took a second for her to realize people were turning to look at her and that Lachlan was no longer smiling at his family but at her. She'd thought he included her when thanking his front-of-house team but…apparently not.

"Without Eliza, this last month would have been harder and nowhere near as much fun."

Her tummy flipped as their gazes met and as he spoke, she felt as if they were the only two people in the room. She knew the fun he was referring to and felt her cheeks heating but couldn't do anything to stop them. Later she would tell him off for singling her out like that and then she would show him her gratitude.

As he continued singing her praise, she felt her cheeks getting redder by the second. Just when it was getting really embarrassing, he finally wrapped up, "You've been my right-hand gal in every decision and I count my blessings for the day you walked into this building."

Thank you, she mouthed back.

"I think that just about wraps up my thanks. Those who know me know I don't like public speaking, so now that I've said what needed to be said, I will leave you all to order and enjoy dessert. Thanks again for coming and, if you've enjoyed your meal tonight, please tell your friends and share on social media. And don't forget to tag McKinnel's."

As everyone applauded at his final words, Lachlan stepped away from the microphone and began circling the tables, chatting to the patrons individually. Eliza wanted to go and congratulate him and also introduce him to her family but, too busy with diners herself, she didn't get the chance to do so. She did see Lachlan shake hands with her dad, kiss Grammy and embark on what looked to be a deep and meaningful conversation before he headed back into the kitchen.

If possible, dessert service was even more of a success than the entrées. It wasn't until everyone was on to coffees or whiskeys that Eliza finally slipped into the kitchen to take a breath.

Lachlan immediately came across to her and touched a hand to her arm. "Why didn't you tell me your dad was Raymond Starr?"

She shrugged a shoulder and answered with a question of her own. "Why didn't you tell me you invited my family?"

He gave her a coy smile. "Are you mad at me?"

"Are you kidding?" she whispered, leaning perhaps a little close when they had the eyes of the kitchen staff on them. "Later, when we're alone, I'll show you exactly how grateful I am."

"As amazing and tempting as that sounds, I wouldn't want to monopolize your time tonight when your grandmother and father are here. Rain check?"

Her heart sank. As delighted as she was to see her family, she'd been looking forward to a private celebration with Lachlan when all the patrons and staff had gone home. "Do you know how long they're staying? Or where?" It suddenly crossed her mind that she'd been so startled by their arrival, she'd failed to ask either of these questions. Perhaps they'd want to stay with her?

"I think they booked into the hotel for the weekend, but you'll have to check with them. And right now, we both need to get back to work." He kissed her with his eyes and then turned to help his staff begin the cleanup.

As Lachlan had predicted, Eliza's family was among the last people to leave the restaurant. Not knowing that her boss with benefits often gave her a lift home, her father insisted she let him drive her to her apartment in his rental car. All the way, he raved about the evening—how outstanding the food had been and how enjoyable the company.

"Does that mean you're going to write a good review?" Eliza asked from the back seat.

"You'll have to wait and see," he replied with a chuckle.

"Tease."

"I must admit I was dubious about your move here," he said as he caressed the steering wheel. "I worried about you being in such a small town, not knowing anyone, but you looked in your element tonight. It's good to see you smiling again."

"Thank you, Dad," she said, a lump forming in her throat. Part of her still felt a little guilty when she felt happy but that part was getting smaller and smaller. "I'm getting there."

"I'm glad."

"Me, too," added Grammy, glancing out the front window. "And I have to admit you were right about this little place being picturesque. New York will always be my first love, but I guess small towns can have their charm, too."

"They sure can," Eliza said. "And I don't start till two tomorrow afternoon, so how about I give you both the grand tour? The river walk is a must and there are some delightful old Craftsman homes to admire."

"That sounds lovely," Grammy said as Eliza's father slowed in front of her apartment block.

Although physically exhausted, Eliza knew she wouldn't be able to attempt sleep with the success of the evening still buzzing through her veins. "Do you want to come in for a nightcap?" she asked.

Her father turned her down, citing the desire to write his review while the food was still fresh in his head, but Grammy jumped at the idea, choosing to stay with Eliza instead of going back to the hotel.

The apartment didn't have a spare room and the couch was too small to slumber comfortably on, but this didn't matter because she and her grandmother had shared a bed numerous times in the past.

While Eliza attempted to make two cups of cocoa without burning down the kitchen, Grammy evaluated the apartment. "It's a little poky," she said, "but it has potential if you add a little more color and maybe a few photos or pieces of art."

"Maybe you can help me shop for something tomorrow morning before you leave?" Eliza suggested.

Grammy's eyes glistened. Along with drinking and flirting with men, shopping was one of her favorite pastimes. "Now you're talking."

They carried the mugs into the small living room, kicked off their shoes and cozied up on the couch together. "It's so good to have you here." Careful not to spill her drink, Eliza leaned her shoulder against her grandmother's. Although they talked on the phone almost every day, nothing was as good as having her here in person.

"It's good to be here," she replied, patting Eliza's knee. "And Lachlan is even better-looking in person than you gave him credit for. Why didn't you tell me you were sleeping with him?"

Cocoa spluttered from Eliza's mouth and this time she did spill some. Grammy had never been one for beating around the bush, but she hadn't been expecting *this*. As she put the mug down on the coffee table, she opened her mouth to deny her grandmother's accusation, but she felt the older woman's gaze boring into her and knew it was futile. "How did you know?" she asked instead, as she reached for a tissue to address the stain on her work shirt.

Grammy smiled victoriously. "A blind person could see the sparks flying between the two of you. I wouldn't have been surprised when he was speaking about you tonight if he got down on one knee and proposed."

"Propose?" Eliza cackled at the absurdity of such an idea. "I've only known the guy a month."

"When you know, you know," Grammy countered. "I'd known Raymond's father two hours before I knew he was the one for me."

Eliza shook her head. Her situation was very different from that of her grandmother and the grandfather she'd never known because he'd died when her father was a child. "That may be true, but my stance on relationships hasn't changed. I'm not looking for love or marriage. We're…" How should she put it? "We're having *fun* together."

When Grammy just raised her eyebrows, Eliza added defensively, "You were the one who said not all relationships had to be serious, that fun and mutual pleasure are valid reasons for being with someone."

"Maybe I did." She sighed. "And maybe for an old woman like me, that's true, but you're still young, you deserve love and companionship as well as physical intimacy."

Before Eliza could say that she didn't want love ever again, Grammy continued, "And so does Lachlan. He might be happy with sex for a little while, but it's clear to see he's a family man and eventually he'll want more. Nora confided in me about his ex-wife—she sounds like a ghastly woman, abandoning those two beautiful children, but not all women are so stupid. Lachlan is not only a handsome man, but he's smart, successful, caring, a good dad…"

As Grammy listed all the things that had gone through Eliza's head only a few hours ago, the cocoa she'd barely drunk grew heavy in her stomach.

"He's a very eligible bachelor and I'm sure there are

plenty of single women in Jewell Rock who'd be happy to take on the role of his wife and his children's mother."

Eliza's shook her head, her heart thrashing about in her chest at the thought of Lachlan being with another woman. "But he's happy with our...arrangement." The last word tripped on her tongue as it suddenly sounded tawdry.

"Are you sure about that?" Grammy turned her head to look seriously at Eliza and took hold of her hands. "Because I'm an old woman. I've seen a lot in my eighty-two years and I think Lachlan already sees you as way more than just a colleague or a quick tumble between the sheets."

The thrashing in her heart slowed almost to a stop as her grandmother's words sank in. She thought of the way Lachlan treated her—how his face lit up when she walked in the door and the tender way he caressed her body when they slept together. But mostly, she thought of the way he tried to get her to talk about Jack and the hurt in his eyes she tried to ignore when she shut those conversations down.

He wasn't a man who was just using her for his body. All the signs were there that he wanted to get to know her more. And then she thought back to that very first postsex conversation. Had he been joking when he suggested he be her boss with benefits? He'd been quick to assure her he was happy with a fling but what if he'd only said so because of what she'd said?

Her mind whirled with confused thoughts. Maybe Grammy was reading more into the situation than was actually there. Maybe she was seeing what she wanted to see because she didn't like to think of Eliza all alone. But alone was safe. Not getting emotionally entangled meant her heart couldn't break, so why did it hurt so much at the thought of Lachlan finding someone else to make a family with?

Because you're already falling in love with him.

But no, she shook her head vigorously. She didn't want to love him. Tears sprang to her eyes at the thought. She certainly didn't want to love Hallie and Hamish.

Grammy squeezed her hand. "I think you're fooling yourself if you think you can keep your body and heart separate where Lachlan is concerned. I know *you*, and I know you want more out of life. Don't let fear and grief stop you from living because doing so won't bring Jack back but it could leave you leading a very lonely life."

"But isn't that what I deserve?" Eliza sobbed, an image of her little boy's lifeless face once again appearing in her head. "If I was a better mother, he'd still be alive."

"Oh, precious girl." Grammy drew her into her arms. "Stop punishing yourself. You were a wonderful mother—you *are* a wonderful mother—and you need to learn to forgive yourself. You moved here to this beautiful town to start again, but you're not allowing yourself to truly do so."

Eliza couldn't stop the tears that fell and she sat there with her grandmother's arms wrapped around her, the old woman gently stroking her hair, until they finally started to subside. "I'm so glad you're here," she said, pulling back a little so she could look into Grammy's wise eyes.

"Me, too. But now this old girl is getting tired. Shall we head to bed?"

Eliza nodded, thankful that her grandmother wasn't going to push the issue anymore. Then she stood, collected their mugs—one empty and the other half-full of now-cold cocoa—and dumped them in the kitchen sink to deal with tomorrow. She lent Grammy a set of cotton pajamas and gave her a new toothbrush, and they both readied themselves for bed.

Within seconds of climbing beneath the covers, Grammy was sound asleep—probably from all the whiskey she'd drunk that night—but Eliza, not wanting to disturb her, lay there quietly, staring into the darkness as she fought the urge to toss and turn. A war of thoughts raged inside her head as she went over and over the conversation they'd had on the couch.

Was her grandmother right? Did Lachlan want more from her?

And if he did, could she risk her heart on love again?

Or should she put an end to their affair and try to protect them both before it was too late?

Chapter Fifteen

Lost in thought and wondering if he would ever conquer sleep, Lachlan took a few seconds before he registered the strange noise coming from outside his bedroom window. He frowned and listened earnestly as another tap sounded on the glass. Flicking on his bedside light, he glanced at Hallie, who looked like a sleeping angel, and tried not to disturb her as he climbed out of bed and crossed to pull back the curtain.

The silhouette of a woman looked back at him and it took a moment for his eyes to adjust in the moonlight and register who it was. *Eliza*. What was she doing here? Was this a booty call? Or perhaps he'd fallen asleep after all and this was some kind of weird dream. Nevertheless, he pushed open the window and whispered, "Eliza?"

"Can you come out?" she asked. Her voice sounded weird and his heart kicked over in concern.

"I'll be right out. Wait there." If it weren't for the damn screen, he would have climbed out the window. Letting the curtain fall back, he yanked on a pair of jeans and a T-shirt and then hurried out to join her as fast as he could.

She met him on the front porch and he finally got a proper look at her. Dressed only in a thin summer dress, she clutched some kind of book to her chest.

"You haven't got any shoes on?" he asked. He didn't either but he'd just climbed out of bed, whereas Eliza had presumably come from her apartment.

"Oh." She looked down at her feet as if surprised by this fact as well and shook her head slightly. "There wasn't time."

He frowned. "Are you okay?"

She nodded, although the expression on her face told him she wasn't completely sure. "I wanted to show you something."

At three o'clock in the morning? He managed not to voice this thought because he didn't want to make her feel bad and if there was a problem, he was glad she felt comfortable enough to come to him with it.

"Okay," he said instead. "Shall we go across to the restaurant? I'd invite you inside but I don't want to wake everyone up."

Again she simply nodded.

"I'll just go get my keys," he said and then retreated inside the house.

"Come on, then," he said when he emerged less than a minute later. He wanted to take her hand but she was still cradling the book like it was a precious treasure so he would have had to ask to do so. They walked the short distance to the restaurant in silence. It wasn't uncomfortable but it wasn't comfortable either. Lachlan had no idea what was going on, whether her late-night visit was a good one or a bad one and he didn't want to put a foot wrong.

When they arrived, he unlocked the door and switched on the lights. "Can I get you a drink?" he asked.

"Coffee?" she said.

Usually he didn't drink caffeine after dinner but it wasn't like either of them were going to get any sleep now. He smiled at her. "Two coffees coming right up. Do you want to sit down?"

"Thank you." She sounded so damn polite—like a stranger almost—as she lowered herself into one of the two leather couches by the door where patrons could sit with a drink while they waited for a table.

Nerves twisting his belly, he set about making two cups of coffee and then carried them over to her. He put them down on the coffee table and hesitated, unsure whether to sit opposite or beside her. When Eliza put down her book on the table, picked up a mug and took a sip, he lowered himself down next to her.

She put her mug back on the table, picked up the book, edged a little closer to him. When she opened up the book, he realized it was a photo album. His heart pinched as he looked down to see the most angelic little child staring back up at him. With masses of thick curls the same delicious color as Eliza's hair and a cheeky smile that filled his whole face, there was no doubt in Lachlan's mind that this was Jack.

"He did like playing with balls," Eliza said, her voice not much more than a whisper.

Tears prickled at the corner of Lachlan's eyes as she answered the question he'd asked her almost a week ago.

"In fact, we had quite a collection of them. He also

loved the color yellow. I could only buy him yellow clothes because he threw a tantrum if we tried to make him wear any other color." She turned the page to the next photo of a little boy curled up with a Big Bird toy that was almost bigger than him.

Lachlan felt like he should say something but no words would come.

"Dad bought him Big Bird and he rarely let it out of his sight. Grammy bought him a packet of the most beautiful crayons. He was just starting to scribble with them but only the yellow one ever came out of the box."

Again she flicked the page and this time Jack sat in a high chair, a bowl on his head and what looked to be custard dripping down from his hair. His smile said he thought the situation hilarious.

"The obsession started to worry me when he refused to eat anything that wasn't yellow, but Tyler told me not to worry too much. That there were plenty of good yellow foods—bananas, cheese, pineapples, eggs, custard—and that he'd grow out of the quirk but..."

She paused, sniffed long and hard, as if trying to hold it together. "He didn't have the chance to grow out of it."

Eliza might be just keeping it together, but there was a lump in Lachlan's throat and he didn't know how much longer he could hold back his tears. He didn't know what to say. Life was so unfair, so terribly unfair, but what was the point in stating the obvious? Should he tell her how adorable her son was? Did she want sympathy and comfort or would she blow up and run again if he tried to give it?

"Why are you telling me all this?" he found himself asking.

She twisted her head to look at him and blinked. "Because I thought you wanted to know."

"I do." He reached out and laid his hand beside hers so their pinky fingers were touching. The warmth from her skin emanated onto his. He wanted to know this and everything else she had to tell, but as much as he wanted to be there for Eliza, he was now all too aware that his heart was on the line.

He was falling hard and fast in love with her. "But I want to know what it means," he said.

"I miss him so much," she confessed. "I feel so empty, like there's a hole inside me that will never go away. The only time I even begin to feel half-human again is when I'm with you and that terrifies me. I'm petrified of getting close to you and to your beautiful children and then losing one of you. I don't think I could ever survive that kind of pain again, but no matter how much I've tried to protect myself, I realized tonight that I'm fooling myself. And not being fair to either of us. I already have very strong feelings…not only for you, but also for Hallie and Hamish."

Hope flared in Lachlan's heart. Her words were music to his ears.

"Of course, maybe I'm being presumptuous." Again her voice shook. "Maybe you're happy with things as they currently stand?"

"I'm not going to deny that I like sleeping with you," Lachlan said, choosing his words carefully, "but from the moment we first slept together, probably before that, it was a lot more than just physical for me. Like you, I'm wary of opening my heart again but you make me want to give love and family a second chance."

She edged her hand even closer and linked her fingers through his. "You do that to me as well, but I've got to admit that taking a risk on both those things— love and family—is a huge deal for me. Not only am

I scared of messing up again, but I'm not really sure I deserve that kind of happiness."

"Everyone deserves that kind of happiness," he said, lifting her hand to his lips and brushing a kiss against her knuckles, happy she didn't pull away.

Eliza was quiet a moment. "Maybe. But this is all a bit overwhelming for me. Do you mind if we take things slow?"

Although in *his* heart he felt ready to propose, he put his arm around her shoulder and drew her into his side. She fit so perfectly there and if it meant being able to hold her like this whenever he wanted, then he could be patient. He would be. "Yes. We can do that."

"Thank you. I don't want the pressure of the staff knowing we're together yet."

He nodded. "But what about my family? I think most of them already suspect there's something going on between us."

Color rushed to her previously pale cheeks. "We weren't very subtle at your mom's lunch, were we?"

He laughed and shook his head.

"You can tell Nora, your brothers and sisters, but do you think we should see how things go before we tell Hallie and Hamish? I adore them but…"

"They already adore you, too," he said, "so maybe that's a good idea." He didn't want to vocalize the possibility that things might not work out between him and Eliza. But Hallie had recently all but lost her mom, so he didn't want her to get too attached to another woman until they were both sure of the future.

"Okay, then." Eliza inhaled and then exhaled deeply. "My grandmother really likes you by the way. And I think my father does, too. He was going back to the hotel to write his review right away."

Lachlan should feel anxious about the prospect of a restaurant reviewer as famed as Raymond Starr commenting on his new venture, but right now with the guy's daughter in his arms, he couldn't even care if he trashed it. "I can't wait to read it," he said.

Then he retrieved the album from Eliza's lap and turned to the next photo. "This is the cutest kid," he said, recalling one of his grief books telling him it was best to refer to the dead loved one still in present tense. "Thank you for showing me these photos of Jack and telling me about him. I hope as time goes by, you'll tell me more, but if you ever need space to grieve quietly, then you tell me that, as well."

"Thank you. I promise I will."

Chapter Sixteen

Eliza stifled a yawn as she smiled at the young couple coming in the entrance of the restaurant. "Good evening, welcome to McKinnel's," she said. "Do you have a booking?"

The guy nodded. "Table for two under Justin."

"Excellent." As she glanced down at the evening's booking register, she breathed a sigh of relief. If they didn't have a booking, she would have had to turn them away and she always felt so terrible when that happened. Whether it was due to the social media efforts she and Sophie had put out to broadcast the new restaurant or her dad's raving review in the *New York Times* a week ago, business had been booming. They'd had a full house every night since opening and the lunch service was always busy, too.

Eliza couldn't be happier with this result, but it was starting to take its toll on her energy levels. Although if she were honest, she couldn't entirely blame the restaurant for her fatigue. Since she and Lachlan had decided to give a relationship a go, they'd been stealing as much time together as they could outside working hours, as well. This was hard due to Hallie and Hamish's needs—not that she begrudged his children his attention at all—so he'd often sneak over to her house in the middle of the night when they were finally asleep.

And they didn't always have sex. Sometimes they just lay together in bed and talked. Other times they'd watch a movie. They made plans for more cooking lessons once things were less crazy at the restaurant and Eliza couldn't wait, but at the moment they were both just struggling to keep their heads above water.

She looked back up from the register and spoke to the couple. "You've got my favorite table right near the window. The view outside is magical at night. Come this way."

As she led them through the restaurant, she had to curb another yawn. If there was time, she'd take a break and get a coffee but the moment she settled this couple, the door opened and another group arrived to be seated. With a sigh, she told the couple their waitress for the evening would be with them in a moment and then made sure her smile was still firmly in place and hurried back to do it all over again.

"Eliza?" Troy—one of the younger waiters—nabbed her the moment she'd settled the group. "Can you come and talk to a woman over here? She wants to know why almost everything on the menu has whiskey in it."

Annoyance flared within her and she felt the beginnings of a headache prickling her scalp. "Did you tell her this is a *whiskey* distillery?"

"I tried, but she still doesn't seem to get it. She says she doesn't like whiskey."

Oh, boy. Telling herself to stay calm—she'd dealt with hundreds of awkward customers in her life—she told Troy to get back to serving his other tables and she'd deal with it.

"Hi there," she said to the lady, pasting a smile onto her face that was so big it hurt. "Would you like me to run through the menu with you?"

"I can read it myself, thank you. I came here because everyone's been talking about the quality of the food but it all reads like boring fare with a dash of whiskey to try to make it original."

Boring? Usually she prided herself on being a fairly patient and tolerant person, but hearing this woman insult Lachlan's talent had her harboring homicidal thoughts. "I can assure you that all the chef's dishes are very original," she said, her tone saccharine, "and flavorsome. If whiskey isn't your thing, however, we do have a lovely salmon dish and a chicken pasta that don't have—"

The woman screwed up her nose as she interrupted, "I don't want salmon or chicken. Let me speak to the chef!"

Not wanting to cause a scene and guessing that once Lachlan opened his mouth to speak, he'd have this difficult customer eating out of the palm of his hand, Eliza said, "I'll go see if he's available for you," and retreated before she said something she regretted.

As she stepped into the kitchen, the aromas of the various dishes hit her like a food truck. Although these smells usually made her mouth water, today she fought a wave of nausea. Trying to ignore it, she called across the kitchen, "Lachlan, do you have a moment?"

He looked up, smiled, said a few words to one of the kitchen hands, who took over his place at the commercial-sized stove and then crossed over to her. "What's up?" Before she could reply, he frowned and touched his hand to her elbow. "Are you okay? You're not looking so great."

"Jeez, thanks." She shook his hand off, still not wanting the staff to suspect anything between them. "I'm just tired, but never mind about me. Can you come and talk to a lady out here?" She explained the problem with the whiskey.

He chuckled. "It'd be my pleasure. Lead the way."

Eliza did as he asked and then happily left to go and chat to more amenable patrons. Lachlan defused the situation, wrote down the table's order himself and then returned to the kitchen. When the meals started to be served, things got hectic and Eliza ran back and forth to the kitchen, trying to help the waitstaff get everything delivered before it got cold.

"Thank you. That smells divine." A gentleman smiled up at her as she put a steaming bowl of whiskey-and-bacon chili in front of him. Usually she'd agree, but as she opened her mouth to reply, another wave of nausea rocked her and she shut it quickly as bile shot up her throat.

Covering her mouth, she turned and fled toward the restrooms, horror washing over her at the realization she'd almost vomited over a customer. *Again.* Locking the cubicle door behind her, she collapsed onto her knees and hurled into the toilet bowl.

No. This cannot be happening.

The door of the restroom opened. She stilled, willing this episode to be over.

"Eliza?" came the voice of one of the waitresses.

"Are you okay? Lachlan saw you rush off and told me to come check on you."

Oh, Lord. Somehow she managed to speak. "I'll be fine. Think I must have eaten something that didn't agree with me."

The waitress chuckled. "Hopefully not from this kitchen."

Eliza could not laugh. There was *nothing* funny about this.

"Okay, then," said the girl after a long pause. "Do you need anything?"

"No. Just go back to work," Eliza managed. "I'll be out in a minute."

She waited until she heard the door click shut again and then she forced herself off her knees. She wiped her mouth with toilet paper, flushed it and then went out to check her reflection in the mirror. It wasn't pretty but she pinched her cheeks to add a little color and told herself to get back out there and worry about *this* later.

Yet, as she opened the door and stepped back into the hallway that led into the restaurant, she almost slammed into Lachlan's chest.

"I'm going to ask you again," he said as he put his arms out to steady her. "Are you not feeling well?"

She wanted to lie, to keep on working, but she didn't want to make another scene. "I've felt better."

"I'm taking you home," he said. "I'll just get my keys."

"No!" She shook her head furiously. "You can't leave now." It was the assistant chef's night off. "I'll be okay," she managed. "I probably just need to sleep it off."

In the end, Lachlan reluctantly agreed to let her go on her own as long as she took his truck and promised to call him the moment she got home.

"I will." Without saying goodbye to anyone else, she grabbed her purse and headed out into the night. As she walked toward his vehicle, her breaths came in rapid jolts and she told herself to chill before she gave herself a heart attack.

This was probably a false alarm anyway. Maybe she really was just sick. She tried to remember the last time she'd had her period but life had been so busy lately she'd lost track. Was it just after she arrived in Jewell Rock? That was well over a month ago now, which would make her late but...

No! She and Lachlan had used condoms every single time they'd made love. Weren't condoms 99 percent effective or something? Probably tomorrow morning, she'd wake up and discover her tiredness and nausea was a new premenstrual symptom.

Clinging to this possibility, she climbed into the truck and started toward her apartment with a quick detour to the drugstore just to be sure. As much as the idea of being pregnant terrified her, she wouldn't be able to sleep if she didn't know for sure.

With shaking hands and hoping nobody there recognized her, she grabbed a pregnancy-testing kit and took it to the counter. Less than ten minutes later, she was in her apartment, staring at the little white stick on her counter.

The word *pregnant* glared up at her.

This felt like déjà vu; the last time she'd been in this situation, she'd been over the moon, but her world had changed since then. She didn't want another baby. She'd only just begun to consider the idea of becoming a stepmom. So much for taking things slow with Lachlan. The fears she'd slowly been starting to conquer these last few weeks reared up inside her once again.

She whirled around and threw up into the toilet. Only this time, she wasn't sure the nausea was down to morning sickness or because she was more terrified than she'd ever been in her life.

Lachlan lost count of the number of times he checked his phone following Eliza's departure. Why hadn't she called yet? Had something happened on her way? An image of her slumped over the steering wheel, the car in a ditch (or worse), haunted him and for the first time since the restaurant had opened—for the first time in as long as he could remember—he burned someone's dinner and had to start again.

If there'd been an accident, you'd have heard about it, he told himself as he tried to focus on cooking. But it was no good. He couldn't get her out of his head. Taking a break he couldn't really afford due to the full restaurant, he slipped outside and tried to call her. When her phone went to voice mail, he cursed and called Annabel.

She answered just as he was about to give up. "Hey, big bro, how can I help you?"

"Are you at home? Eliza left early because she wasn't feeling well and I was wondering if you could go check on her?"

"Sorry. I'm in Bend at Noah's house," she said, naming her new boyfriend.

"Is Soph at home?"

"She's out on a date."

He cursed. Why had his sisters suddenly decided to throw their hearts and souls into dating when he needed them? "Okay, thanks. Bye."

He shoved his phone back into his pocket, then headed back into the restaurant and willed everyone to leave early. Then, when all the desserts had finally been delivered to the tables, he handed the reins over to his barman—who was the most senior employee still there that night—and asked him to close up.

Only outside did he remember he'd insisted Eliza take his truck. He deliberated all of two seconds between taking her bike or jogging to the house and borrowing his mom's car before he jumped on the bike. It might take him slightly longer but he wouldn't have to explain himself to his mom or Blair, which would waste time.

Less than ten minutes later, he saw his truck parked outside her apartment building and pressed his hand to his heart as relief washed over him. But there was no time to catch his breath—he was still worried and knew he wouldn't be able to sleep if he didn't at least check on her before going home. He leaned the bike against a wall, went to the entrance and punched his sisters' code into the security pad to let himself inside.

Less than thirty seconds later, he was pounding on Eliza's front door. "Sweetheart, it's Lachlan."

No reply was forthcoming. He tapped his shoe against the floor, contemplating his next move and was just about to knock again when he heard the click of the lock and the door peeled back.

"You'll wake the neighbors," Eliza hissed.

He put his hand on the door and pushed it enough to let himself inside. "At least two of them are out and all I care about is you anyway." Frowning, he lifted his hand and put it against her forehead. "You don't have a temperature. Is it your stomach? Maybe you should lie down."

She raised an eyebrow as she pulled away from him. "That's what I was doing until someone knocked on my front door."

"I'm sorry," he said, feeling slightly chastised. "But I was worried. You didn't call me to say you'd got home safely."

"I forgot." She hugged her arms to herself.

"Never mind. Let's get you to bed and all snuggled up. I'll look after you." He shut the door behind him and reached for her again, ready to lead her into the bedroom and play nurse, but she all but pushed him away.

Lachlan blinked. He hadn't seen this side of her before but she was kind of cute when she was grumpy. "You're a little feisty when you're sick, aren't you?"

"I'm not sick," she snapped. "I'm pregnant."

And then she promptly burst into tears.

He stood there frozen for a few moments, watching the tears stream down her cheeks but too stunned to do anything about it. *Pregnant?* How could that possibly be? They might have had a lot of sex but they'd also used a lot of condoms.

Finally he found his voice. "Are you sure?"

"I can show you the positive pregnancy test if you don't believe me," she said, her words punctuated by sobs.

"No, of course, that's not necessary," he rushed, feeling like a real asshole. He chuckled nervously and thought of his two pregnant soon-to-be sisters-in-law. "There must be something in the water around here right now."

When Eliza didn't laugh, he took a breath and a tentative step toward her, trying once again to take her into his arms. This time, she didn't resist. And as Eliza's body molded again him, he tried to collect his thoughts.

They'd been so happy the last couple of weeks—the more he got to know Eliza, the more he wanted to know and the more they found out they had in common. He loved their conversations even more than he loved sleeping with her. When she walked into a room, his heart lifted and he always felt a mixture of nerves and excitement. They were in that new, wonderful stage of a relationship where they couldn't get enough of each other and whenever they were apart, he found himself counting down the moments until he could see her again.

It might only be early days and although they'd promised to take things slow, he knew without a doubt that he wanted to spend the rest of his life with her. Getting her pregnant was not ideal but it wasn't the end of the world.

And they couldn't just ignore it.

"Come on, let's go sit down," he said eventually.

She let him lead her over to her couch and as she lowered herself into the chair, he added, "Can I get you anything? Is the nausea still bad? I could go out and get you some ginger soda if you want?"

He remembered that when Linda had terrible morning sickness with the twins, the only thing that helped was anything ginger.

She shook her head, so he sat down beside her and reached for her hand. "It'll be okay," he said.

"I don't know how this happened," she whispered. "We've always been so careful."

And then it hit him. *Oh, God.* "You know that first time we slept together?"

She looked at him warily and nodded.

"That condom had been in my wallet for quite a while." He grimaced. "It could have been out of date."

Her eyes widened and she glared at him. "So this is *your* fault?"

"I don't know." He ran a hand through his hair. "But if you are pregnant, it'll be okay. I love you, Eliza, and although a surprise, the idea of a little baby that's part of you and me is beautiful."

"You...*love* me?"

"Yeah. Yes, I do." He grinned—although he'd suspected as such for a while, this was the first time he'd truly admitted to himself that things had progressed this far for him. He placed a hand against her stomach. "And you know what? I already love this little girl or guy, as well.

"You're probably tired, and today's been massive," he continued, "but tomorrow we should get you in to see the local doctor. Chelsea and Bailey might be able to recommend their obstetricians to you, and of course, you'll need to start on folic acid tablets right away. I'll pick some up tomorrow for you, if you like. And if you're not well enough for work or need to sleep longer then..."

Suddenly registering the expression on her face, he stopped rambling and realized that the best-case scenario to his declaration of love was one of her own, but maybe she was overwhelmed by everything.

"I'm sorry," he said, "we can talk about all this tomorrow but for now—"

She interrupted, once again pushing his hand off her, "You're acting like we're keeping it."

He blinked, confused.

"How could you think I'd be happy about this?" she cried, jumping to her feet.

Lachlan flinched at her harsh words. A baby might not have been in their plans but not for a second would he ever want to get rid of it. Hallie and Hamish were hard work at times but they were also absolute blessings and he'd never once regretted his and Linda's decision to have them.

Is that what she meant? She might not want to go through with the pregnancy. His gut churned at the thought and suddenly Eliza looked more like Linda to him than she ever had before.

"What do you mean?" He couldn't help his icy tone.

She threw up her hands in the air and shouted, "I don't know! I need some time. I need to think about all this."

"Time?" His heart quaked.

"Yes. You promised that you'd give me space if I needed it."

It took a couple of seconds for him to recall the vow he'd made in the early hours of the morning when she'd finally talked properly to him about Jack. But this was different. There was another baby involved now. *His* baby. A child he'd known about less than half an hour but would already do anything to protect.

"This has nothing to do with Jack," he growled.

"It has *everything* to do with Jack," she countered. "And I'm done talking about this with you right now. Your truck keys are on the table by the door. I'd like you to leave."

As hard as it had been to let her go that afternoon in the garage when he'd first found out about Jack's death, it was a hundred times harder to walk away now. He'd never felt more conflicted. He was angry and scared but also worried about her. He didn't want to leave her in this state but it was late, he was losing his cool and maybe they could both do with a little space.

Reluctantly, he pushed to a stand and stared her right in the eye. "Okay. I'll go now. But promise me you won't do anything drastic before talking to me."

She took a long moment to reply. Then she said, "I'll talk to you later."

It wasn't lost on him that she didn't promise him anything and, as he scooped up his keys and headed out to his truck, he fought the urge to turn around and beg her.

Chapter Seventeen

When the plane touched down at JFK airport, Eliza did not feel like she'd come home but she hadn't known where else to go. She hadn't told Grammy, Dad or anyone that she was coming as she didn't want a big welcome at the airport, where she was liable to fall apart. She still wasn't sure whether she was going to tell her family about being pregnant, but she hadn't been able to stay in Jewell Rock a moment longer.

Although Lachlan had let her be last night, she wouldn't be able to think straight seeing him day-to-day and she didn't know how long he'd be able to resist making her talk about their "situation." As everyone around her unclicked their seat belts and bolted upright to scramble in the overhead compartments for their things, Eliza switched her phone on and held her breath as she waited for the inevitable.

Sure enough, within seconds, a message arrived in reply to the one she'd sent Lachlan just before she'd switched off her cell for takeoff, telling him she wouldn't be coming into work for a few days.

I wish you would talk to me.

She read his reply three times and her heart squeezed with the knowledge she was hurting him. The expression on his face when she'd told him she didn't know if she wanted the baby was still as clear in her mind as if he were standing in front of her now, but he couldn't understand how she felt.

Should she reply or should she just leave it?

"Are you going to get up?" came a grumpy voice from beside her. She turned to see the guy who'd been sitting in the window seat glaring at her.

"Sorry," she said, grabbing her purse from beneath the seat in front of her and shoving her phone inside it. Then she unbuckled her belt and rushed to stand, joining the line of passengers slowly shuffling out of the plane.

As she followed the crowds toward the arrival area and then waited by the luggage carousel for her stuff, she noted how crowded this airport was in comparison to the quiet one she'd left only seven hours ago. She'd never really thought about how busy New York was before, but as people bustled around her now, pushing and shoving in an aim to get their things, she wished they would all just disappear.

She'd hoped for silence when she got into a cab but was cursed with a chatty driver. In the end, she told him that she wasn't feeling well and didn't want to talk and he accepted that, so when they arrived at her destination, she thanked him with a generous tip.

"Not a problem. Hope you're feeling better soon," he replied as he lifted her suitcase out of the trunk.

"Thanks." She forced a smile when the last thing she felt like doing was smiling and then let herself into the apartment building that had been her home less than two months ago. It felt like a lifetime ago.

When she got to her grandmother's door, she knocked loudly to announce herself in case Grammy had a gentleman guest. When there was no reply, she used her key and pushed open the door. The apartment was deserted except for the lingering scent of Grammy's perfume. Usually Eliza liked it but today the aroma went straight to her stomach, so she dumped her things and rushed to the bathroom.

As she emerged five minutes later and went to get herself a drink of water, she wasn't sure whether she was happy for her grandmother's absence. Part of her longed for the comforting embrace that only Grammy could give, but another part of her just wanted to be alone. Perhaps she should have gone to a hotel instead or maybe flown somewhere else entirely but when she'd headed to the airport that morning to catch a flight, she hadn't been thinking straight.

Although mentally, emotionally and physically exhausted, she hadn't slept a wink last night or on the plane. Now, standing in the kitchen, her eyes started to droop and she thought if she didn't go to bed, her grandmother might return later to find her asleep on the kitchen floor. With that thought, she found a piece of paper and scribbled a note to leave in an obvious place on the counter in case she actually did achieve slumber before Grammy got home.

Surprise. Came back for a few days' break and am exhausted after an early flight. See you in the morning. xx
Eliza

Then she took herself off to the spare room, which still had much of her stuff in it from when she'd moved in earlier in the year, pulled back the covers on the bed and buried herself beneath them.

Lachlan stared at the roster for the next week and found he wanted to screw it up and hurl it across the restaurant. Five days since Eliza had gone home sick. Five days since he could think about nothing but what she'd told him. Five days since they'd been understaffed.

With a sigh, he dragged his phone out of his pocket and glanced down at the screen for what had to be the five thousandth time. She hadn't replied to the message. His knocks went unanswered but he hadn't even contemplated the fact she'd left town until one of her neighbors saw him turning away from her door and told him she'd seen Eliza get in a cab a couple of mornings ago and didn't think she'd been back since.

He passed his phone from hand to hand, wondering if he should try to call her or message her again. Surely she knew how unfair she was being to him— not only because he didn't know whether he should be looking for another head hostess for the restaurant but because every waking hour, he tortured himself with one question.

Is she still pregnant?

For someone who hadn't imagined ever having more kids, the thought that she might not be haunted him and left his heart cold. But the fact that she'd refused to talk and had shut him out so completely hurt even more. And he missed her more than he thought it possible to ever miss anybody.

He tortured himself with what-ifs and if-onlys. If only...he'd been more gentle with her the night she'd told him. He'd been in shock but he should have realized how hard this would be for her after losing her son not so long ago. Could he have done something, said something different? Unprepared for this news, he possibly hadn't handled the situation as carefully as he should have.

A shadow appeared in the doorway to the restaurant's office and Lachlan glanced up from behind the desk, thinking it was one of his employees. He was about to bark an order for them to get back to work, but he shut his mouth when he saw his older brother standing there instead.

Without a word, Callum stepped into the room and shut the door behind him. In his hand, he held a bottle of McKinnel's finest and two glass tumblers.

"Oh, boy, this looks serious," Lachlan said as Callum lowered himself onto the seat on the other side of the desk. "Is this an official visit?"

Callum had a look of consternation on his face as he unscrewed the lid on the bottle. "I guess you could call it an intervention and I'm here in two capacities—that of your older, wiser brother and also that of the director of this distillery."

"I see," Lachlan said, watching his brother pour amber fluid into the two glasses. When Callum pushed one toward him, he lifted it to his mouth and took a sip. *Why not?*

Callum echoed the action, but when Lachlan took another, his brother put his glass back down on the desk and made an appreciative noise with their tongue. "Man, we're good," he said, nodding toward the bottle.

"We are," Lachlan agreed, although he got the feeling Callum wasn't here to praise their product, and besides, nothing tasted that great at the moment. "What can I do for you?"

Callum leaned back in his chair and clasped his hands behind his head. Although his posture gave off an air of ease, the expression on his face did not. "You can cut the crap and tell me what's really going on with you and Eliza."

"What are you talking about?" Lachlan asked. He'd told his family and the restaurant staff that there'd been a family emergency in New York, which meant Eliza had to go back there for a while. At least, that's where he guessed she'd gone. "I told you, she's visiting her family."

Callum's eyebrows stretched up to his hairline. "You are quite possibly the worst liar I've ever known. If this wasn't affecting the restaurant, I'd mind my own business and tell Mom to mind hers as well, but as it is, I can't. We all know Eliza hasn't gone back to New York for a family emergency—if that were the case, you wouldn't be charging around like a wounded bear and Sophie wouldn't have been fielding complaints from your staff about you being grouchy and unreasonable."

"What?"

Callum nodded gravely. "She wouldn't tell me names but your crew aren't happy campers at the moment and that's not good for business."

So much of the staff was Eliza's, too. In such a short time, so much of his had become theirs. And right now, he didn't really give a damn about business but he guessed that wasn't the answer Callum was looking for. He sighed and took another sip of whiskey. Maybe he should bring Callum into his confidence—he'd had more experience dealing with the fairer sex than Lachlan had lately.

"Eliza's pregnant," he blurted.

"Holy shit. That was fast." Callum chuckled and then grinned. "Congratulations. There must be something in the water round here."

"That's what I said, too," Lachlan replied, "but hold the congratulations."

Callum's smile faded. "So this is why she went back to New York? I know you might not have been planning a baby so soon but surely it's good news?"

"I don't even know if she is in New York," Lachlan admitted. "All I know is that she isn't here and wherever she is, the last time I saw her, she told me she was pregnant but that she wasn't sure whether she could go through with the pregnancy."

Callum frowned. "Jeez. Wanna talk about it?"

Lachlan hesitated a few moments. Despite everything, he didn't want to break the promise he'd given to Eliza not to tell anyone about Jack. But then again, maybe being older really did make Callum wiser, and thus maybe he'd be able to help. He leaned forward and refilled his glass.

"Eliza recently lost a child," he began and Callum listened intently without saying a word as Lachlan filled him in. "She came to Jewell Rock for a fresh start, so it took ages before she opened up to me about any of this. She's still hurting so badly."

Callum finally spoke. "I haven't even met my kid yet and already I can imagine the pain I'd feel if we lost it. I'm not sure losing a child is something you ever stop hurting from. Being pregnant has probably—"

"I *know*. I get that," Lachlan interrupted, feeling the frustration rise within him again. "Even agreeing to start a relationship was a massive thing for her. We definitely didn't plan this pregnancy but her shutting me out is killing me. I don't seem to be a very good judge of character when it comes to women."

"This isn't about you. And don't be an ass by comparing Eliza to Linda. Even I can see they're totally different people. From what you've told me, she's obviously terrified of being a mother, of feeling such intense love and then losing it all over again."

Lachlan threw his hands up in the air. Eliza might not be Linda and maybe Callum was right, but he was still at a loss as to how to handle her or the situation. "Even if that is the case, what can I do about it?"

"Do you love her?" Callum asked.

"Yes."

"Do you want this baby?"

"Yes."

Callum nodded once slowly. "Then there's your answer. You need to do whatever it takes to make her feel safe—you need to make Eliza feel like she has options."

"And what if she doesn't want any of us? The baby or me? Hallie or Hamish?"

Callum shrugged. "You're already a single dad. And a good one. You might not want to do it alone, but you can, and any child would be lucky to have you."

If only it were as simple as Callum made it sound. "How am I supposed to achieve any of that when she won't talk to me? She won't even answer my messages, never mind her phone. I can't force her to talk to me."

"Not sitting there behind your desk feeling sorry for yourself, you can't. But you can show her how much she and the baby matter by going to her. Don't leave her to go through this all alone, even if that's what she thinks she wants. Sometimes in life, you've got to fight for what's important, little brother."

"Even if what's important is in New York—and I can't be certain about that—I can't just go there."

"Why not?" Callum challenged with another irritating shrug of his shoulders.

"Because I can't just leave Hallie and Hamish. And what about the restaurant?"

Callum shook his head. "Hallie and Hamish will be fine with us and what's your priority? Your love for Eliza or your career?"

The answer came quick and easy. "Eliza, of course." In a matter of weeks, she'd become one of the most important people in his world, along with Hallie and Hamish, and the last five days without her in it had been hell. "But I thought as director of this distillery and therefore my boss, you might be against me rushing off to New York. Especially when the head hostess is missing, as well."

As he said these words, he realized this was what he'd wanted to do since he'd turned up at her apartment and found her gone.

"I'm your big brother first and your boss second. Family trumps work every time, buddy, and I believe that you and Eliza have what it takes to make a beautiful family. Chelsea had some restaurant experience years ago, she can help out in front of house and you've got a very capable assistant chef. We'll be fine."

Something a little like hope kicked over in Lachlan's heart. "Are you sure?" he asked.

Callum grinned again and nodded. "What are you waiting for?"

Chapter Eighteen

I should have cancelled, Eliza thought as she walked through Central Park to meet Lilly for lunch at Tavern on the Green. Perhaps it wasn't too late. She couldn't imagine she'd be very good company. But Grammy had apparently run into Lilly at Macy's yesterday and let slip that Eliza was back.

Her friend had been extremely hurt that she hadn't called her and had been on the phone immediately, reprimanding Eliza for not telling her she was home and demanding they catch up for her to dish the dirt.

She already felt enough guilt over leaving Lachlan in the lurch and she didn't need to add being a bad friend to her list of sins, so she'd agreed to a lunch date. After five days of thinking time, her thoughts were no clearer in her head than they were when she'd left Jewell Rock. She missed Lachlan so much that she found herself watching *Mary Poppins* to feel close to him. But every time a wave of morning sickness came over her, her whole body filled with a crippling terror and the thought of facing him left her shaking in her shoes.

She'd decided maybe a little fresh air would help.

Yet now as she walked along the paths toward her destination, she remembered why she favored being a hermit. When you were upset about something, life had a habit of flaunting it in your face. Today, everywhere she looked, there were couples in love, young moms jogging with strollers or pregnant women tenderly caressing their blossoming bellies.

No. I can't do this.

Yanking her phone out of her pocket, Eliza began typing out an apology message to Lilly and as she did so, she turned and started back in the direction she'd come. She was just about to press Send when her foot caught on a crack in the path. A yelp left her mouth as her phone flew out of her grasp and her whole body shot forward. Instinctively, she put her hands out to try to save her fall, but it didn't quite work out. Two seconds later, she found herself lying flat on the path, a small crowd quickly gathering around her.

Her first thought wasn't the pain on her head or the embarrassment of falling so spectacularly in such a public place. It wasn't even, *Where is my phone?*

"You okay?" asked a man, crouching down next to her and depositing her phone on the ground.

"Let me through, I know first aid," boomed a very familiar voice from somewhere above as Eliza attempted to pick herself back up.

"Oh, my God, I know her," shrieked Lilly, dropping to her knees beside her.

Eliza had never been happier to see her friend in her life. She stopped trying to get up and instead burst into tears—it seemed crying was the only thing she was good at these days.

"Oh, Lize." As the strangers dispersed, Lilly helped her into a sitting position, then dug around in her purse and conjured a small packet of tissues as she spoke. "What have you done to yourself? You've got a horrible gash on your forehead." She thrust a tissue against the spot and held it firmly. "Do you think you can stand, or are you feeling dizzy? If you can get up, we should go into the restroom and clean you up. That way, I'll be able to have a proper look and see if you need stitches."

But Eliza didn't care about the blood trickling down the side of her face. She was almost numb to the pain that accompanied it. Her hands rushed to cradle her stomach as she thought about the new life growing there.

What if this fall makes me lose it?

Then the pain came—in the form of a big whoosh to her heart.

"My baby," she whispered.

"Huh?" Lilly blinked and her hand fell from Eliza's forehead as her gaze dropped to Eliza's stomach. "What did you just say?"

"I'm pregnant." Eliza said the words for the first time since she'd told Lachlan. Grammy knew that something was going on but Eliza hadn't been able to bring herself to mention the baby yet. Part of her had thought if she didn't tell anyone, maybe it would just go away but suddenly she knew with absolute certainty she didn't want that.

As terrifying as the idea of being a mom again was, as scared as she was of messing up and experiencing more pain, she wanted this chance and she wanted to have it with Lachlan. Sitting on this hard ground now, she craved his arms around her. But what if she did lose the baby? Lachlan might think she'd got rid of it on purpose.

As these thoughts whirled through her head, her sobs came harder and faster.

"Oh, honey." Ignoring the blood now, Lilly drew Eliza into her arms. "It'll be okay."

Her friend held her until her tears finally started to subside and then she gently suggested they go clean Eliza up. "Do you want to go back to my apartment—Britt will still be out with my mom—or do you still want to have lunch?"

"I don't think I could eat anything right now," Eliza said.

So Lilly gave her a hand up off the ground, then held her close as they headed to find a cab. In the car, she gave their driver her address and then held Eliza's hand the whole way to her place. Neither of them said anything—a silent agreement not to air her dirty laundry to their cabbie—and when they got into Lilly's house, she took Eliza straight into the bathroom and tended her wound before anything else.

When the blood had stopped, the area was clean and Lilly had applied antiseptic cream to Eliza's forehead, she stood back and said, "If you're unlucky, you'll end up with a Harry Potter scar on your forehead."

Eliza almost laughed. Her life might be a shambles but Lilly always had the ability to make her feel a little better.

"So...I would offer you wine," Lilly said, "but in the light of what you've just told me, maybe juice would be better for this discussion. Want to come sit down?"

Eliza nodded and a few minutes later, they were both sitting on Eliza's couch, nursing a glass of juice. She took a sip and then put her drink down on the coffee table. "I'm not really sure where to start."

"How about who the father is?" Lilly said.

"Very funny. I told you I'd started seeing Lachlan."

Lilly nodded. "But you also told me you were taking things slow. Next thing you tell me, you're knocked up."

"It was a shock to me, as well," she said as she told her friend about her resolve not to ever have another baby. "I even told Lachlan I wasn't sure I wanted to have the baby," she concluded.

Lilly's eyes widened. "You thought you might get rid of it?"

"I don't really know," Eliza admitted. "I hadn't thought as far as logistics. All I knew is that I couldn't face the thought of becoming a mother again and so I came back here to try to get my head together."

Lilly reached for Eliza's hand. "And has it worked? Have you made a decision?"

Eliza let out a long, deep breath. "I've thought about nothing else for five days but until that moment I fell today, I was as confused and terrified as ever. I couldn't help feeling that if I allowed myself to feel anything for this baby, it would be a betrayal to Jack. But when I tripped, my first thought was of the baby's safety and suddenly I knew…" She sniffed as tears threatened once again. "I knew that whether or not I want to, I already love this child. And not only do I also love its father, but I love his two gorgeous children, as well. My heart feels like it could burst with love for them all."

"Oh, Eliza." Lilly squeezed her hand. "Just because you love another baby doesn't mean your love for Jack is any less. I know how scary this must be but you are the bravest person I know and you can do this. You deserve to be happy again."

"But what if Lachlan doesn't want me anymore?" She remembered the look on his face when she'd said she wasn't sure if she wanted to have the baby and a chill filled her heart. How could she ever have thought such a thing?

Maybe she'd already ruined things with him.

"I haven't met Lachlan," Lilly began, "and I can't tell you what he thinks or feels, but from the little bits you've told me about him, he sounds like a caring and reasonable person. Go back and talk to him. Tell him what you just told me."

At the thought of seeing him again, Eliza's cold heart sped up. It was time to stop running and face her fears. Time to stop waiting to wake up from her nightmare and start living again.

She lifted her arm and looked at her watch. "I wonder what time the next flight to Oregon is?"

Lilly's face split into a grin. "Leave that to me. You go pack your bags and I'll book you on it."

"I thought you didn't want me to live in Oregon," Eliza said, braving a smile.

"I didn't. I *don't*. But I do want you to be happy, so I'll learn to live with it."

When Eliza turned her key in the lock of her grandmother's apartment twenty minutes later, she wasn't surprised to hear voices. Barely a day went by without one friend or other of Grammy's dropping in for a drink. But she stopped dead in her tracks when she registered the male voice.

No. It can't be. The voice belonged to someone much younger than Grammy's usual gentleman friends and maybe she was hallucinating but it sounded very familiar.

Light-headed, she almost tripped again in her haste to get into the living room and let out a shriek at the sight of Lachlan sitting on the couch. He offered her a tentative smile, but it was Grammy who spoke first.

"Hello, Eliza," she said calmly. "I was just about to message and say you had a delivery. How was your lunch with Lilly?"

"It was fine," Eliza found herself saying and then realized that was a lie. "Actually we didn't eat lunch. I..." Her words failed her as she met Lachlan's gaze and her heart filled with love. It was *so* unbelievably good to see him.

"Good Lord." Grammy pushed out of her armchair, crossed the room and touched her hand to Eliza's forehead. "What have you done to your head?"

Lachlan swore and rushed to his feet. Both of them stood before her, fussing.

She brushed her grandmother off and kept her gaze on him. "It's nothing. I'm fine."

"In that case, I think I'll take myself for a walk around the block," Grammy said and then, with a quick pat on Eliza's arm, she retreated.

The moment the door clicked shut, Lachlan spoke. "Are you sure your head's okay?"

She nodded.

"Look," he began, "I know I said I'd give you time but there's something I want to say and it can't wait a moment longer."

"Me, too," Eliza said. "In fact, I was just coming back here to pack my bag and fly back to Oregon."

"Really? Does that mean...?" His voice broke on the word and he paused a moment before continuing. "Does that mean you've made a decision?"

She nodded. "I'm sorry I've caused you pain and

stress these last few days, but getting pregnant felt like a nightmare. Having Jack was the best thing that ever happened to me and losing him the absolute worst. I'm terrified that something might happen to this baby, that I might make another fatal mistake."

"You didn't make a mistake," Lachlan said, a flash of anger in his eyes. "What happened to Jack was a terrible accident and there are no guarantees in life. I'd be lying if I promised you we won't have hardships, but I *can* promise you this. I love you, Eliza Coleman, and therefore I'll respect whatever decision you make regarding our child. If that means me taking on the baby because you don't think you can, then I will. And I will love it and look after it with all my heart."

Eliza's heart clenched with even deeper love for this man. Already he had his hands full with two children, yet he was willing to take another one on all by himself.

She opened her mouth to tell him but found she couldn't speak past the lump in her throat.

"But," he continued, "I need you to know that I believe in you. I think you can do this, I think you're stronger and braver than you give yourself credit for, but if you choose motherhood again, then you *won't* be alone. If you choose us, I promise whatever we face from now on, whatever highs and lows life throws at us, we'll face them together. I want to be there for both you and the baby. I want the five of us to be a family. But the question is…what do *you* want?"

And despite the decision she'd made in Central Park and as much as Eliza wanted to accept Lachlan's offer, as much as she wanted to believe in herself and them as much as he did, a tiny voice from the past was still crying out to her.

"Tyler made those same vows to me," she found herself saying, "yet when everything—"

"I'm *not* Tyler," he said forcefully and he stepped forward and took hold of her hands, bringing them up to rest on his chest. "But this is your decision."

And as she looked into his lovely blue eyes, she knew his words to be the absolute truth. Life had already thrown a lot of pain and drama at Lachlan but he hadn't turned to illegal substances like Tyler and he hadn't tried to run away from his problems like she had. He was a good, *good* man. The very best man. And he was offering himself and his beautiful children to her.

She'd be an idiot not to accept him.

"Is it my turn to speak yet?" she asked.

Lachlan's lips twisted slightly upward. "Go ahead."

She took a quick breath and then told him about the last five days in which she'd missed him like she'd miss a limb. "I wanted to come back to you, but I still wasn't sure I could face the idea of parenthood again. Then today…" She slipped her hand out of his and gestured to her head. "I slipped badly in Central Park and as I fell onto the pavement, everything fell into place in my head. I realized that this baby is a blessing and so are you."

"Really?" He blinked and sounded choked.

"Uh-huh. I was rushing back to Oregon to beg your forgiveness and tell you how much I love you and Hallie and Hamish and that I want to be a family with you all."

"Really?"

She nodded and laughed. "Is that all you can say now?"

And in reply, he took her face in his hands and kissed her till she was breathless. It didn't take long. His mouth had that kind of effect.

"I love you, too," he said again, "and I'm so proud of you."

She glowed inside but suddenly had a thought. "Who's looking after the restaurant?"

He grinned. "My family and our wonderful staff. Apparently I'm an ass to work and live with when you're not around, so they told me not to bother coming home without you."

She wasn't sure if she believed him or not, but before she could say this, he said, "You know how I told you my favorite color was brown?"

Eliza half laughed, half grimaced. "How could I forget? It's the only thing not quite perfect about you."

Still smiling, he gently took a chunk of her chocolate-brown locks and twisted it around his finger. "Until I met you, my favorite color was blue."

Epilogue

"Mama!"

Eliza jolted from sleep at the sound of her little boy happily calling to her from the crib in the next room, but Lachlan's arms shot out and he wrapped himself around her, preventing escape.

Her body immediately melted at his touch, but she pretended to put up a struggle. "Let me go," she laughed. "I'll bring Henry back in a second."

But even before he could reply, they heard laughter coming from their baby's bedroom, telling them that Hallie and Hamish had got to their little brother first. She relaxed back into the bed and rested her head against Lachlan's chest as they listened to their three children playing happily together.

Sometimes she still had to pinch herself when she woke up to Lachlan lying beside her and the sounds of Hallie, Hamish and Henry began to fill the house. It wasn't always easy holding down a relationship, running a restaurant and parenting three children with very different needs, but there was nowhere else she'd rather be and no one else she'd rather be sharing these responsibilities with.

"What are you thinking?" Lachlan whispered to her, his hands sliding suggestively down her body.

"I'm thinking I want you to feed us all pancakes for breakfast."

He laughed. Even though she was getting much better at cooking—and loved experimenting in the kitchen—he still made better pancakes than her and it wasn't only the kids that loved them.

"All right. You twisted my arm." With a quick kiss, Lachlan rolled out of bed and headed out of their room, saying, "But you can pay me back in kind later."

"It's a deal," she called out to him as she hugged a pillow to her chest and gazed over at the photo that still had pride of place on her bedside table. Only now, the bedside table was in a bedroom she shared with her husband, in a house they shared with the three kids who had become her world and, together with their father, given Eliza a reason to truly live again.

The day Henry was born, Lachlan had popped the question. He joked he'd been waiting for a moment when she wasn't thinking straight, but Eliza knew the truth—he hadn't wanted to rush her into anything. However, by then, they'd already been renting a house together in town while they waited for Mac and his team to build them a forever home, so it felt as if their fate was already sealed and she didn't want it any other way.

They'd waited only a few months before having a simple wedding at the distillery with only their closest family and friends and then the five of them had gone away on a honeymoon to Disneyworld together. She knew people thought they were crazy, going to such a place and taking their children with them, but Eliza hadn't been able to even contemplate the thought of leaving Hallie, Hamish and Henry with anyone else.

Even now, she sometimes panicked when she had to leave their baby with his grandmother or one of his uncles or aunties to go to work, but she loved working in the restaurant and each time, it was getting easier. With Lachlan's patience and the help of a counselor, she was dealing with her grief, her guilt and her fears. And the last thing she wanted to do was stifle Henry because of her past and her hang-ups.

"Mom! Time to wake up!" Hallie burst into the bedroom with Henry on her hip and Hamish not far behind them.

"I *am* awake!" Eliza proclaimed as she turned away from the photo. She laughed as Hallie plopped Henry into her arms and climbed up beside them. "How could I sleep with the noise you three make?"

"So-rry," Hamish said, looking a little sheepish as he stood with his crutches alongside them.

"Don't be silly," Eliza said, grinning at him. "Come up here and give me a hug."

Hamish didn't have to be asked twice and Eliza's heart swelled with love as Henry settled into her lap and the older children snuggled in on either side of her. As Lachlan clattered about in the kitchen making breakfast, she and the twins took turns making faces and trying to make Henry giggle while they waited for the pancakes to be ready.

Just when she thought Henry might explode if he laughed anymore, Lachlan popped his head around the door. "Sounds like I'm missing out on a lot of fun in here, but breakfast's ready."

"Yay! I'm starving!" As Hallie leaped from the bed and rushed past him, Hamish scrambled after her and Henry looked longingly after them both.

Eliza met her husband's gaze and smiled. "The moment this one can walk, we're in trouble. He'll be chasing after them for sure."

Lachlan nodded as he stepped up to the bed and held out his hands for their baby son. "True," he said, scooping Henry up into his arms. "But I wouldn't have it any other way. Now, are you coming to join us in the kitchen or doth the lady require breakfast in bed?"

She laughed. "I'm coming." As much as that idea appealed to her, sitting down and eating with her family appealed even more and so she tossed back the covers and climbed out of bed.

A few moments later, Eliza was sitting at the table, surrounded by the people she loved most in the world. Family, food and laughter, she thought, as she glanced from face to face—these were the simple things in life and they were the best.

* * * * *

MILLS & BOON

Coming next month

BABY SURPRISE FOR THE
SPANISH BILLIONAIRE
Jessica Gilmore

'Don't you think it's fun to be just a little spontaneous every now and then?' Leo continued, his voice still low, still mesmerising.

No, Anna's mind said firmly, but her mouth didn't get the memo. 'What do you have in mind?'

His mouth curved triumphantly and Anna's breath caught, her mind running with infinite possibilities, her pulse hammering, so loud she could hardly hear him for the rush of blood in her ears.

'Nothing too scary,' he said, his words far more reassuring than his tone. 'What do you say to a well-earned and unscheduled break?'

'We're having a break.'

'A proper break. Let's take out the *La Reina Pirata*—' his voice caressed his boat's name lovingly '—and see where we end up. An afternoon, an evening, out on the waves. What do you say?'

Anna reached for her notebook, as if it were a shield against his siren's song. 'There's too much to do . . .'

'I'm ahead of schedule.'

'We can't just head out with no destination!'

'This coastline is perfectly safe if you know what

you're doing.' He grinned wolfishly. 'I know exactly what I'm doing.'

Anna's stomach lurched even as her whole body tingled. She didn't doubt it. 'I . . .' She couldn't, she shouldn't, she had responsibilities, remember? Lists, more lists, and spreadsheets and budgets, all needing attention.

But Rosa would. Without a backwards glance. She wouldn't even bring a toothbrush.

Remember what happened last time you decided to act like Rosa, her conscience admonished her, but Anna didn't want to remember. Besides, this was different. She wasn't trying to impress anyone; she wasn't ridiculously besotted, she was just an overworked, overtired young woman who wanted to feel, to be, her age for a short while.

'Okay, then,' she said, rising to her feet, enjoying the surprise flaring in Leo di Marquez's far too dark, far too melting eyes. 'Let's go.'

Continue reading
BABY SURPRISE FOR THE
SPANISH BILLIONAIRE
Jessica Gilmore

Available next month
www.millsandboon.co.uk

LET'S TALK

Romance

For exclusive extracts, competitions
and special offers, find us online:

 facebook.com/millsandboon

 @millsandboonuk

 @millsandboon

Or get in touch on 0844 844 1351*

For all the latest titles coming soon, visit
millsandboon.co.uk/nextmonth